MW00981538

ROOTED

When The Trees Whisper

J FIC

Mary Ridgeway

36341219

authorHOUSE®

AuthorHouse™
1663 Liberty Drive
Bloomington, IN 47403
www.authorhouse.com
Phone: 1-800-839-8640

First published by AuthorHouse   12/31/2009

ISBN: 978-1-4490-4782-5 (sc)
ISBN: 978-1-4490-4783-2 (hc)

Printed in the United States of America
Bloomington, Indiana

This book is printed on acid-free paper.

CHAPTER ONE

The black and white squares of the linoleum floor stared back at Wendy as she sat in the chair outside her Mothers' room at the hospital. Wendy silently wondered "what is wrong, what are they doing in there and why won't they let me see her?"

She watched as nurses and doctors went in and out of the room with gloomy faces.

"She's going to be alright, I just know she is. She has to be, I need her." Tears overflowed from the corners of her eyes. Her dangling feet began to swing back and forth. Her hands held so tight in prayer that her fingers were beginning to turn a bluish color. The strain of not knowing what was happening was almost too much for her.

She stared back at the black and white squares..........."One, two, three, four........." She counted the black ones.

The day had started out well. They had eaten a wonderful breakfast of bacon, sausage, eggs and pancakes with her Mother's famous homemade Huckleberry Syrup. Hot chocolate with melting marsh mellows steamed from everyone's cup. That Huckleberry Syrup had won the blue ribbon at the county fair three years in a row.

No one had much to say as they all ate their breakfast. Her Father sat at the head of the small table, her Mother on his right and her on his left. Just the three of them, which was fine with Wendy. She didn't really want to share her parents with a sister or a brother. Her world was wonderful just the way it was.

"Wendy?" her Mother said a bit nervously. "How would you like to go on a picnic today? All three of us will go," she said glancing at Wendy's Father.

"Oh, goody! I love picnics!" Wendy squealed. "Where will we go?"

"How about your favorite spot in the little meadow across the stream by the tall trees that you love so much?" her Father suggested, taking another bite of the delicious pancakes.

"Can we go right now?" Wendy asked anxiously.

"Well. Dear, we've just eaten our breakfast. Don't you think we should wait until noon or one o'clock when we will be hungry again?" Her mother smiled at Wendy's anticipation.

Wendy frowned. "I guess so but maybe we could leave a little bit earlier so we can walk down the trail through the trees," she suggested. "I've never been there before and you always said that you would take me there some day."

"Well, maybe we can do something about that today," her Mother told her. "But, I still have the kitchen to clean, beds to make, dishes to do, the laundry to hang outside, sandwiches to make and the rest of our lunch to pack."

"That's a lot!" Wendy said frowning as she stared at her plate. "It will probably take you until dinner time to do all that."

Wendy's Mother smiled once again. "No, I don't think so," she said looking at her daughter. "Maybe you can help me?"

"How can I help you, Mama?"

"Well, I do need to water all the flowers outside before we go, so maybe you could do that for me, okay?"

"Okay! I'll go do it right now!" she said, springing up out of her chair and heading for the front door.

"Wendy! You don't have any shoes on!" her Father told her.

"Oh, yeah, shoes. I'll go upstairs and put my shoes on and then I will go out and water all the flowers," she said running quickly up the stairs to her room.

Jim and Abby looked at each other and smiled. Wendy was so precious to them both. "Well, what do you think she will say when we tell her?" Wendy's Mother asked her husband, Jim.

"I really don't know. But, your idea of a picnic is a good one," Jim said, wiping his face with his napkin. "Is that where you are going to tell her?"

"Uh huh. I think the surroundings will be perfect." She looked at Jim with worried eyes. "I don't know what her reaction will be...I'm worried about how she will take the news. I really dread telling her." Abby said as she looked down at her folded hands. Tears were beginning to form in the corners of her eyes.

She didn't want Jim to see them.

"She has to know and it would be better if she learned it from us than from someone at church," he warned her gently.

"I know, I know," she said shrugging her shoulders.

"My dear, sweet, adorable Abby, Are those tears I see in your eyes? You worry entirely too much about things, do you know that?" he said reaching out to hold her hand in reassurance.

"Well. Maybe, but she is so sensitive."

"And I wonder where she gets that from!" Jim teased. "Anyway, it is what makes her so special. I wouldn't want to change her in any way."

"Yes, I know, but, when it comes to things like this, her sensitivity scares me."

"Don't let it. Wendy is very mature for her age," Jim said, scooting his chair away from the table and standing up. "Maybe that is why she gets along better with older people than she does with other children."

"She does, doesn't she?" Abby stated thoughtfully. "I really think she would prefer being around grownups than children her own age. She seems to have more in common with us."

Jim smiled. "You had better be getting started on the kitchen before Wendy comes back down those stairs and finds you sitting idly around," he chuckled. "Remember, she wants to leave as soon as possible. And, I for one want to get this thing over with as soon as possible so that we can take the appropriate steps for the future."

"Me, too," Abby told him as she also got up from the table and stretched to her tip toes to kiss her husband.

"I'll be back soon," Jim called to her as he walked out of the kitchen.

"You'd better or Wendy will never forgive you!" she teased. "Oh, and say hello to Josh for me, will you?" she called to him.

"I always do!" Jim smiled as he went out the front door. He had to be the happiest man on earth to have such a loving wife and daughter. Not everyone ran home to their wives the minute they got off work, but he was different. He couldn't wait to see his little family. If it wasn't for the guys wanting him to be down there every Saturday morning, he wouldn't go.

Every Saturday for about five years now, Jim had gone down to the hardware store in town where all the men from around the area gathered to talk about the previous week. He would bring home all the news to share with his beloved Abby over a cup of coffee. But, not today, today they would not be sharing any conversation unless it was on a blanket out in the field surrounded by food and ants!

Abby loved her life on their small farm. Not only was Jim a forest ranger, but, he was a farmer in the true sense of the word. He planted and grew alfalfa for the local ranchers and for their own cattle.

"Where are the clowns, send in the clowns," Abby sang as she cleared the table.

"Okay! I'm ready!" Wendy said, rushing through the house, out the front door and around the corner of the house to where the hose was curled up in circles on the ground.

"Was that my daughter or a whirlwind?" Abby laughed as she caught a glimpse of Wendy already watering the flowers.

Wendy was careful not to have the water on too hard so that it wouldn't hurt the flower's soft pedals. The fragrance was different and equally enjoyable at each flower bed. The Petunias smelled the strongest next to the roses. Wendy couldn't figure out which scent she liked the best, but the pansies were the cutest she decided.

Wendy turned the gentle spray off when she heard Ralph whining behind her. "What's the matter, Ralphy?" she asked as she knelt down and hugged her dog.

Ralph licked her face.

"I love you, too," she said, giggling, "but, I can't play with you right now. I have to finish watering Mama's flowers so we can go on a picnic, she explained as she got to her feet once again.

Dragging the hose to another rose bush, she heard Ralph whine again. Turning, she noticed that he was limping.

Wendy dropped the hose and went over to where Ralph stood on three legs. His right front paw was being held gingerly in the air.

"What happened? What did you do?" she asked, gently probing Ralph's paw. "I can't feel anything," she told him. "Maybe I had better

4

go get Mama; she knows how to fix you all up when yc There's nothing she can't fix. You stay right here, I'll be right don't you go anywhere." She shook her finger at him in wa ran into the house, banging the screen door.

"Mama? Mama!" Wendy called to her Mother.

"What's the matter?" Abby asked, drying her hands on a towel as she walked out of the kitchen. A worried look cros face. She could tell by the tone of Wendy's voice that somethi wrong.

"It's Ralph; he is only walking on three paws. His other c hurting him. He's crying, Mama. Can you help him?" she asked.

"I can try," she said reassuringly. Where is Ralph?"

"He's out in front of the house," she said positively. "I told him stay put."

"Well, let's go take a look at Ralph and find out what his proble is, shall we?" she said following Wendy out the front door where Ralp still sat where Wendy had left him.

"What's the matter boy?" Abby cooed. "Does your paw hurt?" she asked while she examined his tender paw. "Look here, Wendy, he has a sticker in his paw. Can you see it?" she asked pointing to the sticker.

"Can you take it out for him?"

"I think so," she told her, pulling on the sticker.

Ralph yelped.

"There you go," Abby told the dog, patting him on the head and rubbing his ears. "It's all over now," she consoled him.

"He cried just like me when I had a splinter in my finger and you had to take it out with a needle," Wendy told her, hugging her dog lovingly.

"He'll be okay now," Abby told her daughter.

"Are you going to put some of that stinging stuff on Ralph's paw like you did on my finger when you took my splinter out?"

"No, I don't think so. I think he will be okay without it."

"Good, I don't like to hear him cry and he would have cried if you had put some of that stuff on his sore paw," she declared.

"Why don't you walk over there towards the fence and call him and see how he walks."

"Okay." But, Wendy didn't need to call Ralph over to her. He followed her on all four paws, tail wagging.

"There, see? He is fine now." Abby smiled and got to her feet.

"You can fix anything!" Wendy said proudly. "That is what I told Ralph just before I went into the house to get you. I told him that you could fix anything and you did!"

"Well, I can fix most things, but, unfortunately, not everything," she said a bit sadly.

"Are you okay, Mama?" Wendy asked.

"Yes, Sweetheart, I'm fine. You had better finish watering the flowers and I will go do my work, okay?"

"Okay," Wendy told her still wondering what her Mother had been sad about. She didn't hurt Ralph that bad.

Abby washed her hands and began making the sandwiches for their picnic. Spur of the moment picnics were not her favorite. She preferred fried chicken, potato salad, deviled eggs, olives, pickles, potato chips, fresh fruit and vegetables and brownies or a cake or maybe a pie. Now that was a picnic! But, this time they would all settle for sandwiches, pickles, olives, potato chips, left over hard boiled eggs and the rest of the Huckleberry pie form the previous night's dinner. Actually it all looked pretty good when she had it all together.

After packing it all neatly in the picnic basket and paper bags, she filled the gallon thermos jug with lemonade. "At least now when Jim returns home we can all leave right away and get this over with," she thought as she reached above the refrigerator to retrieve the paper plates, cups and plastic utensils.

"Is there anything else I can help you with?" Wendy asked as she came around the corner to the kitchen.

"Have you fed Ralph today and filled his water bowl with fresh water?" she asked.

"Nope, but I will do that right now."

Abby smiled at her daughters' obvious enthusiasm.

After making the beds, doing the dishes and hanging the clothes out on the clothesline to dry, Abby sat down with a cup of coffee anticipating Jim's return.

"Mama, where is Daddy? What is taking him so long?" Wendy asked, anxiously.

"Oh he probably got carried away talking to all the men down at the hardware store," she said looking at the clock. "You know how ol' Josh likes to talk. He would keep all of them there all day if he had his way," Abby smiled.

"What time is it?"

"It's almost noon," she said standing up and kissing the top of Wendy's head.

"It's already time for lunch and we haven't even walked down there yet!" she pouted.

"Your Father...." Abby was cut off in mid sentence by the ringing of the telephone."

"Hello?" Abby said when she answered the phone.

"Hi, Sweetheart, I'm going to be a little late. I am still down here at the hardware store. Our car decided not to start and a few of us are trying to get it going again."

"What do you think is wrong with it?"

"We think that the fuel line is all plugged up so we are in the process of putting a new one on the car right now," he told her.

"Wendy is pacing the floor waiting for you to come home. She is very anxious and so am I," she informed him.

"I can sympathize with you both, and I will hurry as fast as I can, okay?" he promised. "Tell Wendy not to worry, Nothing will keep us from our picnic today," he laughed.

"I will tell her, but I don't think it will make things any easier on her," she chuckled into the phone.

"I love you and I will see you soon," he told her, and then he hung up the receiver.

"Was that Daddy? Is he on his way home? Are we still going on our picnic?" Wendy asked all at once.

"Yes, that was your Daddy and no he isn't on his way home quite yet, but he will be in a few minutes and yes, we are still going on our picnic."

Wendy hung her head.

"Why don't we walk down to the barn and see the new calf?" she asked her daughter. "Have you thought of a name for it yet? It's your very own calf, you know."

Wendy's eyes brightened immediately. "Oh! Can we?" she said jumping up and down.

"Sure. Come on, let's go," Abby told her affectionately.

Wendy was deep in thought as they walked through the field to the barn.

"Whatcha thinking about?" Abby asked her.

"Hershey. That's what I think I'll name my calf," she decided.

"Oh, okay, I'll bite. Why are you going to name her Hershey?" Abby asked looking sideways at her daughter.

"Because, then when she grows up and I milk her, maybe she will give me chocolate milk."

Abby tried not to laugh but wasn't very successful. "You're funny; did you know that, Kiddo?" Abby asked ruffling Wendy's hair. "And, I love you this much." She said stretching her arms out to her sides as far as they would go.

"And, I love you this much." Wendy told her Mother as she copied what her Mother had just done. "Come on, Mama, I'll race you to the barn!" she said running as fast as she could to outdistance her Mother's longer legs.

"You're cheating!" Abby said as she also began to run as fast as she could to catch up with Wendy.

"I won!" Wendy said breathlessly as she turned around to see how close her Mother had come to beating her to the barn.

"Mama," Wendy called. "Are you hiding from me?" Wendy giggled. "I'll bet I can find you!" she whispered as she tiptoed back outside the barn.

"Mama!" Wendy screamed when she saw her Mother lying in the dirt outside the barn. "Mama, what happened?" Wendy gently touched her Mother's arm. "Mama? Please talk to me," she cried.

Abby slowly opened her eyes. "Go to... The house.....Call Mandy.........you know Mandy's number...." Abby tried to catch her breath. The pain was too intense for her to move. "Tell her what..... Happened.....   Tell her to call.......Ambulance." Abby told her then she fainted from the pain.

Wendy began to cry as she ran as hard as she could to the house. Once inside, she dialed Mandy's telephone number just the way that her Mother had taught her to do in case of an emergency.

The phone rang twice on the other end before Mandy finally picked it up. "Hello?"

Wendy was crying so hard that she couldn't talk.

"Wendy, is that you, darling?" Mandy asked. "What is going on, Sweetheart?'

Wendy tried to talk but was unable to stop crying. Her throat felt like it was closing up. She could hardly breathe.

"Calm down now, Sweetheart, and tell old Mandy what's wrong? What are you crying so hard about?"

Wendy took some deep breaths before she answered Mandy. "It's Mama." She cried. "She fell. She can't get up."

"Okay Wendy, I want you to get hold of yourself. Where is your Father?"

"He's down at the hardware store," she screamed.

"Now Wendy, you need to calm yourself down right now. You can't do anyone any good when you are so upset. You need to go back to where your Mother is and stay by her. I am going to call an ambulance and then I will come right over to be with you, okay?" Mandy asked. "Did you understand me, Wendy?"

"Yes," Wendy replied more calmly.

"Alright, you hang up the telephone and go stay by your Mama until someone gets there." Mandy said. "Go now."

"Okay." Wendy hung up the phone and ran back outside and headed toward the barn where her Mother was still laying on the ground.

"Mama?" Wendy tried to wake her. "Mama? Please wake up and talk to me." Tears flowed freely down Wendy's face when there was no response from her Mother. "Mama, I love you. I'm right here beside you and I won't leave. I promise. Just say something to me, Mama," Wendy sobbed as she brushed her Mother's hair away from her forehead.

Wendy didn't know how long she had sat by her Mother rocking back and forth on the ground watching for any sign that her Mother was awake.

"Send in the clowns, there ought to be clowns," Wendy sang to her. How many times had she heard her Mother sing that very song as she worked around the house? "Sing the song with me, Mama" Wendy pleaded to deaf ears.

Mandy was the first to arrive. Wendy stood up and waved to her so that Mandy could find them.

"Over here, Mandy, Hurry!" Wendy cried once again, relieved that someone was finally going to help her Mama.

Mandy rushed over to where Abby was laying on the ground. One look had told her the story of what had happened. Abby had caught her foot in a gopher hole and had fallen.

"Abby?" Mandy called, gently patting her friend's hand.

There was no response. It was then that Mandy saw all the blood on the ground around Abby. "Oh, Dear God in Heaven!" And then she turned to Wendy. "Sweetheart, I think it would be best if you went down to the house and waited for the ambulance. That way you can show them the way to the barn."

Wendy began to cry uncontrollably. "It's all my fault! If I hadn't made my Mama race me to the barn she would still be okay."

"Wendy, now listen to me," Mandy told her in a firm voice, "How many times have you raced with your Mother before and nothing happened?"

"Lots of times," Wendy whimpered.

"This was an accident, that's all. Your Mama tripped in that gopher hole and fell. It could have happened to you or anyone."

"I wish it had happened to me. I wish it was me instead of my Mama."

"Come here, Sweetheart," Mandy told her holding her arms out in invitation.

Wendy didn't hesitate as she gladly curled her body in Mandy's loving arms.

Mandy held Wendy until the ambulance came. Jim was just behind them. His face was drained of all color when he saw his beautiful Abby lying in a pool of blood.

"I think she has lost the baby," Mandy told Jim.

"Baby? What baby?" Wendy asked staring at her Mother.

"Oh dear," Mandy shook her head in sorrow, "I thought you had already told Wendy about the baby. I'm so sorry Jim."

"It's okay. We were going to tell her today when we went on a picnic. I guess it doesn't make any difference now. Abby has evidently had a miscarriage," Jim said sadly.

Jim walked over to where the medics were gently putting Abby on a stretcher to take her to the hospital. He held her hand in his. "Abby?"

There was no answer.

"Is she going to be alright?" Jim asked one of the medics.

"It is too early to tell anything, but she has lost a lot of blood and that is what is keeping her from waking up. We have to get her to the hospital as soon as possible."

"I'll follow you in my car," Jim said.

"Why don't you go in the ambulance with Abby and Wendy and I will follow you in your car," Mandy suggested.

Jim nodded without saying anything and got into the ambulance.

"Mandy, was my Mama really going to have a baby?"

"Yes, Darling, she was but I'm sure she can still have another one when she gets better," Mandy told her encouragingly.

Wendy thought about this new information for a moment." That is my fault, too," she said, tears flowing down her cheeks once again.

"What was your fault?" Mandy asked her.

"It is my fault that she lost the baby because I was just thinking this morning how nice it was that I didn't have a brother or a sister. I wanted to keep my Mommy and Daddy all to myself. And, now, Mama has lost the baby." Wendy jumped up and tried to run.

Mandy grabbed her by the arm. "It is not your fault. None of this is your fault. Do you understand me? Things happen and that's just the way it is. It is called life. We have good times, bad times, happy times and sad times." Mandy choked out the words as she also began to cry.

"Don't cry Mandy. Maybe we can find the baby that Mama lost and everything will be okay again," she hiccuped.

Mandy held her little charge tightly. "Such a wonderful child. So loving and caring," she thought to herself. "We had better get going so that we will be there when your Mama wakes up." Mandy held Wendy's hand as they walked down to the car.

Mandy; how do you describe an angel? She wasn't a hair above five foot with gray hair that she always wore in a neat little bun on top of her head. A small pair of glasses rested half way up her nose. Her eyes were always lit with the joy and peace that came along with age. She was a little on the heavy side, like most women in their sixties. She looked like the perfect Grandma. Her voice was always gentle and her smile was genuine. She was kind to everyone and she never had a bad thing to say.

Wendy did not want to let go of Mandy's hand when they had reached the car.

"You can sit right next to me in the front seat. We will hurry as fast as old Mandy can drive safely," she said squeezing Wendy's hand for reassurance.

They went straight to the emergency room where they were told that they could wait outside the room.

Wendy sat in a chair outside her Mother's hospital room, thinking. It might be okay after all if she had a brother or sister. It wouldn't be so bad. At least then she would have someone to play with besides Ralph.

Mandy had gone to get something for them to drink and was just now returning with coffee for herself and some hot chocolate for Wendy.

"Has your Daddy come out of the room yet?" Mandy asked her.

"No, just lots of nurses and doctors."

"Well, I'm sure he will be out soon to tell us all about it. Just be patient," Mandy patted Wendy's hand lovingly.

Wendy grabbed Mandy's hand and held on to it tightly. She was afraid. She didn't like hospitals.

The door to Abby's room opened. Slowly Jim walked over to Wendy and picked her up and held her in his arms, tears making a path down his saddened face.

"Mama is alright, isn't she?" Wendy asked as she pushed herself far enough away from Jim's chest to see his face. "I can go in to see her now, can't I?"

Jim sat down in the chair where Wendy had been sitting next to Mandy. "Your Mama is with the angels in Heaven now, Sweetheart." Jim tried to be strong for all of them.

"But, she can't be," Wendy started to cry again. "Make God give her back! He can't have her! I need her!" she sobbed uncontrollably.

Mandy hung her head and cried silent tears of sorrow.

"Shhhh, now. She is with Jesus. Jesus needed her more than we did, I guess. Maybe He needed another angel to sing in His Heavenly choir. You know how much your Mother liked to sing and how beautiful it sounded," Jim told her. His very heart and soul were breaking. His strength was being drained form his body. The emptiness in his chest cried out for his Abby, his other half. He felt lost without her. But, he knew that Wendy needed him right now and that he had to be strong.

He had to be strong for her and for Mandy. Abby would have expected it of him, and he would do anything for his Abby.

"Did she ever wake up at all, Jim?" Mandy asked drying her tears on her apron. She had hurried so fast to be with Wendy at the farm that she had forgotten to remove her apron.

"Yes," Jim choked back his tears. "She woke up long enough to smile and whisper to me."

"What is it that she said," Mandy asked, "that is, if you don't mind telling me?"

"She said that she loved me and to take care of Wendy for her. She told me to tell Wendy to keep singing the song and that she would miss all of us very much." Jim began to cry, streams of tears making trails down his cheeks. He could hold them back no longer. "She knew that she wasn't going to live. I kissed her and she smiled. She looked so content. Her eyes closed and she was gone. She was gone so fast." He shook his head in disbelief. "It was just this morning we were all fine and now my Abby is gone."

"I want to see my Mommy," Wendy told him, calmly.

"I don't know…" Jim looked at Mandy for some sort of guidance.

"I think it would be best if you let her see her Mother for herself. That will make it all real for her. Otherwise, she will always wonder. She is really too young to understand truly what has happened." Mandy counseled him. "But, be prepared for her reaction." She warned.

Jim stood up and carried Wendy in to see her Mother for the last time. They had already pulled the sheet up over her head. Jim gently removed the sheet to see his beloved Abby still smiling, even in death.

"She looks so pretty, Daddy," Wendy told him, softly. "She must already be singing in the choir. Look she is smiling."

"Yes, Sweetheart, she is smiling. Now you can remember her that way always." He hugged her tightly.

"Mama always smiled."

"Yes, she did. She loved us so very much and she was always so very happy because she had you."

"Where are the clowns? There ought to be clowns. Send in the clowns," Wendy sang softly. "I love you, Mama," she cried and hugged her Father.

CHAPTER TWO

"I feel very lost in my trunk," Predictor told Old Log, sadly.

"Why should you feel lost in your trunk?" Old Log asked, "No one has ended. We are all healthy. The sun is shinning and it is a beautiful day."

"I don't know. I just feel a deep loss as though something bad has just happened. Yet, I can not quite put my limb on it." Predictor answered deep in thought..

"You remind me of a Walk-to. They always seem sad and unhappy," Old Log chided him.

"Yes, I suppose I do at that," he said, mentally shaking his thoughts away. "I guess that I am being pretty ridiculous. We are all here," he said, looking around. "At least as many as there should be, which is not that many any more. We used to outnumber the Walk-To's at one time."

"Yes, I know," he answered sadly, "But we are enough to carry on, don't you think? That is......if the Walk-To's would realize what they are doing and leave us alone. And, I can almost guarantee that that is not something that is going to happen any too soon," Old Log told Predictor, sorrow heavy in his trunk. His branches drooped in despair as he thought of all the friends he had lost in the past.

"I think otherwise, Strong One. I do not think that there are enough of us left to carry on. We are so few. Soon we will only number enough that you can count us on your branches. It is not only the Walk-to's who are endangering us, but, you must remember all the other things.........such as fire, disease, niggets...And...never forget the great winds. There are many, many things that are a danger to us, surely you will agree.

I do not like the Walk-To's either, but, it is not entirely their fault," Predictor argued.

"Why do you defend the Walk-To's? They certainly have done nothing to deserve such loyalty from you! They are destructive, self-centered, greedy, mean, nasty, hypocritical, wasteful and very unintelligent." Old Log hissed in anger.

"Do not judge all Walk-To's the same, Old Log. There are some Walk-to's that actually go out and spend days and days planting our seedlings in meadows and fields where other trees have been cut down."

"They only plant them so that they will have more of us to cut down. And, soon, there will be no more seedlings to plant," Old Log retorted in anger.

"Would you judge all trees the same? Would you judge me to be cruel and angry and grumpy just because Old Bitter Bark was? There are good trees and there are bad trees. Just as there are good and bad Walk-To's. Do not judge every tree by the shape or color of his leaves," Predictor cautioned his long time friend.

"You will never convince me that there are any good Walk-to's. There is no such thing, Tall One. I have lived long and have yet to see a good Walk-to. No.....I do not believe there are any," Old Log said, folding his branches in front of him, his mind made up.

"So be it, then. Talking to you is like talking to a boulder......... cold, hard and unmovable," Predictor criticized as he turned his trunk in another direction so that he would not have to look at Old Log.

"It is much too nice of a day to be arguing! Look at the sunshine! Feel its warmth and listen to the sounds of life all around you! Do not talk of ending, talk of life! Why just look.....Old Log and I have a new seedling about to push its way into the world. Life goes on, see?" Many Branches said happily as she pointed to the ground where it was just beginning to bulge and break open.

"And just what is there to be so excited about? So what? So we have a new seedling coming up. Big deal!" Tickler said with disdain. "It will probably turn out to be a puny stick like Thin-As-Grass!" He said with a hearty laugh.

Thin-As-Grass pouted and gave Tickler a dirty look. But Many Branches was not about to lose an argument, especially this one to Tickler.

"Oh, you think so, do you? Look, Tickler, it may not be of any importance to an old piece of driftwood like you, but, it is to Old Log and me. We have waited many long cycles to watch one of our own seedlings grow. And you have the nerve to stand there and make jokes about it? How could you be so cruel? And, how could you be so rude to Thin-As-Grass?" she asked with a frown of disbelief on her pretty face. "That which is important to one of us is supposed to be important to all of us." Many Branches declared as she stiffened her branches and rustled her leaves. "So there!"

"My! My! You have quite a temper! A hidden dark side to such an otherwise sunny disposition!" He said, teasing her. "You know what they say about a stuck up tree, don't you?........They make good telephone poles! Ha! Ha! Ha! Ho!" Tickler shook with laughter as he held on to his trunk as though he was in great pain.

Tickler was the Thickets clown. He was always teasing and joking whenever someone would listen. He was rarely funny and hardly anyone ever laughed at his jokes. Sometimes, when Tickler thought he was being funny, it would hurt someone's feelings instead. Like Thin-As-Grass. Tickler was never very careful about what he said.

Tickler wasn't very tall, only about eleven lippets tall, one lippet equaling about three feet. He had many bushy branches that sprouted little green pitlies in the springtime. Then, in the fall, they turned brown and hard with a green covering and they fell to the ground below. That is when the Bushy Tails would busy themselves with the task of gathering them all up and storing them away for the Big Slumber in the winter.

The Walk-To's called Tickler a black walnut tree. Of course this meant nothing to any of them. The trees had their own language and way of saying things.

Tickler always seemed lonesome and sad as though his thoughts were some where else. He tried to cover up his depression by telling jokes. The members of the Thicket all loved him and they enjoyed being around him, most of the time, but, like everyone else, he could be a nuisance at times.

"Both of you had better shut up before you wake Predictor up from his nap again and he predicts your ending! It would not do to wake him up….. No, not at all!" Old Moss cautioned them grimly as his voice became a menacing whisper like that of a stealthy cold wind.

Old Moss was very wise and could never be accused of cloudy or muddy thinking. His demure and high office demanded the highest respect from everyone, yet, he needn't demand it as it was freely given to him by all. He had great perception and memory, even to the slightest detail of the background of every member of his Thicket........except for Old Sap. And no one knew how old he was.

Old Moss had the most knots of any tree in his Thicket. He had proven himself to be the ablest thinker and had studied all manner of things. He grew very tall, but his branches weren't as strong as they had once been. He stood a good twenty lippets away from any of the rest of the trees. He was very well rooted in all directions because he had plenty of room to stretch.

The members of the Thicket had chosen Old Moss as their Thicket Councilor because he had proven himself over and over again to be the ablest thinker among them. They all wanted a strong-willed leader, someone that would be fair and think things through before he answered or gave a decision.

So, many, many cycles ago they had devised a test, a hard test with only one acceptable answer. It was a question that whispers from many Thickets around said was answerable in many ways and this is why it was so difficult. Very few were even considered eligible to take the test. But.....Old Moss had taken it and he had passed.

"It is already too late. I am awake again. What is going on? Can't a tree get any rest around here anymore? Why did I have to be planted next to a bunch of insomniacs?" Predictor complained with a sigh, peeking with only one eye as though maybe it was only part of a dream and maybe all the noise would just disappear.

Predictor was very tall with limbs that seemed to reach the clouds and beyond to the Land of Sweet Waters and Cool Breezes. He towered above all the rest of the trees in the Thicket. It was said by some of the trees in the forest that Predictor was able to predict things only because he talked back and forth with the angels above the pillows of God. He was the Thicket's Tree Prophet. And, he did his job well.

Predictor had a few more knots than Old Log, but not as many as Old Moss. He had smooth, grainy bark on a round sturdy trunk. His branches were loaded with long, sharp needles. He loved to talk, but it was mostly about things that were going to happen in their future.

"Nothing! Absolutely nothing is going on, Old Friend, Predictor. Nothing at all! Ha! Ha! Haw!" Tickler shook his very trunk with boundless laughter. "Wouldn't you call that puny little thing, NOTHING!"

"You had better watch it ol' boy or you will have very many large lumps all over your trunk. If I could move like a Walk-To you would be very sore right now," Many Branches threatened as she shook her branches in Tickler's direction.

Many Branches stood next to her husband, Old Log. And, just in front of them both was where their new seedling was beginning to grow. Many Branches was named for quite obvious reasons. The name fit her well. She was not nearly as tall as Old Log, but she had many beautiful branches that were very long and full of large, beautiful olive green leaves. Her bark was the smoothest that anyone had ever seen. It had no bulges to show her age and there were no pits or holes from the Stiff **B**eaks.

Many Branches was very intelligent and had more knots than any of the other mothers of the forest for miles around. She loved young seedlings and mere twigs and they loved her in return. It was her job to teach them the customs of their Thicket.

Old Log was a little taller than his wife, but not as tall as Predictor. Old Log had a gnarled and twisted trunk that denoted much hardship and strength. He had many fine large knots. There were only two other trees that had more knots than he did. One was Old Moss and the other was Predictor. Old Log was stronger than anyone in the Forest. His branches and limbs were like thick, sturdy steel rods. He had large, olive green leaves that graced the wind as it mingled in and out, touching each tree with its breath. Old Log's roots grew very deep and were spread far and wide like fingers on a giant piano.

Old Log was wise and crafty, a politician, so to speak. He had the coolness of a spring breeze, yet, the firmness of a rock when it came to settling disputes among the many members of the Thicket. He was their trouble shooter and peace maker. He was often consulted about important matters when another opinion was necessary.

Many Branches and Old Log were very proud and excited as their son poked his head up out of the rich brown earth where his seed had lain for so long.

Old Log reached out and hugged his wife as they watched their son straighten and stretch as though he had merely been asleep and was just now awakening.

"I still say that it is of little or no importance at all. The seedling will probably be dumb and have no knots at all when he is of age and fully grown. We have not had a good, intelligent seedling grow in this Thicket for many cycles. So why should it be of any importance to the rest of us? What we need is someone who will be smart enough to be our next Thicket Councilor when Old Moss retires as he has said he is just about ready to do. This seedling will probably be nothing more than a scrawny little bush. Yes! We should name him 'Scrawny Little Bush!'" he teased. "I think it will fit him well," he said, looking from the small seedling to where Many Branches was glaring at him. "Do you like it, Many Branches?" Tickler continued to tease her unmercifully. Then he glared at the little seedling as though he was a bird and the little seedling was a worm and Tickler was about to swoop down and immediately devour him.

"No, she doesn't. And, for that matter, neither do I!" Old Log told him in a cold terrifying voice as he, at last, broke his silence. His voice became thick with rage like the angry thunder of a storm brewing in the skies. "I suggest, Tickler that you go tickle someone else's fancy and leave my wife alone to nurture our son, Little Bark, as I so named him just now." He glared at Tickler. "It is my right to name my own son, is it not?"

"Yes, as you well know, it is within your rights to name your own seedling," he told him, "But, just remember what they say.....A name can lame a tree to shame, so name for fame and not for blame."

"You remember your tree lore better than you remember your manners," Old Log hissed as he tried to anticipate what Tickler's response might be.

But, Tickler was caught off guard and too surprised to offer a response to Old Log's comment for the moment.

When the silence that followed had become awkward and uncomfortable, Old Log added, "I was just about to take a nap, won't you join me?"

"Thank you. I think I will," he agreed quite readily as a great gasp of air escaped his trunk. He had been holding it too long. It was not a very good idea to have Old Log as an enemy. He had, once again, pushed too far with his teasing,

With that, Tickler's thoughts became his own as he watched a long eared fuzzy hopper come up out of his perfectly round hole in the ground, carrying what looked like a turnip in his mouth, stopping every now and then to take a bite and look curiously around.

Tickler had often wondered about that hole. He thought that it was probably not an unbecoming place to live, though it was very dark and had no sunshine, which he preferred. It was, more than likely, dry and sandy. Warm in the winter and cool in the summer. He doubted that it had too many wiggly worms, blickets or other uninvited guests crawling around in it.

He imagined that it probably had many tube shaped tunnels leading to little storage rooms here and there. There were probably far off exits that only the long-eared bushy tails knew about.

The tunnels and rooms all intertwined with the many roots of the trees of Old Moss' Thicket. Old Moss and all the other trees could have choked off the many tunnels with their enormous roots, but they shared a fond kindred for the little guy as they watched him go about his every day business of gathering food and scurrying around this way and that. It always seemed to be in a hurry which the trees found very strange. Why did one hurry? There was plenty of time.

"You are not sleeping, Tickler. Do you spurn my invitation to nap in the sun?" Old Log asked in a cold and icy tone that sent chills up and down Tickler's trunk.

"And, if I did, what then?" Tickler asked, bravely, with all the mental force at his command. It was not wise to talk to Old Log in such a manner that he was doing. Old Log was highly respected and with that respect a certain amount of fear was also present.

"Is there a small matter that I may prove myself of any assistance, no matter how small and meager that assistance might be?" Weeper cried in a tiny apologetic voice. "I am but a day-to-day tree, not knowing how to think beyond one day. My abilities are small but my heart is big. There is just too much tension and arguing going on among us these days. I just hate to see anyone angry with anyone else. It makes me feel so lost in my trunk," she wept as though her heart was about to break.

Weeper was a beautiful, full tree with long branches that hung all the way to the ground in cascades of light green and pale yellow colors. It made her look as though she was bowing in constant prayer. The Walk-To's called her a Weeping Willow, which seemed to fit her personality better than any name that they could have given her. So, they called her Weeper for short.

Sometimes the Walk-To's children would come and play games as they hid from one another in her branches. Others came and sat under her as though she were a giant tent and told each other secrets. At other times, especially when it was raining, the animals would run under her long branches to stay dry.

"It is over, Weeper. Do not concern yourself any longer. We are all good friends and an occasional disagreement sometimes helps to clear the air. Sleep now and worry no more," Old Moss told her firmly, but kindly. Then he turned up his leaves to soak up the sun and swayed to and fro in the gentle breeze. His mind began wandering to stories of distant lands of long ago.

No one spoke for a long time as they all seemed to be enjoying the warm splashes of sunlight that gently caressed their leaves. Some were watching as the song-with-wings fluttered away in exaggerated excitement when a bushy tail ran up Tall Tale's trunk and out on a limb to sit and scold the song-with-wings for being such cowards.

At long last, Tall Tales broke the silence. Stretching and yawning at the new day, he cleared his throat and said, "Many Branches, I have a tale to tell you of long ago. Do you wish to hear it?" he asked, picking a few dead leaves from his limbs and dropping them to watch them slowly float to the ground as they waved back at him.

"If it pleases you to tell me, Tall Tales, then I will be attentive," she sighed. Many Branches, like all the rest of the members of their Thicket, tolerated Tall Tales and his stories out of love and friendship and the deep understanding that had come with the cycles of association and familiarity. She had heard each one of his stories at least a thousand times, she thought, and they had become very tiring to her.

"Very well," he said, louder than was actually necessary. But, it was a few moments before he ventured forth with his tale. He thought that the longer he waited, the more the suspense would build up and the more the suspense, the more trees that would listen.

Tall Tales was very tall and slender in his trunk. So slender, in fact, that Tickler was always teasing him saying that he hoped a good strong wind would not sneak up on him and catch him unaware and blow him over like an old weak Walk-To. But, Tall Tales had simply ignored him like someone would ignore a mosquito buzzing in the air, unable to reach it to put an end to its incessant buzzing.

Tall Tales branches were short and pointed straight up, unless he was telling a story and then he usually waved them around and used them to illustrate an important part of his story. His limbs had hundreds of leaves that were of a dark green on one side and a pale gray on the other. They looked almost musical when they twittered and rustled in the breeze. The Walk-To's called him a Poplar tree. Tickler had often teased him about it saying that Tall Tales was far from being popular.

Tall Tales had quite a few knots, but they weren't of much size, being very small and almost unnoticeable. He loved to tell stories....tall tales....that his Father before him and his Grandfather before him and so on down the line had told for many, countless cycles and generations. Everyone thought that his stories were interesting the first few times that he told them. All the young seedlings and mere twigs for many Thickets around would hush and barely move for fear of being unable to hear. Each one stood gazing as though they were being slowly hypnotized by Tall Tales' voice. A tree had to have a very special voice to be the Thicket's story teller and some Thickets didn't even have a story teller.

"Well, what are you waiting for?" Many Branches asked in an irritated tone. "Don't tell me that you are trying to think up a new story to tell us?" she asked, hopefully.

"No.....not new, just changed here and there," he assured her thoughtfully. He frowned. Had he told her this story before?

"Won't you be happy and in your best voice in about a week when Little Bark will be old enough to listen and understand your.......tall tales, as it were.....like all the rest of the young seedlings? I'm sure he will be quite attentive," she tempted him.

"Yes, I quite agree with you. It will be a refreshing change to have someone listen who can appreciate a good story when they hear one," he told her as he stuck one limb on his trunk as if he were disgusted with the whole idea of telling his story.

"Well, what are you waiting for, the Great Lifting?" She had become tired of waiting. She had other things that demanded her attention right now, one of them was her son, Little Bark.

"Oh, dear, oh me, there is going to be another argument, I just know there is and then everyone will be angry with everyone else and I won't be able to get any sleep just worrying about it," Weeper sobbed in her tiny, apologetic voice. "If it is I that you are waiting for, Tall Tales, please forgive me for not taking notice. I am, after all, a weak minded tree and I do not always notice things as easily as do the others. Anyway, please begin your story."

"No....." Tall Tales sighed. "I have changed my mind. I do not want to tell my story now. No one wants to hear it anyway"

"Oh, dear! You are angry and it is all my fault. If I were not so weak minded, I am sure things would be of better state. But, as it were, I have not been blessed with the foresight of the others. I am but a day-to-day tree......not knowing how to think beyond my outer bark. Again, Tall Tales, I apologize for being unable to perceive that it was I whose attention you favored. Please tell me your story, I would like to hear it," she coaxed him.

"It is really okay, Weeper, I just don't feel the inclination to tell it anymore," he said forlornly, staring at the ground in front of him.

Old Log had been listening for quite some time before he finally broke his silence again. "Tall Tales, tell us your story, we are all attentive now," he said, firmly, silencing any more protests that Tall Tales might have had. He knew that Tall Tales had only carried on that way to get everyone's attention. And, he knew that Tall Tales was really very anxious to tell his story.

"Well, alright.........if you insist," he said with a long sigh, pretending as though he would really rather be doing something else. "Many cycles ago, when the Nibblers ran free and the humped buffs roamed the hills and valleys, there was a tree, a very special tree. They called him Day Dreamer because he was always dreaming about walking. It was all he ever talked about. He yearned to walk the earth like the Walk-To's do now and see everything that they were able to see.....but....alas, he was still well rooted. Then, one day as he was praying to the Great God of All Things to let him walk, the ground opened up and swallowed him whole. And, do you know what?" he asked, looking around at each tree.

"He got his wish, and now he walks the earth day in and day out. But you can't see him…. No….no one can see him. He is a see-through, cursed to wander the earth without rest forever, never to be taken home to the Land of Sweet Waters and Cool Breezes," he finished, pompously folding his limbs in front of him, standing straight and tall and matter-of-factly.

"There once was a tree, told of long, long ago,

Who prayed to God to let him roam.

So God opened up the earth below,

And gobbled him up like the heat does the snow.

And now he walks the earth evermore,

From land to land and shore to shore.

No friends has he like me and you,

For he has been cursed forever a see-through," Rhymer told everyone as he wiggled his little leaves in silent laughter.

Rhymer was a cute little bush that grew at the base of Tall Tales trunk. He loved to speak in riddles and rhymes. And, most of the time, it was just to tease Tall Tales.

"Too bad you aren't a tumble weed," Tall Tales chided him, "and then maybe you would just roll away."

"Leave the little bush alone," Old Sap warned, "he harms no one with his rhymes and I rather look forward to them after your stories."

"I still feel lost in my trunk," Predictor said, sadly. "It is almost as though one of us has ended. But, that is silly. We are all here, aren't we?"

"Yes, we are," Old Moss assured him. "However, I also am feeling a little sad. There is no apparent reason. It must be that the weather is about to change. Maybe it is going to rain," he added looking at the sky.

CHAPTER THREE

The ride home seemed to take forever, but Wendy was glad to be away from the hospital. It smelled like medicine. She wanted the familiar smells of home. Flowers on the kitchen table. Flowers in the living room and on the chest in the hallway. Fresh pies or bread baking in the oven. She wanted to hear her Mother's gentle voice singing Send in the Clowns.

There would be no more pies. There would be no more freshly baked bread. There would be no more singing coming from the kitchen.

"Oh, Mama," Wendy cried softly.

Her small body was shaking as she sat between her Father and Mandy in the front seat of the car.

Mandy folded her arms around Wendy and held her lovingly. "It's okay to cry, Wendy. Let it all out. It will make you feel better," she told her. Mandy was having a hard time controlling her own grief. Abby had been like a daughter to her and a best friend all rolled up in one. She knew she would miss her tremendously. The empty, hollow feeling was almost unbearable and she knew it must be even more devastating for Jim and Wendy. How would they be able to manage without Abby? Who would cook their meals? Who would wash their clothes? Who would do the hundred or so tasks that Abby had done so lovingly.

Mandy looked at Wendy. Who would look after Wendy when she came home from school? Who would be there to meet her as she climbed down the stairs of the school bus? Who would comfort the child when she was hurt? Who would help them both through their grief?

Her thoughts went to her own life. Her own children were all grown and had children of their own. Her husband was retired and could take care of himself during the day. She could come over early in the morning to fix their breakfast, do the dishes, clean the house, make the beds, and do the laundry and all the other things that had to be done to keep a home running smoothly. She could help Jim get Wendy off to school in the morning and be there for her when she came home on the bus. It could work. She could ask her husband, Bill, to take over some of the duties at home. "Yes, it could work," she thought to herself.

The first thing she would have to do is talk to Bill and then to Jim. She smiled in satisfaction, her eyes resting on Jim. Her smile faded when she saw the empty almost blank look on his face. He was driving slowly as though he was in some sort of a trance. His whole body seemed to sag in hopelessness and despair.

"Abby, my sweet, precious Abby. What will I do without you? How will I manage? How can I face a day or a night without you? Your very presence was like a sunshine always glowing around me." Jim's thoughts were like knives being thrust into his chest. Tiny stabs of his own slow death. A book closing in his life. A very precious book. A short book, so very, very short. They had made so many plans for the future and the new baby. The new baby. If it hadn't been for Abby being pregnant with his child, she would still be here with him. They would still have a future. They would still be a family.

He turned briefly to look at the other love of his life, Wendy. What about her? How was he going to be of any comfort to her when he was hurting so badly? His chest felt like it was being squeezed, crushed with a devastating emptiness that he had never felt before in his life. He wondered what Wendy was feeling? Did she really comprehend what had happened? Did she know that her Mother was never coming back? Did she know that she would never see her again in this life? How did a seven year old child think about situations like this? Did she realize that this was permanent? Did she realize that her Mother wasn't going to just get up out of that hospital bed and come home? Did she think that this was a cartoon where bad things happened but everyone just got up and continued on? How could someone so young comprehend something like this when he was having such trouble accepting it himself?

Another stab of pain, sharp and unrelenting tore at his chest as their home came into view. Abby, his wonderful, precious wife would never be there again to greet him as he drove up the driveway on his way home from work.

Jim parked the car and opened the door. Tears pooled in his eyes as he stood looking at the rose bushes and the flowers that Abby so lovingly took care of. Pansies and Petunias lined the walkway to the steps of the house. Azaleas and Rhododendrons snuggled against the outside walls. A special flowerbed of Sweet Williams was tucked in one corner of the fenced yard. Gladiolas stood tall in full bloom just outside that freshly painted white picket fence. Everything was so perfect. Abby had made it perfect.

"Come, Wendy," he called, reaching his hand out to his daughter.

Wendy slowly scooted over to his side of their car and got out. Tears were pooling in her eyes and slowly trickling down her cheeks, but she wasn't making a sound.

Jim stooped down and held Wendy in his arms. Then, as though on cue they both released their grief in each others arms.

Mandy stood watching. It seemed as though her heart was being ripped from her chest at the sight of her dearly loved neighbors sorrow. Her own release of sorrow and grief would have to wait until she could go to her own husband and her own home. Now was not the time. They needed her presence right now, not only to comfort them, but to bring some sort of normalcy back into their lives. They needed her strength. They needed someone to help them carry on with their lives and she was going to be the one to do it for them and her dear, sweet friend, Abby.

Mandy was the first to enter the front door. The smell of food permeated through the house as she walked into the kitchen. "News spreads swiftly in this small community," Mandy said to herself as she gazed upon enough food to feed a small army. Evidently the people of the valley had heard the news of Abby's death and had brought food over to Jim and Wendy knowing that in their grief they would not feel up to fixing something for themselves.

Wendy's eyes brightened and a smile lit up her face as she came in the front door. The smell of freshly baked bread, fried chicken and chocolate cake gently pressed upon her senses.

Swiftly she ran to the kitchen. The freshly baked bread and fried chicken were on the table. The chocolate cake was on the counter next to the canisters and the cookie jar was filled with freshly baked chocolate chip cookies. There was food everywhere. Mandy was putting something in the refrigerator. But, no Mommy. Her Mother wasn't there. And, she never would be again.

"Mama? Oh, Mama!" Wendy cried out and ran up the stairs to her room realizing that her whole life was changed forever.

"Let her go, Jim," Mandy told him as he began to climb the stairway to follow his daughter. "She needs a little time, a little space of her own to work this out in her mind." Mandy said walking over to him. "You both do. That is why all your neighbors brought you all this food and then quietly left. They haven't abandoned you, you know. They just understand that their presence right now would be disturbing to you." She smiled and patted his arm. "They will be over tomorrow in droves. Right now I think it would be good for you to go for a walk or sit quietly out on the porch and gather your thoughts together."

Jim looked at Mandy, his eyes expressing what his voice wouldn't let him.

"Your welcome," Mandy told him.

Jim went out the front door and down the walkway and out the front gate. He began walking, not knowing or caring where he was going. The earth felt food under his feet. The brisk walk began to clear his thoughts. He would need to find someone to come over every day to help him with Wendy and the housekeeping. He would have to tell his boss at work that there would be no more of his working overtime. He needed to be at home in the evenings for Wendy. And, he didn't know that much about cooking. Abby had always done all the cooking except when they had a barbeque outdoors. He needed someone to do the chores around the house during the week. He could do them on the weekends. He would have to advertise in the local paper or perhaps tack a note on the church bulletin board. That was it. He would try the church first. He knew everyone at church and he couldn't think of a single soul that he couldn't trust with his daughter.

He hung his head. There would never be anyone to take his Abby's place. No one could fill her shoes.

Standing at the edge of the field, he looked at the trees and the gently flowing brook. Today was supposed to have been such a special day. Both he and Abby had been apprehensive about telling Wendy about the new baby so they had decided on a picnic, a family outing where they could gently break the news to her.

Anger gripped him as he bent over and picked up a rock and threw it as hard as he could. They should have just told Wendy at breakfast. If they had, maybe Abby would still be alive. If the car had started he could have been home when he should have been. If he just hadn't gone down to visit with the guys at the hardware store this morning. If......
If.......If. Hindsight was always so much clearer than foresight.

Jim stood watching a small cluster of clouds as they moved slowly across the blue sky. Birds were singing. Bees were humming. Squirrels were scolding him for intruding in their domain. The breeze gently touched his face, drying the tears as they escaped his eyes.

His hands were trembling so he put them both in his pants pockets. How could everything around him be so alive when he felt so dead inside? He shook his head. This was not what Abby would have wanted. She would have wanted him to gather himself together and carry on without her. She would want him to set an example for Wendy, be strong for their daughter.

And, he resolved himself to do just that, as he turned around and began the walk back to his home. Correction.......their home. Wendy's and his. He could and would make it a home again. A happy one. Somehow.

"It is Mama's favorite," Wendy said as she stood watching Mandy wrapping the fried chicken in aluminum foil. "She would have liked to have had some for dinner. She liked potato salad, too." Wendy stared at her feet. "I only like my Mama's potato salad. She makes it taste so good. Everyone else's tastes funny."

Mandy put the chicken in the oven to heat for Jim and Wendy. "Your Mama was a very special person and just between you and me, I liked her potato salad the best, too." She told her with a quick wink.

"When did you eat my Mama's potato salad?" Wendy asked.

"Oh, I've had her potato salad lots of times.. I always watched for her to set hers down at the church picnics so that I could be sure to grab some before it was all gone. And, I have been over here for barbeques every now and again, remember?" Mandy smiled at her.

"I guess I won't be eating potato salad any more," Wendy said as tears began to form in her eyes once again.

"Oh, now I don't know about that. You see, about two months ago, I asked your Mother for her recipe for potato salad and she gave it to me." Mandy wiped her hands on her apron and crossed the room to where Wendy was standing in the doorway.

She reached out and lifted Wendy's chin so that she could see her eyes. "Would you like me to make some for you?"

"Maybe sometime," Wendy answered, "But, right now I'm not very hungry. I don't feel very well. My stomach hurts and I feel like I want to throw up." She replied, holding her stomach with both hands.

"It's just nerves, child. You've been through a lot today. Both you and your Daddy have been through a lot." Mandy sighed. "I guess we all have."

"Where is my Daddy?" Wendy asked.

"He went for a short walk. He should be back soon," she informed her.

"I think I will go see if I can find him," Wendy said, turning to walk to the front door.

"I don't know if that is such a good idea, child. You might get yourself lost and then we would all be frantic trying to find you," Mandy tried to explain.

"I promise I won't go far," Wendy told her.

"Oh, alright, but, don't go so far that you lose sight of the house. That way I can see you."

"I won't Mandy," she promised and went out the front door.

Ralph came bounding up to her, tail wagging.

"I don't want to play right now, Ralphy," Wendy said, pushing him away. Ralph whined.

"Oh, Ralphy, I'm so sorry. I didn't mean to make you sad," she consoled him. "Come here," she patted her legs in invitation.

Ralph jumped at the call from Wendy and came to her with his tail wagging once again with happiness.

"You know there is something wrong, don't you, Ralphy?" she said as she petted his large head with her small hands. "You can feel the sadness, too, can't you? I'll bet that you are going to miss Mama about as much as I will." Wendy sat down on the ground in front of Ralph. "No, no one will miss her as much as I do." She sobbed.

Ralph licked her face.

"Are you okay, Sweetheart?" Jim asked his daughter as he walked up to the gate.

"Yes, I guess so," she pouted. "And, no I'm not. I'll never be okay again. Not without my Mommy."

"I know how you feel, Pumpkin, but I don't think that Mommy would want you to be so unhappy," Jim told her as he sat down on the ground beside her and Ralph. "I know it hurts, but right now your Mommy is in Heaven with Jesus. And, there is no happier place to be. She is probably looking down at you right now and wondering why you are so unhappy. And, that is making her unhappy."

Wendy looked at the sky. "Do you really think that she can see us, Daddy?"

"I really think she can, Sweetheart. And, you wouldn't want her to be unhappy, would you?"

"No."

"Well, then, let's go inside and eat something and then maybe we can sit and talk if you want to."

"I don't really want anything to eat, but I would like to sit on your lap for a while," she pouted and put her arms around her Father.

"Anything you want, little one. Anything you want." He said hugging her as tight as he could without hurting her. She was so precious to him. Especially now. "Let's go inside," he said, picking Wendy up in his arms and carrying her into the house.

"Jim? Pastor Richards called and wanted to know when you wanted to get together with him to make the arrangements for the Funeral," Mandy told him.

"Later. I'll call him later," he said as he carried Wendy into the living room and sat down in his chair.

Wendy immediately curled up into a ball on his lap. She snuggled as close to him as she could and was fast asleep.

An hour later, Mandy entered the room to find them both asleep. Tears formed in the corners of her eyes and slowly made a path down her cheeks. They both looked so vulnerable, so lost. As soon as Jim woke up she would tell him of her plan. Turning, she went back into the kitchen and called her husband and told him that she was going to stay as long as they needed her. She asked if he would be okay and he told her that he would be just fine and to let him know if there was anything that he could do to help.

"I love you, my wife," he told her.

"I love you, too, my husband," she replied and hung up the phone. How blessed she felt to have such a wonderful husband. They had celebrated their forty fifth wedding anniversary last August, forty five of the most wonderful years of her life.

Her thoughts turned to Jim and Abby. They had only been married for eleven years. Such a shame to cut a good marriage off in it's prime. And, the baby, it would have been so good for Wendy to have had a baby brother or sister. She knew deep down in her heart that Jim would never marry again. The kind of love that Jim and Abby and Bill and she shared only came along once in a life time, if you were blessed. No, she was almost positive that he would remain alone with Wendy. Wendy was his whole world now. She could tell by the look on his face when he had carried her into the house. He would now devote his whole life to making his little girl happy. Mandy smiled and then made herself some coffee and sat down at the table to wait for them to awaken. Sleep, blessed sleep, helps mend the heart of its wounds and the body of its ailments.

Jim slowly opened his eyes hoping that he had just been dreaming a horrible dream, but it was all too real as he looked down at his sleeping daughter. Slowly, so as not to wake her, he got up out of his chair and gently laid Wendy on the sofa and put an afghan over her. He then checked to see if she was indeed still asleep. She was.

He walked silently to the kitchen. "Mandy! What are you still doing here? I thought that you went home a long time ago."

"I wanted to stay to see if you needed me to help put Wendy to bed. You know, neither one of you has had anything to eat since your breakfast this morning. You should eat something, Jim. You are going to need all the strength you can muster for the next few days," Mandy warned him.

"I am a little hungry," Jim said heading for the refrigerator.

"You just sit down at the table and let old Mandy wait on you," she ordered.

"I can't let you do everything around here. You have been here all day. What will Bill think if you don't go home and fix him some dinner?" Jim asked.

"He has already made himself a chili dog with onions and cheese all over it." She smiled. "Now, all I have to do is go home tonight and give him some antacid for his stomach!" she chuckled.

"Well, you have been a true angel from Heaven in our time of need. How are you taking all this? I know that you and Abby were best friends," he questioned her waiting to see what her reaction would be.

"I don't mind telling you, Jim, that I am going to miss her as much as I would my own daughter. My heart aches for the loss of her. My heart aches for both you and Wendy." She glanced his way. "You seem to be holding up pretty well, Jim, are you?"

"As well as can be expected when half your life is taken from you. Abby wanted me to take care of Wendy and I can't very well do that if I can't keep my grief under some sort of control. I would be absolutely no good to her or anyone else if I fell apart. It's hard; let me tell you, it's very hard. The ache and the emptiness that I feel in my heart threatens to cut me in two. But, Abby's last words strengthen me again." He folded his hands in his lap. "We used to say that we were each others strength. Well, it's true even in death she gives me strength that I never thought I had."

Mandy gave him two plates full of food. Fried chicken, potato salad, baked beans, corn on the cob, pickles, olives, a dinner roll, mashed potatoes and gravy, coleslaw and Jell-O fruit salad. She opened a bag of potato chips and set them down on the table beside his two plates. She then poured him a nice cold glass of milk.

"This is enough food to feed the whole valley!" Jim exclaimed looking at the food that Mandy had set on the table for him to eat. "I said that I was a little hungry."

"Like I said, you're going to need all the strength that you can muster up for the next few days. It is going to be hard on you both and you need your nourishment to keep going," Mandy sighed. "I only wish that I could get Wendy to eat something."

"Maybe she will when she wakes up," he offered

"Maybe," she agreed. Then she sat down at the table with Jim. "I was going to wait until I spoke with Bill about it, but, I feel the need to tell you now so that you won't have that to worry about with everything else," Mandy stated.

"What is it, Mandy?"

"Well, I was thinking earlier today about your situation now that Abby is gone. You will need someone to come over in the mornings and help get Wendy off to school, and make breakfast and make you both lunches. You will also need someone who is familiar with the house and someone that knows Wendy so as not to traumatize her any further. You'll need the wash done, the beds made and so on. Dinner has to be cooked in the evening and someone has to be here with Wendy until you get home from work," she explained.

"Yes, I know. I have been thinking about that very same thing today. I thought I would put a notice up on the bulletin board at church or maybe advertise in the paper," he told her. "Why? Did you have someone in mind?"

"Yes, I do. Me."

"Are you forgetting that you have Bill to take care of? What would poor Bill do with you over here all day?" he asked, concerned that she was just distraught and not thinking clearly.

"What he always does. He'll putter around in his shop and do some gardening and he will help me with the chores at home. Don't you worry about Bill; I'll keep him plenty busy enough. He won't have time to miss me," she chuckled.

"I'll accept on two conditions. One, it has to be completely okay with Bill and two, I want to pay you," he said, adamantly.

"You'll do no such thing! I wouldn't hear of it! No! I won't accept one penny from you!" she told him firmly, folding her arms in front of her.

"Then the deal is off and I will have to find someone at church to help out," Jim said just as firmly.

"You are a stubborn man, did you know that Mr. Jim Wardly?" she accused, pointing a finger at him.

"Yes, I know. Abby accused me of being stubborn a couple of times, but my being stubborn still stands. Bill has to okay it and I want to pay you or no deal."

"Fine! Go ahead and pay me. I'll just spend it on Wendy."

"Now who is being stubborn?" Jim chuckled.

"I am. After all it is my right as a member of the female gender to be stubborn, to change my mind and make a happy home for some dear friends of mine who happen to need me right now." She smiled at Jim.

"You know, you really don't have to pay me. I want to do it for you and for Abby, not for money."

"Yes, I understand your feelings, but, please understand mine. I would feel better if I was paying you. That way you and Bill can take that cruise to the Bahamas that you have been talking about for the past ten years."

Mandy laughed. "That's really all it is, just talk. I don't think we would ever actually do it."

"Why not? It sounds great. I only wish that Abby could have lived long enough so that we could have gone on a vacation like that together. Do it, Mandy......before.....before it's too late," he said sadly.

"Of course, Jim. I'll accept your terms and I'll even put most of the money away for that vacation if it will make you feel better."

"It will." He said.

"Then, it is all settled. I'll be here every day at six thirty in the morning to make your breakfast and get Wendy off to school. Then I'll stay in the morning and do the laundry, make the beds, dust the furniture, wash the dishes and whatever else needs to be done. Then I will go home and spend a couple of hours with Bill and be ready at two forty for the bus when Wendy gets home. I'll stay with her and make your dinner in the evening, wash up the dinner dishes and see that Wendy takes a bath and brushes her teeth and does her homework. I'll even read her a bedtime story like I used to do for my children when they were small."

"What about Bill's dinner?" Jim asked curiously

"I thought that every now and then he could come over and eat here with us," Mandy suggested.

"What a wonderful idea. He is welcome every night not just now and then." Jim gladly offered. "Wendy always calls him Grandpa anyway so he's just like one of the family, like you are, Mandy. You are more of a Grandma to Wendy than her own Grandmother was."

"That's a nice compliment and I will pass it on to Bill." She smiled contentedly.

"What was that?" Mandy asked when she heard a noise.

"I think it is Wendy," Jim said, scooting his chair away from the table.

They both went to the living room to investigate.

"Daddy," Wendy cried. "I had a dream," she sniffled. "I dreamt that Mama was sitting right here beside me and told me that any time I want to talk to her I can send her a letter."

"Where are you supposed to send this letter, Sweetheart?" Jim asked as he knelt down on his knees next to the sofa where Wendy was still laying with the afghan tucked tightly around her.

"Mama said to go down to the hardware store and ask Josh for a balloon.........one that floats. She called it a hemean balloon."

"Do you mean a helium balloon?" Jim asked her in surprise.

"Yes! That's what she said!" Wendy said excitedly. "She told me to tie the letter to the balloon and let it go in the air and that she would get it and read it." Then Wendy frowned. "But, she said that she couldn't write back to me because there was no way for her to send it. But, she said she still wants to hear from me!"

Both Jim and Mandy looked at each other in astonishment. Could it really have been Abby? Or, was it just a dream? Had Wendy's mind given her a way to accept her Mother's death? Had her mind given her the link that she so desperately needed to her Mother? Jim shook his head. There was still the matter of the helium balloon. Jim and Abby had always called them floating balloons whenever they had bought one for Wendy. Where did Wendy hear the word helium?

"Honey? Where did you hear the word helium before?" Jim asked

"Just now in my dream. Mama said that it had to a hemean balloon or the balloon wouldn't float high in the sky for her to reach it."

"Did your Mommy say anything else?" Mandy asked in wonder.

"She said that she was very happy and that she wanted all of us to be happy too." Wendy smiled. "Can I send Mommy a letter tomorrow, Daddy?" She asked.

"You sure can, Pumpkin. We'll go down and see Josh first thing after church tomorrow morning and get you that balloon." He hugged her and thanked God with all his soul and all his heart for giving him such a precious gift.

"Are you hungry?" Mandy asked her in a quivering voice.

"I'm starving!" Wendy said throwing the afghan off her body and running to the kitchen.

Jim and Mandy stood there looking at each other.

"We may never know the answer to our question," Jim told her, "But, I really think that it had to be Abby. Somehow she communicated with Wendy through a dream. Wendy has never heard the word helium before in her life, unless she heard it at school, though she has never mentioned it to me before." Jim shook his head. "It had to be Abby," he smiled contentedly.

"It's the only answer," Mandy told him nodding her head.

Wendy ate some fried chicken, Jell-o salad, baked beans and corn on the cob, but she refused to even taste the potato salad.

"Would either of you like a piece of cake?" Mandy offered.

"Only if you have one with us," Wendy told her enthusiastically.

"I think that I might have enough room in my stomach for a small piece."

"It sounds good to me, but just a small piece for me, too. I ate way too much dinner." Jim told Mandy as he sat down at the table with Wendy and rubbed his stomach.

Mandy reached into the cupboard and got three small plates for their cake.

"You better make mine a small one, too, please," Wendy said as she copied her Father and rubbed her stomach. "It's pretty full in there."

When Wendy had finished eating she got up out of her chair and went over to where her Father was sitting at the table and gave him a kiss. "Goodnight, Daddy," she told him and then walked over to where Mandy was sitting. "Thank you for trying to help my Mommy today, Mandy. It wasn't either of our faults." She gave Mandy a big kiss on the cheek. "I love you."

Mandy was moved to tears. "I love you, too," she told her. "I'll be up in a minute to tuck you in."

"I love you, too, Daddy."

"Come here and give me a big hug, Kitten. I need one about now, don't you?" he asked her.

Wendy immediately ran to her Father's outstretched arms.

Mandy felt contented.

"You know, Sweetheart, you don't have to go to bed yet, it is still early," Jim told her.

"I know, but the sooner I go to bed, the sooner I can get up in the morning and write a letter to Mama!" she said, smiling.

After Wendy had left the kitchen, Jim asked Mandy, "What was that all about?"

"What was what all about?"

"What did Wendy mean when she said that it wasn't either of your faults about Abby's death?"

"Oh," Mandy smiled. "She has come to terms with herself about what happened today, that's all. You see," Mandy told him while she began to clear the dishes off the table, "she blamed herself for Abby's death. Wendy challenged Abby to a race and they both ran to the barn. Only, as you already know, Abby didn't make it. She also blamed herself for the loss of the baby. It seems that just this morning she had been thinking about how nice it was that she didn't have any sisters or brothers to have to share you and Abby with. So....when Abby lost the baby, she thought it was her fault."

"I wonder what set her mind in the right direction?" he asked, sipping on some hot coffee.

"I don't know," Mandy frowned. "She sure is taking all this a lot better now that she had that dream."

"If it was a dream," Jim cautioned her.

"Miracles do happen, Jim."

"Yes they sure do and I think that we have just witnessed one today."

Mandy did the dishes and went up stairs to tuck Wendy into bed. She was already asleep. Mandy stood for a moment and thought about what life held in store for her little foster grandchild. That is what this precious child had become to her, a foster Grandchild.

Jim came into the room and saw that Wendy was asleep. "She looks happy," he whispered.

"Yes, I know she does." Then she asked, "What time will you need me to come over in the morning?"

"How about seven thirty?" he asked her. "I think that will be soon enough to eat breakfast and get ready for church."

"Sounds good to me," Mandy concurred. "But, remember, you need to stop at the hardware store on your way home. Wendy wants to send a letter to her Mother."

"It's a good thing that Josh opens up for a couple of hours every Sunday for folks that need something after church."

"See you in the morning," Mandy told him. "I'm going home to give Bill some antacid!" she smiled and patted Jim on the shoulder.

"I don't know how to thank you for all that you have done today. If it hadn't been for you, this could have turned out a lot worse than it did. I'm happy that you were there for my family when we needed you. I'm so thankful that you were there with Wendy. Thank you," Jim told her.

"You don't need to thank me, Jim, but, you are very welcome. Goodnight."

"Goodnight, Mandy."

The next morning Jim woke up to a noise coming from Wendy's bedroom. He got up out of bed, put on his bath robe and went to investigate. Wendy was sitting at her mirrored dresser with pencil and paper trying to write a letter to Abby.

"Hi! Daddy!" she called when she saw his reflection in the mirror.

"Good Morning, Kitten," he replied, smiling. He was thankful that Wendy was doing well, but his heart was missing pieces that he would never put together again, not until the day he died and held his beloved Abby in his arms once again.

"How do you spell, Ralphy?" she asked, erasing something that she had written on her piece of paper.

"R-A-L-P-H-Y." her told her.

"I'm telling Mama how much Ralphy misses her."

"Tell her that I miss her, too, will you?" he said shakily.

"I already did," she assured him.

"Did you sleep good last night?" Jim asked her.

"I slept pretty good. I kept waiting for Mama to come and sit on my bed and talk to me, but, I guess she was busy practicing with the rest of the choir," Wendy told him thoughtfully.

"Yes, I guess she was."

"There, I'm finished. Do you want to write something to her on my paper, Daddy?" she asked him, her eyes were bright with anticipation.

"Yes, I think I will," he replied as he took the paper and pencil form hr small hands.

He read Wendy's letter.

Deer Mama I love you and I mis you Daddy mises you to so duz Ralphy I mis seeing yur fase but it is nise to no that I can rite you a leter I hope that you ar hafing fun singing in the qire I wil rite to you agin I love you mama.

My Dear Sweet Wife, Abby, My heart aches for you, but, my soul soars for you at the same time. I know that you are at peace and with Our Lord Jesus. Wait for me, Darling. I'll be there with you when it is my time and when I have made sure that all is well with our daughter. Thank you for giving her this special letter delivery system. It has changed her life. I miss you, my sweet Abby.....so very much. Your loving husband, Jim.

"Hello? Is anyone awake up there this morning?" Mandy called up the stairs.

"We are both up and writing a letter," Jim called back to her. "I need to get dressed then I will be down."

"I'll start on some breakfast," she said, turning and heading for the kitchen.

Bill came over and ate breakfast with them and they all decided to go to church together.

Before and after the church services, everyone from miles around stopped to give their condolences to Jim and Wendy. So many people had loved her. He realized then, that the funeral service would be enormous. These were the people that he went to church with. He knew a lot more that didn't go to the same church and he knew that they would probably be coming to Abby's funeral as well.

He estimated about three hundred people.

When they finally arrived at the hardware store, the story of Wendy's dream had already reached Josh. He had a bouquet of five balloons tied together and ready for Wendy to send her letter to her Mother. He refused to take any money for the balloons.

"After church every Sunday, you stop by my hardware store and I will have a bouquet of balloons ready for you, okay?" Josh asked Wendy.

"Okay," Wendy answered, "Thank you Mr. Holbreck," she said as she turned to her Father. "Daddy will you tie my letter to the balloons so that it doesn't fall off before it reaches Mommy?"

"I sure will, Kitten." He took the letter and tied it tightly to the balloons and then he handed it to Wendy. By then, there was quite a crowd of people standing around silently watching as Wendy released the balloons into the air. Many of the people had tears streaking down their faces. Many just stood somberly as the balloons slowly floated out of sight.

The funeral was even larger than Jim had anticipated. Seven hundred and seventy seven people signed the guest registers at the church. The gathering was held at the county park and almost everyone attended, each bringing their favorite dish of something to eat. The newspaper reporter was there and he said that he had never seen such a beautiful funeral in all his many years of reporting. It had also been the largest he had ever attended.

CHAPTER FOUR

Months passed by as Little Bark became strong and his roots became firmly planted in the ground so that the Nibblers could not come along and uproot him. During this time he had gained much knowledge from his friends and family. Tall Tales taught him about the world of make believe with each story that he told. Predictor taught him that things aren't always as they seem, you must think every emotion and dream out to the fullest before coming to a conclusion. Old Log taught him all about his family heritage. Old Sap taught him to take one day at a time and enjoy it to the fullest. Many Branches taught him his manners. She taught him the things he could do and the things that he should not do. She taught him how to love, how to be compassionate, and above all, she taught him to listen with his heart. Old Moss taught him the ancient history of the huge ones of long ago. He taught Little Bark to think before he asked questions, because, if you looked hard enough, the answer was already inside you. Old Moss became his mentor, his strength and his courage. Tickler taught him to laugh at himself and not be so critical. Fuzzy Moss taught him how to compete, and, win or lose; it was just fun to compete. Rhymer taught him humility. Weeper taught him how to be considerate of others, to think of the other tree before himself. Thin As Grass taught him just how truly blessed he was. Twiggy taught him a different kind of love.

"Tell me another story, Tall Tales," Little Bark begged him.

Of course, Tall Tales pretended to be bored with the whole idea. The thought of someone actually asking him to tell one of his stories was almost too much for him to handle.

"Yes! Please tell us, Tall Tales," Fuzzy Moss and Twiggy pleaded in unison.

"Oh, alright, if it will please you," he mused as he fiddled with his limbs in anticipation, preening for his momentary oratory. "Once upon a time, long, long ago, there lived a cleptor of trees that built great ships out of their enemies and sailed across the big water to distant lands. And.......there on the shore to greet them were huge fire-breathing dragons that stood taller than any tree ever grown. The dragons were fierce looking.....and....trees being what they are, did not want to be burned up by their hot breath. So, they set sail to a different land. This time they wore a sword at their side made of the finest shiny steel. They all went ashore to see what they could see. Slowly.....ever so slowly....they crept with eyes in every direction, ready to run at the first glimpse of trouble, unaware that they were being watched by see-throughs who could not be harmed by the blade of a sword. Nay.....and they didn't know that the see-throughs were even there," he whispered in a mysterious voice, "Until the see-throughs ooooooood and booooooooood at them and the see-throughs picked up rocks and began to throw them at the invaders. The rocks bounced off their trunks with a painful thud. So...back aboard the ship they went to sail to another shore where they set anchor once again and went ashore. Slowly they crept along, inching their way inland with eyes as big as the moon. Stealthily, quietly they inched along, shaking all the way. Suddenly a hoard of giants the size of which was unimaginable came straight up out of the sand and started after them! Well, this was much too much for the timid trees who only liked to fight with trees that were smaller than themselves. So, they hastily retreated back to their ship and set sail for their own land. That night when they set anchor in their home port and were all fast asleep , the ship that they had built out of their enemies came alive and slayed every one of the sailors," he finished proudly as he looked around at all the mere twigs and seedlings. They all looked mesmerized.

"There once was a cleptor of trees
Who made ships of their enemies.
They all set sail one day
Without delay,
To distant shores, all three.
A fire breathing dragon on one
Another, see-throughs to shun.

And then on the last,
A giant stood fast,
As homeward their journey begun.
Alas, as they slept
Their enemy crept
To end their sailing days.
And, with long roots
All clad in boots,

They stamped them to a maze," Rhymer said, proudly, glaring at Tall Tales, waiting for him to say something. He was not disappointed.

"One of these days, I shall put an end to you! Mark my words!" he said, shaking his branches in anger directed solely at Rhymer.

"I think, Tall Tales, it would be better for your own personal physical condition if you leave poor, little Rhymer alone and pick on someone your own size. Do you get my meaning?" Old Sap said menacingly.

Tall Tales shot an evil look at Rhymer and left it at that. It was not a good thing to have Old Sap angry with you.

Little Bark stood nonchalantly, thinking about the story. It would be nice to be able to travel from one place to another the way he heard that the Walk-To's did. "Oh, Well," he sighed.

"By the look on your face, Old Moss, you must be thinking about the same thing I am." Predictor said.

"And just what might that be?" he asked?

"I am trying to understand the lost feeling I have in my trunk. It will not go away and there is no apparent reason for it to be there. I cannot put my limb on it. It is a sadness that goes right to my core," he told Old Moss. "Is this what is bothering you also Old One?"

"You are right. I have been thinking about it. My trunk is too old to be hurting this way for no reason. Something must be wrong somewhere. We just haven't put our limb on it yet. We are all here and we are all well so it is evidently not anything to do with our Thicket. Therefore, I cannot tell you why we are feeling as we do, but I will put some more thought into it and see what I can come up with." Old Moss told his friend.

"Thin-As-Grass?" Many Branches called to her friend as she raised one of her branches and wiped her brow. "It is very hot. How are you feeling today?"

"I am not so good," she whined like an old, tired Walk-To. "My roots are too crowded and they are beginning to dry up and become brittle from the parched, hard ground. And, Tickler is constantly soaking up what little water I do manage to find. My needles are all turning brown and they are starting to fall off. Soon, I will be bald! And, as you probably already know, I am very weak from no sun. I think some day I will wither away and end and I doubt very much if any of you would miss me at all," she said, searching Many Branches face for any sign of sympathy.

"I would miss you very much, Dear Friend. Do not talk of ending. You may have some of my water," Many Branches offered. "Can you reach it?"

"I cannot take so precious a gift from you. It would not be right."

"It will be just fine. I have plenty. Can you reach it?" Many Branches repeated her question.

"I think so......I'm.....trying...but... I am so weak," she complained as she stretched her roots as hard and as far as she could. She looked a little like a rubber band about ready to snap. "Yes! Yes! I can reach it!" she cried excitedly thanking her friend for her precious gift.

Thin-As-Grass was always whining and complaining because she was unlucky enough to be rooted between Many Branches and Tickler and because of this, she didn't get enough sunshine and her roots were too crowded. She was already many cycles old, about twenty, and she was only about five lippets tall, very short for her age. She had only seven spindly branches with just a few tiny limbs sticking out like stiff weeds from her skinny trunk.

"Thin-As-Grass.....You look more like a Walk-To than a Walk-To does!" Tickler teased her for the thousandth time.

Poor little Thin-As-Grass, even the niggit seemed to pick on her more than anyone else, crawling all over her bark. Maybe it was because they thought she was easy prey.

"Old Moss!" Predictor directed his thoughts at his old friend in a frightened voice.

"What is it, Good Friend? You must calm yourself or you will shed all your needles!" he said when he saw that his friend was very upset. "What is it that has upset you so?" Old Moss was curious. Predictor didn't usually become so excited over anything.

"Listen, Old Friend and listen well to what I am going to say. It is not good," he said, looking around to see if anyone happened to watching them. "Something is going to happen, something very bad. I dread telling you about it, but, I feel that I should. Soon, very soon I think, there will be a fire, a terrible fire. It will consume many Thickets and many trees will perish, perhaps even some from our own Thicket," he said, sadly, and then he continued after a short pause. "It will be started by a Walk-To. He will come by in his stinky-go and he will throw one of those little sticks of smoke out along the road, there it will catch the weeds on fire and spread to the trees. We cannot stop him. And, when it happens, there is no way to put the fire out," he said and his branches drooped in sadness.

"Good Friend," Old Moss told him after much thought," It is good that you have told me of this. Now we can prepare ourselves for the worst. We must think this thing through thoroughly. Do you know'" he asked, his voice wavering, "do you have any idea when it is to happen?"

"I have searched my knots until they ache and I cannot come up with a time. No, Old Friend, I guess we are not supposed to know when it is to happen. We are only supposed to know that it definitely IS going to happen and there is absolutely nothing that we can do about it. It is so frustrating!" he said in desperation.

"Do you know how many of us will perish?" Old Moss asked a bit apprehensively. He was a little afraid of the answer, afraid that he was going to lose one of his family, because that is what Old Moss thought of each member of his Thicket. They were all family and he didn't want to lose any of them. "Oh, God, I would gladly end in their place," he prayed silently to himself.

"No, I guess we weren't supposed to know that either. I am sorry, Old Friend, I am afraid that I am not of much help to you with this vision," Predictor told him, apologizing as though he had complete control of his dreams, which he didn't.

"It is just meant to be kept from us, I guess, Good Friend," he said, consoling Predictor as best he could. "Do not feel that you have failed. There are some things that we are meant to know ahead of time, and others that The Great God of All Things thinks that it is best we do not know, though I do not know why He would warn us of the fire and then tell nothing about the rest."

"But, there is a reason…..there has to be a reason that He forewarned us, but, what is it?" Old Moss thought to himself. Then after a short pause he continued. "Tell me, please, if you can…..do you know if it is a long time or a short time? Does if feel as though it is eminent and soon or maybe far off in the distant future?"

"I tell you the truth, Old Friend, I know nothing more than I have already told you. It feels like it might be soon, but, then again, I can't be sure. I would hate to say one thing and then have it turn out to be another," he paused for a moment and looked down to the ground in sorrow, "Are we going to warn the others?"

"Hmmmmmmmmm………That I must think about with all my knots, Good Friend. We mustn't be too hasty. Haste in this case anyway, could very well mean waste. It may cause unnecessary worry. We do not want to cause a panic among all the Thickets. It might prove a disaster as it did many cycles ago when you predicted the great winds. Ha! Ha! Oh, yes, what a mistake that was! Do you remember what happened when we forewarned everyone?" Old Moss asked as he raised one eyebrow and gently leaned toward his life long friend.

"Oh, yes! I do! Even before the great winds finally came, we had many casualties. Many limbs and branches were broken in all the excitement and panic, and, as I recall….two friends were uprooted also," He said, holding his chin with one of his branches in thought.

"Yes, so you see, I have a very large and weighty decision to make. It makes me feel lost in my trunk to think about it," he sighed as their conversation was abruptly interrupted.

"Old Moss?" Little Bark called to his Mentor. "Old Moss! Do you hear me?" he asked, stretching over so far that he almost fell over. Old Teacher of Many Things, can you spare a moment of your time? I must speak with you!" he demanded.

"Yes, what is it, Little Bark? I am quite busy doing some very serious thinking of my own," he told him, listening with only half an ear. "Can't it wait until later?" he asked without really concentrating on Little Bark.

"Old Moss, I need your full attention! I must know something right away," Little Bark shouted as though he was out of breath.

"Calm yourself, Little Bark," At last Little Bark had Old Moss' attention. "What is this all about? What has you trembling like that? Look at your leaves; they are all shaking and about ready to fall off. You are much too young to worry like this. How many emergencies shall we have today?

"What do you mean by that? What other emergencies have there been?"

"Nothing that need concern someone so young. Now, tell me, what is on your knots?"

"Great Teacher, what I have seen is enough to rot even the strongest roots with worry. Tell me, Old Moss, what is it that makes gray and black clouds and is red, yellow, and blue with angry tongues that eat away at our limbs and branches until we end?" Little Bark was describing a fire although he had never before seen one.

"Where did you see this, Little Bark?" Old Moss asked trying to appear unconcerned.

"I saw it in a dream as I slept. What is it?" he asked again, angry that Old Moss had answered his question with a question. Old Moss was famous among all the Thickets for doing this. It was a rarity when he didn't.

Old Moss and Predictor looked at each other in amazement! Little Bark was only a few moons old and yet, he had already proven himself to be a tree prodigy. Now he had proven himself to be a Tree Prophet as well. This was unheard of in all the memories that Old Moss could remember which was a very long time.

"Please tell me, Old Ones. What is it that I have seen in my dreams?" he pleaded.

"Little Bark, listen carefully. You are to tell absolutely no one else about what it is that you have seen in your dream. Do you understand?" Old Moss asked in a demanding voice, looking first at Little Bark and then back to Predictor.

"I understand and I won't tell anyone."

"Do you promise?" Old Moss asked with raised eyebrows. Trees, unlike the Walk-To's, never went back on their word for any reason. If a tree made a promise, it had to be kept until the tree that had made him promise released him from that promise. It was the way of the Thickets, a rule to be kept no matter what.

"Yes! Yes! I promise! I promise on all my roots and all my knots! NOW! WHAT WAS IT THAT I SAW IN MY DREAM?" he almost screamed in desperation.

"How many knots do you have now, Little Bark?" Predictor asked, curiously, trying to distract him. He was making entirely too much noise and they did not want the attention of the whole Thicket.

"I have only five. Quit changing the subject and tell me WHAT IS IT THAT I HAVE SEEN IN MY DREAM!" he demanded in no uncertain terms. This time, however, he had lost all control and all the trees from four Thickets around had heard him and stopped what they were doing to listen. Nothing exciting ever happened around the Thickets, at least anything to shout about, anyway. "Is it the dragon that Tall Tales told of in his story?" Little Bark asked in a smaller voice when he looked around and saw that everyone was staring at him. All were quiet, even the constant chattering of the bushy tails and Freckles, the Spotted Owl, ceased their discord as an eerie, deadly silence fell over the forest. No sounds could be heard except for Little Bark's voice which was almost a whisper.

"I will tell you later," Old Moss whispered as he, too, glanced around uneasily, afraid that someone might have overheard them talking. "

"Oh, Teachers, they can be so secretive at times!" he thought to himself, throwing his branches up in desperation. "But, it must be important or they would have told me without all this evasiveness."

"Did you hear what Little Bark said?" Predictor whispered to his Old Friend as he stared at Little Bark in wonder. "He said he has five knots! No tree in my memory or anyone else's, for that matter, has ever had five knots in less than one full cycle! If there was, I would surely have heard about it before this!" Predictor gasped for air as he rushed the words out in one breath.

"Ah, but there is one other one. He already has four and is just now growing his fifth and he is less than one full cycle, also!" Old Moss informed him.

"Who?" Predictor demanded, looking all around at each tree. "Surely not someone from our own Thicket?"

"Yes, he is. You must have had your top in the clouds for a long time not to notice him. See…..over there by Tall Tales and Rhymer," he said as he pointed in their direction.

"Who is his Mentor? Who is teaching him?" he asked with a surprised look.

"Old Sap, Tall Tales, Old Log and just about everyone else in the Thicket, including myself." Old Moss' heavy lids dropped even lower over his cool, dark eyes. "Where have you been while all this has been going on?" he asked his friend.

"Off in dream land, I guess," Predictor said in a puzzled voice. "Why have I not been consulted concerning his teachings? I am, after all, supposed to be teaching all the young seedlings and mere twigs," he said indignantly.

"Fuzzy Moss is wary of talking to you."

"But, why? I have never said anything to him to make him wary of me! I have never talked to him at all! I did not know of his existence until now."

"Well, never the less, he is wary of you and it is something that the two of you will have to work out between yourselves. It is not something that I can remedy for you. He thinks you are spooky," Old Moss laughed.

"What do you mean by spooky?" Predictor was rapidly losing his patience with Old Moss because he would not stop laughing.

"He thinks you are spooky because you have dreams about things that are going to happen and then they happen. It seems that he has heard a lot about you and he doesn't understand how or why you do it. I guess it kind of scares him."

"Well, he's not alone there! It has scared me since I was a Mere Twig and had my first vision. Hmmmmmm.......I thought that Little Bark was to be our next Thicket Councilor when you retire?"

"It is a close race between the two seedlings, a race that only one can win," Old Moss said sadly, his voice dim as though it came from a long distance. "We've all got to remember that just because we expected Little Bark to be our next Thicket Councilor, does not mean that we can shirk our duty and responsibility towards Fuzzy Moss. After all, The Great God of All Things might have something else in mind for Little Bark. We want to give them both an equal opportunity to do their best." Little Bark was Old Moss' favorite; though he told no one and he did not let his feelings get in the way of his duty to Fuzzy Moss.

Fuzzy Moss was a Will-of-the-Wind seedling. He came from somewhere close or far away, carried along by the wind or perhaps on the fur of an animal, it didn't really matter. It happened all the time, but, the fact still remained that it did happen and Fuzzy Moss was not considered an outsider because of it. He was a member of their Thicket and as such he therefore had all the same rights, privileges and responsibilities as the rest of the Thicket.

That was the way of things. Trees learned at the Time of the Great Planting not to be prejudiced.

Fuzzy Moss was not a great oak like Little Bark, he was an elm. He would grow very tall and strong like Little Bark, but, perhaps, he would not be as sympathetic and understanding. Elms were known to be stern and prudish.

"Old Sap, are you awake? It is I, Tall Tales. I wish to tell you a story," he called.

"I'm awake now, thanks to you. Go away! I'm tired and I wish to sleep. Besides, I have heard your stories at least a thousand times. You never change them or think up a new one," he paused as his curiosity got the better of him. "Is it a new one or just one of your old ones?" he asked, hesitantly, his voice old and shaky.

Old Sap was Little Bark's Grandfather. He was very special, very special indeed. He was skinny and twisted and brittle and very old, but he was still well rooted. His roots were strong and long and very deep in the ground. He slept most of the time swaying in the breeze.

No one knew exactly how old he really was, not even Old Sap. If you asked him how old he was, he would say, "I am as old as my bark and ten thousand times older than my leaves." He could remember being a seedling long ago when there were very few "Walk-To's. In fact, he could remember when his father had told him that he was one of the first seedlings to be born after the Great Planting, many, many cycles ago. Old Sap had always been there. There wasn't anyone for miles around in any direction that was older than he was, so, therefore, no one was able to tell him how old he actually was.

"It is a good story and I am sure that you will enjoy it very much," Tall Tales assured him with no intention of taking no for an answer.

"Oh, alright," Old Sap stretched and groaned as he turned his curiosity and attention towards Tall Tales.

Tall Tales cleared his throat and began his story. "Many cycles ago there was a very special tree, the only one of its kind. He was very short and very round. In fact, he was so big around that he was said to have had a great huge tank inside of him to hold thousands and thousands of pintles of water. Day after day he stored up water until he could store no more. All the other trees began teasing him because he was so fat. They told him that he was water logged and they called him a sponge and Old Water Belly. Until…..one day…..there was a great huge fire heading directly for them. All the trees looked to one another in desperation. They trembled so hard that they shook the ground around them, including where Old Water Belly was standing. The vibration from all of them trembling with fear shook Old Water Belly's tank so hard that the water tickled his branches. Soon he could stand it no longer and he lifted his whole trunk about two lippets high and pulled the plug! None too soon, as the fire was just beginning to scorch their branches. All of the water from Old Water Belly's trunk gushed out like a giant tidal wave and quenched the fire to mere steam. The fire was out! And, from that day on, no one ever made fun of Old Water Belly's trunk again. He was their hero!" Tall Tales said, proudly.

"I've heard it," Old Sap said as though he were speaking to himself.

"Old Water Belly shook like jelly until it tickled him so.

His trunk he lifted as water he sifted out of his trunk below.

And out went the fire as 'twas everyone's desire ,

Much to alls content.

No one made sore, their hero no more

Good tidings did not relent."

"Oh, shut up Rhymer!" Tall Tales shouted menacingly. "One of these days I shall tie all your spindly little stems together and choke you until you end!"

"I must caution you," Old Sap said as his eyes narrowed and his voice held a definite tone of disapproval. "Do not harm the little bush, I rather like his rhymes. They are a definite improvement over you stories," he said, curving up his lips in a slightly sardonic smile.

"Without my stories, he would not have any rhymes. He is too dumb to think up his own," Tall Tales retorted sarcastically, undaunted by Old Sap's steely gaze.

"I think not. I think he could probably outdo you two to one in stories, and, his rhyme, yours don't."

"I can! I can!.......

There once was a tree who stood by me

That was always forever a grump.

Until one day he heard them say

Let's cut him to a stump.

From that day on a smile upon

His lips did not erase.

And, without a doubt warm fuzzys gave out

For a grin on every face," Rhymer ended his oration with a hug for himself and Tall Tales.

"Let go of me, you tumbleweed!" Tall Tales warned him.

"What are warm fuzzys?" Old Sap asked.

"Oh, I thought that everyone knew what warm fuzzys and cold pricklies were. Let's see.......which would you rather have, a warm fuzzy or a cold prickly?" he asked him.

"A warm fuzzy, I suppose. It depends on what it is. It sounds better than a cold prickly if my imagination serves me correctly."

"Well, when you say...'Good morning! How are you? You sure look wonderful today!'......that's a warm fuzzy and it makes them feel good. Then that tree will pass out another warm fuzzy to another tree and soon everyone is smiling and happy and handing out warm fuzzys to everyone else. On the other limb, if you were to say....'Why don't you go back to sleep you grumpy old nag!'...... that is a cold prickly and then that tree will pass out another cold prickly and soon everyone is in a bad mood. Warm fuzzys are so much nicer."

"I have never thought of it that way before," he said in deep thought. "But, it does make sense,"

"Bah! He's just babbling," Tall Tales snapped at him.

"That is a cold prickly," Old Sap warned him.

CHAPTER FIVE

"Old Moss, It is I, Little Bark. Do you have time for my question now?" he asked in a whisper so that he did not call attention to himself.

"What question is that, Young One?" Old Moss asked as though he had forgotten.

"Can you tell me now, old, wise and elusive one, what it was that I saw in my dream a few days back?" Little Bark knew that Old Moss was just skirting the issue, though Little Bark could not understand what all the secrecy was about,

"Must you know, Little One? Is it necessary to your peace of knots to know something that will only cause you worry and much anxiety?" Old Moss asked in a very old and very tired voice.

"There he goes again," Little Bark thought to himself, "answering my question with a question."

"Yes, Old One, Great Teacher, I must know. I do not know why I must know, other than the evident curiosity I have, but, I must know. Maybe it isn't just mere curiosity after all, when I stop to think about it. I can not sleep, I can not eat, I can not drink and I can not think of anything else. It is as though The Great God of All Things wants me to know. Your answer can not possibly cause me more anxiety than I am already feeling from not knowing."

Old Moss paused and looked at Little Bark with old and wise eyes. He could remember when he was a Mere Twig like Little Bark. Little Bark was so much like him. It was times like these that made him wish that he was not the Thicket Councilor. Good tidings were always a joy to tell, but this?

Old Moss looked around to see if anyone had been listening to their conversation. All were busy primping and preening and greeting each other on the new day.

It was a beautiful day. Old Moss loved the early morning skies when they were so soft with just a brush of pink clouds to gently reflect the sun as it began its journey in the east. The Song-With-Wings were very cheerful this morning as thy hopped and flew from one branch to another. Even the bushy tails seemed unusually happy today, although Freckles the Spotted Owl was nowhere to be seen.

"I feel lost in my trunk, Little Bark. I do not like to have to be the one to tell you something like this," he paused before going on. "It is not something that we trees like to talk about. It is not a happy subject, indeed, it is a terrible one," he said, fiddling with his many limbs in thought. He looked down to the ground and then he took a deep breath and closed his eyes. He didn't want to see the look on Little Bark's face when he told him. A tear escaped his eyes and journeyed down his trunk. "It is called a fire," he whispered. "It burns us to ashes, Little Bark. It consumes us until we end and are no more than just a pile of charred ashes. It is a very slow and painful ending."

"It is as I had imagined," Little Bark told him as his limbs drooped in sadness and he began to think, think so that it really counted. He didn't want to end, and he didn't want any of his family or friends to end, either. "I must think.....think!......THINK! Think until it hurts. I can't let everyone down," he thought to himself.

Moments went by as they both thought about the fire. Old Moss was the first one to break the silence.

"Did you happen to see in your dream how many of us or who they were that will end on that day?" Old Moss asked him as he had asked his good friend, Predictor but a few days before. Perhaps Little Bark had seen more in his dream than Predictor had.

"No....no I did not. The Great God of All Things evidently does not want me to know or He would have made it clear to me. I don't even know when it is to happen. I only know that it definitely IS going to happen no matter what we do. We don't have Old Water Belly in Tall Tales story to save us. We only have ourselves" Little Bark said sorrowfully. At that moment, Little Bark sounded very old and very mature for his age.

Although Little Bark's reaction was much better than Old Moss had anticipated, he still dreaded having had to tell him. Old Moss was very proud of his young student, very proud, indeed.

"You know, of course, Little Bark, that the Great God of All Things never lets us know about things ahead of time without a reason. So there must be something that we can do to prevent it," Old Moss instructed him.

"Yes, that was my first thought. But, what.....? And, if we can't prevent it, what can we do to save ourselves?

"Barky? Barrrrrrk eeeeeeeeeee!" Twiggy called to him in as loud a whisper as she could without interrupting Old Moss.

"Yes, Twiggy, what is it?" he answered her almost rudely. He had too much heavy thinking to do to be disturbed by anyone, even Twiggy.

Twiggy was a small tree, a perfectly shaped fir tree with nice full branches that were kept in perfect shape by the nibblers who would only eat the straggly little growths that stuck out here and there. She looked very dainty as most female Mere Twigs did.

Twiggy was older than Little Bark by about two cycles. She loved Little Bark and he loved her, also. It didn't matter that they were two different kinds of trees. If you loved someone as much as they did, it didn't matter.

Twiggy wasn't at all like the other Mere Twigs in the Thicket. She was smarter and had more knots and she didn't giggle every time he looked at her like the other female Mere Twigs did. She was always fun to talk to and very rarely did she talk unless she had something important to say.

"Something is coming this way. Can you hear it?" she whispered, secretively.

"No, no, I don't believe I can," he told her as he leaned forward and strained to hear.

"Something is really coming! I can hear it! And, it is not a nibbler or any other friend. It is so loud, Barky! I am surprised that you can not hear it!"

"Maybe it is closer to you than it is to me, I don't know. And, don't call me Barky. My name is Little Bark," he told her as he strained to hear.

"Somebody help me! I'm lost," it cried.

"What was that?" Little Bark asked, his curiosity aroused to the fullest.

"That is what I have been trying to tell you about! What is it?" Twiggy asked.

"I don't know, I have never seen one before. It talks the language of the trees.....and ....Look! It's moving!" he said in astonishment watching it come up the path.

Little Bark turned to his Father, Old Log. "What is it that is coming down the path and is talking in the language of the trees, Father?"

"Oh, that's just a Walk-To. Pay no attention to it and maybe it will go away."

"A Walk-To! WOW!" Little Bark said in surprise.

"Yes, they come by here every once in a while. It has been a very long time since one has ventured through our Thicket. Not long enough though. They bring nothing but trouble when they come. They do not belong in our world or anywhere around us. The Walk-To's are intruders. We were created before they were. They belong to some other world. It is an alien, horribly different, fast paced world. We do not belong in their world either," he told him as he watched the skinny Walk-To. "This must be the first one that you have ever seen?"

"A real life Walk-To! Wow!" he said in awe. "Yes, it is the very first one I have seen! Do they all look like that one? Where did it come from? Are there any more?"

"Hey! Slow down! One question at a time, Son! They don't all look the same, exactly. Some are taller and better built than that one. And, as far as I know, there are thousands of them all over the place. Like I said, every now and then one of them will wander down our path and hopefully pass on by. But, there are some that you must be wary of. They are the ones that bring....."

"No! Old Log!" Many Branches cried as she cut Old Log off in mid sentence. "He is too young to be told of such horrors. Let him enjoy his youth. He will need to know soon enough. Please say no more."

"Go on, Father, tell me, please?" Little Bark pleaded.

"No, My Son, I cannot. Maybe when you are older and have more knots, but, not until then. It will do you no good to know now anyway. Your Mother is right," he said, looking down at him with his face softened by an understanding smile. In his youth, Old Log had hungered to know everything, also. Now he just wished that he didn't know so much.

Little Bark wondered what he had meant by the remark 'ones that you must be wary of' that His Father had said, and, why did his Mother stop him? What had he been going to tell him? Little Bark did not ask. He knew better than to argue with his parents.

"Father, can you tell me what the Walk-To meant when it said it was lost?"

"It is very hard for me to explain in words because it is something that you feel deep down in your trunk. Why don't you ask Old Sap, he could probably tell you?" and Old Log turned to watch the Walk-To as it ran up the path.

"Old Sap, are you awake?" he called, but there was no reply. "Grandfather! Wake up!" he shouted.

"Hmmmmmmmm.....What is it this time, Little Bark? Have you lost your first leaf? Or Maybe you have a girlfriend, huh?" he said teasingly. "Or maybe you are wondering about wondering! Ho! Ho! Ho! Haw! Ho!" Old Sap laughed, shaking the very ground beneath them.

Little Bark began to laugh. Anyone that heard his Grandfather's laugh couldn't help but laugh right along with him no matter how excited or upset they were.

"Grandfather, what does lost mean?" Little Bark asked, scratching his chin in wonder,

Old Sap stretched his old tired limbs and tried to gather his thoughts. It wasn't easy for him to stay awake these past few weeks. "Oh......That's really not too hard a question," he chuckled, "it's the answer that's hard!" and he thought for a moment. "A long time ago, before you or your mother and father were seedlings," he said in a more serious voice, "There was a tree, a very dear tree. His name was Whisper. He was called this because he had a very small voice that sounded like a whisper. He was a very dear friend of mine, yes, very dear indeed. We used to talk for hours and hours and dream together. Why, he was the best....but, anyway. He was a good friend. No one knows how old he was when his sap stopped pumping, but, you know when he ended and no longer was, I missed him terribly and I had a lost feeling in my trunk. It hurt very badly, way down deep inside my trunk. It still hurts when I think about him. Time will heal it someday, that's what they say, anyway. I guess that the more time that passes, the easier it gets. But, I do wish that I could go to the Land of Sweet Waters and Cool Breezes and be with him. Do you understand what it is to be lost, now, Little Bark?" he asked sadly.

"Yes, I do. I'm sorry I put you through this, Grandfather," he said, compassionately. "But, the Walk-To was crying 'Help me I'm lost!' Is she mourning like you did over Whisper?"

"No…. I don't think so. I have heard of that kind of lost before….a long time ago, But, you should probably ask Old Moss about it," Old Sap said as he quickly dismissed all thought as definitely as he knew how and relaxed his branches and fell instantly back to sleep.

"Old Moss, I have a question for you. I need your teaching, again," he called.

"What is it, Little Bark? Have you had another dream?" Old Moss asked curiously.

"No, Old Moss, I haven't. I need to know something. What does it mean to be lost?"

"Ahhhhhhhh…….so you have heard the Walk-To! What do you think of it, Little Bark?" Old Moss asked him as he glowed with the anticipation of Little Bark's answer.

"Oh, Old Moss! Sometimes you can be so frustrating! Do you know that you always answer my questions with a question?" he said rather sharply with his brows scrunched down in a frown.

"I do…..? Well, I don't mean to. It is just an old, nasty habit that I have picked up somewhere along the way. I have had it for cycles. I guess I have done it most of my life. What do you think of the Walk-To?" he demanded, ignoring the frown on Little Bark's face.

Little Bark thought about it for a minute. He knew that there must be lesson in this somewhere, but, where? "It is small," he began, hesitantly, not wanting to sound too dumb, "and it looks very weak. It has long, silky yellow….something growing out of the top of it. It has only two spindly branches with no leaves or needles on them. It has two long, skinny roots, but…..they aren't stuck in the ground! They are……'t is moving! It is going somewhere! I have seen the animals move on r paws, but, never something that speaks the language of the trees!" aid in amazement.

"Exactly! The Walk-To's can move and that is why they sometimes get lost. They go somewhere and then they can't find their way back," he explained, carefully.

Little Bark thought about his new information for a moment. Being lost was hard for him to understand. Trees never move so therefore, they can't get lost. They just stand in one spot all their lives, except for the rare occasions when one was dug up and moved by a Walk-To.

He finally dismissed the thought and went on to say, "But, the Walk-To speaks our language, how can that be?"

"You misunderstand, Little Bark. We can understand them, but they cannot understand or communicate with us. We speak in thought directed at one another except when there are no Walk-To's around. Then, we speak with our mouths. You did not even notice the change when I spoke with my mind and you answered with yours, did you? So subtle is the change that most of the time you don't even realize it. If the Walk-To's were to hear us talk, it would sound to them like gibberish. They cannot understand us, but, no matter what language they are speaking, we can understand them in our own language. The Great God of All Things has blessed us with this….this gift is what I call it," Old Moss explained to him, patiently. "Do you understand, Little Bark?"

"It is quite complicated, but, yes, I do understand, I think. I would like to try an experiment, if I may?" Little Bark told him as he thought at the Walk-To with all the power of his knots. "It didn't work. It didn't even know that I was thinking at it. It is rather dumb, is it not, Old Moss?"

"In some ways, yes. In other ways they are as far beyond us as the stars are away from us in the sky," he said while looking up at the sky as though he were imagining the great distance.

"Hello there! Can you hear me? Why are you so upset?" Little Bark cried out to the Walk-To.

"What was that?" Wendy cried, looking all around her. Her eyes were huge with fear. She couldn't figure out where the strange noise had come from. "It is me! Right over here!" Little Bark tried to tell her.

Old Moss just smiled to himself. He had tried talking to a Walk-To a long time ago with the same results.

"Oh, Father! Where are you? I am so afraid," she said, shaking all over. "What am I to do? I am so lost and there are so many strange and frightening noises," she cried softly. Then, as she was drying her eyes with the back of her hands, she saw Twiggy for the first time. "Oh! How beautiful and perfect you are, little tree! I must tell Daddy all about you! That is, if I can ever find my way home again," she said, sitting down next to Twiggy. "I am so tired. I think I will rest here for a while, right next to you, little tree," she said as she curled up under Twiggy's branches and was soon fast asleep.

"Well, it did not understand me either way. I think it is really quite dumb. I don't see much intelligence at all. Don't you think that is should keep searching for whatever it is that it is searching for?" Little Bark asked Old Moss while he gazed at the Walk-To in wonder.

"Sometimes, maybe, but it looks rather young so it is probably better that it stays in one spot so that it will be easier for another Walk-To to find it," he explained.

"Does this mean that we might get to see another Walk-To?"

"Yes, it is quite possible. Usually where there is one, there is another not too far away."

"Wouldn't it be better if they were both searching? That way they double their chances of finding one another?"

"Maybe, but, that way, they also double their chances of losing each other, also," he cautioned.

"Yes, I can see that, but why didn't it remember where it was going so that it could just retrace its tracks?" Little Bark speculated.

"That, I can not tell you," he answered, thoughtfully.

"I think it is because it is too young and too dumb," Little Bark speculated.

"You may have something there. Maybe it is too young to find whatever it is trying to find."

They were both interrupted by a frantic call from another Walk-To.

"Wendy? Wendy?" Jim called as he ran up the path. "Wendy!" he cried in relief when he saw his daughter lying under a tree, fast asleep. "Wendy, are you alright?" he asked, gently touching her shoulder. "We have been so worried about you! You have scared poor old Mandy so badly that she is at home this very minute crying her heart out," her

Father told her. He was so relieved to find her safe that he threw his arms around her and gave her a big hug.

"Oh, Daddy, I am so glad that you found me. I was so worried. I looked and looked and looked for the way home, but I couldn't find it. I got so tired that I laid down here to rest for awhile. I must have fallen asleep. I heard some very strange noises, Daddy," she told him in a sleepy voice.

"What kind of noises?" he asked her. He was concerned that there might be a rogue bear running around in the valley instead of up in the hills where it belonged.

"I don't really know. It was kind of like an animal was trying to talk to me, only he couldn't speak our language and it was all mumbled up. It was really scary. It might have even been a ghost!" she said, wide eyed with fear.

"You were probably dreaming it all," he comforted her. "Why did you come to the forest, Wendy? You know that you are not supposed to leave the house without either Mandy or me," he scolded her gently.

"Mandy was busy making cookies and you were at work and I wanted to look for a Christmas tree for our Christmas this year....... And..Oh! Look! Daddy, look at this tree! Isn't it just perfect? See how its limbs are so even and beautiful? Can we dig it up and take it home at Christmas time and decorate it all up pretty?" she asked without taking her eyes off of Twiggy.

"It is very beautiful, indeed. So perfect. I have not seen one like it for a long time. We will see when the time comes. It is a while, yet, until Christmas. Right now, you must come home with me. It is getting dark and poor old Mandy is worried sick about you," he said as he took her hand and led her out of the forest.

Wendy looked back, "Goodbye for now, Perfect Little Christmas Tree. We will be back to dig you up at Christmas time!" and they disappeared down the path through an opening that looked like an arched gate under stout, curved branches.

"I still say they are dumb, very dumb," Little Bark commented as he watched them disappear. "I tried to communicate with the large Walk-To and it was like talking to a dead twig on the ground. There is little or no intelligence at all," he said, disgustedly.

"Then you have not heard of the story of the great Walk-To who once talked to the trees thousands of cycles ago and told them of the Great Lifting?" Tall Tales asked Little Bark.

"No....I do not remember you telling me about it, but, I have no time to listen right now. I must think of a way to communicate with the Walk-To's."

"Barky?" Twiggy called to him, "What is a Christmas Tree?"

Little did she know what she was asking.

Mandy came running out the door when she saw Jim and Wendy coming up the walkway. "Where have you been? I've been worried sick about you!" she scolded her gently.

"I went for a walk and I got lost in the forest, but Daddy found me and we saw a perfect little Christmas tree. Daddy is going to dig it up at Christmas time. And, we can decorate it and put lights on it and everything!" Wendy told her with her eyes shining brightly.

"Why didn't you ask me to go for a walk with you? I would have gladly gone, you know," Mandy told her.

"I went to the kitchen to ask you, but you were busy baking cookies. Daddy was at work, so, I went by myself." Wendy frowned. "You wouldn't have liked where I went anyway, Mandy. There were all kinds of strange noises and it was really spooky. I even got scared."

"Well, thank goodness you are safe at home again," Mandy hugged her.

"I'm going to go to my room and write to Mommy and tell her all about the Christmas tree that I found!" Wendy told them as she ran up the stairs to her room.

"She really had me scared, Jim. I don't know what ever made her go off like that without at least telling me."

"I'll have a talk with her. Sometimes she can be the smartest, wisest little girl I know of and other times, well, she just doesn't think about the consequences of what she does. I'm sure she didn't mean to scare either one of us."

"She hasn't missed sending a letter on Sunday in all these months, has she?" Mandy asked, shaking her head.

"No, she hasn't. It's really amazing when you think about it. That dream made the difference between her being depressed and being the happy little girl that she is now. I know that Abby did it for her. I know in my heart that the dream was really Abby trying to ease the pain for Wendy. I only wish that she would come to me in a dream sometime so that I could see her beautiful face once again and see her smile at me," Jim bowed his head as he walked into the house.

Mandy followed him not knowing what to say. "I'll go finish dinner. Bill will be eating here with us tonight," she called to him over her shoulder as she went to the kitchen.

"Good, I haven't seen him in about a week," Jim told her.

"Yes, I know. He has been working about twelve hours a day in his shop. Says he's making something for Wendy for Christmas. Won't tell me what it is though. Maybe you can squeeze the information out of him after diner and then you can tell me."

"If Bill isn't telling you what it is, I know that he won't tell me," Jim pondered.

"You're probably right. He won't let me anywhere near the shop. I've tried sneaking a peek, but he even has sheets over the windows! And, he locks the door when he leaves to go fishing or to town."

"Well, you can bet that it is something really special then," Jim told her.

"Oh, I'm sure it is, but, you know how bad a woman's curiosity can be," she chuckled.

That Sunday Wendy sent her Mother a letter on the balloons telling her all about the tree that she had found in the forest for their Christmas.

CHAPTER SIX

Dusk deepened and a heavy mist lay among the trees of the Thicket as though they were all a part of a gigantic thick soup. Above the mist, the sky was clear and the stars were popping out one by one as it got darker and darker.

The moon was edging its way across the sky constantly changing the shadows of the trees into hideous, distorted, crawling shapes like black ghosts. Silent black ghosts. Silent and foreboding like the emptiness of death. The moon's pace was slow, but, relentless.

There, in the cool hours before dawn, Little Bark rested and wondered at the journey of the moon. Where was it going? Why did it travel almost every night? Was there something chasing it? Or, maybe it was trying to grasp something that was just beyond its reach?

"Why are you not at rest, Little Bark?" Old Moss yawned and looked at him out of one eye as though to keep a half grasp on a favorite dream to which he might return.

Little Bark drew a deep breath and let out a long, slow sigh. He was watching Freckles, the spotted Owl, swoop down between Old Moss' branches and snatch a moth out of mid air.

Freckles was a very special song-with-wings because he had saved Rhymer's life and possibly Tall Tales as well. Many cycles ago, a Walk-To came down the path and lit a stick of smoke and threw the stick of fire that he had lit it with almost on top of Rhymer. Freckles saw this and swooped down and picked it up in his beak and flew away with it. So, this made Freckles a very special song-with-wings, though no one particularly liked his singing.

"I know not, Old One. Maybe it is youth that keeps my eyes open. I guess, maybe, my mind is not yet competent enough to understand or to reason out why I am unable to sleep. Maybe it is because I feel too comfortable and secure and am waiting for someone or something to come along and snatch away my happiness.....I don't know. Maybe I'm just depressed tonight or, maybe, I am dreaming of an adventure I wish to share and am afraid if I close my eyes or tell anyone, it, too, will disappear. I do know that I feel a deep sadness, a foreboding, if you will, of some sort of impending danger that I cannot quite put my limb on. I cannot pin it down to a single thought. It is merely a feeling as yet. Maybe I am being a bit too hasty in my thoughts. If only I had more data upon which to build my conclusion....maybe...." he said, sadly, with the sound of emptiness in his words that comes from the sorrow of something that has happened in the past or the heavy dreaded feeling of something terrible that is going to happen in the near future.

Old Moss opened his other eye as he let go of his half grasp on his favorite dream, completely shutting the door to the world of dreams to turn to the world of reality. He stood very quietly looking at Little Bark while Little Bark watched.......something....a little creature, yet, not so little and almost indescribable to tree. He watched it as it crouched or huddled or lay on his branch. It was not a spider, though it had legs like thread glistening in the moonlight. It did not resemble, at all closely, a beetle. It was large, unlike a flea, and long, unlike the fly. It had silky wings like a butterfly, but, not the same shape or color. Its head was a cone-shaped mass of hundreds of tiny eyes, all of which seemed to be looking at him.

"What sort of adventures would you be thinking of to share?" he asked quietly as he watched Little Bark flick the ugly creature to the ground where it laid on its back, its tiny feet kicking in protest, only to be gobbled up by Freckles.

"Would you really like to know, or are you just trying to keep me company?"

"I really want to know," Old Moss told him, cautioning him to be quieter. It would not do to wake everyone in midst of their nightly slumber.

"Well," he whispered, "I would like to travel to the lands that I have heard of in Tall Tales stories where there are dragons and see-throughs and huge giants to do battle with! I would like to sail across the big water in large ships to far shores for exciting adventures! I would like to meet all the many different kinds of trees that there are all over the world! Bless Me! But, I do sound a bit like the tree that was swallowed whole in Tall Tales story!" he said in surprise, thinking that it might be better to change his mind about wanting to move like a Walk-To. "Hmmmmmm....I mustn't be too quick with my yearnings and my wishes or I may find myself up to my tip top in trouble!"

"You are a wonder to behold, for sure, Little Bark. You talk of things you barely know anything about. You have been listening much too intently to Tall Tales stories and not concentrating enough on what Predictor and I are trying to teach you'" he counseled him.

"Have you never had the desire to go to see the mountains and hear the pine trees next to a great waterfalls singing as the water rushes by? I have heard it said that they sing like the voices of many angels," he said, imagining what they must sound like. "Have you never wished to explore the caves and canyons and swift rivers, the rocky beaches and great caverns that Father talks about? Don't you ever wonder what it is that is over the next hill or around the next corner? Don't you ever wonder why we are here on this earth or what our purpose might be?"

"Not that I can remember....no," he said, thinking, trying to remember. "And, as for our purpose, who knows? But, I am getting very old, too old, and I do not remember my youth that well these past few moons," he said in a distant voice trying to remember long forgotten memories. He could remember that he had a good youth, better than average, but, he couldn't remember the small details like he used to anymore. He knew, with much sorrow, that many friends had come and gone since then. Good friends. Old Moss' memory was fading day by day.

Little Bark watched his teacher as the blanket of happiness was slowly replaced with a sheet of sadness. "How long has this forest been here, Old One?" Little Bark asked, changing the subject.

There was a long pause before he spoke. "Well, most of the trees have lived here for a very, very long time. Some since the unthinkable remote time of their origin," he said, eyebrows drooping as he studied his young student.

"Ahhhhhhhhh! Old One, you are trying to trick me and elude my question. What kind of an answer was that........ 'Since the unthinkable remote time of their origin'? Of course the trees have lived here since their beginning, but, when was that beginning?" he asked, cleverly, trying to outdo his old teacher.

"Hmmmmmm......he is learning quickly! I must sharpen my mind for future battle!" Old Moss thought to himself. "Some since the day of the Great Planting, I think, others, not so long, but, enough of this. Go to sleep now and dream of your adventures," he told him firmly as he relaxed his watchful vigil and fell immediately back to sleep in search of his favorite dream.

"I wish I could do that," Little Bark thought to himself as he listened to the rhythmic tone of Old Moss' snoring. He snored so loud that Freckles gave up his watchful throne and flew away to find a more peaceful and quiet perch.

"I must ask someone someday what the Great Planting is," he whispered.

Everything was very quiet in the Thicket. Old Moss fell into a deep sleep and his snoring ceased. Not the usual, comfortable quiet, but, the empty, cold, fearful quiet of a tomb.

The moon had hidden itself behind a cloud as though it were in some sort of danger that had been pursuing it all night. As Little Bark listened, really listened, he thought he could hear the mournful cries of lonesome trees of by-gone days, trees that seemed to be reaching out from their graves to grasp their icy cold limbs upon his heart to warn him of some untold danger. He wondered what it was that they wanted as a dark shadow fell upon him. He felt as though he was the only tree left standing in the Thicket and a huge giant had sought him out to devour him in its mighty jaws.

Suddenly he felt very small as though he were being squeezed from one world into another. It was an unwholesome, cruel world, he thought as he looked around, a world of ill tidings and perils which were only felt, not seen.

To the left were many jagged mountains, the like of which he had never seen. Or, had he? They were purple and green and blue, striped here and there with white. In the middle was a giant cave with a subdued light shining out of its mouth. There was a vast deep chasm surrounding it with boiling red hot liquid rock to stay anyone from venturing too near. The scene was a familiar one.

Directly in a straight line to the right, there was a great light buried behind some hills. It was unlike the sun as we know it today and great shadows crept down the mountains as it slowly disappeared. A cool and clammy mist clung to everything in its wake.

The cave entrance had a giant cylindrical mouth with stairs that went almost straight down with but the slightest slant. Here and there it mildly turned from left to right with an empty room every now and then. At last it came to an abrupt halt at a huge doorway with great white pillars to hold it up. Carved on the huge doors were the heads of many animals. Beyond the door was a great hall with many trees sitting around huge tables made of white marble.

The trees were feasting from great pots of stew and flat, round cakes of bread, and, each one had a huge cask from which it drank ill smelling ale. All about them were Walk-To's combing the needles of the trees and polishing them to a bright, brilliant shine, others were waiting on them, bringing them more stew and cakes and ale. Little Bark could not believe his eyes! "This is madness!" he almost said out loud. "What kind of cruel trick is being played on me?" he thought as he continued to look around.

The trees were talking to one another in loud and boisterous tones, enjoying one another's friendship in drunken merriment. At their sides, hung swords and great knives and battle axes! The tools of War!

Little Bark noticed that all the trees that were sitting around the tables were of the same kind, and over against the great rock walls of the huge room were cages with different kinds of trees in them! "They're prisoners" Little Bark shouted in horror.

Suddenly there was silence, a deafening silence, the kind that pierces your ears and makes them ring.

"Oh, No! They have seen me!" he said as icy limbs of fear ran up and down his trunk.

A tall, strong, gnarled, bearded tree got up from the table where he had been sitting and came toward him. Little Bark's first reaction was to run as fast as he could, but, alas, he was still well rooted.

Little Bark bravely stood his ground with chin up high as the Old Bearded tree reached out to him and stared him eye to eye. Kind eyes? And, were those tears?

"Tell them….. Warn them all before it is too late! Tell them they mustn't…."

"Little Bark? Little Bark!" Many Branches called to her son. "Little Bark, wake up! You are having a bad dream, dear."

"Wha…… What happened? What's going on?" he asked, looking around in confusion." Where did he go?"

"Where did 'who' go, Son?" she asked, slowly looking around her. "I have seen nothing. Nothing has been here. You have just been dreaming, dear. It's morning…..see?"

"Why did you wake me?" he asked, closing his eyes again to try to recapture the dream.

"Because, you were shaking and mumbling about something in your sleep. You were shaking so bad that…..say, what were you dreaming about anyway?" she asked him, curiously.

"Oh, it was nothing. Nothing at all," he said quickly, opening his eyes once again and looking around him. There…..way over there…. were the hills and mountains of his dream. Only they were changed somehow and, where the cave hole had once been, there were now many houses. There wasn't a feeling of foreboding around him as it had been in his dream, either.

"What is it that is over there above the hills, Tickler?" Little Bark asked as he saw that Tickler was watching the same thing he was.

"It is the end of the world," he said, feigning sadness.

"What?" Little Bark cried out in astonishment.

"It is the end of the world. Soon it will be here and it will all end."

"Do not let the Thicket-cricket fool you, Little One," Predictor cautioned him.

"Stay out of this you old piece of driftwood!" Tickler warned him."

"I will not!"

"You two sound like a couple of badly spoiled Mere Twigs! Do not listen to either of them, it is nothing," Tall Tales told Little Bark, giving both Predictor and Tickler a stern look. "If you wish, I will tell you what is happening. It is no real mystery as they would have you believe."

"Please, spare us!" Tickler said, grabbing his trunk as though he was going to faint.

"I think that I would like to hear what Tall Tales has to say," Little Bark decided. This was something he had never seen before. The more he watched it, the more frightening it became. Maybe Tickler was right. Maybe it was the end of the world.

"Over there, just above the hills, there is a great battle being waged between good and evil. See how the mountains are crowded with black, fluffy clouds? First, there is God's lightening bolt as He warns the evil demons to cease their constant bickering and like gigantic broken tongues of fire, it reaches down to touch a tree or a bush. Then, there is the thunder as the evil demons curse and swear. Then, there is rain...... such rain as you have never seen before as the Angels pour the water from the brim of their golden buckets. The fires are put out, and then there is another battle between God and the evil demons. God always wins and then the sky will be clear again." Tall Tales told him.

"That was a very good story, Tall Tales. I do not ever remember you telling it before," Old Sap told him with one raised eyebrow.

"I just made it up, Old One. Pretty good, huh?" he asked, proudly.

"Yes, it was very nice, very nice, indeed. I wish that we could talk with God in person. I feel a need in my soul, an emptiness that only the utter Peace of God can fill. It would be wonderful, would it not, to talk to Him and have the Great Lifting now?" he asked with a heavy heart.

"Yes, it would be wonderful," Tall Tales agreed.

"You know, Tall Tales, you should really spend your days thinking up new stories to entertain us all."

"What? No way! I can think of much better ways to spend my time, Old One! Entertain yourselves!" he said, rudely.

"So be it, then, I was just trying to be nice, but, I see that you still have not learned how to accept a compliment gracefully," and with that said, Old Sap snapped the line of thought in two like a pair of scissors cutting a string.

"Father," Little Bark called, "why can't I hear or understand Grandfather's thoughts when he doesn't want me to?"

"Because, when we are thinking about something that we do not want anyone else to know about, we think on a higher level. All of us have two different levels of thought patterns or wave lengths that we think with. One, everyone can hear and understand, the other, only that tree, himself, can understand and hear. That higher one is different for everyone. No two trees are the same; they are all different, as different from one another as we are different from the Walk-To's. Do you understand?" Old Log asked his Son.

"Yes….I think so. I must do it, also."

"Yes, everyone does. You don't think about it, you just do it. It is just natural, I guess."

"Do the Walk-To's do it? I mean, maybe they think at each other the way we do, only on a different level altogether?"

"No, I do not believe so. As far as I know, they talk to one another with voices only."

Little Bark thought about his new information for a long time as he tested his own thought levels to see if they worked.

"Is the storm coming this way?" Twiggy asked Many Branches as she watched the Northern skies.

"No, it should stay where it is for a while and then it will move away. I don't think that it will reach us. Let's hope not, anyway. We don't want a fire."

Old Moss and Predictor looked at her and wondered if she knew that there was going to be a fire some time in the future.

"Well, Little Bark, did you finally get some sleep last night?" Old Moss asked as he stretched and groaned. He thought that it was a good idea to change the subject.

"I got a little, I suppose," he said. He wondered whether or not he should tell his teacher about his dream. 'No, I don't think he would believe me', he thought, making up his mind to remain silent.

Later, he would regret his decision.

"Maybe you nap too much during the day." Predictor told him.

"I hardly ever nap during the day," he said, feeling insulted at the idea. "Napping during the day is for young Seedlings and Old Trees, not for strong, hard thinking Mere Twigs like me."

"I do not feel so good," Weeper sighed, trying to sound ill.

"What is wrong?" Thin-As-Grass asked her in a tiny, whining voice.

"I feel weak and tired."

"Then, go to sleep!" Tickler told her rudely.

"I know what she needs," Tall Tales told them.

"What does she need?" Fuzzy Moss asked.

"She needs Healer," Tall Tales told him.

"Who is Healer?"

"Do you want to hear about him?"

"I guess so," Fuzzy Moss said hesitantly.

Tall Tales straightened up his trunk and settled his leaves as he began. "Once upon a time, many, many cycles ago, there was a tree named Healer. He was very, very special. He was the only one of his kind; there were no others, ever. He was not like you and me, his trunk was made of soft crushed petals like that of Roses and it had the aroma of many lilacs in the spring. His branches were made of feathers from Angels Wings, soft and light. His leaves were like Lilly Pads, and, every Spring he would sprout one gold leaf that would fall to the ground. And, there it has been said in the folklore of the Ancient Ones, that a Walk-To would pick it up with great care and put it on a velvet pillow. He would take great care of it because it had the power to heal all manner of sickness. Anyone or anything that touched that leaf was instantly healed. But, the leaf only had healing powers for one day, then, the leaf just melted away to nothing." He said, looking around for some sort of appreciation. "That's it, the story is over."

No one said anything.

"Well, didn't anyone like it?" Tall Tales asked, sadly, disappointed that no one had said anything.

"I think it was beautiful!" Thin-As-Grass told him wiping the tears from her eyes. "If I could only touch that leaf, I would never be sick again."

"I liked the swords and the dragons and Old Water Belly better," Fuzzy Moss told him.

"I liked it," Little Bark said, finally, after much thought.

"I've heard it before," Old Sap snickered.

"There once was a tree with a special leaf
Who could heal all manner of sickness and grief.
But, only for one day in the middle of spring
Comfort and healing and strength could he bring.
Then to the ground the leaf fell with a thud

To slowly disappear down into the mud," Rhymer said, as he wiggled and giggled with pride.

"Why,….Why do you grow at the base of my trunk? Why couldn't you have grown over there by Old Moss or someone? Why did you have to grow here? I wonder what it was that I ever did to deserve such punishment?" he asked in wonder.

"I like the Little Bush and his rhymes. They are quite refreshing. You should be honored to have someone think so highly of your stories that he makes up rhymes about them," Old Sap warned him with cold eyes.

Tall Tales just stared at Rhymer and said nothing, but, he wondered why Old Sap always stood up for the crazy little bush.

CHAPTER SEVEN

The summer days were like carbon copies of one another. The morning sun was warm with just a hint of a cool breeze. The afternoon was white hot, unbearably dry. The ground was hard and cracked and the weeds and grass were slowly ending as the sun beat down upon them without mercy. The leaves of the trees were wrinkling into a leathery, wilted mass and the needles were turning brown. The trees of Old Moss' Thicket longed for rain to soothe their dry, parched roots.

Nothing seemed to change much in the Thicket as the days slowly etched their way into mere memories.

"Tell us a story, Tall Tales," Fuzzy Moss begged.

"My throat is too parched to talk right now," he told him.

"Oh please, Tall Tales," Twiggy pleaded.

"Oh, alright," he cleared his throat. "Long, long ago, many more cycles than even Old Sap can remember, there was a tree that lived on a tiny piece of land way out in the middle of a lake, all by himself. He was very different from all the other trees. At first, the trees that would come to visit him would soon shy away and leave because they were afraid. They were afraid to look at him because he had a great big trunk with a huge window in it and when they looked into that window they could see a picture of the whole world from way up high in the air like the moon or a Song-With-Wings sees it. It frightened them very much. They didn't understand.

Then, one day, Look-See, as he was called, told them not to be afraid, that the window would not hurt them, but, that it could bring them much joy and happiness. He told them to look into the window and pick a place where they would like to visit. When they had done this, he zoomed in on the area and told them to step through his window. He warned them that they could only remain there for one cycle and not a day longer. At the end of one cycle, they must call to him so they could return or they would be turned to stone forever. That is why you see so many petrified trees."

"On a tiny piece of land far out on a lake,

His trunk made the trees with fear, to shake.

Because in his trunk was a huge window

Where they could see the earth below.

Go for one cycle and see all that you could

But, return not a day later or be petrified wood." Rhymer said, looking at Tall Tales.

Tall Tales pretended not to notice him, that way, just maybe, he would go away.

"That is my favorite story by far. It is undoubtedly the best one you have ever told, Tall Tales," Fuzzy Moss told him as he hugged himself with awe. "It would be so wonderful if it were true. Wouldn't it be wonderful if we could see the whole world and everything in it? Just think of the things we could see and do!" he said his mind wandering with the imagination.

"It is not good to wish to walk like the Walk-To's, Fuzzy Moss," Predictor warned him.

"Nonsense," Tickler argued. "Are you going to stand there and tell me that you believe all those stories that Tall Tales has been telling us all these cycles?"

"Some of them, yes," Predictor replied defensively.

"Then you are even more stupid than I originally thought, though I don't see quite how it is possible."

"Why must you be so nasty all the time? Can't you be nice?" Predictor asked with eyebrows frowning in disgust. "You are always so disagreeable."

"I am nice!"

"No, you're not!"

"Yes, I am!"

"No, you're not!"

"I'm hot," Thin-As-Grass told them as they all looked at her in wonder.

"What did you say, dear?" Many Branches asked her, doubting her ears.

"I said, I'm hot!"

"That is what I thought you said. We are all hot, my dear. It is summer. It is one of the worst dry seasons that we have had in the history of the Thicket, but, we will all survive it, we always do." Many Branches reassured her with a smile.

"But, just look at my poor needles, they are all brown and dry," she complained.

"Yes, we all look a little like tall, stiff weeds, don't you think so?" Weeper asked as they all laughed.......even Thin-As-Grass.

They all rested that afternoon when a nice cool breeze began to caress their eager branches. The sun seemed to have mellowed from a heavy constant stream of piercing rays, to a gentle touch of warmth like the soft fur of a kitten.

Little Bark was slowly pulled from the land of sleep as a caterpillar crawled lazily across his limbs, stopping long enough to lift its tiny head to look all about. Alas, the tiny creature lost its footing in its eagerness to chase down a particularly tasty tidbit. It hung precariously from one of Little Bark's leaves, clinging desperately, afraid to even breathe as it looked down to the ground below.

'What a cute little fellow,' Little Bark mused giving the little caterpillar a boost until it had regained its footing.

As he helped the little caterpillar, he could see Twiggy busy doing something out of the corner of his eye.

"What is it that you are doing?" he asked her curiously.

"Uh.....nothing!" she said, startled. "Why do you ask?' she said, putting whatever it was behind her so that he couldn't see.

"What are you hiding?"

"Nothing, nothing at all."

"Come on, what is it?"

"Really, it's nothing. Go back to sleep."

"I don't sleep during the day," he said, a bit irritably. "And, if it is nothing, then why don't you want me to see it?"

"Because.....that's all.....just because," she told him, sticking her nose up in the air in defiance.

"You know," he said as he stuck out his lower lip and pouted, "You're not supposed to hide anything from me."

"Who said I'm not supposed to hide anything from you?" she asked with stern, frowning eyes.

His pouting evidently wasn't working. "I did. I thought we were friends...best friends....and best friends don't hide things from each other."

"Oh...well...when you put it that way...I guess...well, alright, but you've got to promise not to tell anyone."

"Yes, yes, I promise!" he told her with anticipation.

"Okay," Twiggy agreed as she looked around to see if anyone else was listening. "I have a boyfriend," she whispered shyly through her branches.

"YOU WHAT?" Little Bark shouted, forgetting his promise.

"What's going on here?" Old Moss asked them, sternly. "Are you two quarreling?"

"Uhhhhh....no....no....not really. No we weren't. Besides, we never quarrel....we just discuss loudly," Little Bark said as they both giggled.

"Then kindly carry on your discussion quietly so that the rest of us can get some well deserved sleep, will you?" Old Moss asked as he dismissed the matter....but not totally.

"Barky!" Twiggy called in anger, "I thought you promised that you wouldn't say anything?"

"I did...and, I do. It was just a surprise, that's all. Who is your boyfriend? Is it someone I know? Is it Fuzzy Moss?" he asked looking to where Fuzzy Moss stood talking to Tickler.

"No, I'm the only one that knows him, no one else. And, I don't want anyone to know anything about him. Not who he is, where his roots grow or anything....nothing....nothing at all. It is no one else's business but mine and his," she said, sticking her nose up in the air in stubbornness.

"Why don't you want me to know anything? I will never tell anyone. I promise. And I'm honest. I keep my promises. And....well...I thought, well....I love you," he said, bashfully, suddenly turning away from her surprised stare. He looked at the ground in front of him.

"You.....love.....me? How? When? Where? Why?" she asked boldly, though she was stunned to her very roots. She had always secretly been in love with Little Bark but, she never thought that he might feel the same way about her.

"I love you because you are not like the other female Mere Twigs. You are intelligent and pretty.....and...I don't know, I just do," he told her, wishing all the time that she would change the subject.

"I didn't know, Barky. I really didn't know. You never, ever told me this before."

"No, but I thought we had an understanding."

"What sort of understanding was that?" she asked, coyly.

"Well...you know....I thought...well...I thought.....maybe you loved me, too," he said, bashfully.

"I do very much, and I like Long Needles...OOOPS!" she gasped, biting her lower lip at her dumb slip of the tongue.

"Sooooo, His name is Long Needles, huh? Well, it is a good name, a strong and proud name," he said, matter-of-factly

"He is very nice, Barky. I wish I could see him. Maybe someday," she said, wishfully.

"What is it that you are hiding behind you?"

"Oh, that! It is just a letter that I am writing to him."

"How do you send it?"

"See that Song-With-Wings, the pretty gray one over there by Rhymer?" she asked as she pointed to where Rhymer grew at Tall Tales roots.

"Yes, I see it."

"Well, it takes my letter to him in its beak, then, it brings one back to me from Long Needles. We have been doing this all summer," she said with a hint of pride.

"How did you meet Long Needles?" he asked her, curiously.

"He heard about me through the whispers of many trees. He says I must be very beautiful the way everyone talks about me."

"He's right, you know. You are very beautiful," Little Bark told her, boldly, becoming more relaxed about telling her of his feelings.

"Thank you," she said, shyly.

"Predictor, it is I, Fuzzy Moss. I must ask you a question. Are you awake?"

"Yes, what is it, Young One?" he asked a bit groggily.

"How long do the Walk-To's normally live? What is their life span?"

"It varies, as it does with us. Some live as long as one hundred cycles, but, most of them end when they are about sixty or seventy."

"Why do they live for such a short time?"

"Because they are puny, spindly, weak and high strung. They worry entirely too much and they never rest. Never. I have never seen one of them relax or nap in the afternoon except the little golden Walk-To that was here the other day. Rest is essential to a long life. They sleep when the sun goes down, but, never during the day. And, because they don't rest, they become sick and eventually end." He told him. This was not his favorite subject. Oh, the Walk-To's were alright, in their own place, which was nowhere around him.

"How come we live so long? Surely just taking a nap in the afternoon won't make that much difference. We live many, many more cycles than seventy or a hundred. Look at Old Moss and Old Sap, they are six or seven or more times that!"

"Yes, what you say is true, but, we do get lots of rest, warm sunshine and we are easy going. We let very few things bother us. Worry is not very often a word in our vocabulary. Oh, yes, there are times when we worry. The Walk-To's worry all the time. And, maybe it is because we are so strong and our roots are so long and firmly planted. You must have seen the little golden Walk-To the other day. Do you remember how small its roots were?" he asked. "Well, they won't get much bigger than that."

"No! Do not listen to him, Fuzzy Moss. He knows nothing about such things," Tall Tales warned him.

"Who says I don't" Predictor demanded.

"I said, that's who." Tall Tales told him.

"Then, pray tell, what makes us live so long if you know so much?"

"I will be glad to instruct you both," he said, proudly. "Our trunks are tall and strong and our roots are long and deep and way down deep in the ground, about fifty lippets, there is a river with beautiful sky blue waters. The Walk-To's call it the Fountain of Youth. We call it the River of Life. When we drink from this River of Life, it keeps us young and strong, but, if we relax our vigil and our roots don't grow deep enough, or if they become too brittle, we cannot drink and we end at a very young age."

"Really?" Fuzzy Moss asked, bewildered, thinking about his own roots and wondering when he would be able to reach the River of Life.

"Yes, it is true," Tall Tales reassured him, "but, I have had some friends that have ended in other ways, also."

"Who?"

"One of the dearest friends I ever had. Shorty was his name. He ended when a great wind came and blew him down. He was a Douglas fir, the largest one in the world. He was about seventy lippets tall and sixteen lippets around his middle. We were very good friends, very good friends. I miss him. It was sad, very, very sad," he told him as a lump came to his throat.

"How old was he when he ended?" Fuzzy Moss asked him.

"He was somewhere around twenty five hundred cycles, I think."

"Wow! It had to be a very strong wind to knock him over!"

"It was."

"Tell us another story, Tall Tales," Fuzzy Moss asked him. He loved to listen to his stories.

"What would you like to hear about?"

"Tell us a love story," Twiggy suggested.

"Okay....well....let me think. You know, you have never asked for a love story before, but, I think I have one for you. A very long time ago when trees wandered the earth like the Walk-To's do now, there was a tree that was desperately in love with another tree. They were so much in love with one another that they were always together wherever they went. That is, until one day at the start of World War Three, thousands of cycles ago, there came word to her from far away over the big water that her father was ill and would soon end. She wanted desperately to see him again before he ended, so, she set sail on a great ship. Sad Sap, as he was so named, swam out to a giant boulder that was just about a mile off shore. There he crawled slowly up the side of it to watch as the ship sailed farther and farther out to sea. He watched until it was completely out of his view. At that very moment, The Great God of All Things planted us all forever. To this day, it is said that Sad Sap still stands on that big, huge boulder way out there in the ocean, watching and waiting for his long lost love, hoping that some day she might return to him."

"That was beautiful," Twiggy told him with tears in her eyes.

"Yes, it was very beautiful. I do not ever remember you telling that one before," Many Branches told him, curiously.

"That is because it is a new story. I just now made it up," he said, proudly.

"Even I liked that one," Old Sap told him, smiling. "You haven't got another new story up your branch, have you?" he asked with a glint of hope in his eyes.

"Not right now. It is too hot to think. Maybe later when it cools down I will tell you another."

I really did like that story that you just told us, Tall Tales," Old Sap reassured him.

"I'm glad that you did. You know, you are not very easy to please when it comes to story telling," he said, affectionately. He really did love Old Sap.

"No, I guess I'm not. I guess I just get tired of hearing the same old stories all the time. It is really quite refreshing when you are able to think up a new one or change an old one around a little."

"There once were two trees that were so much in love
They could see naught but the stars up above.
Until one day bad news was her grief
On a long journey at once she must leave.
So he swam out to sea and climbed up a rock
Standing and staring with no one to talk
Watching the ship as it went on its way
Hoping to see his love on another day.
For God at that moment planted us all
Her name on his lips forever to call," Rhymer wiggled in satisfaction.

Tall Tales, as usual, was not impressed with Rhymer's poem. He just stared at Rhymer and wondered how he could rid himself of such a pest. Yet, this time, he didn't say anything because he didn't want to upset Old Sap, who, for some strange reason, liked the little bush.

"That was very good, Rhymer," Many Branches praised him.

"Thank you," Rhymer giggled.

All were quiet for a while as everyone rested and thought about Tall Tales story and how lonely poor Sad Sap must have felt out there all alone.

"What was that thing that just floated by?" Little Bark asked his Father.

"Where?" Old Log asked as he looked all around him.

"Over there by Twiggy. It just floated by her."

"Oh, that! That is just a fairy."

"What is a fairy?"

"It is something that floats by every now and then and if you can catch her, she must grant you one wish…any wish that you ask her."

"Really? Where does she come from?" Little Bark asked, puzzled.

"She grows on a weed. The wind carries her on its breath. No one has caught one for hundreds and hundreds of cycles. They are too fast and too sneaky. When you grab for her she swerves out of the way and scurries away. They are really very hard to catch, but, as I said, a long time ago one was caught," he said, tempting Little Bark's curiosity.

"Well…..?"

"Well, what?"

"What did he ask for? What was his wish?"

"Who?'

"Whoever it was that caught the fairy the last time?"

"Oh, he wished that he could fly."

"He what?"

"He wished that he could fly. He thought about it all the time when he was growing up. He knew that trees once walked the earth a long time ago, so he didn't want to do that. But….to fly ….to fly would be to do something that no other tree had done."

"So, did he get his wish?"

"Yes."

"Well, where did he fly to?"

"All over the place. Nowhere in particular and everywhere you could think of. But, he was sorry that he had wished it," he said, tempting Little Bark's curiosity again.

"Why?" Little Bark asked.

"Because he forgot to tell the Fairy when he made his wish that he wanted to be able to come down whenever he wanted to. So, he is still flying around up there somewhere."

"Oh," Little Bark said, as he thought about it very seriously. One had to be quite careful and not too hasty when making a wish or one might find oneself in quite a mess!

"Fuzzy Moss," Tickler called to him, "What have you been thinking about all this time? You haven't said a word since Rhymer told us his poem."

"I was just thinking about the Walk-To's and how happy they should be. They can walk to wherever they want to and we just stand here day in and day out. Take Sad Sap, for instance, he lost his only true love and the ability to walk at the same time. I wonder if the Walk-To's realize how blessed they really are?"

"I do not know the answer to your question," Tickler told him, thinking about the time when the little Walk-To was there in their Thicket. She seemed sad. Maybe she didn't know just how lucky she was to be walking. The little Walk-To......there was something different about her.

CHAPTER EIGHT

"It is a beautiful day, much better than yesterday when it was so hot, is it not, Old Log?" Many Branches asked happily as she looked at the sparkling moistness of the dew on her leaves and felt the warmth of the sun on her limbs and branches.

"Yes, it is," he agreed as he, also, looked around. "It is great just to be alive and living among friends," he told her, smiling.

"Have you watched our son lately, My Husband?" she asked, proudly." Have you seen how much he has grown and how very strong he is getting, like you?" Many Branches visibly swelled with pride as she nudged Old Log with her limb.

"How could anyone not notice? I have never before seen a tree of our kind grow so fast. If he keeps it up, he will pass me by in just a few cycles. His growth is astonishing," he said, shrugging his branches, a bit bewildered. "But, he is my Son, he is my joy and I love him and I, also, am proud of him. I have not only watched him grow in strength and height, but, also in his lessons and knowledge." He smiled as he looked at his wife. "He has eight knots now, you know."

"No, I didn't know. He will be eligible for the test soon, then, don't you think, My Husband?"

"I don't know about that. I do know that you have to be very intelligent and have many knots before you are even considered as a candidate for the test. And, remember, many Branches," Old Log cautioned her, "even then not everyone is given the test. He is very bright and gifted and he already has more knots than anyone ever has had at his age, but he has a ways to go yet," he told her, gently. "Also, have you forgotten about Fuzzy Moss? He is almost up with Little Bark in knots and size," he warned her, softly.

"Yes, I have been watching him, also," Many Branches frowned. "But, I just can't imagine anyone else but Little Bark as our next Thicket Councilor," she told him matter-of-factly with a hint of concern evident on her face.

Old Log laughed. "That is the mother in you talking now, Many Branches, not your knots!" he teased her. "We will just have to wait and see what happens. If it is The Great God of All Things will that Fuzzy Moss be our next councilor, then that is the way it shall be. We can only hope for our son."

It was a beautiful day. It was warm, but not too warm and the Songs-With-Wings were singing in their best voice today. A gentle breeze lazily touched each of them as they talked of the new day.

Even the long-eared-fuzzy-hoppers seemed to be a bit bolder today as they hopped here and there chasing the bushy tails that simply ran up a tree and perked up their tails and scolded them in warning.

"You haven't answered my question that I asked you when the little Walk-To was here. Have you forgotten?" Twiggy asked Little Bark.

"Which question was that?" he asked half-mindedly.

"You know.....what is a Christmas tree? The little Walk-To wants to dig me up for its Christmas tree and I want to know what one is," she said, worried that she wouldn't be planted back where she could be with all her friends.

Little Bark cleared his mind. "I'm not quite sure just what it is, Twiggy. I have thought about it for some time since the Walk-To was here, but, I do not know. I think we should ask Old Moss. I have not heard of one either."

"Oh, no, not me! Don't include me in this!" she shuddered, her eyes as big as the full moon, "You and Fuzzy Moss are the only Mere Twigs that he likes to talk to. I don't think that Old Moss likes me very much. Besides, he gives me the bark bumps! He's so very old and wise. It is like talking to one of the ancients. He scares me. And, he's too darned elusive with his answers. I have heard him answer a few of the questions that you have asked him and most of the time he doesn't make any sense to me," she explained, shaking as though she had a bad chill run up her trunk.

"Oh, Twiggy, it is all in your imagination. He's not going to eat you for breakfast, you know. He really is a very understanding tree, once you get to know him," He looked at her and she was still shaking. He wanted to put his branches around her and comfort her and tell her that everything was going to be alright, but, he didn't dare.....yet. "I have an idea," he said after a short pause, "I'll count to three and we will both ask him, okay?" This was his way of trying to get Twiggy over her fear of Old Moss. He never had been afraid of him. He could have asked him and left Twiggy completely out of it, but, he wanted Old Moss and Twiggy to be friends. He wanted her to be able to ask him anything she felt she needed counseling with.

"Okay," she agreed, reluctantly.

"Okay, now get ready! One....Two....Three! OLD MOSS!" They both yelled in unison.

"Heavens to earth!" Old Moss jumped in surprise. "What is the matter with the two of you? You scared the leaves right off my limbs! I shall probably end ten cycles sooner than I would have had you not frightened the bark right off my trunk! Now, what is so imperative that you felt the need to terrorize the whole Thicket?" Old Moss sounded a bit irritated.

Little Bark was trying to caution him about becoming angry with them. He was afraid that Twiggy would never try to speak to Old Moss again. He had to admit that he felt a little intimidated himself.

"We have a very important question to ask you," Little Bark said, a little dramatically.

"Why did you feel it necessary to yell so loud? I am right here where I have always been. I cannot move, remember? I am just as rooted as the rest of you. At least, I think I am still well rooted. After such a fright it is a wonder I do not topple over. Is it that you think that I am growing deaf or something? My ears are even ringing!" he scolded them.

"I didn't yell loud, he did!" Twiggy said, pointing to Little Bark.

"Hey, you little bump on a log! You yelled just as loud as I did! Don't put all the blame on me and get me into trouble!" he told her abruptly. Then, as he looked at Twiggy, he realized that he had almost made her cry.

"Well, it was your idea," she pouted.

"I'm sorry," he told her compassionately.

"Enough, both of you!" he told them both firmly. "You could have asked me ten questions already while you have been bickering back and forth. What is it that seems to be so important?" Old Moss' curiosity was getting the better of him.

"We want to know, Great Teacher, what a Christmas tree is," Little Bark told him as they both began to giggle at scaring Old Moss so thoroughly.

"Ahhhhhhhhhh! Now that is indeed an interesting question. What makes you ask?"

"There you go again, Old Moss, asking a question when I have already asked you one. Why do you always answer my questions with a question?" His frustration was very evident in the tone that he used.

"I do not know why I do it," he pondered, "except many cycles ago my Father told me that it is best to acquire all the necessary information before you answer a question. That way your answer will always be well thought out and you will not be called a fool," he admonished them, failing to keep his voice stern in light of their evident amusement.

"Oh," little Bark said raising a quizzical eyebrow at his teacher.

"Now, to get back to your other question, why do you ask about a Christmas tree?"

"Do you remember a while back when the little Walk-To was lost and she came down our path and sat right in front of Twiggy?" Little Bark asked as he cautioned Twiggy to be quiet with a frustrated wave of his limb. She was still giggling.

"Yes, I remember. I remember very well. I am not so old, you know, that I cannot remember from one day to the next what has happened in the Thicket," Old Moss told him, insulted by his question.

"Oh…..yes…..well…..sorry," Little Bark stammered at his own boldness. "Well, anyway," he said staring at the ground, "that Walk-To stood right in front of Twiggy and told her Father that she had found a perfect tree for their Christmas tree. Then, she pointed to Twiggy," he explained. "Now, Old, Wise and Elusive One, I have answered your question, now answer mine if you will. What exactly is a Christmas tree?" Little Bark was finally beginning to relax a little as Twiggy began to control her giggling.

"A Christmas tree is a very special thing, Twiggy. You must feel honored and very proud to have been chosen by the Walk-To. You know," he smiled down at her, "only the most beautiful and perfect trees receive this honor," he complimented her. "I have heard it said in many whispers from other Thickets that the Walk-To will come and dig you up and take you to its lair. There a whole bunch of Walk-To's will gather around and dress you up with all manner of pretty things! Then, they will all stand back and look at you and smile and say how very beautiful you are. You must stand tall and very straight and make us proud of you. You will do that, won't you?" Old Moss asked hopefully.

"Yes," she whispered in a tiny, shy voice.

"Will they bring her back here to us?" Little Bark asked. "Because if they don't, I will feel very lost in my trunk," he said, sadly, looking at Twiggy with worry and concern.

"Yes, I have heard that they bring them back, but they no longer have all the pretty things on them. I guess they are not yours to keep," he paused in thought and then went on. "They will dig a new hole and plant your roots deep again," Old Moss smiled at Twiggy with the pride of a Father. "You are so lucky to be chosen. I am so excited for you! You are the very first one to be selected out of our Thicket that I can ever remember," he told her, gaily fluttering his branches in happiness for her. "And, believe me; I can remember hundreds of cycles ago!"

"Twiggy doesn't need anything to make her pretty. She is already pretty without putting anything on her limbs." Little Bark was not convinced that this was such a great honor. He didn't trust the Walk-To's. He was afraid that they might think that Twiggy was too beautiful to bring back to the Thicket and they might want to keep her near their lair so that they could look at her every day. A sudden feeling of great loss stabbed his trunk to the very core. Was it a premonition or just fear for the one he loved?

Twiggy blushed at the compliment.

The morning skies were fast turning from their soft pink lace to their scorching hot afternoon whiteness. It seemed to make the trees feel a bit lazy as most of them slept.

The breeze would have felt good, but, it had died away and there was no hint that such a blessing would return that afternoon. Quite to the contrary, it promised to be a very hot, dry and stale day.

"Daddy!" Wendy called as she ran up the front steps and through the front door. "Daddy!"

"I'm in the kitchen with Mandy," he called to her.

"Oh, Daddy, you have to come outside and see the smoke that is coming from the forest! I think that it is a fire!"

"What are you talking about?" he asked her with concern as he scooted his chair away from the kitchen table and followed Wendy out the front door. Mandy was right behind them.

"Oh, dear," Mandy said, anxiously when she saw all the smoke that was clouding over the forest.

"I've got to call this in," Jim said as he returned to the house. The telephone was already ringing.

Jim was just hanging up the receiver when Wendy and Mandy returned to the house.

"It is a fire. I have to go to the station and help," he told them as he changed from his street shoes into his working boots. He reached down and gave Wendy a kiss on the cheek. "I'll be back as soon as I can." And he went out the door.

"Take care, Jim," Mandy called to him as he got in the car.

"I will,' he called back, waving to them both as he drove away.

"Sniff? Sniff?" Many Branches was sniffing the air. "Sniff? Sniff?" She could smell something but she couldn't quite put her limb on what it was. "Sniff? Sniff?"

"What on earth are you doing, Many Branches?" Old Log asked tilting himself towards her as he gave her a thoughtful stare. He looked around to see if anyone else had been watching her. He was a little embarrassed by her unusual actions. Thankfully no one had taken notice.

"I think I smell gud in the air from too many of the Walk-To's stinky-go's," she told him as she wrinkled her nose and tried to wave the foul odor away.

"That is not the gud from the Walk-To's stinky-go's that you smell in the air, Many Branches, it is the smoke from a fire!" He stiffened with fear as he looked around to see where the fire might be.

Many Branches began to shiver with horror and apprehension. "Oh, Great God of All Things........help us!" she cried.

Old Moss, Predictor, Tall Tales, Fuzzy Moss and Little Bark had already noticed the smoke and they had been in conference on what should be done for quite some time.

"I think Little Bark's idea is the best," Predictor told Tall Tales.

"Maybe so........maybe not. Anyway, to my knowledge it has never been tried before. Fuzzy Moss says that if we all wave our branches at once, very fast, we may blow the fire away from us. I think he has a good idea," Tall Tales stated, firmly.

"But, to our knowledge, that has not been tried with success, either. I have heard it said that some trees have tried it and they perished in the fire. We have been told to trust in God of All Things and all manner of things will be done for us. See how He feeds us and gives us water when we are thirsty and keeps our roots warm in the winter during the Big Slumber? And, you have seen how He dresses our branches and limb tips during the spring. If we trust Him we need not worry." Predictor argued.

"Well, then, Predictor, what do you predict will happen?" he asked, sarcastically, spitting the word 'predict' out of his mouth. "Can you tell us what is going to happen? Hmmmmmm?"

"Stop this bickering this very instant! I'll not have you two arguing over something so vital and precious as all our lives! What is the matter with the two of you, anyway? You are acting like seedlings." Then as Old Moss calmed down a little, he continued. "We need more opinions on such a grave matter. We will ask Old Sap, Old Log and Tickler and see what they have to say," Old Moss instructed them. He then explained to Old Sap, Old Log and Tickler Fuzzy Moss' suggestion and then Little Barks. "We will take a vote among ourselves as is the custom of our Thicket. All those in favor of Fuzzy Moss' idea will let their branches droop and all those in favor of Little Bark's suggestion will point them straight up. Are you ready? Now......GO!" he said as he watched everyone hesitate.

Little Bark was the first one to stick his limbs straight up.

Fuzzy Moss was the first to let his droop.

Predictor pointed his limbs up so hard that you could hear them creek and groan with the unaccustomed strain.

Tall Tales immediately drooped his branches and stuck his nose up in the air defiantly.

Old Sap rubbed his chin in thought. To his knowledge, nothing had ever worked, but, of the two ideas, he wanted Little Barks, for his own reason, so he stuck his branches straight up.

Tickler did not really want to agree with anything that Tall Tales wanted, but, he thought that Fuzzy Moss' idea sounded more acceptable. Waving your branches was actually doing something and it might just blow the fire out. So, he drooped his branches.

Old Log hesitated. He loved his son very much. He thought about Fuzzy Moss' suggestion and then Little Barks. In his heart, Old Log was a strict believer in The Great God of All Things. He knew the power that God had and to believe in Him without a doubt took great courage. He also knew that it would only take one weak link in the chain of intense thought to undo the strength of their quest. Just one tree that had a tiny doubt and they would be doomed. He looked around at each tree. He thought about each one individually. They were all trustworthy. They were all determined to come through this fire. They all seemed determined to live. Therefore, he stuck his limbs straight up.

It was now up to Old Moss. His vote would either make it a tie or a decision in Little Bark's favor. They were swiftly running out of time. He looked at Little Bark, then at Fuzzy Moss. Then he looked to the sky as if he might find the answer there somewhere. That is when he made his decision. If he was already looking toward The Land of Sweet Water and Cool Breezes for help then he knew what his decision must be. He stuck his branches straight up.

It was settled. The voting was done. No one argued. No one said anything. They all had to accept it. It was the law of the Thicket.

"Let us tell the others," Old Moss said, grimly.

"I think that since it was Little Bark's idea, he should be the one to tell them." Predictor suggested.

"That is fine with me," he agreed quite willingly.

"Listen everyone!" Old Moss called as he tried to get everyone's attention. "We have some very bad news for all of you. Now, this concerns each and every one of us so PLEASE LISTEN! Little Bark will tell us all about it," he told them as he prompted Little Bark to begin speaking.

Little Bark cleared his throat. It felt dry. "There is a great fire coming toward our Thicket," he said as he looked around. "I see that most of you are already aware of the fact. Do not worry. I know it is easier to tell you not to worry than to actually do it, but, I have an idea that just might save all of us."

Everyone began to mumble to one another in low voices, even some from other Thickets around them.

"Quiet now everyone," Little Bark told them as he looked toward the fire. It was coming faster now. He could feel the heat as it crept closer. "The fire is almost upon us and we haven't much time. I want you all to reach down and gather enough dirt to put at least one lippet all around your trunk, around the bottom like this," he said as he showed them what he wanted them to do. Everyone quickly complied. "Now, I want you to reach back in your memory, way back to when you were young seedlings and your parents or councilor taught you about The Great God of All Things. Do you remember them telling you that God said, 'Ask and it shall be done' and if you have faith and believe hard enough, you can move mountains? Well, we need that faith now, from each and every one of you. Do you all remember your teachings?" he asked as he looked around. They all assured him that they did. "Now, what I want you to do is, everyone join branches....that's it, that's the way," he said as they all did what he asked them to do. Little Bark reached over and took Twiggy's branch and squeezed it lovingly to give her the reassurance that she needed. He could see that she was very afraid. "I love you," he whispered for her ears only.

"I love you, too, Barky," she whispered with tears in her eyes.

"Now, I want all of us to join our minds.....merge them together into one huge mind directed at me. Yes, that's the way." Little Bark gasped as he felt the touch of all of them at once. It was as though his mind had suddenly opened many doors and rooms that were previously closed and had never before been used. "Now, I want you to believe with all your knots and without a doubt in your mind that we will be saved and that God will spare us all. There must not be the slightest hint of a doubt or we are all lost," he cautioned them as he looked toward the fire again.

For moments that seemed like hours nothing moved and then the expanding tongues of fire licked ever closer and closer and then disappeared only to return relentlessly eating away at all the bushes and weeds in their path.

A scant thirty seconds was all that remained before the fire would overtake and engulf them. They were fast running out of time. Time, that elusive element that indicates happiness or tragedy at its own whim.

Only twenty seconds! And, then the hellish flames would lick furiously and hurl themselves with all their destructive might at the Thicket.

Death seemed inevitable.

Nevertheless......

"Now, I will need you to concentrate and believe with all your knots. You must believe that the fire will go around us. You must believe that it will not even stop long enough to scorch our branches with its heat. No one must doubt for a minute or we will all be lost. Are we in agreement?" he asked as he looked at Twiggy with a longing that he barely understood. He wanted to comfort her, to tell her that everything was going to be alright, but, his duty was to be focused on everyone right now.

They were all in agreement.

"Okay! All together now............CONCENTRATE!"

The walls of flame blew upward and outward as huge chunks of ash and debris were thrown angrily to the heavens above and then floated as though in slow motion as they flared down toward the earth again, lighting upon some helpless, immovable, innocent object that happened to be in its path. The temperatures were blinding.

They all held together tightly as they concentrated and believed with everything they had in them. That is, all but one.

CHAPTER NINE

"It is over!" Twiggy was the first one to break the silence.

"Yes, it is over! Thank You Great God of All Things," Little Bark prayed as he looked up to the Great Heavens. His voice was filled with emotion. He had taken a huge chance that his plan would work. Everyone had to cooperate and concentrate to their fullest. If it hadn't worked……..If it hadn't worked none of them would have been left to criticize him.

"Are you okay, Twiggy?" he asked as he looked her over good to see that nothing had hurt her.

"I'm fine," she said with tears of happiness in her eyes. Little Bark was still holding her limb as though he would never let it go again.

"I meant what I said, I do love you," he said, feeling joy and happiness well up inside of him.

"I meant it, too," she said squeezing his limb.

It seemed that in the last few minutes, when their future was uncertain, they had found out just how much they did love each other.

"Will you become my betreethed? My wife? Forever to come?" he asked her.

"Yes, I will be betreethed to you, Little Bark, gladly and with all my heart," she said, proudly.

"I love you," he said again as though he couldn't say it enough.

All of them began to relax and look around. There were still many trees left standing, but many trees had been leveled to the ground and bushes had become mere dust. The terrain around them had been hideously changed.

Little Bark did not know it at the time, but many Thickets had been listening to him and only here and there, around them was a tree burnt beyond recognition. Some had been burnt to the ground. These were the ones that had refused to hold branches or had not believed hard enough, the ones that had not linked minds with them.

"Can anyone see what happened to the trees up on the hill?" Fuzzy Moss asked.

"It is too smoky to see, but, I think they are gone, all of them. I can feel it in my branches," Old Moss said, sadly.

"Da only ting dat ya feeellll in yurrrrr branches is ald age creepin up on ya!" A voice from very far away told him.

"By my roots! Look! It's Old Thunder Stick! He has survived!" Old Moss was elated. His friend had made it through the fire. Tears of joy were in Old Moss' eyes.

"Yah, by da barrre moss on me trrrunk I surrrrrrrvived! Ya di' no' tink dat I'd ah made it, di' ya?" he asked, happy to be able to surprise his old and dear friend.

"Why you old wart! You'll out last us all! It doesn't even look as though the fire came near you, Old Thunder Stick, Old Pal. What did you do, blow the fire away or what?" Old Moss asked his friend of many cycles.

"Ah, nay! Nothin' so drrrrrrrrastic as dat, me Frrrrriend. I just prrrrrretended I wuzzz invvvvizzzzible and da' ting di' no' see me. It rrrrraged arrrrround me, but, it nevvvverrr evvven cum a lit'l bit close. Not evvven a lit'l bit close! An' how mi' I ask di' ya all surrrrrrvive such ah torrent o' flames, ye Ol' Poop?" he asked affectionately.

"It is a very long story and I'm sure you are probably just as tired as all of us are. Maybe we can talk later," Old Moss told him in a tired voice as he, again, thought about what they had all just been through.

"Tiz trrrue, tiz trrrue, fur shure. I tuu need me rrrest af'er such a bat'l. Boooot, mind ye, lat'r I wan an' expect a fuuull acountin' o' wha' 'appened," he said coughing from the smoke and the ashes.

Old Thunder Stick was a very tall tree, a Scotch pine about sixty lippets tall. He stood on the very top of the hill amidst a huge field all by himself with no other trees around him for hundreds of lippets. He was named Old Thunder Stick because he had been hit by lightning three times. He had survived all three except for some singed bark here and there. He only had three branches left, all sticking out of one side of his trunk. He was very funny to look at.

"If anyone was going to survive something like this, it is Old Thunder Stick!" Tickler joked, trying to relieve the tension he felt inside. "I swear he has nine lives!"

"Sometimes you do make some sense, Tickler. It reminds me of a story I once heard about....."

"No stories right now please, Tall Tales," Many Branches said in a tearful voice. "My nerves are all bundled up ready to explode like a Stinky-go that goes over a cliff."

"Relax now, Many Branches, it is over. It has been a bad and traumatic experience for all of us to go through, but it has been good in a way, also. We all survived, didn't we?" Old Log asked. "And, we have learned a valuable lesson from it all, haven't we?"

"I guess so, but my nerves...." She said as she tried to calm down.

"I feel a great loss in my trunk, though I cannot put a limb on what it is," Old Log said, sadly. "It is as though someone were calling to me from the ashes."

"I feel sad, too," Weeper cried.

"You always feel sad," Thin-As-Grass told her. "I am the one who should be sad, why just look at my three branches! You all held on to them so tightly that they have wilted even more than they did before! And, look! Just look at the dirt all over my trunk! Why I should...."

"Where is Grandpa?" Little Bark interrupted her. Now that the smoke was clearing he had noticed that Old Sap was no longer standing where he should have been.

Silence came over everyone for many Thickets around as they looked around at each other. Old Sap was no longer standing where he had stood for so many, many cycles. There were only ashes where his mighty trunk once stood.

"Oh, God, NO!" Many Branches screamed, covering her eyes with her limbs.

"Yes, I am afraid that Old Sap is gone. I guess he was just too set in his ways to change his way of thinking, or, maybe, he just wanted to end. He was always talking of the day when he would end and be in the Land of Sweet Waters And Cool Breezes with his friends." Old Log paused and thought before he went on, "Did any one of you hold branches or roots with Old Sap during the fire?" he asked, looking around at each of them.

"No," they all said, looking at one another.

"Then it is as I have said. He must have wanted to end. He was very old and tired. He often spoke of the day when The Great God of All Things promised to take us all home at the time of the Great Lifting. I guess he just couldn't wait any longer and the fire gave him the perfect opportunity to end." Old Moss stood very still. He, too, felt very old and very tired. "Maybe he was too old to concentrate and didn't want to jeopardize the rest of our lives by being a weak link." Everyone and everything was silent. Not even the Song-With-Wings uttered a sound. It was as though everyone was in shock. The silence was cold and eerie as everyone's thoughts wandered far back to visions of better times.

A cool breeze began to blow the rest of the smoke away and little drops of rain began to fall from the dark, gray clouds that hung like giant pillows in the sky. They fell to mingle with the tears that were shed for Old Sap.

Hours passed by before Old Moss finally relaxed his branches from prayer and looked around him. The rain had cleansed the air and it was fresh smelling once again. Old Moss' eyes were sad, sad with the loss of a loved one, swollen in grief because he could not be with him.

"We must have a Raften for Old Sap as soon as possible," Old Moss said with a quivering voice.

"What is a Raften, Old Moss?" Twiggy asked.

Little Bark looked at her in astonishment. She had actually talked to Old Moss! 'Either she is feeling brave or she is in a state of shock,' he thought to himself. He really didn't know which, but, what he did know was that it took a lot of nerve on her part for her to ask him a question.

"This is the first question you have ever asked me, Little Twig." He called her by the name he had called her when she was just a seedling. "Why haven't you ever come to me before?"

'There, he had done it again,' Little Bark thought. Never in his short life could he remember Old Moss ever answering a question without first asking a question of his own.

"Because......I was afraid," she said, softly.

"What were you afraid of?" Old Moss asked her. "I have never before bitten anyone, nor have I struck anyone down with a mighty blow!" he winked as he teased her.

"I guess I was afraid of myself. I guess I was afraid that my questions would be considered dumb and that you would laugh at me. I don't know exactly," she replied with a little more bravery.

"Do not be afraid that your questions might be dumb, Little Twig, not from you, anyway. You are much too intelligent. You must never be afraid to talk to any one of us. We are all your family and your friends. We have no one else. You must never hesitate to say what is on your knots," he told her, lovingly." And, now to answer your question, a Raften is a time of remembering, a time of sharing thoughts of our loved one who has passed on from this life into the next. The Walk-To's call it a funeral, I believe," he said as his thoughts wandered to another time, another day, another Raften long, long ago.

It had been his Father's Raften. The Walk-To's had come along one day and without warning they started up a loud, growling, smelly thing that chewed away mercilessly at his trunk. His Father had ended that day for no reason. It would be a long time before Old Moss would forget the sight and sound of the growling ripper. He still often wondered why the Walk-To's had cut his Father down. There was no reason behind it that he could think of. His Father had been strong and perfect.

"Old Moss," Old Log called him back from the past. "We must begin."

"Yes, we should," he said looking around. "Everyone join limbs or roots," he told them. "This time, Rhymer, you may recite the Poem of All Ages. Do you know how it goes?"

"Yes," he said, sadly and began;
"Old Sap was standing next to me
A very tall and sturdy tree.
He stood so long
And his roots were strong,
But, now he has gone away.
We will miss him, everyone
But will see him when our life is done
Standing on that sandy beach
With young and sturdy limbs to reach

And greet us on that day."

Rhymer had done well.

There was a long silence.

"I remember his gentle swaying as he slept in the warmth of the sunshine. It made me sleepy just to watch him," Many Branches was the first to tell what she had liked about Old Sap the most.

"I remember his kind teachings. He never once raised his voice in anger to me, though, sometimes, I dare say, I deserved it. He always showed great patience with me. I shall miss my Father very much," Old log said as he bowed his head in sorrow.

"I remember his laugh. No one could laugh like my Grandfather. It was always so outgoing and full of joy and so spontaneous. When he laughed, it made me laugh even when I was feeling sad. His laughter had a way of easing the tension and worry. It always made things seem better. I shall miss his laughter very much," Little Bark said, sadly. He felt as though his trunk was being ripped in half, the pain of his loss was so deep.

"I remember him snoring all the time. It was a gentle and serene kind of snore, but, it didn't bother me," Weeper said, quickly so as not to offend anyone's feelings. "No….I apologize if that is the impression that I gave. I am but a day to day tree, and I do not know much about speaking publicly…..and, for this, also, I beg your pardon and your indulgence. But, he did have a snore that slowly hypnotized me until I, myself, was asleep. I will miss it very much as I will him," Weeper cried.

"I remember all of his funny jokes and how he used to tease everyone when he was younger. Those were good times when we laughed and it made me happy," Tickler said as his mind wandered back to the days of yore when Old Sap and he had traded jokes back and forth, one trying to outdo the other. It seemed, somehow, that Old Sap always got the better of him, but, he didn't mind because it was like trying to be taller than Predictor, he knew he couldn't do it, but, it was still fun to try.

"I remember his great stories. They were so full of joy and excitement. No one could outdo him in story telling and they all had a good moral to them. He is the one that I owe most of my story telling ability to. I shall miss his stories very much," Tall Tales told them, wearily.

"I remember when I was hot and thirsty, he gave me some of his water and then he fanned me with his branches until I was cool. You see, I cannot fan myself because I have so few branches. He was always very kind to me. I shall miss his caring tenderness very much," Thin-As-Grass told them, sadly.

"I remember his courage. He was very brave and he taught me to be brave, also. There were many times when I felt like I would fail at something and he always gave me the courage to do it. I, too, shall miss him very much indeed," Fuzzy Moss told them.

"I remember when he would encourage me when I was small and I thought I would never be anybody, ever. I thought I would just be an old, dumb tree that no one cared anything about until he told me that everyone is a somebody, God doesn't make sawdust. Only the Walk-To's make sawdust. Now, look! Soon I will be a Christmas tree! Old Sap did not live long enough for me to tell him, I forgot," she cried.

"He knew, Little Twig," Old Moss reassured her, "I told him and he was very proud of you, very proud indeed."

"I remember his strength of character the most because it seemed to overflow on all of us. He never weakened, even in the end he did not hesitate to do what he did. He knew that he wanted to be in The Land of Sweet Waters and Cool Breezes with Whisper and the rest of his friends, so he did it without telling us anything about his plans. I guess he knew we would all try to either talk him out of it or want to go along with him. He didn't want to be the weak link in the chain. He probably thought that if he held limbs with us that he wouldn't be able to concentrate and we would all have ended. He was a good example of strength to us all, even though I do not agree with how he ended," Predictor said with a growing lump in his throat. "God put us all on this earth for a certain amount of time and it is not for us to decide when we are to end."

Everyone thought about this for a moment. The silence was comforting while everyone gathered their thoughts once again.

"I remember a great, but, gentle friend. He wasn't just a friend to us, but he was a friend to all the animals, and the Song-With-Wings. He was even a friend to the Walk-To's. I remember his laugh, his courage, his gentleness, his caring, his great insight into things, his patience, his encouragement and most of all, his love for everyone. Yes, I will miss my great, but, gentle friend who used to sleep and snore and sway in the cool breezes." Old Moss said as he looked where Old Sap had once stood so proudly. The tears that he had been holding back for so long finally squeezed their way out of his sad, old, tired eyes and ran down his old, rough trunk.

They all hung their branches low and bowed their trunks as they prayed a silent prayer that God would put Old Sap next to a clear, bubbling brook where he could drink Sweet Water and sway in the cool and gentle breezes without a care in the world to worry him.

"And, now we must get on with the business of life," Predictor told them.

"But....I, too, remember him. I remember how he used to defend me and scold Tall Tales, in a very gentle way, of course, when Tall Tales had threatened to end me. He is the only one that ever stuck up for me, He was my best friend and now he is gone. I shall miss him, very much," Rhymer said, sadly, but, proudly.

"I'm sure we all will," Old Moss told him in a gentle and understanding voice.

They all slept out of sheer exhaustion.

When they woke up, the sun was shining and the air was clear and clean.

"Old Moss," Little Bark called to his teacher, "What is that roaring noise like small thunder that I hear?"

Old Moss listened for a moment as the terrible noise brought back sharp and painful memories. "You have so many questions for such a young Mere Twig. I don't remember ever asking that many questions when I was your age, but then, I must have. Anyway, why do you ask?"

"Because I want to know. You know, of course, that you did it again," he told Old Moss with a brief smile on his face. There wasn't much to smile about today.

"I did 'what' again?"

"You answered my question with a question again," he replied. "But do not worry; I think I am finally getting used to it. I think that I would miss it if you didn't do it now,"

"I do not think that I really mean to do it, it just happens. Now, why do you want to know about the noise? After all, it is just a noise," Old Moss said, stalling for time to think.

"Old Teacher, how am I ever going to increase my knots if I can't ask questions?"

"This is true, Little Bark, but there are some things that it is best that you don't know, just yet, anyway. We will talk of your small thunder another day. Perhaps tomorrow, perhaps cycles down the line of time, who knows?" he said as he fell into a deep and restful sleep.

Why wouldn't Old Moss tell him about such a small thing as a noise? What was so bad about it? "Teachers!" he said, frustrated at the whole world.

CHAPTER TEN

"What is it young one?" he sighed as he pulled his thoughts back to the present. He found that his thoughts were almost always in the past lately, back in a time when it was a joy to wake up and feel the sun or the rain on his leaves. Things were changing. He felt it in his roots and he didn't think they were changing for the better.

"How long does it take the pain inside to go away?"

"What pain is that, Little Bark? You aren't sick, are you?" he asked looking at Little Bark with more scrutiny and concern.

"No, I'm not sick, not like you are thinking anyway. I hurt inside every time I think about my Grandfather. How long does it take for the pain to go away?" Little Bark asked, embarrassed because a tear escaped his eyes. He was too old, he thought, to be crying.

"Sometimes it never goes away, Little Bark. We just have to remember the good times that we shared with him and have the belief that we will see him again soon when we end. It is hard, but, with time, it gets a little easier." He sounded very far away; as though he were remembering something that had once hurt him the way the ending of Old Sap had hurt Little Bark.

"It is a hurt that I hope I never have to bare again. It is too heavy of a burden for me to carry. It hurts so badly," he cried. He didn't care who saw him. He felt empty.

"Barky?' Twiggy whispered to him.

"What is it?" he snapped at her. "Leave me alone. I do not want to talk to anyone right now."

"Barky, listen to me, there is nothing to be ashamed of. When something hurts as bad as losing someone you love, there is no shame in crying. It is a release from that grief. Just remember that there are trees that are still alive that love you as much as you loved your Grandfather. There is a reason to go on with life. There always is."

"I know. You are right, but right now it just hurts too bad to think about anyone else except my Grandfather. It is as though he didn't love us enough. It is as though he didn't want to be with us anymore. That is what hurts the most. He didn't care enough about us to stay with us."

"I think that he cared so much that he didn't want to endanger any of us by being the weak link in our concentration," she explained.

"It still hurts. He could have tried. I miss him."

"It is always so. We do not mourn for the tree that has left us because deep down in our trunks we know that they are better off in The Land of Sweet Waters and Cool Breezes. We are mourning for ourselves because we won't be seeing that tree for a long time. Just remember, Barky, you will see your Grandfather again."

"But, there was so much that I wanted to say to him. I don't even think I ever told him that I loved him. I always thought that there was plenty of time to tell him things like that. I never really just talked to him like I do with you or Old Moss. Maybe he thought that none of us loved him."

"He knew that we loved him. We didn't have to tell him, either. He just knew. You don't have to tell someone that you love them, you know. If they cannot see it in your eyes or the things that you say, then they are blind. Believe me, Barky, your Grandfather knew and he was so very proud of you." Twiggy wanted to hug him and tell him that she loved him. She wanted to make the pain that he was feeling go away. She wanted to see him smile again.

A tear escaped and ran down her face as she watched him. There was nothing she could do to ease his pain and she knew that she would hurt as long as he did.

Little Bark looked at Twiggy with sad, loving eyes," I love you," he whispered.

Twiggy sighed as though a huge weight had been lifted from her. "I love you, too, Barky. Nothing will ever change that."

"We have our whole lives together. That is a very long time," he smiled.

"Yes." She replied, shyly. At least she had made him think of something else besides his Grandfather. A whole life with Barky sounded so good to her. She never knew she could love someone as much as she did Barky.

"I never expected to be betreethed at such a young age, Barky," she confided to him.

"You haven't changed your mind, have you?" he questioned her with a worried look.

"No, never! Don't be silly, Barky." She looked at him coyly. "You haven't changed your mind have you? I mean, you asked me so suddenly and all, I just thought that you might have changed your mind."

"Never in a million cycles," he assured her. "I want no one but you. I think of no one but you. I dream about you as I sleep. You are in my thoughts all the time. You are the only one for me, ever. I love you so much I can't seem to put it into words. If I bared my very soul to you, only then would you understand the depth of my love for you."

Twiggy was beaming with pride. Life couldn't get any better than this. To have someone to love like Little Bark was everything to her.

The day seemed to warm up a bit with the Song-With-Wings singing in a cheerful way. Everything seemed to be renewing itself since the fire. The animals were slowly returning and even Freckles had returned to his familiar perch in Old Moss' branches. The more things changed, the more they seemed to remain the same.

The mood of the trees had changed the most. It didn't seem that there was much to be happy about these days. Hard luck seemed to be their bread in the recent weeks that had passed, but, no one was complaining. It did no good to complain.

At least they had been spared from the fire.

"Tickler?" Fuzzy Moss called.

"Yes, what is on your knots, Young One?" he asked. Tickler was almost afraid for Fuzzy Moss to ask him a question lately. Fuzzy Moss was already smarter than he was in so many ways. It just wouldn't do to have Fuzzy Moss ask him a question that he could not answer. No, Tickler did not like that at all.

"Why hasn't the little Walk-To come back to see us?"

Oh! This was a relief to him, an easy question to answer.

"I think it is because of the fire. I would suppose that they are just as afraid of fire as we are, even though they can run away from it. I have heard of them burning in a fire a few times, though. Most of the time it is when they are asleep in their lairs."

"I am glad that we do not have to sleep in a lair, then." He paused in thought. "I miss seeing the little Walk-To."

"I was afraid that was what you were going to say. Have you taken leave of your senses? Don't you know that they are the cause of the fire that we just barely came through alive?" He looked at Fuzzy Moss in despair. This was the young tree that he had thought was so much smarter than he? Maybe he should re-evaluate his estimation of Fuzzy Moss' intelligence.

"Yes, I know, but the little Walk-To seemed so special."

"It was only special to you because it was the first one that you had ever seen. Stop making more out of it than it was. It really is quite common for them to come walking down our path, especially in the hot season. They like to walk through us and enjoy our shade."

"No, I think that you are wrong, but, I will not argue with you. The Little Walk-To is special and not only because it was the first one that I have ever seen, either. You just have no second sense about these things like I do, and, mark my words in your memory, there is something very special about that Walk-To," he said, firmly.

"I will remember. And, you remember this, Fuzzy Moss, any friend of the Walk-To's is not a friend of mine." He glared at him, disapproving of the affection that Fuzzy Moss had for the young Walk-To.

On the other side of the meadow, far away from the trees, Wendy was running in the front door, letting the screen door bang as she hurried to the kitchen to see Mandy. She could smell the aroma of fresh baked bread and she could hear Mandy singing as she mixed the dough for a batch of her favorite peanut butter cookies.

"Hi, Mandy!" she called as she entered the kitchen and climbed up on the bar stool in the breakfast nook. "May I have some dough?"

"Of course you can," Mandy said with a smile on her face. She loved Wendy as though she were her own daughter. "I'd feel mighty bad, Little One, if you didn't want some of Old Mandy's dough. But, not too much now or you'll spoil your dinner."

"I don't think so, Mandy. I think I could eat a horse! Except I love horses too much to eat them! Is Daddy going to be home in time for dinner?" she asked, hopefully.

"He said that he was going to try to be home. They still have quite a mess to clean up from the fire the other day. There are a lot of trees that need to be cut down or else they might fall down on some unsuspecting soul out for a walk one of these days. That wouldn't be very good, now would it?"

"No, I suppose not. I just wish that we didn't have to cut down any trees at all. But, you are right; I would hate to see a tree fall on someone or an animal. People can take care of themselves, but animals are so trusting and they don't look around for any trees that might fall on them," she paused, watching Mandy wash her hands at the sink." Did I tell you that I petted another deer the other day, Mandy?"

"No, I don't remember you saying anything about it," Mandy said as she turned to look at her. Who was this child that the animals weren't afraid of? It seemed as though the animals could sense something special about her.

"Well, I did! And it had a little fawn with it. I wanted to pet it too, but, I was afraid that I would frighten it away, so I just petted its mama," she declared as she stuck her finger in the cookie dough for another taste.

Mandy pretended that she didn't see her. "I'll bet she was soft what with winter coming on and her getting a winter fur on her."

"She was," she said, thinking of the feel of her fur. "Mandy, do you think that the government will give some more money to feed the deer this winter when it snows?"

"My dear child, you shouldn't be worrying about such things. God will take care of the deer and all the other animals. He always does. He keeps them warm by giving them extra fur in the winter and He finds other ways to feed them than just your Father. Don't worry your pretty little head about them, they'll be just fine." Mandy wondered why such a young child would care so much about animals and trees. Why, at her age she was playing with dolls and flirting with boys, but, she wouldn't change a hair on Wendy's head if she could. She thought that Wendy was pretty close to being perfect.

Wendy had turned eight years old on her last birthday a little over a month ago, but Wendy still remained a delicate child with a small frame. "Too small," her Father had said more than once, "to carry such a big, loving, caring heart." Wendy's big sky blue eyes, beautiful platinum blonde hair and sincere smile would melt anyone's heart. She had begun to look a lot like Abby.

"I'll just bet that you are the best cook in the whole world, Mandy!" Wendy said, eyeing the cookies that Mandy had just taken out of the oven.

"Well, I don't know about that, little one," she smiled and handed her a cookie, "Why don't you try one out for me and let me know if they are any good?"

"Ummmmm! They are delicious! What would Daddy and I do without you, Mandy?" Wendy frowned as she licked her fingers.

"Oh, I think that you could take care of yourselves just fine. But, I'm not going anywhere, so you just put that kind of thought out of your pretty little head. My, but you are the worryingest child I've ever come across!" she said, shaking her head in wonder. "You act so grown up all the time, child. Why, I hardly ever see you playing with other children. Don't you have any friends to play with?"

"I have Ralph and all the animals in the forest," she assured her. "I don't need anyone else, besides, I have you and Daddy. That is all I need."

"Well, I guess if you're happy, why change anything, huh?" she winked at Wendy.

"I love you, Mandy," she said, happily.

"Hey! Is anyone home?" Jim called as he entered the front door.

"Hi, Daddy! You made it home in time for dinner," she shouted as she ran and jumped into his arms.

"I missed you, too, Kitten," he said, kissing her on the cheek and ruffling her blonde curls. "Just think, when you are a teenager and have lots of boyfriends, you won't let your old Dad ruffle your hair up anymore," he teased.

"Oh, Daddy, I don't need any other boy friend than you!" she said as she ruffled his hair with both her hands and then gave him a big hug.

"Hmmmmmm, we'll see about that when the time comes. You just remember this conversation when you are sixteen and you want the keys to my car to go into town to be with your friends," he chided her.

"I don't know if that day will ever come, but, if it does, you can drive me, okay?"

"It's a deal, Kidddo, but I don't think that you will want me to be tagging along with you."

"Somehow I don't think that we will have to worry about it," she said, sadly.

"Now listen here, Kitten, I told you a long time ago that I didn't want you talking like that anymore, remember?" he gently reprimanded her.

"Yes, I know, but I have this feeling deep down inside me…like….. like I won't ever be sixteen. I have these dreams all the time. I told Mommy about them when she was alive. They don't go away and they don't get any clearer either. I can't see what happens. I just know that it is very sad," she said with tears in her eyes. She was looking into her Father's eyes." Daddy, I miss Mommy very much." Tears rolled down her cheeks. "Hold me tight, Daddy, and never leave me."

"You never have to worry about that, Pumpkin. I'll be here for as long as you need me," he said, tears escaping the corners of his eyes. He missed Abby so very much.

At six feet, three inches tall, Jim was a large man with a large frame. His steel gray eyes had a special kindness about them and, when he smiled, they became almost non-existent as his cheeks pushed up on them with an almost ear-to-ear grin. His curly, wheat colored hair was cut short and combed neatly back with a little curl hanging down in the front. His dimpled smile would capture the heart of any woman.

"Hey, what's going on here? Are you two keeping secrets from Old Mandy again?" she teased.

"Nope! We were just coming in to see what was for dinner. I'm starved! I think I could eat a horse!" he told her.

Both Wendy and Mandy burst out with laughter.

"Okay, what's the joke?"

"It's nothing. I just told Mandy that I was hungry enough to eat a horse not five minutes ago, that's all!" she giggled.

"Oh, is that so? Well, then, we had better go into the kitchen and see what wonderful dinner she has prepared for us tonight," he said as he put Wendy down and they followed Mandy into the kitchen.

"I'm afraid it's just pot roast, mashed potatoes and gravy, some biscuits, a bit of salad and an ear of corn for tonight," she said, apologetically.

"Ummmmm! Wonderful! Sounds like a feast fit for a King!" he said, hungrily.

They all sat down around the dinner table eyeing the delicious food that Mandy had prepared for them.

Mandy always stayed with them for dinner when she could. She knew that her husband could fend for himself when she was needed at Jim's and she always took a plate of food over to him when he didn't come over.

"Are we ready?" Jim asked, looking at them both. They all bowed their heads and closed their eyes in prayer. "Father, we thank You for this food that You have so abundantly blessed us with. We thank You for the hands that prepared it and we pray that those less fortunate than ourselves will truly be blessed by You. Thank You for our good health and all the many blessings that we take for granted each day, In Thy Son Jesus name we pray. Amen."

"When I ate dinner at Aunt Pat's house last year, they didn't thank Jesus for their food, they just sat down and started eating, but, after I took one look at the food, I thought it was best to say my own prayer. She doesn't cook so good," Wendy shook her head. "I think that it was the only thing that saved me from getting a stomach ache."

Mandy and Jim laughed.

"Some people don't do the same things that we do. They don't always believe the way we do, so, I guess, we just have to say an extra prayer for them," Jim explained.

"Mama always said that we should thank Jesus for everything that we have, but, I can remember when I had the chicken pox, I didn't thank Him for them, because I didn't want them. Instead, I prayed that He would take them away and He did!"

"I think we are only supposed to thank Him for the good things, Sweetheart," he chuckled.

"Did you ever have the chicken pox, Mandy?" Wendy asked.

"Oh, My! Yes! And what a sight I was! It was on my fifteenth birthday as I recall. I was supposed to be going to a dance with my steady beau at the time. But, I couldn't hide my chicken pox from my Mother, so I ended up not going." Mandy shook her head. "What a shame it was, I had such a pretty new dress all laid out nice like, just ready to put on. I had new bows for my hair and my boyfriend had brought me a corsage. We were going to do it up right that night. He was a real gentleman, he was." She sighed. "Maybe if I had gone to that dance, I would have married that one, but I guess The Dear Lord had other things in mind. He certainly knows best. And, besides, I never would have met Bill." She smiled. "I don't know what I would do without him; it would be like losing half of me after all these years. And, that other fella has been married four times! So, you see, Our Lord knows what is best for us."

"I'm glad you married Bill. I like him a lot," Wendy told her, and then paused with a frown. "Did you itch all over?" she asked as she shivered at the thought.

"Oh, boy, did I itch! I itched on top of my itches!" she chuckled.

"Daddy, did you ever have the chicken pox?"

"Oh, you might say that. We were on a camping trip when I was a young boy and I woke up in the middle of the night just itching from one end to the other," he told them as he reached for more mashed potatoes and gravy. "My Dad said that I must have gotten into some poison oak. They put Calamine Lotion all over me. It was sticky and the smell was awful. But, the next morning, I had a very high fever and I started to cough a lot so my Mom insisted that we go home to see a doctor. I got pneumonia from my chicken pox. Boy was I sick!" he shook his head remembering how long he had had to stay in bed.

"I wonder what all that noise is about." Jim pondered as he got up from the table and looked out the window to see why Ralph was barking. "It's Milly! Come here, Wendy," he motioned to her. "Milly is here."

Milly lived about seven miles down the road. Since Abby had died, Milly had come over at least once a week to visit. She always brought freshly baked goodies and an occasional present for Wendy.

Milly's hair was gray with streaks of white. It was sharply drawn back in a soft bun with tiny flowers surrounding it. Tiny glasses rested on the brim of her nose. She was plump and always wore an apron wherever she went. Her smile was warm and loving. Wendy thought the world of her.

"Hi, Milly!" Wendy called to her as she ran to greet her.

"My goodness, Sweetie, you sure have grown a lot in just one week!" Milly said, hugging Wendy. Then she handed her a small present that she had wrapped in the funny paper from the Sunday Edition. "And, you, why I always did say that some lucky young filly ought to horse shoe you, you handsome devil," she said, pinching Jim's cheek the way she always did.

Jim just smiled as he thought about his beautiful Abby. No one could ever fill the empty void she had left when she had died. It was supposed to get easier as time went on, but not for him, because every day that he was without his Abby, his heart felt heavier and all the more empty.

"How have you been, Milly?" Mandy smiled as she dried her hands on the front of her apron. Mandy liked Milly's caring ways. She could tell that Milly cared deeply about Jim and Wendy.

"Just fine! And, you?" she asked as she handed Mandy some cinnamon muffins and an apple pie that was still warm from the oven.

"Oh, I'm still kickin'. Sometimes it feels as though my joints need some oiling. They get so stiff, some times I'm afraid I won't be able to move!" she chuckled.

"I doubt that, Mandy. I've never seen anyone with as much energy as you have. I still don't know how you keep up with Wendy the way you do," Jim told her.

"Ahhhh, she's mighty mellow compared to some children. Why, now, for instance, just take my Grandson, I can last about two hours, three tops, with that young un. He's a handful, that one!" she said, her eyes big and round.

"May I open my present, Milly?" Wendy asked, wondering what was inside the small package.

"Of course you can! That's why I brought it for you!" She knelt down in front of Wendy. "Go on, open it."

"Okay," Wendy said as she tore at the wrapping, but only after she had carefully removed the bow. It was such a pretty bow that she thought she would save it to put in her hair.

Inside the wrapping was a little yellow box. Wendy carefully opened it and removed the tissue covering the little treasure. There in the small box was a little music box with a picture of a cute little clown on it and a little handle that she turned as it played 'send in the clowns, where are the clowns…..'

Tears welled up in the corner of Wendy's eyes as she hugged the little music box. "Thank you…..Thank you so much," she cried as she ran out of the kitchen and up to her room.

"Well, I'm glad she liked it," Milly said, a bit worried.

"I'm sure she loves it. That is the song that her Mother used to sing when she was busy in the kitchen," Jim said with a far away look in his eyes. "Excuse me, I think I will go up and see if she is okay." He wiped his mouth with his napkin and headed up to Wendy's room.

"I hope I haven't done the wrong thing," Milly said, a worried look on her face as she watched Jim go up the stairway.

"No, I don't think you have. It's her favorite song, too," Mandy told her.

"Yes, I know. She told me the other day. I was in McMinnville at Rutherford's on Third Street and I happened to hear a little boy playing with one and I recognized the song immediately. So I bought it for her." She shook her head.

"Well, no harm done. You can tell that she loved it. She held it close to her heart and you don't hold something that you don't like close to your heart." She patted Milly's hand. "Let's have a cup of tea. I need to catch up on the latest news of the neighbors," Mandy told her as she put the tea kettle on to boil.

Jim stood in the doorway of Wendy's bedroom. Her back was turned toward him as she sat playing the little music box, quietly singing the words through her tears. Her Mother had sung that song to her so many times. Jim felt as though his heart was being ripped right out of his chest as he watched her. She looked so small and fragile, like a sad, delicate porcelain doll.

Wendy put the little music box on her nightstand and laid face down, drowning her sobs in her pillow.

Jim walked into her room, sat next to her on her bed and held her close in his arms. "It is okay, Kitten, I miss her, too."

"It hurts so bad in here," she told him, pointing to her heart, sobbing with the ancient loneliness of a loved one who had died.

"I know, Sweetheart, but just remember all the wonderful things we did together with her and remember that some day when we all die, we will see her again in Heaven. Won't that be wonderful?" he asked, giving her an extra squeeze.

"I wish I could be with her now," she cried, sadly.

"But, then I would miss you."

"I want you to come with me," she sniffed.

"But, our lives are not finished here on this earth. God has something planned for each of us while we are here and our work isn't done yet." He looked at his daughter with strained heartstrings pulling in his chest. It felt like his chest was going to explode with the overload. He loved her so much. She looked so much like Abby, the same platinum blonde hair, and the same huge caring blue eyes. His little 'Alice in Wonderland'.

"I wonder what God wants us to do. If we knew, then we could do it and go see Mommy," she said, anxiously

"Only God knows what He wants us to do. We don't want to upset His plans, now do we?"

"No, that wouldn't be right. He would be very angry with us."

"Then, I guess we will just continue to love each other and when our life is done and Jesus calls us home, we can see your Mommy again." He smiled. "I love you, Kitten. Just always remember that I love you," he said as he hugged her one more time. "Now, don't you think that it is time that you and I go downstairs and visit with Milly? She came to see us both, but, especially you."

"Okay," she pouted.

"Not until I see a smile on that pretty face! Here, go in the bathroom and wash your face. I'll meet you downstairs," he said as he began to walk out of her room.

"I know that tomorrow isn't Sunday, but can I send a special letter to Mommy? I want to tell her all about the music box that Milly gave me."

"You sure can, Sweetheart. We will do it the first thing in the morning if you like."

She gave him one of her winning smiles and went into the bathroom to wash her face. When she was done, she went to her dresser and picked up the little music box. She hugged it to herself like a small kitten, slipped it into her jeans pocket and ran down the stairs.

"Here she comes! It's good to have you back with us, Sweetie! I thought that you were mad at me about something." Milly winked at her.

"Oh, Milly, I couldn't ever be mad at you," she said, earnestly.

"Then come here and sit down on my lap. Your Father and I have been talking and I asked him if I could take you on a picnic tomorrow. How would you like that?" She asked, smiling.

"Oh! That would be wonderful! Can Ralph come with us?" she asked, excitedly.

"Well, I guess so," she said looking up at Jim.

"No, Sweetheart, I think you had better leave Ralph at home. Okay?" Jim told her.

"I guess so. He would probably eat all of our lunch anyway," she said, matter-of-factly.

They all laughed.

"I'll write my letter to Mommy tonight and you can send it to her for me tomorrow morning when you go to work," she said looking at her Father. "Will you do that for me, Daddy?"

"I sure will," he told her. "After you get done writing it, put it on the kitchen table and I will take with me."

"I'll go write it right now!" Wendy said as she ran up the stairs to begin her letter.

"I guess I had better get going. I want to be here bright and early in the morning," Milly told them as she headed for the front door. "Wendy is still writing letters to Abby, is she?"

"Yes, she sends her one every Sunday without fail."

"But, tomorrow isn't Sunday?"

"I know. She is sending Abby a special letter to tell her all about the little music box that you brought her today." Jim smiled. The dream that Wendy had on that night had changed her whole life. It had given her a way to talk to Abby. A miracle? He thought so.

"I'm glad that she liked it," Milly said as she walked out the front door to her car and drove away.

Mandy cleaned up the kitchen and went home to be with Bill.

Jim went out and sat in the swing on the front porch, his thoughts far away.

Wendy tiptoed down the stairway and put her letter on the kitchen table. "I miss you, Mama," she whispered and went to her room.

The next day came faster than Wendy had thought possible. Milly had called and said that she was just leaving her house and that she would be there soon. Jim had already left for work at four thirty, taking Wendy's letter with him.

Mandy was just finishing up some extra sandwiches for them in the kitchen.

Wendy brushed her hair until it shined like the rays of the sun through a window in the clouds on a dreary day. Her hair was so fine and pretty. She heard a car drive up in the driveway just as she was finishing her hair. She ran to the window and saw Milly sitting in her car.

"She's here! She's here!" Wendy cried out as she ran to the kitchen and grabbed the stuffed picnic basket. Then she gave Mandy a kiss on the cheek.

"You have a good day, Pumpkin," she called as Wendy ran out the door.

"I will! Bye!" she called over her shoulder as she ran to Milly's car.

"Hi, Sweetie! How's my best girl today?" Milly smiled at Wendy's enthusiasm.

"I'm fine!" she said happily, scrambling into the front seat. "Where are we going?"

"Now, if I told you, it wouldn't be a surprise, now would it? You like surprises, don't you?" she asked as she carefully backed out of the driveway.

"Yes, I do!" she told her. "Do you want me to close my eyes?" Wendy asked, squeezing her eyes tightly shut.

"No, that's okay. It's going to take about forty five minutes to get there so buckle up your seat belt."

"Daddy always makes me buckle up my seat belt even if we just go to the store."

"Well, it's always a good idea. You never know when it will save your life," Milly told her.

"I saw a program on television about seat belts and I don't see why everyone doesn't buckle them on. They would if they had seen the program that I saw," she said, adamantly. "Daddy says there are a lot of people who would be alive today if they had just taken the time to put their seat belt on," she explained.

"Yes, I know," Milly said a bit sadly.

"Why are you so sad all of a sudden, Milly?" Wendy asked with a frown.

"Oh, it's nothing. I lost someone I love very much because she didn't have her seat belt on," Milly told her. She looked at Wendy with sad eyes. "And, I sure don't want anything to happen to you," she reached over and squeezed her hand.

"Who was it, Milly?" she asked, cautiously.

"You are the one for asking questions," she said, looking into Wendy's big blue eyes. Her daughter's eyes had been blue, sky blue." It was my daughter, little one. It happened a long time ago."

"I'm sorry, Milly, I shouldn't have asked, that way you wouldn't be sad right now. It hurts so bad when someone dies. I sure miss my Mama." Wendy looked down at the floor of the car and swallowed hard. She didn't want to cry, but she could feel the tears beginning to well up in her eyes.

"Hey, I've got an idea!" Milly said. "Why don't we stop up here at the animal farm and pet some of the young animals! Doesn't that sound like fun?" Milly asked, trying to get Wendy's mind off of her Mother.

"That would be fun!" she brightened immediately. "Daddy always said that he would take me there some day, but he never has time. Oh, how exciting!" Wendy could have bounced up and down had it not been for the seat belt that firmly held her in her seat.

"Child, you are so good for me, you're just like a tonic," Milly said, lovingly.

"What's a tonic?" Wendy asked, curiously.

"Well, it's like taking some mint for your tummy when you don't feel good. It makes you feel better," she explained.

"Do I make you feel better, Milly?"

"You sure do, Sweetheart."

"You make me feel like a tonic, too" Wendy told her.

Milly just laughed. She understood what Wendy had meant. They were good for each other.

Wendy unbuckled her seat belt when Milly pulled the car into the parking lot of the Animal Farm.

"Hey! Wait for old Milly! You're going too fast for me!" she called to Wendy as she ran to the door of the Animal Farm.

Milly paid the two dollars entrance fee and they both walked in. Just inside the door was an old woman dressed up like an Indian, sitting on a huge pile of colorful blankets. A large bowl of sacks of grain to feed the animals was lying on her lap. A little farther ahead, there was a doorway that was draped in very heavy burgundy material. Behind the draped doorway, Wendy could hear all kinds of animals.

"Are you ready, Milly?" Wendy asked in anticipation.

"I sure am!" she smiled.

Once through the doorway, Wendy could see some baby goats standing near their mamas. All of them came over to Wendy as she approached. Milly stood back and tried not to frighten them. She had been told about Wendy's extraordinary gift with the animals. She secretly wanted to see for herself. And, there she was with the mama goats and their babies, petting them all.

There were four baby calves in the next coral and they all came over to greet Wendy without hesitation as soon as they saw her,

Milly was thrilled.

Next to them, in a smaller area were two miniature horses. "Oh, look, Milly!" Wendy said as she pointed to them. "They are so tiny. I think Ralph is bigger than they are!" she exclaimed as she petted first one then the other.

The next coral had Shetland ponies, which were larger than the Miniature horses had been, but Wendy loved them and petted them just as much. Next to them were regular horses with their foals. None of the animals were afraid of Wendy so far. Baby pigs, deer and their fawns, turkeys, chickens, rabbits with their little bunnies, Llamas and baby llamas, sheep and lambs, all came up to her when they saw her.

They had spent about an hour before they came upon some baby cougars and their mamas. Milly knew that this would be the supreme test if Wendy had a true gift with the animals. These were animals that belonged in the forest. They weren't like the animals that Wendy had petted so far. But, as Wendy approached them, they also, came over to the gate for her to pet them. This was indeed unusual and Milly was elated.

The bears and their cubs also came willingly over to Wendy's gentle voice as she approached them.

Milly just stood back in wonder.

"Well, did you enjoy yourself?" Milly asked her.

"Oh yes! They were all so cute! I just wish that they didn't have to be all cooped up like that," she said, kicking a small rock as they walked back to the car. "Thank you so much, Milly. It was great! I love the animals so much. We couldn't have gone anywhere that I would have liked better." She clapped her hands. "Where are we going now?" she asked.

"You'll see," Milly told her with a sly look. She knew that Wendy also liked the trees, so she had planned to take her to Silver Creek Falls, a beautiful, peaceful area not too far from Salem.

"How come you didn't pet any of the animals?" Wendy asked as Milly drove out onto the highway.

"Oh, I probably would have scared them away. Besides, I had fun watching you. The animals love you just as much as you love them."

"I sure hope so. I love trees, too, and I love you and Daddy and Mandy and Ralph!" she said, proudly.

"And, we all love you, too!"

"There sure are a lot of cars on the road today," Wendy commented.

"Yes. It seems that more and more people are moving to Oregon." Milly sighed. "I would hate to see this area become like Los Angeles or New York. They have way too many people living there. The traffic is terrible. I've been there, so I know," she told Wendy adamantly. "But, don't get me wrong, I like people, just not so many in one place."

Milly turned the car into the entrance to Silver Creek Falls. "There are lots of tables for us to sit and eat our lunch and there are lots of tall trees to keep us company. And, way over there, behind those trees," Milly pointed to her right, "there is a trail that we can take to go see the big water falls. But, let's eat first, shall we? I'm hungry," Milly said, rubbing her stomach in emphasis.

"Me, too," she said, helping Milly unload the car. "It is so beautiful here, Milly. I wish I could build a house right here in this very spot and live here the rest of my life," she said, hugging herself as she looked around. "Then, I could hear the water falls and all the birds singing all the time. Can you hear the birds singing, Milly?"

"Yes, I can. They are pretty, aren't they?" Milly agreed as she spread a tablecloth out on the picnic table.

"Maybe Daddy will build us a house here if I ask him."

"I don't think they would let anyone build a house in a state park like this," she cautioned her.

"Then, I'll just stay here and sleep under the picnic table."

Milly chuckled. "I don't think that your Father would like it very much if I came home without you," she said, shaking her head. "Let's eat, we've got a lot to see today, Milly told her as she took a big bite of her sandwich.

Wendy was almost too excited to eat, but, she finally managed a half of a sandwich and a leg of fried chicken, some cookies and a Tootsie Roll Pop.

After they were satisfied with their lunch, they began the long hike down the trail to the big water falls. It was just warm enough that they only had to wear a sweater. There were a lot of people that were walking the same trail that they were. Some were on their way down and others were coming back up.

Wendy caught her first glimpse of the waterfalls as they came around a corner of the trail. "Oh, Milly, it's so big and beautiful!"

"It is gorgeous, isn't it?" she said, looking with awe at all the water that was falling from such a long way up the side of the hill.

Squirrels were running with their tails straight up in the air, scolding them as the continued down the trail to get a closer look.

"Would you like to go all the way down?" Milly asked her. "You can walk right under the water falls, you know."

"Oh, let's do it, Milly!" she said, jumping up and down.

Milly smiled with contentment as she took Wendy's hand and they walked behind the water falls.

The noise from all the water falling made it impossible for them to talk to each other.

Wendy could feel the spray gently touch her face. It felt good to her. They stood there for a long time drinking in the beauty of all that they saw. Mellowed, they both walked back up the trail to the table and grabbed another bite to eat. Then they loaded up the car and headed home.

"Thank you for such a wonderful day, Milly," Wendy said, sleepily.

"You are very welcome. Thank you for such a wonderful day. I can't remember when I've enjoyed myself so much," she told her.

"I wish it could always be this way," Wendy told her as she snuggled up close to Milly in the front seat and was soon fast asleep.

CHAPTER ELEVEN

Jim entered the house about five thirty. He could smell the tantalizing aroma of chicken frying in the kitchen. He could also hear Mandy singing happily as she set the table for dinner.

"Hello!" Jim called, smiling, expecting Wendy to run up to him any second.

"Hi!" Mandy called as she came out of the kitchen. "You're home early tonight, aren't you?" she asked wiping her hands on her apron.

"I suppose I am. I just couldn't concentrate on my work today," he told her as he looked around. "Where is Wendy?"

"They haven't returned yet," Mandy told him, a frown on her face. "I'm really worried."

"Didn't Milly give you a time that they would be back?" Jim asked as a shiver of anxiety pierced his body.

"No, as a matter of fact, Milly never even came into the house. When Milly drove up, Wendy ran out to her car. I did see that it was Milly though," she quickly reassured him. "I mean, Wendy didn't get into a stranger's car or anything."

"Well, they will probably be along any minute now," he tried to sound confident. "When will dinner be ready?" he asked, sniffing the air. "I'm starving! And, if I'm not mistaken, that is my favorite dinner I smell, isn't it?"

"Anything I cook seems to be your favorite dinner!" she teased him with a big smile that didn't quite reach her eyes. She was still very worried about Milly and Wendy.

She patted his arm. "Dinner will be ready in about thirty minutes," she called over her shoulder as she walked back into the kitchen.

Jim crossed the room to where the console television was placed in front of the living room window. He reached down and turned it on. It was time for the news. He took his newspaper from Ralph who had been waiting patiently; tail wagging, with the newspaper in his mouth.

Jim sat down in his favorite easy chair, patted Ralph on the head and began to read the front page.

The television news caster broke his concentration.

"And, this just in from our news desk. There has been a two car collision on highway twenty two just outside of Salem. The ambulances are there now. There are three people known to have died at the scene. Stay tuned to this station for further details as they are made available."

Jim dropped the newspaper as a stab of dread shot through his body.

Mandy came running in from the kitchen, her hands folded on her chest.

They stood staring at one another not wanting to believe the worst.

"We don't know for sure that it is them," Jim said, clenching his fists as tight as he could to control the emotions that were threatening to overwhelm him.

"No, we don't know that it is them," she agreed. "But, Dear Lord in Heaven they are so late," she cried, grabbing her throat to keep from choking as her heart raced inside her chest.

Jim put his arm around her. "I couldn't live without my little Wendy," he confided. "I couldn't survive two deaths. It just can't be possible." His whole body was shaking.

"Everything's going to be alright," Mandy told him as she straightened her shoulders in resolve. "Who knows? They may be just about to drive up in the driveway now," she said with as much encouragement as she could muster. "I'll go finish dinner. I'm sure they will both be very hungry when they get here," Mandy said as she patted him on the shoulder.

Jim stared at the picture of Wendy and Abby that was on the table beside his chair. It had been taken about a year and a half ago when they had both dressed up as clowns for Halloween. Abby had been so full of life then. They had made so many plans for their future. But, it had all changed in the blink of eye.

Jim's thoughts were interrupted when the telephone rang.

He just stood there staring at the phone, afraid to answer it.

Mandy came running back in from the kitchen, her hand over her heart in anticipation.

Neither of them wanted to answer the telephone.

Finally, Jim reached for the phone; a feeling of dread overwhelmed him. "Hello?" Jim whispered hoarsely.

"Hello, is Jim Wardly there please?" a man on the other end of the line asked.

Jim's mouth suddenly became very dry. The words stuck in his throat. He sat down with his head in one hand and the telephone in the other.

"This is Jim Wardly," Jim whispered quietly.

"Sir, this is Sheriff Howard Dawson." He paused for a moment. This was the worst part of his job. He could do almost anything else, but, he hated making calls like this one. "Sir, it's about your daughter," and there was another long pause as the Sheriff cleared his throat. "There has been an accident. A two car collision." The Sheriff paused once again. "We regret to inform you that Milly Anderson and your daughter were killed in the crash. I'm so sorry."

Jim didn't want to believe his ears. The blood drained from his face. He dropped the phone. He would never see his little Wendy again. "Oh, God, no. This can't be happening," Jim moaned, both hands covering his face. First Abby. Now Wendy. He couldn't bare the thought of living without them.

"What is it?" Mandy asked, tears streaming down her face as she picked the telephone receiver up off the floor where Jim had dropped it. She listened to see if anyone was still one the line, didn't hear anyone so she hung up the phone.

"It's Wendy and Milly.......they were in that accident." He began to tremble from head to toe. "Oh, My God," Jim cried as the truth finally hit him like a sledge hammer in his chest. "They are both dead. I wonder how her husband is taking the news? I wonder if the Sheriff has even called him yet."

"That isn't something that you need to worry about right now," Mandy told him as she slowly walked over to Jim and sat down beside him on the arm of his chair. She put her arm around him. "Oh, Jim," she cried, "I'm so sorry. So very sorry. I don't know what to do or say to make things better for you." Not Wendy. Please Lord, not our little sunshine. Her thoughts were in turmoil.

Jim straightened his shoulders in determination. "I've got to go down to the Sheriff's Office," he told her blankly, almost void of emotion.

"Do you want me to go with you?" she asked.

"No, "I'll go by myself. You stay here and take care of things," he paused and looked around. "There will probably be telephone calls and people coming over to express their condolences," he said, sadly. "It's happening all over again, isn't it?" His knees felt weak. His heart felt empty. His soul was bruised.

"I'm so sorry, Jim, if I could take Wendy's place, I would gladly do it." Mandy sobbed.

"No Mandy. Don't even think like that, although, I had the same thought just a minute ago."

The telephone rang again and Jim looked at Mandy. "News travels fast in this small community, doesn't it?" he said as he went to answer the phone.

"Hello?" Jim said.

"Hello is Jim Wardly there, please."

"This is he," Jim said.

"Mr. Wardly, this is Sheriff Howard Dawson. Sir, I'm so very sorry. There has been a mistake. Your daughter was not one of the casualties. Her identity was mistaken. It was the child of the driver of the other car."

"Oh! That's wonderful! I mean…..that's not wonderful for the other people…..but….it's such good news for us!" He motioned for Mandy to come over and sit by him. He covered the phone and said, "Wendy is alive! Our little Wendy is alive!" he cried with joy. His muscles felt weak. He was shaking worse than before.

"Oh, Thank You, Lord!" Mandy said out loud, her hands folded in prayer. "Jim I'm so happy! What happened? How could they make such a mistake? Don't they know what they have just put us through?" Then Mandy became really outraged." Why, if I wasn't so happy, I'd go down there right now and punch that Sheriff right in the nose!" She grabbed Jim's arm, all concern again. "How is Wendy? Is she okay? Where is she? Is she in the hospital?" Mandy's questions poured out one after another.

"Wait.......wait! I can't answer all your questions and the Sheriff's too!" he said as he put his arm around her. It was then that he realized that Mandy was the closest thing that Wendy would ever have to a real Grandma. His parents were both gone and so were Abby's.

"How is my daughter? Is she going to be alright?" Jim asked, just happy that she was alive. He knew that she could possibly be in a coma or maybe paralyzed for the rest of her life, but she was alive! And, he would quit work and take care of her if it was necessary.

"She seems to be doing just fine," the Sheriff said, happily. "I was at the hospital when they brought her in. She wasn't awake at the time. She had been knocked out when she hit her head. The people that stopped when they witnessed the accident pulled her from the car and that is why we thought she was the other people's daughter. They had pulled everyone from the cars, afraid that the cars would catch fire and explode. Everything was such a mess; we couldn't tell who was who. However, they are transporting her by ambulance to the McMinnville Hospital. They thought it would be less traumatic for her and more convenient for you because it is closer to where you live. They need you to meet them there to sign some papers and your daughter has been asking for you and someone named Mandy. She seemed to be calm enough, but, she wants to see you as soon as possible."

"Mandy and I will be there right away," Jim paused. "Can you tell me what happened?" His voice was serious once again as he remembered that Milly was one of the casualties.

"The final word isn't in yet, but, from what we can figure out so far, the driver of the other car had a heart attack and came across into the lane that Mrs. Anderson and your daughter were in. According to the witnesses that pulled everyone from the cars, if it had not been for Mrs. Anderson, your daughter would not be alive right now, Mr. Wardly."

"Why? What did she do?"

"She threw herself on top of Wendy. Evidently Wendy was asleep on the front seat."

"Thank you for all your information, Sheriff Dawson. We will head down to the hospital." Jim hung up the telephone and turned to Mandy. "Let's go," he said.

"Do you really want me to go with you?" she asked, hopefully.

"Of course I do. I realized tonight just how much you love her. Come on," he said, smiling, "let's go see our little girl."

"I'll just go turn off the stove in the kitchen," she said, stumbling. "My knees are a little weak. This has been quite a night of ups and downs."

"Yes, it has, and my knees are weak, too. But, remind me to get down on them tonight and thank Our Dear Lord for giving us back our Wendy."

"Amen to that!" she agreed wholeheartedly as she grabbed her coat and purse.

It took them eleven minutes to get to the hospital. The ambulance had already arrived and was parked at the emergency entrance. The paramedics opened the ambulance doors and rolled the gurney toward the emergency room. Jim and Mandy followed a little distance behind.

Jim couldn't wait any longer. "I'm her Father," he called to them.

They stopped so that Jim and Mandy could see her.

"Daddy?" Wendy called to him.

"Yes, Sweetheart, it's Daddy and Mandy is here, too. How are you?" he asked as his eyes studied her from head to toe.

"I feel okay. I'm just really sleepy and a little sick to my stomach and they don't want me to go to sleep," she complained.

"She may have a concussion," one of the paramedics told him.

"It's okay, Sweetie. They will take some x-rays and see if everything is okay and then you can go to sleep, okay" he smiled in relief. His little girl was going to be just fine.

"Okay." Then Wendy looked at her father. "How's Milly?"

Mandy looked at Jim with a warning look on her face.

"We don't know yet, Pumpkin," he lied. It was just a temporary lie. She would know the truth soon enough.

"Mama got my letter that you sent to her this morning. She told me to tell you that she loves you very much and that she is watching over us all. She says that she is our Guardian Angel."

"When did you talk to your Mama, Sweetheart?" Jim asked in confusion.

"When I was on my way to Heaven. She told me that you needed me more than she did right now because she has Jesus and God and all the other Angels with her, but, if I died and stayed with her, you wouldn't have anyone, so I came back to be with you."

Jim stared at Mandy.

"Mandy?" Wendy called.

"I'm right here, Sweetheart," she said as she held out her hand to Wendy.

"Mandy, I'm going to be okay, now. You and Daddy don't need to cry any more," she said, shaking her head.

"I love you," Jim said as they wheeled her into the emergency room.

Jim and Mandy sat in the waiting room watching first the clock and then the emergency room doors. It seemed like it was taking forever, but in reality it had only been a little over an hour.

"Would you like something to drink, coffee, juice or a soda?" Jim asked Mandy.

"No thank you, Jim. I think I would probably choke on it right now if I tried to drink something," she smiled wearily.

"I have heard about people who have died and then come back again. What Wendy told us was truly amazing." Jim shook his head. "I still wish that Abby would come to me in a dream or something so that I could talk to her and tell her how much I miss her," he told Mandy, sadly.

"Maybe it will happen sometime, Jim. You never know what causes a person to be able to communicate with their loved ones that have passed on."

"I always did say that Wendy was a very special little girl and she has proven it over and over," he said, thoughtfully.

Finally, the emergency room doors opened and the doctor came out with a smile on his face.

Jim felt relief.

Mandy relaxed.

"I'm happy to report that there doesn't seem to be any damage at all. No concussion, no fractures of any kind. She's a mighty lucky young lady coming through an accident like that one with just a few bruises."

"But, she was covered with blood," Mandy told the doctor.

"Yes, she was. It was Milly Anderson's blood, not Wendy's. We've got Wendy all cleaned up now, though and, if it is alright with you, we'd like to keep her overnight for observation."

"That will be fine," Jim agreed. "May we see her now?"

"Well, you could, but she is sleeping pretty soundly right now. That is one of the reasons that we would like to keep her overnight," he explained. "You can go to room 202 on the second floor and take a peek if you like, but, please don't wake her."

"Okay. We will just take a peek at her from the doorway so that we don't wake her up. What time can I take her home tomorrow?"

"Anytime after eleven should be fine. We want her to eat some breakfast and make sure all her plumbing is still in good working order," he smiled.

Jim shook his hand, "Thank you, Doctor. Thank you so much."

"I don't deserve that thank you, Jim, but Milly Anderson sure does," he smiled, weakly. "She gave up her life for your daughter."

Jim and Mandy went up the elevator to the second floor and found Wendy's room. Jim just stood there looking at her, a trace of tears trickling down his cheeks as he said a silent prayer of gratitude and thanks to Jesus and to Abby.

Mandy stood in much the same manner, quietly watching to see if Wendy truly was breathing.

Then they turned to each other and smiled in relief and joy.

"Come on Mandy, I'm taking you out to dinner," he said guiding her down the hallway.

"I don't think that I can eat," she said, looking at him, sorrowfully.

"I know, we all lost a special friend and true neighbor."

Mandy was surprised after dinner at just how hungry she had been. They were both stuffed full of food as they drove home.

"I'll get Wendy some clean clothes together for you to take to the hospital when you go to get her tomorrow. Her other clothes are soaked with blood," Mandy shivered. A single tear slowly made its way down her cheek.

Jim patted her hand with understanding.

The next day, Jim drove to the hospital with Wendy's fresh, clean clothes while Mandy cleaned up the mess from the uneaten dinner of the night before.

Jim could see Wendy as he entered her hospital room. She was just sitting there with her back to him coloring in a color book.

"Hi, Kitten!" he called to her.

"Hi Daddy!" she said hopping down off the bed and running to him, "I thought you would never get here!"

"It's only seven-thirty! I can't even take you home until eleven-thirty," he warned her and ruffled her hair, being especially careful not to touch the area where she had hit her head.

"Oh, Poooooooo! I want to go home now! I feel fine," she pouted.

"Well, you can't go home until the doctor says that you are ready to go home, and, remember, he did say maybe. He doesn't want to send you home too soon," he smiled as he looked at her from top to bottom. She had a bruise on her left arm a bump on her head and her lip was swollen, but that was all. There were no cuts, no scrapes, and no broken bones. She looked pretty good for just being in a car accident that had killed three people.

Jim suddenly felt sad for the people that had died and especially the ones that they had left behind. He knew all too well what kind of pain that was; he had experienced it when Abby had died not long ago and again, when he had gotten that telephone call last night. It made him feel weak.

"I must have bitten the inside of my lip, it hurts," she told him, licking the inside of her lip with her tongue.

"Is that all that hurts?" he asked her.

"No, I hurt all over! I feel like I have been wrestling with Ralph all day! I'm sore!" she told him.

"You will be for a while," the doctor said as he came into the room. "Hello, Jim," he said as he took Jim's hand in a friendly handshake. "I heard about the first telephone call that the Sheriff made last night. That was unfortunate indeed," he said as his heart went out to this man who stood before him.

"Yes, but, everything is okay now," Jim said, returning his handshake whole-heartedly. "I'll take that first call any day as long as the second one comes along afterwards!" he smiled.

"Can I go home now?" Wendy asked the doctor.

"We would still like to keep you here at least until eleven. Did you eat your breakfast?"

"Not the first one. But, the nurse brought me some oatmeal and toast and I ate that," she told him as she wrinkled her nose. "I don't like soft boiled eggs."

Jim and Doctor Sawyer both laughed.

"How does your tummy feel now?" Doctor Sawyer asked.

"It feels like it wants to go home to Mandy and get good food. They don't cook so good in here."

"Well, we'll see what can be done about that. I'll be back around eleven o'clock to examine you," he said, smiling and turned to Jim. "I'll see you in a few hours." And then, he left the room.

"He's nice. I like him. He is the one that brought me the color book," she said as she opened it up. "Look at what I colored!"

"That's beautiful, Sweetheart," Jim told her, and it was beautiful. Wendy had a way of blending in the colors that made it look like a painting instead of just something that she was coloring with color crayons.

"When can we go see Milly, Daddy?" she asked, smiling brightly at the thought.

Wendy knew by the look on her Father's face that something was wrong. She got down off her hospital bed and slowly walked over to him. "What's wrong, Daddy? She's going to be okay, isn't she?" she asked, worried.

"Yes, Little One, she is going to be alright, but not the way that you are thinking." He looked at his precious daughter hoping that she was strong enough to hear the bad news. "Come and sit on my lap." He told her as he put his arms around her and held her tight.

"Milly died in the crash last night and now she is with Mommy and Jesus and her own little girl. She has no more cares or troubles where she is. She is in Heaven."

Wendy began to tremble. "Oh, Daddy," she sobbed, "why does everyone that we love have to die? Why can't we be happy and have everyone that we love here with us? I am so afraid that everyone that I love is going to die," she cried as she hung on to him afraid that he, too, might die and leave her.

"You didn't die and I love you very much," he told her, gently brushing her hair off of her face. "I was so happy when they told me that you were going to be okay."

"Mama said that you would be happy," Wendy told him.

"Did she say that last night when you were unconscious?" he asked.

"What does unconscious mean?" she asked.

"It means when you were asleep and going to Heaven. Did she tell you then?"

"Yes," she cried. "Maybe I can send a letter to Mama for Milly, and Mama can give it to her." She was sobbing. "I miss them both so much,"

"We will do that just as soon as you feel up to it, Pumpkin."

Wendy just laid in his arms and cried until she fell asleep with exhaustion. Jim had let her cry. He knew that it was best for her to let her feelings out. It wasn't good to keep anger and sorrow all tied up inside her. It only made things worse.

Jim's eyes were not dry, either. It had finally hit him that Milly wouldn't be coming over any more. She wouldn't be bringing her love and her wonderful baked goodies for Wendy. There would be no more loving little gifts. No more picnics or afternoon excursions. He bowed his head and closed his eyes and he, also, was soon asleep with Wendy in his arms.

In the forest near Jim's ranch, the trees were just waking to a new day, all except one who had been awake while the others had slept.

"Predictor?" Little Bark called to him.

"Yes, Little Bark, what is it?" he asked while he yawned and stretched.

"I was awake all night with a feeling," he told him, frowning with thought.

Predictor looked at him with curiosity. Predictor knew very well that Little Bark had the same gift that he, himself, had. Feelings and dreams were not to be ignored. "What kind of a feeling?" he asked a bit apprehensively.

"It is the little Walk-To. I have a feeling that something has happened to it," he said, frowning in thought.

"What makes you think that something has happened to it? It looked okay the last time it was here. I know that they are puny and weak, but it did not look like it had anything wrong with it." He tried to encourage him, knowing that he liked the little Walk-To.

"Yes, it looked alright," he agreed, "But I just can't shake this feeling that something bad has happened to it."

"Well, I for one certainly hope that nothing has happened to it. Twiggy would be very upset. If something happened to the little Walk-To then Twiggy couldn't be its Christmas tree. Twiggy would be very disappointed," Predictor warned him. "She is looking forward to being all dressed up, you know."

"Yes, I know, but maybe it would be better if she wasn't its Christmas tree," he said, pausing in deep thought. "I have a feeling about that, too. I don't think that I want her to be a Christmas tree. What's the big deal about it anyway? She would go away and I would miss her too much. And, from what I've heard, she will be gone for quite some time. And, another thing that worries me, remember what Old Moss said that sometimes the Walk-To's don't even plant us back in the same place where they have dug us up. I can't bare the thought of losing her now. I love her too much," he said, earnestly

"Don't worry about things that have not even happened yet. We must always think about them and try to change the things that we can change, but we must not dwell on them. Everything will be just fine," he said, winking at Little Bark. "Just fine." But, deep down in his trunk, he could feel doubt. Things didn't always go the way a tree wanted them to.

Doctor Sawyer came into Wendy's room and found them both fast asleep in the chair. As he looked at them, he couldn't help feeling happy for them. It must be a wonderful thing to know such feelings for each other. As for himself, he never had the time for a family of his own. His work kept him too busy. The days were very long and he didn't think that it would be fair to any woman or child to live most of their lives without him being at home.

He reached over and touched Jim's shoulder. "I see that you have both been napping in my absence," he said, quietly.

"Sorry about that, Doctor Sawyer, we were just talking about Milly Anderson. I told Wendy," he whispered, looking at him with saddened eyes.

"How did she take the news?" he asked, concerned that Wendy had had just about all the turmoil she could handle right now.

"She cried a lot and then fell asleep in my arms. I fell asleep right along with her. I didn't exactly sleep last night.

"You should have said something or called me. I could have given you something to help you sleep. Sleep is very important to you both right now. Sleep heals the mind, body and your soul," he advised as he listened to Wendy's chest and stomach with his stethoscope.

"You don't know my daughter very well, then. As soon as we are out of here, she will want to do something. She isn't one to just sit and think about things."

"Well, maybe that would be best in this case, then. We really don't want her to brood about her friend's death. Brooding doesn't accomplish anything. It only makes matters worse." He looked Jim in the eyes. "You need to take care of yourself, too. You need lots of rest after such an ordeal. Your body and mind need as much mending as Wendy's right now. Go home and get some rest when you can. If you feel like taking a nap during the day, do it. It's your body telling you that it still needs rest. We call it 'shut down' time."

"I will take your advice, but, Wendy must come first," he said as he gently carried his sleeping daughter to the bed. "I guess I had better wake her."

"Yes, and then you can go down the hall and check her out of the hospital at the desk. There will be some papers for you to sign and then you can take her home. I will go get the nurse so that she can help your daughter get dressed. I see that you brought her some clean clothes. I'm happy that you had the foresight to do it for her. Otherwise we would be sending her home in a hospital gown. Her clothes have been disposed of," he said as he went out the door.

Jim thought about her clothes and how badly they had been stained with Milly's blood. It made him shiver.

He reached over and kissed Wendy on the forehead and gently shook her. "Hey, Little Girl, it's time to go home. Are you ready to get out of here?"

"Yes, I am. I want to go home," she said, rubbing the sleep from her eyes.

"The nurse will be in to help you get dressed in just a moment. I'm going down the hall to sign some papers and then I will come right back to get you and we can head for home. Okay?"

"Okay," she said, her voice still trembling a little.

"I love you, Kitten. I'll be right back," he said as he went out of the room and down the hallway.

"I love you, too," she whispered, but he didn't hear her.

The nurse had Wendy all washed and dressed when Jim returned for her.

"Ready to go?" Jim asked her.

"Yup!" Wendy said, happily.

Wendy seemed to calm down once they were on the road home. She had relaxed considerably.

"That was awful," Wendy said after a long silence.

"What was awful?" he asked her, not knowing whether she was talking about the car wreck or the stay in the hospital.

"Everything. I don't remember the car crash at all. I must have been sound asleep. I only know that when I woke up, the first time, there was blood all over my shirt that I was wearing and Milly wasn't moving. She was on top of me. I thought she was hurt, but I didn't think that anything was bad wrong," she said, sadly, trying to hold back the tears that were threatening to spill from her eyes. "That is when I went back to sleep and saw Mama," she added, staring at her clenched hands.

Jim knew that she was going to be okay if she was already able to talk about it. She was trying to be strong. She was facing the truth. She had already accepted it in her heart and her mind.

"Let's not think about it any more. Let's think about getting home and how happy Mandy is going to be to see you," he told her with a big smile.

"I can't wait to see her. I missed her this morning. She must have been very busy or something." She smiled and looked at her Father.

"She stayed at our house this morning to clean the kitchen from last night. When we heard that you were hurt, we just left the dinner sitting there all night."

"I hope we aren't going to eat it tonight," she said, wrinkling her nose at the thought.

"No, I'm sure that all the food has been thrown away in the garbage by now," he laughed.

They drove into the driveway and Mandy came running out to the car to greet Wendy.

"How's my girl?" she asked, happily. Wendy was looking much better than she had hoped.

"I think I'm okay," she said, looking at her arms and legs. "Yes, I'm okay," she said happily. She reached up and gave Mandy a big hug. "Mama told me to give you a big hug from her for taking such good care of Daddy and me," she said with a big smile.

"Well, when you write another letter to your Mama, you can tell ther that it is a pleasure," Mandy didn't know how she felt about all this that was going on between Wendy and Abby, but, it seemed to keep Wendy happy and that is all that mattered.

"You are afraid for me, aren't you Mandy?" she asked. Wendy could feel the doubt coming from her. "You don't need to be. We all have a Guardian Angel. Mama is watching over us right now. I can feel her. She is here with us right now."

"I'm sure she is, Sweetheart," Mandy agreed, hugging her and trying not to squeeze her too tight. She was afraid that she might hurt her. "I missed you."

"I missed you, too, but now I'm home," she said looking all around for Ralph.

"Ralph is in the house waiting for you," Mandy said, in anticipation of Wendy's next question.

They all walked in the front door where they were greeted joyfully by Ralph jumping up and down and barking, his tail wagging with pure joy.

Wendy knelt down and petted him and hugged him until he was calmed down.

"Shall we go into the kitchen and have some peanut butter cookies and a nice cold glass of milk?" Mandy asked as she headed for the kitchen.

"That sounds good to me!" Wendy grinned from ear to ear at the thought of Mandy's homemade cookies.

"After we have some cookies and milk, I think I will go home for a while," Mandy told them. "I don't think my husband knows what I look like any more!" she laughed.

They all sat around the table and ate the cookies and milk and then, as Mandy had said she was going to do, she left for home, telling them that she would return that afternoon.

"Daddy, can we go to see if my tree is still standing today?" Wendy asked as she looked out the window.

He looked at her and smiled. She was such a gentle child with a special insight to other people. "If you feel up to it, but I think it is still there. For some reason, that area was not touched by the fire. No one can explain it. It doesn't make sense. I have been a forest ranger for nine years now and I have been to many forest fires….but, this one had to be a freak change in the wind or something." He looked at his beautiful daughter. "Yes, we will go to see your tree if it will make you happy. You had better bring your sweater with you though. It could turn cold by the time that we get back. This time of the year the weather is very unpredictable. And, Mandy would skin me alive if I don't make sure you are warm enough." He chuckled.

Wendy walked over to the table and took her sweater from the back of the chair where she had left it hanging. Then she carefully draped it over her arm to wear later. It was too warm to wear it. It was only twelve forty-five and the day had already promised to be a warm one. Wendy doubted that she would even need her sweater, but, she didn't mind taking it with her.

Wendy remembered watching her Mother knit that sweater. She had thought that her Mother was making it for someone else, but, she had knitted it for Wendy's birthday just before she had died. Wendy had promised herself that she would take good care of it so that she could give it to her own little girl some day when she grew up and got married. If that day ever came. There were still those dreams that she couldn't quite make out. They had a warning in them somewhere. She shook her head to rid herself of all thoughts except being with her Father.

Wendy and her Father banged the screen door shut as they walked out the front door together. They walked down the short stairway to the cement walk. There was no need to ever lock the door; they lived so far away from everyone that Jim never locked it, not even at night.

"Ummmmm! Aren't they beautiful?" she asked her Father as she pointed to the flowers that bordered the walkway. There were many different varieties and colors, but Wendy's favorite was the Pansies because they looked like they had little faces.

They had a large yard, green with the smell of being freshly mowed. It was delicately bordered with a white picket fence that needed a fresh coat of paint. Jim had promised himself that he would paint it some time this summer. He just didn't care about it that much any more since Abby had died. She had been a perfectionist and had wanted everything just so, and Jim loved her for that. He had loved everything about his wife.

The big rose bush over in the corner of the yard needed tying up and a little pruning, but, that, too, could wait along with the weeds that needed pulling in the garden.

"We had better shut the gate so that Ralph doesn't run off," Jim said as they passed through it.

"Can't Ralph come with us, Daddy?" she asked him as she stuck her lower lip out pouting, pleading for poor Ralph.

"Oh, I guess so. You know, don't you, that you are spoiled absolutely rotten and that I love you so much," he told her as he stopped long enough to give her a big hug and open the gate for Ralph.

"I love you, too, this much…." She said as she spread her arms out as far as they would go.

"Ralph! Stop it! Oh, just look what he did! He got my dress all dirty!" she said as she tried to brush the dirt off.

"It's okay, Mandy will wash it all up nice and pretty again. Ralph's just a little over zealous that he is going to go with us," he said while he patted Ralph on the head to calm him down.

"What does zealous mean, Daddy?" she asked him, curiously.

"It means excited…..overly happy, something like that."

"Oh, I see," she said as she stepped way around a beetle so that she wouldn't bother it.

Jim looked at her. She was so compassionate. She couldn't stand to see anything hurt. He was just glad that she hadn't seen Milly after the accident.

The walk through the meadow was an easy one and very pretty. One that they were enjoying very much.

Wendy especially liked seeing the animals. She had seen two rabbits as they had chased each other back and forth across the trail, and, then there was the squirrel that had scolded them as they had come around a corner.

Farther down the path they were surprised when they had startled hundreds of birds of all different sizes and colors and the noise that they made as they all fluttered and flew away was almost musical.

"Ohhhhhh! Father! That scared me! And, did you see Ralph?" she laughed. "He jumped at least three feet in the air! I thought he was going to run home!" she said with huge eyes, laughing out of control until the tears were rolling down her cheeks. She had to stop and hold her tummy because it hurt from laughing so hard.

"I was surprised to see that many birds all in one place! So was Ralph!" he told her as they both laughed until they could laugh no more. It was good for them to laugh.

At the edge of the field they both came to an abrupt stop.

"Look Daddy!" Wendy whispered in excitement as she pointed to a doe and her fawn drinking water at the creek.

"They are beautiful, aren't they?" he told her as they tiptoed as quietly as possible, trying not to startle them.

If it had been just Wendy and her Father, and Ralph had stayed home, things might have been different. Wendy would have been able to walk right up to the doe and her fawn, but, as it was, it was of no use. The deer seemed to know that he was there through some sort of special sense that all animals have.

First, they just stared at Wendy and Jim but, when they saw Ralph; they hopped and bounded out of sight to the safety of the great tall trees of the huge forest as fast as they could.

"Ralph! Come back here!" Jim ordered, "Come back here right now!" he said, pointing to the ground in front of him.

Ralph stopped in mid run as he was chasing the deer and turned to look back at Jim. Then, he took one last look at the forest and slowly walked back to Wendy's side.

"That was a bad dog, Ralph. That's a no-no. You must not do that any more," Wendy told him firmly, but gently, all the while she was petting his soft fur.

Ralph was a good dog, generally speaking. He had his faults just like any other dog, but, he had been an excellent companion for Wendy, especially way out there in the country where they had lived with no other children to play with. She had some friends at school, but she didn't get to see them very often.

Ralph was a cross between a collie and a German Shepard. Perhaps a little more German Shepard than Collie. He had an even temper and he was an excellent watchdog. No one would ever harm Wendy with Ralph around.

"The deer were so graceful, weren't they, Daddy?" she asked as she looked up into his eyes.

"Yes, they were. I think they are one of the most beautiful animals that God has ever created. I love their big brown, innocent eyes. What animal do you like the best?" he asked her.

"That is so hard for me to say. They are all so perfect and special. Each one is different. Let me see," she said as she stuck her finger between her teeth as she thought about it. "I think I like the horse the best," she finally said in a whisper.

"Why are you whispering?"

"Because I don't want to hurt Ralph's feelings," she said, matter-of-factly.

Jim laughed. "You are really quite something, do you know that, Kiddo?" he asked as he squeezed her hand gently. "It is a good thing I built this little bridge last summer or we would not be able to cross today. The water is way up, look," he said as he pointed to the creek. "it is overflowing its banks."

"How come the water is so high, Daddy? We haven't had any rain for a long time," she asked, puzzled at how high the water was.

"It may not have rained around here for several weeks, kitten. But, it has sure been raining up in the mountains. And, when that happens, all the water rushes down here to the valley for us to drink, take baths and to cook." He explained to her.

"Oh, My! Look how black everything is way over there!" she said as tears came to her eyes and she pointed to where some trees had been burnt and were standing like tall, black, hideous statues, a reminder of what can happen when people were careless. "It would be just awful to be a tree and have to just stand there, unable to move or run from the fire. What a horrible way to die," she cried.

Jim had felt the same way many times. He had wished more than once that he could get his hands on the people who were responsible for such utter waste.

"Daddy? Do you know what caused the fire yet?" she asked as she looked up into his eyes once again.

"Yes…Careful now," he cautioned her as they crossed the tiny, narrow bridge. "We are pretty sure it was a cigarette that someone carelessly threw from the window of their car along the highway. Do you see, over there on the other side of the road?" he asked her as he pointed far away." There was no fire on that side, but, there was on this side. We found a cigarette where we think the fire might have started," he said as they stepped down off the bridge and watched Ralph slowly walk across the little bridge. Then they all entered the forest.

Wendy became very quiet. The trees were overpowering to her. She stretched her neck to look up at them.

"Oh, Daddy, aren't the trees just beautiful? I think I love them more than any animal in the world," she whispered in an awed voice. "I wish they could talk. Think of all the stories they could tell about all the things that they have seen over the years. They look so old and wise,'

"Stand tall and straight, Twiggy. The Walk-To's are coming. It is the little one that picked you out for its Christmas tree and its Father. They are both coming and they have a barker with them," Tickler warned her.

"Where? I cannot see them! Where are they?" she asked with much excitement.

"There…right there….see them? They are coming around the corner and down the path toward you, dummy!" Tickler told her.

"Don't call her that!" Tall Tales scolded him soundly.

"I'll call her anything I like!" he shouted.

"The little one is very pretty for a Walk-To, isn't it?" Twiggy asked ignoring them both.

"What? Are you blind or something? It is short and skinny and ugly like all the rest of them," Tickler told her in an angry, disgusted tone.

"No! No! I am not talking about its branches or its roots or even how short it is. I am talking about.....well....there is just something special about it that is different from all the other Walk-To's. I don't exactly know what it is. Can't you feel it, too" she asked, wondering why he was so adamant about how he felt about the Walk-to's.

"You haven't seen enough Walk-to's to make an educated comparison." He told her stiffly "And, no I can't. All I feel is anger and contempt every time I see one of them. They are so careless and they don't think about anyone else but themselves," he told her as he looked down at the Walk-To's as though they were germs under a microscope.

"You're just jealous," she chided him as she had finally had enough of his contempt.

".....are so old and so wise." Wendy finished her sentence just as she came around the corner.

"It certainly isn't talking about you, Tickler!" Tall Tales teased him as they all laughed. Except Tickler, that is.

"Oh, Father! My tree is still here!" Wendy said as she came running up to Twiggy.

If Wendy could have reached around Twiggy she would have given her a big hug, but, as it was, she could only caress her branches.

"Yes, it is just as I thought. The fire didn't touch this section of the forest. I can't for the life of me understand it," he told her, his thoughts wandering.

"I wish I could take her home right now," Wendy told her Father. "Isn't she beautiful?"

"Yes, it seems to be even more beautiful than the last time we were here." He agreed. "But, we must wait until just before Christmas to dig it up," he said as he reached for her hand. "Come on, Sweetheart, we have been dawdling all afternoon and it's getting late. We should be getting back to the house before it gets dark. Besides that, Mandy will have dinner all ready for us. Are you hungry?" he asked.

"Yes," she said, sadly. "I wish that Mama was here to see my pretty tree," she said, frowning. "Why does it hurt so much in here to think about her and Milly?" she asked pointing to her chest,

"It is because we miss them so much. We are used to having them around us to talk to and now that they are gone, it has left an empty feeling in our chest. They are with God now and they are waiting for us. We will see them again someday," he explained to her once again. "Let's go home, remember you have just been hurt in an accident and you should be resting a little."

"When I get home, I will write a letter to Mama and tell her all about the fire and how my Christmas tree didn't burn down," she told him as she began to skip along beside him. Ralph plodded along beside them, panting from the heat.

"The little Walk-to was sad, was it not?" Old Log asked Twiggy.

"Yes, it was. The big Walk-To said that its Mother was with God. Does this mean that the Walk-To's go to the Land of Sweet Waters and Cool Breezes as we do when we end, Old Log?"

"There has been much speculation on that subject, Little Twig. Many very wise trees have thought for ages on just this one thing. We are not really sure, but, it is whispered that all living creatures that The Great God of All Things has created will go to the Land of Sweet Waters and Cool Breezes. There, it is promised that we will all live equally. No one will be better than anyone else. We will not be better than the bushy tails or the nibblers and the Walk-To's will not be better than us."

"Did you hear the Little Walk-To, Predictor? I told you that I felt that something had happened to her and it did." Little Bark told him.

"Yes, so you did." Predictor was very impressed with Little Bark's observation.

"I like the little Walk-To, Old Log, do you like it?" Twiggy asked in a compassionate voice.

"Yes, I do. I didn't think that I would ever be hearing myself say that about a Walk-To. But, yes, I do. It seems different from all the others."

"I think there is something very, very special about it. I can't quite put my limb on it, but I will."

"The only thing SPECIAL about it," Tickler teased Twiggy, "is that it has picked YOU for its Christmas tree. And, that is the only reason that you think it is so special," he declared.

"No…. I don't think so. I have searched my knots and have not come up with an answer, but, mark my words, that Walk-To is special," she told him. "And, you're just jealous because it didn't pick you for its Christmas tree!" she said, haughtily.

"Can……you…….imagine….me…a….Christmas…tree? Ha! Ha! Ho!" He laughed uncontrollably. "That would be a sight to see!" and he laughed all the harder.

"Enough! Both of you! My nerves cannot take much more of this! My roots have become weak from the fire, as it is, without having to put up with any more arguing. I think that I might become so weak that I cannot stand and I shall tumble over to the ground if it continues," Thin-As-Grass cried.

"There, there, Thin-As-Grass, they were only discussing the Little Walk-To and, I agree with Twiggy, there is something special about it," Many Branches told her, thoughtfully.

"I, too, agree with Twiggy and Many Branches," Fuzzy Moss told them. "There is something different about that little Walk-To. It is not its appearance, but, maybe something inside it. It is something to think about."

Little Bark had been watching and listening. He had kept his thoughts to himself. He could remember the last time that the little Walk-To had come. At that time he had also thought that there was something special about it, but, because it had been the only one that he had ever seen, he had said nothing. It had been the first Walk-To that either Fuzzy Moss or Twiggy had ever seen, also, though, and they had said something. But, Little Bark liked to have all the facts first before he drew upon a conclusion and opened his mouth with an opinion.

"Ek-hem!" Tall Tales cleared his throat a bit loudly. "There isn't a Walk-To alive that deserves as much attention as you are all giving that one. Why, I've seen bigger, taller, stronger Walk-To's than either one of those and I still think they are all puny."

"Look! Tall Tales, down by your roots! The Walk-To left foot prints in the moss where they stood!" Fuzzy Moss pointed out in excitement. Then his thoughts wandered as Isaac Newton's must have done on that famous day with the apple. "Where does the moss come from that covers the ground over our roots and up the side of our trunk, Tall Tales?"

"Ahhhh! It is good that you have asked me this question instead of Old Moss or Predictor. They know nothing of this, but I do," he said as he began. "Not so very long ago, in a place the Walk-To's call California, there lived hundreds of tall red trees, as big as any fifty of us and as tall as the stars in the sky. Most of them had stood there since the great planting. Among those great trees was one they called Stirdy Air. He was always happy and full of joy and he swooshed and stirred the air with his branches in happiness. Until one day when a huge hairy Back Scratcher with long claws and sharp fangs came along. He stopped by Stirdy Air and began scratching and rubbing his back on Stirdy Air's rough trunk. He pushed harder and harder until he finally loosened Stirdy Air's deep roots. The harder he pushed, the looser they became. Then, all of a sudden, the Back Scratcher gave one long hard shove and Stirdy Air toppled over. Now, all the members of Stirdy Air's thicket were very angry. They loved Stirdy Air very much and they all felt very lost in their trunks. So they all joined branches so that the great Back Scratcher could not move and they began choking him until he ended. Then, the Big Reds, as they were called, stripped that giant Back Scratcher of all his fur and they laid it down on the ground. So now you know where the moss comes from that covers our roots and trunks to keep us warm during the Big Slumber."

"Oh, I am so sure, Tall Tales!" Predictor said while brushing his trunk with his branches. "You have just lived up to your name," he laughed.

"It is as I have said. I heard all about it from the whispers of other Thickets," he said, defending himself.

"And, I suppose that you believe everything that you hear?" Predictor asked him with one raised eyebrow.

"Of course not, do you?"

"No, and only half of what I see,"

"I liked the story, whether it was true or not," Old Moss told them both.

"Long ago, a Back Scratcher came
To push, to mangle and to lame.
Up came the trees roots as over he went

While all the others squeezed without relent.
And, all his breath he gave away
His fur to warm us from that day," Rhymer told Tall Tales, proudly.

"If you do not cease your incessant rhyming, I will personally put an end to you!" Tall Tales told him in an angry voice.

"I, for one, like his rhymes," Tickler told him.

"Then let him make them up about your jokes and your sarcasm!" he shouted as he folded his branches on his trunk and glared at Rhymer.

Rhymer had found a new friend and champion to defend him.

CHAPTER TWELVE

"Oh, Father! Look! The front door is standing wide open!" Wendy said as she came running up to the gate. "We shut it when we left. I wonder who could have been here."

"It was probably Mandy. I'm sure everything is okay," he told her clasping her hand in his as they both walked through the gate. "Hello?" he called, "Is anybody here? Mandy, are you here?"

There was no answer.

"Come on, Wendy, no one is here. If there was a stranger in the house, Ralph would have torn his leg off by now," he said as they both came up the walkway to the steps and in the front door.

"SURPRISE!" Everyone shouted all at once as they popped up from behind the furniture.

"What is this?" Jim asked, as he looked around at all his friends in astonishment.

"Happy Birthday!" they all said in unison.

"My birthday?" Jim thought, rubbing his forehead. He really hadn't thought about anything except the accident and Milly's death. "It is my birthday today, isn't it?" he said in surprise as he looked around. He saw a big beautiful birthday cake and all the presents and decorations. "I hadn't even thought about it. My mind has been too occupied by other things."

"Yes, we know. That is why we decided to do this with Wendy. She planned it a long time ago before her accident," Mandy said, proudly. "We thought that since she was doing so well that it would be okay to go ahead with her plans."

"Gosh! I forgot all about it!" Wendy said, truthfully. Then she turned to her Father. "Happy Birthday, Daddy!" she said as she ran and got him his present and handed it to him.

"Why, you little Sweetheart!" he told her as he gave her a big hug. "So, this was all your idea, huh?"

"Well, it was my idea, but Mandy helped me a lot. She called everyone and set the whole thing up," she said, matter-of-factly. "Open your present, Daddy," she said with anticipation.

"Oh, okay," he told her as he tore the wrapping paper off the small present. "Well, will you look at that!" he said as he held up a hand knit muffler. "It's beautiful! Did you knit this all by yourself?"

"No, Mandy showed me how and she helped me fix all my mistakes. Do you really like it, Daddy?"

"Yes, Sweet Pea, I love it. And, I love it all the more because you made it for me with those little hands of yours. It sure will come in handy this winter when I am out in the cold and the snow," he smiled, "Thank you!" He gave her a big hug.

Wendy loved her Father's hugs. It was his way of showing her how special he thought she was and how much he loved her.

It was her way of feeling secure and showing her Father how much she loved him, also.

The party lasted for hours as they all ate cake and ice cream and watched Jim open the rest of his presents. It was a gay time, a time of renewing old friendships and remembering the ones that were no longer with them. They had all agreed that they would definitely miss Milly. Her presence was missed by everyone at the party, but it had felt good to be able to talk openly about it. It had felt good to be with old friends again.

Months passed by and Christmas was almost upon them.

"Burrrrrrr! It is getting cold, Many Branches. Either that or I am getting so old that my sap is freezing in my trunk," Old Log said as he shook from the cold.

"Oh, come on now! You aren't that old, my husband. I think that the Big Slumber will be upon us very soon. It doesn't seem possible though. It seems as though we were only yesterday talking of how dry it was. Now, look, it is raining all the time," she told him as she looked up at the sky.

"Mother, what is happening to our leaves? Look, they are turning gold and red and yellow and orange! They are so beautiful! What does this mean?" Little Bark asked as he held up his branches to show her. "It is happening to you and to Father, also!" he said in surprise.

"It is pretty, isn't it?" she said looking at her own leaves." It means that the Big Slumber is almost upon us." She told him as she looked up at the sky again. If her knowledge of the weather was as precise this year as it had been for many, many cycles, it was going to snow. The clouds were rapidly covering the sky.

"What is the Big Slumber?" Little Bark asked. "I have heard almost all of you use this term, but I have not yet had it explained to me."

"It is a time when the weather gets cold and our sap slows way down and we rest. Our leaves turn all different colors and they fall to the ground where they help the moss keep our roots warm. It is a good time. We dream many dreams of all sorts of wonderful things. You will like it, I'm sure."

"Must we sleep if we don't want to?" Little Bark asked her.

"It is true that we do not sleep all the time, no, but I am sure that you will find that you will want to sleep much more than usual, my son. It is only natural."

"Not me! I am strong and I do not need as much sleep as you or Father do," he said, proudly.

"We shall see," she told him as she thought about the day that someone had first told her of the Big Slumber. She had reacted in much the same way that Little Bark had just done.

"Old Moss, why isn't Twiggy turning different colors like most of the rest of us are?" he asked him, curiously.

"Do you not see a definite difference between yourself and Twiggy, Little Bark?" Old Moss asked him.

"There, my day is complete, Old Moss. You have just answered my question with a question of your own again. If you should ever answer my question without first asking one of your own, I think I should topple over and end at that very moment from shock," he told his beloved tutor. "And, yes, there is a difference in our leaves. She has pointed little needles and I don't."

"She is called an evergreen. She and some of the rest of us never do turn the beautiful colors that you do. It is only for trees with leaves."

"Well, don't her roots get cold in the time of the Big Slumber? We've got our leaves to keep our roots warm. She has only the moss and a few puny needles that are not even worth mentioning."

"No, not so much as would your roots if they were not covered with your leaves. You are used to having two blankets to warm you, we need only one," Old Moss explained carefully.

There was a long pause as Little Bark thought about all of his new information.

"Does this make a difference? I mean Twiggy and I … well…..we are betreethed. Does it make any difference that we are not of the same kind?" he asked, shyly.

"It makes no difference at all. If you two love each other, that is all that matters. Life used be otherwise before we were all planted long ago. There were different tree nations and they were forbidden to love any but their own kind. Now it is different," he carefully instructed his young student. "I think that it is wonderful." He said, but he didn't add that all along he knew that they had felt something special for one another.

"Tell me, Old One, how do the Walk-To's stay warm during the Big Slumber, their bark seems very soft and not of very good texture."

"It is said in Whispers that they live in cabins and houses built out of trees. In those houses, they build a place out of stones to build a fire to keep them warm."

"They build houses out of us?" he asked in disbelief.

"Yes," Old Moss told him, sadly.

"What is a house?"

"It is a….well, it's a ……Hmmmmmm……in so many words, it's a……well, it is square, but not all the time. It has holes to see out through and to let the sunshine in. It has a door that opens and closes for them to walk in and out of," he told him, shrugging his branches. "And, that is the best way that I can explain it to you. When you reach my height, you will be able to see the Walk-To's farm house…. you know, the one that was here to look at Twiggy."

"Do the Walk-To's sleep all during the Big Slumber, too, like us, Old Moss?' Fuzzy Moss asked.

"No, they have to wake up every day and eat and keep the fire going to keep warm."

"I'm glad we don't have to depend on a fire to keep us warm. That fire that we had was too warm for me!" Fuzzy Moss told him.

"What was that?" Twiggy asked when she heard a loud buzzing noise that sounded like a whole swarm of angry bees.

"That, my dear Twiggy, is a little stinky-go. They are very noisy and they stink very badly. They usually only have one Walk-To on them, unlike the big stinky-go's that sometimes have as many as eight Walk-To's riding around inside it," Little Bark told her. "I wonder why the Walk-To's want to ride when they can walk?" he wondered.

"How did you know what that noise was?" she asked him with a frown. "I am older than you and I do not ever recall anyone telling us about it?"

"Old Sap told me about it long ago," he told her, proudly.

Then his memory went back to a day long before when he had heard a noise like small thunder and he had asked Old Moss what it was and Old Moss had told him he was too young to worry about such things just yet. He wondered if he was old enough now.

"Old Moss, can you tell me now what the noise like small thunder was that I heard on the day of the fire?"

Again a sharp pain struck Old Moss' memory as he thought about his Father and his terrible ending.

"What makes you ask about that now?" Old Moss asked.

"You did it again. You answered my question with a question.
"Sorry."

"I want to know because I want to know," he said, exasperated.

"Not yet, Little Bark, but soon."

"But, Old Moss, how can it be worse for me to know about this noise than the fire we have all just lived through?" he asked, frustrated at being treated like a seedling.

"It is not worse in a way, but it is in another. I think it is best that you wait for a while. But soon, Little Bark, soon, then I will tell you all about it. It is sad and we have had enough of sad things for a long time."

"How about it, Fuzzy Moss, Twiggy, Little Bark? Would you like to hear a story?" Tall Tales asked. He turned to Old Log. "Would you like to hear a story, Old Log?"

"Is it a new one, or just rearranged?" Many Branches asked him.

"It is a new one. I've never told it to anyone before," he told her as he proudly began. "There once was a tree long ago that stood in a mighty forest. His name was Old Rubber Trunk because he was afraid of everything. He was not strong and had no bark. All the other trees made fun of him because he was afraid of the animals and the Song-With-Wings and even the flying flowers. He was afraid of any creature that flew or crawled or walked near him. Until, one day, when a big huge Walk-To came to their Thicket and put up a funny looking thing like a giant green bee hive. Then he brought many things from his stinky-go and he put them on the ground. Then he went around and gathered old dead twigs and leaves and piled them up in a great big pile. Then he took a little stick of fire and lit it. The pile of dead twigs and leaves began to burn, higher and higher the flames rose as hotter and hotter it got. All the other trees were very afraid and didn't know what to do, but, Old Rubber Trunk did. He told everyone to take a deep breath and blow the fire out. They all did as they were told and the fire went out. Well, needless to say, this frightened the Walk-To. He looked all around him, his eyes huge with fear. Quickly he packed up all his things and ran to his Stinky-go and hurried away. Old Rubber Trunk was never called a coward again, although he always remained afraid of the creepy, crawly things," he finished with a smile of satisfaction on his face.

"It was good, I liked it," Old Log told him.

"Yes, I liked it, too," Many Branches told him.

"It was okay, I guess, but I liked the one about Sad Sap better," Twiggy told him.

Fuzzy Moss and Little Bark just shrugged and said nothing.

"There once was a tree named Old Rubber Trunk
Afraid of the crawling and flying and gunk.
Along came a Walk-To who built a large fire
The flames started growing higher and higher.
The trees shook with fear their branches hung low
Until Old Rubber Trunk said "Let's everyone blow!"
The fire went out to everyone's relief

Old Rubber Trunk's bravery had been very brief.

The Walk-To was frightened and he ran away

Old Rubber Trunk a hero to this very day," Rhymer proudly recited.

"You left out the part about the others teasing him," Tickler told him.

"Oh, okay. There once was a tree…"

"Oh, shut up!" Tall Tales told him.

"Pick on someone your own size, you overgrown weed," Tickler told him.

"Who's an overgrown weed, you old withered piece of grass," Tall Tales retorted in anger.

"I'm warning you, don't bother the little bush again," Tickler hissed.

"He's not worth the effort," Tall Tales sneered.

The moon rose higher and higher and the wind grew very loud. It was chilled with the icy fingers of winter. It twisted and stretched the white fog into ever changing shapes that looked like see-throughs running in a panic from an unknown terror or an angry dragon that was unwillingly awakened from his slumber.

Thus the weeks passed as the chilly wind sang through their branches.

One morning in December the wind had died down to give the trees a few more hours of warmth as the sun gently caressed their colorful leaves then slipped away to the ground below to warm their roots as though they had cozy, furry slippers on them……all except Thin-As-Grass and Twiggy who were in the shade.

Across the meadow Jim stretched and yawned as he awakened to Mandy's cheerful singing in the kitchen. He could smell the wonderful aroma of bacon frying and fresh coffee brewing. The sun was warm as it filtered in on him when he sat up in bed. "It's going to be wonderful day," Jim said as he looked outside. "My! My! Old Man Frost was here last night. It looks a lot like it snowed, doesn't it, Ralph," he smiled as he petted the dogs head. "The sun should melt it soon, though. Come on, let's go get some breakfast."

Jim threw on his bathrobe and slippers and stumbled down to the kitchen. There he washed his hands, sat in his chair at the table and sipped on his coffee.

Ralph brought him his newspaper.

"Breakfast will be ready in about five minutes, Jim. I've got to put the toast down and make some hot chocolate and we can all eat," Mandy told him as she dried her hands on a towel that was hanging on the oven door handle.

"Oh, good morning, Mandy. Where were you when I came into the kitchen?" he asked, puzzled.

"I was in the pantry," she told him.

"Isn't it a beautiful morning?" he asked her.

"Yes, it sure is, but you had better enjoy it while you still can because I don't think there are going to be too many more like it," she said as she refilled his cup. "When my arthritis starts acting up like it has been this past week, it usually means that the bad weather isn't too far away."

"Yes, I know what you mean. My hip that I broke a couple of years ago has been giving me some trouble and it only gives me trouble when it starts getting cold," he agreed with her. "Where is Wendy? Hasn't she come down yet?" Jim said as he scooted his chair back and walked to the bottom of the stairway.

"Wendy?" he called to her.

There was no reply.

"Wendy, would you like some breakfast? It's all ready and waiting on the table," he called to her again.

"Is she coming down?" Mandy asked as she walked from the kitchen to the stairway beside Jim.

"I don't know. I don't hear her. It isn't like her not to answer me. I wonder what's the matter with her. She never sleeps this long," Jim told her in a concerned way. "I'm going up and see what's wrong I'll be right back," he said as he climbed the stairs.

Jim looked around the room. Wendy was still in bed.

"Wendy, are you alright? What's the matter?" he asked as he felt her forehead, it was a little warm, but not bad.

"I just don't feel very good this morning. My stomach hurts and I have a headache," she told him, holding on to her stomach with both hands. She frowned. "And, today was supposed to be a special day for us. We were supposed to go to the forest and dig up my Christmas tree for our Christmas. It's only five days away, you know. It will soon be here and we won't have a tree up for Santa Claus. Then where will he put the presents?"

"Oh, we'll have a Christmas tree, don't you worry your pretty little head about that, Sweet Pea. I'll go get you your tree but I think it would be best if you stayed here. You can't go out in the cold weather when you aren't feeling well. It would probably only make you worse than you are now," he said as he brushed the hair out of her face with his fingers. "Mandy will stay here with you, okay? I won't be long." He told her as he kissed her cheek and started to leave the room.

"Daddy?" she called.

"Yes, what is it Pumpkin?" he asked as he peeked around the door to her bedroom.

"Is Mandy here yet?" she asked, hopefully. She really missed her mother and Mandy sort of filled the void she felt in her heart.

"Yes, I am here, Wendy," Mandy said as she entered the room. "What seems to be the problem here? Aren't you feeling well?" she asked as she felt Wendy's forehead. "She is a little warm. I'll bring some children's aspirin and some juice up here for her. I'll be right back," she told Jim.

"Well, I think that you are in good hands. I'm going to go now. Take care of her Mandy, we don't want anything to happen to her!" he said as he followed Mandy out of the room.

Mandy went downstairs and Jim went to his room to shave and get dressed for the day. Then he grabbed his jacket off the hook in little nook in the hallway and went out the door without any breakfast.

It was quite cold outside, even though the sun felt pleasantly warm on Jim's face. He could see his breath as he walked. There was still a hint of frost in the air as he grabbed his shovel and began to walk across the field to the forest where Wendy's tree was standing.

The little bridge that he had built had been wet, but not icy. But, the sun had not reached the ground around Twiggy yet, to soften the dirt so that he could dig her up.

Try as he might, he couldn't budge the frozen ground. "This will never work. I should have brought my ax with me," he said as he leaned on his shovel and looked at Twiggy. "I'll just have to go and get it," he sighed.

Jim started back down the path toward home again.

"What is an ax, Father?" Little Bark asked as he watched the big Walk-To disappear down the path.

"Where did you hear that word?" Old Log asked frowning and rubbing the sleep from his eyes.

"Were you asleep when the Walk-to was just here?" Little Bark asked.

"Yes, I must have been," he answered him with a frown. "Was it the same Walk-To that wants Twiggy for a Christmas tree?" Old Log asked in a worried tone.

"It was the little Walk-To's Father," Little Bark replied.

"Was the young Walk-To with him?"

"No, he was alone. What is an ax, Father?" he asked once again.

Old Log looked at Twiggy with tears in his old, tired eyes. He felt lost in his trunk. How could he tell her that she was going to end? How could he tell her that the Walk-To had decided to cut her down instead of digging her up?

There she was, standing so tall and so straight and so very proud and pretty. To forewarn her would only mean to make her worry and unhappy. "I cannot tell you now, for reasons of my own, but, soon, though I think you will find out for yourself. Brace yourself, Young One. I know that you and Twiggy have spoken of love and I think it is important that she know, right now, this instant, how much you love her," he said as he looked at him out of the corner of his eye. "I was not always sleeping while you talked, you know."

"Why is it so important that I tell her right now?"

"Just do it and don't ask any more questions."

Little Bark blushed as he called to Twiggy. "Twiggy?" he called to her.

"Yes, Barky, what is it?"

"You are very beautiful and I will miss you very much while you are gone to be the Walk-To's Christmas tree. I guess......what I am trying to say is...I love you so very much.

Tears poured down Old Log's tired face as he witnessed their tender moment of love.

"I love you, too, Barky. Very much," she told him in a small, shy voice. "Why is Old Log crying?" she asked when she saw the tears on his face.

"I love a good love story, I guess and I'm going to miss you very much while you are gone, too," he told her. It wasn't the whole truth, but what he said about missing her when she was gone was the truth.

"Can you tell me Old Log, what these little flakes of frozen white fluff are that are beginning to fall all around us?" he asked as he put all thoughts of his other questions away for now.

The clouds had slowly inched their way across the sky and were now shedding their frozen tears. The sun was gone now, but the clouds were a bright white so that the forest did not overly darken.

"Do you mean to tell me, Little Bark, that you do not know that on this day, the angels of the Great God of All Things are shedding their feathers from their wings?" he asked him.

"No, no one has ever told me anything about it. This is the first that I have ever seen. They must do it like we do our leaves. Does it happen very often?"

"No," he sighed still looking at Twiggy. "Most of the time it happens just before or during the Big Slumber," he told Little Bark. "It is going to be a long, cold winter. I'm afraid that I can feel it in my limbs and my roots. They ache when our winters are hard, but then, again, maybe I'm just getting old."

By this time, everyone in the Thicket was awake to see Twiggy go.

"Something is coming!" Thin-As-Grass cried.

"It must be the big Walk-To. He must be coming back to get me already. Isn't it wonderful and exciting?' Twiggy asked Little Bark as she shook with anticipation.

Little Bark just looked at her with a hopeful, but worried look. He knew deep down inside that something was dreadfully wrong with this whole situation, but he still couldn't put his limb on it. He could only wait and hope that everything would turn out all right.

"It IS the big Walk-To! He's coming Twiggy! Aren't you excited?" Weeper asked.

"Oh, Twiggy, you are so lucky to have been chosen for this honor! Now, stand very tall and proud for us! That's it! You look so pretty," Many Branches told her with pride as the Walk-To came around the corner and up the path. "OH! GOD! NO!" Many Branches screamed as she saw the ax in his hands. "Oh, God, please don't let him do this, Please No!.........He can't do this! Old Log! Do something!" she pleaded as the tears streamed down her face. "Can't you do something?" she cried as she reached out her limbs to her husband.

Old Log merely closed his eyes as tears squeezed their way down his sad, tired, old face. His trunk was being ripped apart with the pain he felt for Little Bark and Twiggy. There was nothing he could do.

"What is wrong with all of you?" Twiggy asked as she looked around at each of them. "This is supposed to be a day of happiness and delight and …..What is happening?" she screamed as the Walk-To began to chop away at her trunk. 'Ouch!...........Oh, God it hurts! It hurts me! Stop! Please make him stop! Little Bark help me! It hurts me so badly! Why is he doing this to me?" she screamed as she looked at everyone. "Help…..me…..please….help…me…it… hurts….so…..much. Is he… angry…with….me….for…something? Won't you help, please?" she called to Little Bark.

"I can't do anything!" he cried, tears of hate and frustration and anger streamed down his face. "Old Log, help her!" he cried as he reached up and touched her branches to calm her and ease her pain, "I love you, Little Twig," he told her as tears continued to pour down his face. "I love you so very much."

"None of us can do anything," Old Log, said sadly. "If I could take your place and bare your pain for you, Little Twig, I would without hesitation, but, I can't. No one can. You must remember, Twiggy, be strong and proud, no matter what happens. And, remember, also, that we all love you very much and we will miss you while you are gone," Old Log told her as he watched her fall to the ground.

"I am so sorry," Tickler told her with tears streaming down his face. "Forgive me for everything I have said in the past."

"I think I'm going to be okay….it doesn't hurt so much any more…I…I…….feel kind of numb," she told them. "Maybe it isn't going to be so bad after all," she said as the Walk-To began to drag her down the path. "Maybe I will grow some new roots and he will bring me back and plant me here among all my friends again. Take care! Goodbye for now! I will see you all in a little while. Watch for me, Barky, I'll be back soon. I love you, Barky, remember that always, okay?" she called as she disappeared out of sight.

All were very quiet and lost in their trunks, as they looked where Twiggy had once stood so delicate and pretty.

"I hate all Walk-To's! I hate them! I hate them! I HATE THEM! I wish I could end that Walk-To," Little Bark screamed in anger. "I wonder how he would feel if I took an ax and chopped the little Walk-To down. I wonder if he would hurt inside like I do." Little Bark sobbed.

"Revenge is not yours, I'm afraid, Little Bark," Predictor told him gently.

"Someday, maybe, if I live long enough, I will see them all punished," he said as he began to calm down a little. "Is she going to come back, Old Moss?" Little Bark asked as he looked up at his teacher.

"I don't know," he lied. "I have never heard anything about one of us being cut down for a Christmas tree before, I have only heard of the ones who were dug up and then brought back and replanted," he told him, untruthfully. He knew deep down in his trunk that they would never set eyes on their little Twiggy again in this life.

If circumstances had been different, Little Bark might have noticed that Old Moss had not answered his question with a question, but, as it was, he felt lost in his trunk and could think of nothing else but his precious little Twiggy. His beautiful, shy, sweet, little Twiggy. Why did it hurt so much to think about her he wondered? She would be coming back, wouldn't she? Already Little Bark was counting the minutes until he would see her again.

Much heartache might have been spared for Little Bark had Old Moss merely told him the truth, but Old Moss thought that he had done the correct thing in not telling Little Bark.

Two full weeks went by. A cold, chilly breeze blew the fluffy flakes of Angels Wings here and there as the ground was covered with about an incklet of snow, (an incklet being about one foot}.

It was much deeper in the drifts that gathered around the trunks of the trees. All of Old Moss' Thicket were deep in their slumber. All except Little Bark who was waiting for his beloved Twiggy to return.

"Hello! I'm back! I brought you your little Christmas tree!" Jim called as he banged the door shut behind him. "Wendy?" he called again, "Wendy, come see your tree!" he said excitedly as he heard a big thump and then the sound of hurried footsteps. Wendy and Mandy both came thumping and thudding down the stairs.

"Well, isn't she pretty?" Jim asked Wendy.

Wendy's eyes were huge like saucers as her hands flew up to her face in shock. "Oh, Father! How could you?" Wendy screamed when she saw that her Father had chopped her little tree down instead of digging her up so that they could replant her after Christmas.

"The ground was too hard," he tried to explain. "It was frozen. I couldn't even budge the earth around its roots with the shovel. It was like trying to dig through cement." He paused, saddened by Wendy's reaction. "There was just no other way," he told her sadly. He felt hurt that he hadn't pleased Wendy. He felt hurt because she was hurting.

"Oh Daddy, then you should have left it there!" she sobbed as she ran back up the stairway to her room and shut the door.

"I have never seen her act that way toward me before," Jim said in astonishment as he looked at Mandy.

"I will go talk to her. She is very upset," Mandy told him as she started up the stairway to Wendy's room.

"Wendy?" she called as she knocked on her bedroom door. "May I come in?"

"Yes," Wendy called out, her voice was trembling.

Mandy opened the door and stood there for a moment looking at Wendy with compassion and understanding.

"You know that you mustn't ever talk to your Father like that again," she cautioned her as she sat on the edge of Wendy's bed. "He loves you so very much. Don't you think that you are being just a little unfair? After all, he got you your tree. He told me that you had picked it out and that you had your heart set on that particular one. He said that you both went and looked at it several times. Isn't it the one you wanted?" she asked as she stroked Wendy's hair.

"Oh, Mandy, you don't understand. It is the tree that I wanted, yes, but......Oh, Mandy!" she sobbed into her pillow. "Why did he have to cut it down? It was so very beautiful!" she cried.

"It still is very beautiful. It will be even more beautiful when we have finished decorating it all up, don't you think so, Sweetheart?" she tried to encourage her.

"Yes, but it will die now and all because of me. If I hadn't been sick this morning, if I hadn't wanted the little tree so badly, Daddy would never have cut it down. Now it is all my fault that it is going to die," she cried uncontrollably as Mandy held her in her arms.

Mandy did understand a little. After all, Mandy loved trees, too. It had always made her feel sad when she would see all the pickups going down the road towards the city dump with the dying trees. Trees that had given so much happiness to everyone were merely tossed away like so much garbage to be forgotten. "Such a waste," she would always say.

"Dry your tears now and come down stairs with me and we will help your Father decorate the tree. We don't want your little tree to go to waste, now, do we?" she asked as she held Wendy's chin up and looked into her eyes. "You would not have wanted it cut down for no reason, now, would you?"

"No, I guess not," Wendy told her as she got up off her bed and wiped her eyes and her cheeks. Then she straightened her clothes. "It just seems like such a terrible waste though, Mandy. It makes me feel so sad that it will die just because of me, just because I wanted a pretty tree to look at for Christmas. Now it will have to die just because of me. Daddy always digs our Christmas trees up and then he plants them back where he got them." She looked into Mandy's eyes. "It is all my fault, isn't it, Mandy?"

"No, it is no ones fault, Sweetheart. Why, every year millions of trees are specially grown for Christmas. Some of them are cut down and others are dug up and replanted after Christmas," she explained. "I will admit it does seem to be a tragic waste. I have asked myself the same question that is going through your head right now many, many times and there is no right answer. People just don't think before they do things," she said, looking down to the floor in thought. "But, what is done is done. We can't change it now, can we?"

"No, I guess not, but someday, someone will be very sorry they cut them all down like that every year. They are eventually going to run out of trees. Someday when I grow up, I am going to do something about all the bad things that people do to the trees," Wendy told her, matter-of-factly.

They walked hand in hand silently down the stairs. Wendy saw her little tree in the living room already standing tall and proud in the tree stand.

"It is so pretty," Wendy told her Father as she ran across the room and caressed Twiggy's branches.

"It will be even prettier when we have decorated it all up," he said with a sigh of relief. Wendy no longer seemed to be upset.

"Did you put some water in the stand for it to drink, Father?" she asked, worried.

"Yes, I sure did," he told her as he looked with understanding at his daughter.

It took them two hours to decorate Twiggy. They all agreed that she was the prettiest Christmas tree that any of them had ever seen.

Twiggy was in awe of the place where the Walk-To's lived. At first she had been afraid of the fire in the wall of the building until she had discovered that it couldn't get out and that it couldn't harm her. It actually made her feel warm and cozy like the sun on a cool spring afternoon.

She had watched with pride as the Walk-To's had put pretty lights on her branches like fire dancing on their very tips. There were all different colors of lights! Some had been as blue as the sky, some as red as the coals of a fire. Others were as green as the grass and as yellow as the sun. She watched them string colored popcorn and then gently lay it on her from branch to branch. Then they put beautiful colored balls all over her limbs and they twinkled and sparkled with the reflection of the many lights. Finally, they draped her branches with a shiny silver string that looked like the ice cycles that came during the Big Slumber. Then, the big Walk-To put a shiny gold cross that lit up and blinked on and off like a tireless beacon on the very top of her.

All the Walk-To's gathered around her when they had finished.

"Oh, Father, she is beautiful, isn't she?" Wendy's face beamed with pride.

"Yes, I think it is the prettiest tree we have ever had, and you picked it out!" he said as he pinched her nose between his fingers as though he was trying to steal it off her face.

"It is definitely the most beautiful tree that I have ever seen, and I've seen a lot more of them than both of you put together!" Mandy told them with sparkling eyes. She was happy that everything was turning out okay.

"I am beautiful, aren't I?" Twiggy had wanted to say to them but, alas, she could tell no one. "Oh, I wish that Little Bark and Old Moss and all the others could see how very beautiful I am!" Twiggy said as she looked at her branches with pride. "I don't know what they were all so worried about."

Christmas Eve came and with it came the excitement and the anticipation of the next morning.

"I'm going to bed now, Daddy," Wendy told him as she pretended to yawn.

"But, it's only seven-thirty! You won't go to sleep, you know that don't you?" he warned her.

"Well, maybe I can. Anyway, I'm going to try. That way tomorrow will get here sooner!" she smiled, anxiously.

"Okay, go ahead, but I think you will be making a big mistake. You do this every year and every year you are still awake when I go to bed at ten," he smiled. "Come here and give me a kiss good night," he told her as he held out his arms.

She reached around his neck with her small arms and hugged him with all her strength. "I love you so much," she told him, sitting down on his lap.

"This much?" he asked her as he stretched his arms out as far as they would go.

"This much!" she said as she also stretched out her arms as wide as they would go.

"I love you, too, Sweetheart," he told her.

"I'm sorry that I said what I did today, Daddy," Wendy apologized.

"It's okay. Don't even think about it anymore. I don't like cutting down trees any more than you do. I only wanted to make you happy," he told her.

"You have made me very happy," she told him as she glanced at Twiggy and smiled. "I wish that Mama could be here with us," she told him, sadly.

"Me, too. I miss her very much."

"Good night, Daddy," Wendy told him as she climbed down off his lap and started up the stairs.

"Good night, Pumpkin," he called to her.

"Good night, Mandy," Wendy called to her.

"Goodnight, love, see you in the morning'" Mandy said contentedly.

That night a Walk-To came in the middle of the night and it was very dark. Twiggy couldn't see who it was. It put pretty boxes with colorful ribbons and bows under her branches next to her trunk.

The next morning, the Walk-To's rushed to her side and began opening the boxes. There was such merriment and joy as Twiggy stood tall and watched, not quite understanding what was going on, but, she was enjoying their happiness knowing that she was a part of it.

"Oh Daddy! Look!" Wendy gasped in excitement. "Look at my new bicycle! Isn't it beautiful? And, look! It's green just like I wanted!"

"Yes, it's very pretty, Pumpkin. Do you think that you can ride it?" he asked her.

"Oh, yes, but not in the snow!"

"What else did you get for Christmas?" Mandy asked as she came in from the kitchen.

"I got a doll with blue hair and she talks and crawls. And, I got a baby stroller and doll clothes and a mirror and brush set for my hair and combs, pretty combs for my hair! I got a watch! Isn't it pretty?" she told her excitedly.

"Wow! You must have been a very good girl this last year!" Mandy told her as she winked at Jim. "Well, what did Santa bring you, Jim?"

"A nice pair of warm slippers, some socks, a fishing pole, waders, a new ax and a book on guns that I have always wanted. Oh, and I can't forget my new hat!" he told her. "What did Santa bring you?'

"Oh my! I got so much! Let's see......I got a new set of beautiful china with little pink flowers all over them and some new pots and pans. I got a bathrobe and some slippers and a pretty broach with all the colors of the rainbow in it....Let me see....Oh, and I got a new coat, a new purse and an umbrella and boots!"

"Wow! You must have been a good girl, too!" Wendy told her as they all laughed.

"Here is a present from us to you," Jim said as he handed her a pretty green package with a big red bow on it.

"For me? You shouldn't have done that, but I'm glad you did!" she said with an excited chuckle.

"Open it, Mandy!" Wendy told her, excitedly.

Oh, alright," she said as she sat down on the sofa and began to unwrap her present. "Oh, how beautiful," Mandy told them with tears welling up in her eyes as she held up a bell made of the finest crystal with birds and trees and deer engraved on it. And, as she turned it around and around, the crystal changed color, soft pastel colors like a rainbow. "Thank you so much!"

"There is a card for you, too," Wendy told her.

"Oh, I didn't see it," she said as she opened it. "What is this?" she asked as she held up an envelope that looked like a plane ticket.

"It's a plane ticket so that you can go to Florida to see your Mom," Wendy told her.

"I don't know what to say!" she gasped as she cried tears of happiness.

"You deserve much more for all the kindness you have shown to me and Wendy," Jim told her, sincerely.

"Yes, we love you, Mandy." Wendy told her as she put her arms around her.

"How about some breakfast? Are you guy's hungry yet?" Mandy asked them as she put her bell back in the box and put her card and plane ticket in her purse.

"I'm starving!" Jim told her, enthusiastically.

"Me, too!" Wendy said as she rubbed her tummy.

"Then let's eat! I have it all ready to put on the table," Mandy said on her way to the kitchen. "Bill went over to see Josh and his family after I fixed him his breakfast, so he won't be eating breakfast with us this morning. But, he did tell me to tell you to have a very Merry Christmas and that he would be over later today," she told them.

Later that day, more Walk-To's came over with more boxes all decorated with pretty bows and ribbons. They all sat around a big table and talked. And, on that table there was the biggest Song-With-Wings that Twiggy had ever seen. Only now it had no head, no feet and no feathers. It was all brown as though it had been in the sun too long.

There were many other things on the table that she didn't recognize and the Walk-To's ate them as though they hadn't had anything to eat in a cycle. "I sure have a lot to tell Barky when I get back," she told herself.

There was a knock on the door. It was Bill.

"Hi! How's everything going?" he called as he entered the house.

"Well, hello! We thought that you weren't going to make it over today," Jim told him as he shook his hand.

"I had to finish something in my workshop. It's out in the car. It's for Wendy for Christmas," he told them.

"Do you need some help bringing it in?" Jim asked.

"I might, although I got it in the car by myself.'

"I have been waiting to see this for the whole summer," Mandy told them.

Jim and Bill went out to the car and brought a large package into the house.

Wendy's eyes were huge as she looked at the package. "This is for me?" she asked.

"It sure is!" Bill told her.

"Can I open it?"

"That's what I brought it over here to you for!" Bill laughed as Wendy tore the paper off the huge box.

"Daddy, can you help me open the box, I can't get it open," she said, anxiously.

Bill reached down and cut the box open with his knife.

"A doll house!" Wendy cried out, "Look, Daddy, it's a doll house with little furniture and tiny people in it!" she said excitedly.

"So this is what you have been spending all your time on in the workshop," Mandy said, smiling at her husband.

"You made this?" Wendy asked in surprise.

"I sure did!" he said, proud that she had liked it so much.

"It's beautiful! I love it! Thank you ever so much!" she told him as she stood and gave him a big hug.

"It's really nice of you to do something like that for her," Jim told him earnestly.

"My pleasure," Bill grinned from ear to ear. All the work had been worth it to see the look on Wendy's face.

That night Wendy came over to Twiggy and looked at her with sadness in her eyes. "Oh, little tree you are drying out already," she said sadly as she checked the little bowl in the stand to see if it had any water in it. There wasn't any, so Wendy hurried to the sink in the kitchen and drew some water and poured it in the stand for Twiggy.

"Soon we'll have to take the tree down," Jim told her. "It is getting dry and it might burn down our house. We wouldn't want that to happen, now would we?" Jim asked her.

"No, I guess not, but, I feel so sad, Daddy. I still wish that you could have dug her up instead of chopping her down," she told him as she touched Twiggy's dry needles. "I want to name her," she said trying to think of a name. "I think I will name her Twiggy. It sounds like a good name for her."

Twiggy was fascinated. How did the little Walk-To know what her name was? She just had to tell all the others about this!

A week passed by and Twiggy began to get weaker and weaker with each passing hour.

Then, one night after Wendy had gone to bed, Jim looked at Twiggy. "Tomorrow we shall take you down," he said as he looked at her brown needles.

"I wish I could talk to him," Twiggy said to herself. "I feel so very weak and I am very sick. If he doesn't take me back to the Thicket soon, I think I shall end. I want to see all my friends again. I wonder how Barky is. I wonder if he misses me as much as I miss him."

Jim was about to turn around and go to the kitchen for another bite of turkey until he looked at Twiggy once more. "I don't think that I will wait until morning. It will be hard enough on Wendy to see it gone, she needn't watch us undecorated it," he told Mandy as they both began the task of taking everything off of Twiggy's branches. They carefully put everything away for next Christmas.

"Oh wonderful! They are going to take me back to my friends! I can't wait to see Barky and tell him all about my adventure! They will be so proud of me! Old Moss was right though, I don't get to keep all the pretty things but at least I get to go back and see all my loved ones!" she giggled with pride.

"Wendy is such a sensitive child, isn't she?" Mandy asked him, compassionately.

"Yes, she always has been. Even before her Mother died, she was somehow different from all the other children her age that we knew. She loves the trees and the animals. It's almost an obsession with her. The animals seem to sense this because they come right up to her with no fear at all. Just a couple of months ago, I stood in the yard and I watched her as she was playing out in the field and a doe walked right up to her and nudged Wendy as though they were long lost friends. Wendy touched her and petted her and fed her some nice green grass right out of her hand. I watched her for over an hour as the rabbits and the squirrels came right up to her for a nibble of the cookies that she had taken with her," he said, thoughtfully. "You know, Mandy, sometimes I think that it is as though nature made a mistake and made Wendy a human being instead of a tree or an animal. She really loves them you know?" he said, wistfully. He wished that he hadn't had to cut the little tree down. "If only the ground hadn't been so hard," he thought out loud.

"What did you say?" Mandy asked him

"Oh, nothing, I was just thinking out loud."

The last string of lights was now coming off as Jim looked at the bare little tree.

"There now, that didn't take as long as I thought it would," he said as he finished undecorating Twiggy. Jim wiped his hands on his pants and looked at Mandy. "I guess I will take it out back with the pile of leaves."

He pulled Twiggy out of the stand and dragged her out the back door and threw her on top of an old pile of dead, dry leaves.

"It is a good thing that the snow is not covering the leaves. I wonder if it will still catch. Then Wendy will never know what happened to her little tree," Jim said to himself as he walked to the garage to get a can of gasoline and then to the kitchen for some matches.

Jim paused for a moment looking at the little tree with a sense of eminent disaster. He could not quite put his finger on what it was that was bothering him.

"Oh, well, the day has been a long one and it must just be my nerves," he shrugged as he began to pour the gasoline over Twiggy and the pile of leaves. He was using the gasoline to make sure that nothing remained for Wendy to see.

"What is he doing?" Twiggy asked as she felt the liquid drench and sting her branches and needles. "It smells awful like the Walk-To's Stinky-Go." she said as she watched him take something out of his pocket. It looked like a little stick. "What is it?" she asked with a feeling of dread. "OH, NO! It is fire! It is a little stick of fire! What is he going to do with it?"

Jim leaned over slowly and touched the burning match to the gas soaked leaves.

"Oh! God! What is he doing?" Twiggy screamed. "Oh, God, please help me! Somebody help me, please! It is burning me....please help me!" Twiggy screamed with all her knots.

"What was that?" Wendy asked as she woke and sat up in bed with a start.

"Help me! It burns!" Twiggy screamed again.

Wendy quickly climbed out of bed and ran down the stairs in search of the voice she had heard screaming for help.

"Oh, please, someone help me...it...burns me so....it hurts so bad.....

She couldn't believe her ears; she could hear her little Christmas tree screaming! "FATHER! NO!" Wendy screamed as she fainted and fell to the floor in the doorway.

"Call the doctor," Jim told Mandy. "I'll carry her into the living room."

While Mandy was busy calling the doctor, Jim laid Wendy on the sofa and stroked her hair. She opened her eyes.

"How are you feeling? You gave us quite a start, you know," he told her fondly.

There was no reply. Wendy just stared straight ahead with no expression on her face.

"Are you okay, Wendy?" he asked as he tried to get her attention.

There was still no reply. Wendy didn't even blink her eyes.

"The Doctor said that he would be here as soon as possible. Is she awake?" Mandy asked.

"Yes, I think so, but I can't get any sort of a response from her. Look at her; she has a funny look in her eyes. She just stares as though she is in some sort of a trance," he told her, worry evident on his face.

"She might be in shock. I have seen people go into shock before and she looks like she is in shock," she told him in a very worried voice. She gently held Wendy's hand.

"That tree must have meant more to her than I had realized, but surely not enough to cause her to faint. I thought she was in bed asleep. In fact, she was sound asleep. I remember because when I went up stairs to get the boxes to put the decorations in, I looked in on her and she was sound asleep. I didn't make any noise at all. I even tip toed away from her door. I wonder what woke her up?" he said, frowning.

Wendy closed her eyes and a tear escaped down her cheek as she fell into a fitful and restless sleep. Mandy and Jim both looked at her.

There was a knock on the door. Mandy got up and walked over to the front door and opened it. "Jim, the Doctor is here," Mandy called to him.

"Please show him in."

"Hi, Jim, what seems to be the problem? I hear that you have a sick little girl," he said as he felt Wendy's forehead. "She's not hot."

"She fainted! She came running down the stairs and came to the back door and saw that I was burning the Christmas tree and she screamed and fainted!" Jim told him with a hint of disbelief in his voice.

"Maybe she had a nightmare. It isn't uncommon, you know," Doctor Shumway said.

"Wendy? Wendy?" the doctor called to her as he patted her hand to wake her up. "Wendy! Wake up!" he demanded.

Her eyes opened once again, but she still had a blank look in them and on her face.

"Wendy, how are you feeling?" he asked her with a very concerned look on his face.

There was no response. She didn't even look at him.

"Get me a blanket, immediately!" There was urgency about his voice that made Jim's blood run cold.

Jim brought three blankets and gently laid them over Wendy. He felt so helpless.

"Is she going to be alright?" Jim asked.

"I don't know. What happened?"

"I told you what happened," Jim answered him in an exasperated tone of voice. "She just came running down the stairs and out the back door. When she saw that I was burning the Christmas tree, she screamed and fainted. Then we called you because we couldn't get any kind of a response out of her. She just opens her eyes and stares..... that's all. That's everything that happened," Jim said as he paced back and forth across the floor. He was very irritated that the doctor was still asking him the same questions.

"A nightmare would not throw her into shock this way. I think we had better take her to the hospital right away. That way she will have medical attention around the clock until we can figure this thing out," he said as he put his stethoscope back into his bag. "I'll call an ambulance," he said as he got up. "Where is the telephone?"

Mandy pointed to the table in the corner of the living room with one hand and held the other over her mouth in disbelief.

CHAPTER THIRTEEN

"It is so cold and I am so sleepy," Little Bark whispered to himself as he trembled from the cold, icy snow. "I wonder when the Walk-To will bring Twiggy back."

It had been a little more than two weeks since the Walk-To had come and chopped Twiggy down. All the other trees of the Thicket had fallen asleep for the Big Slumber, but Little Bark had fought to stay awake. He had to be awake to welcome Twiggy back home.

Day after day he had watched down the path, but there was nothing coming. He became very discouraged.

"What if she never comes back? What if she has ended?" His trunk felt very heavy. He felt very lost in his trunk. He loved her so much, he couldn't even think of life without his Little Twiggy.

Then, one day as Little Bark stood shivering in the cold, a leaf blew to him and on it was a message from Twiggy written with soot from the ashes in tiny letters. Little Bark was very excited as he began to read.

"Little Bark, I hope and pray that you get this message. Tell them all that I was so beautiful. Tell them that I stood very tall and very proud. And, tell them that it is not so great to be a Christmas tree. It is a very slow ending. Being a Christmas tree is but to trade a lifetime of happiness for a moment of glory. I was so pretty, but now, I go. The Walk-To is burning me. Oh, Barky, tell everyone that I love them and I will miss them all very much. Tell them I will be waiting for them in The Land of Sweet Waters and Cool Breezes. It is time…..Oh, Barky, I shall miss you….so….much…"

"NO!" Little Bark screamed. "NOOOO!"

"What is it?" Old Moss asked alerted immediately by Little Bark's tone of voice.

"Old Moss, it is Twiggy! She has ended!" he sobbed uncontrollably.

"How do you know of this, Little Bark? I do not see her anywhere," he told him in a concerned voice as he looked all around.

"She told me on this," he said as he showed Old Moss the leaf that had blown in on the wind.

There was a long silence as Old Moss read the message and tears came to his old eyes. He felt very lost in his trunk. All of a sudden Old Moss felt very old and very tired. He wondered why there was so much sadness in the world. He wondered why he had ever wanted to be the Thicket Councilor.

"She was such a pleasure to have around, always joyful and always primping. She was a beautiful tree, but I guess her beauty was eventually her downfall. I shall miss her even though she did not talk to me very much," Old Moss said, sadly.

"I think I shall end, Old Moss. I feel so lost in my trunk that I think I shall split right down the middle and fall to the ground. I cannot believe this pain that I feel. I thought I hurt when Grandfather ended. This is a thousand times worse," Little Bark cried. "I loved her so much. She was so young and so full of life. She never said an unkind word toward anyone. Oh, God, it hurts so much. I don't want to live anymore. Maybe Grandfather was right. Maybe we should all end and then we won't ever have to hurt like this again."

"I can understand how you feel. It does feel that way, doesn't it? But, you won't end, Little bark and, in time, that ache in your trunk will lessen and you will be able to think of other things. It doesn't hurt you as much to think about your Grandfather now that some time has passed. Just look around you, you have all of us and we love you as much as you loved Twiggy. We would all feel very lost in our trunks should something happen to you. Do not talk of ending, Little Bark," he said as he thought of the time Old Firm Roots lost his wife to a strange disease of the trunk. He had also talked of ending and just three weeks later, he did end despite everything that they had tried to do for him. He just quit eating and drinking and finally he ended. Love is a strange concept, it could strengthen you with happiness and joy so that you could tackle any problems that came along or it could rip your trunk open with limbs of grief.

Old Moss looked down at Little Bark. Little Bark certainly had been through a lot in the first cycle and a half of his life. It had been very hard, and, it didn't look like things were going to get any better.

In the week that he had slept, he noticed that Little Bark had somehow changed. He had grown a few inches taller, but that wasn't quite it. "Ahhhh! Yes, the Little One is maturing beyond his cycle. "Yes, he should," Old Moss thought to himself. "He has been through much worry and sorrow for such a short life. He will make a good Thicket Councilor when I retire….that is, if he can answer the question when they give him the Big Test. Of course, Fuzzy Moss could very well answer it also and then he would become the Thicket Councilor. Well, no matter, The Great God of All Things would surely see to it that the right one was chosen. He could only hope that the right one was to be Little Bark."

"Little Bark?" He tried to get his young student's attention. "I have something to tell you. I need you to pay attention," Old Moss said, trying to get him to pay full attention to what he had to say. "A long time ago, there was a tree with a very special name. His name was Hang-In-There. Can you tell me where and why he might have gotten his name?" Old Moss asked him. Old Moss knew that he must get Little Bark thinking about something else for a while or Little Bark might end like Old Firm Roots had done many cycles ago.

"No, Old Moss, I do not know and I do not want to think about it right now. My knots are all muddled and jumbled up like a mixed up wind does to my leaves. I cannot think of anything else but my poor Little Twiggy. She ended all alone! Do you understand? She had absolutely no one there with her who loved her. It must have been terrible. She must have been so lonely. My knots hurt and I feel so lost in my trunk. I just wish I could have been there with her if she had to end. What a terrible way to end. She survived the fire with us and then the very Walk-To that helped put out the fire set fire to Twiggy. I don't understand," he cried. Then he looked at Old Moss. "Shall we wake the others and tell them of Twiggy's ending?"

"Yes, I suppose we should," he said, sadly. He realized that his plan had not worked. He could only hope that Little Bark was strong enough to want to live and that he wouldn't go into a deep depression like Old Firm Roots had done.

"Old Log, Many Branches, Predictor, Tickler, Tall Tales, Fuzzy Moss, Thin-As-Grass, Weeper, Rhymer, all of you wake up!" Old Moss called to them.

"What is it?" Many Branches asked in a sleepy voice as she stretched and yawned.

"Why have you awakened us?" Old Log asked in a stern, but worried tone. He knew that it must be something bad; because that was the only time any member of the Thicket could wake anyone else during the Big Slumber. It had to be an emergency.

"Yes, what is it? Don't you know that this is the time of the Big Slumber?" Predictor admonished him as he rubbed the sleep from his eyes.

"Oh, you are so cruel to wake me. I need all the rest I can get. I don't get enough sun and water for my roots and now you even wake me and take away my precious sleep," Thin-As-Grass complained.

"Yes, I agree. It had better be an emergency. I was dreaming a wonderful dream and just as I was about to learn to walk like the Walk-To's, you woke me!" Tickler was always very grouchy when he was awakened in the middle of the Big Slumber.

"It must have been me. Have I bumped one of you with my branches or stretched my roots too far? If so, it was but an accident and I shall endeavor to be more careful. Maybe I snored too loudly and woke you up. For this I am very sorry, also," Weeper cried, apologetically.

"It might have been me," Rhymer told them. "I do have a habit of moving too much while I sleep and I have been told that it makes much noise. If so, I am sorry and I will try not to wiggle so much,"

"I am glad that you woke us, I have a kink in one of my branches. It might have fallen off had I slept all through the Big Slumber that way," Fuzzy Moss told them.

"You know, this reminds me of a story I once heard about a Thicket that had been woke up during the Big Slumber. Everyone was shouting and angry and...... Tall Tales was cut off abruptly.

"Listen! All of you listen. I have some very bad news for you, news that will hurt deeply. We have heard from Twiggy. She has ended," Old moss told them in a quivering voice.

"How do you know this?" Old Log asked.

"In the final moments of her life she wrote Little Bark a letter on a leaf. It was a miracle that he even received it. He will read it to all of you."

Little Bark read them the letter. He had to stop every now and then because it hurt so badly to read it.

"I had thought that it was so on the very day that the Walk-To cut her down. Twiggy thought that she might grow some new roots and be replanted again, but none of us has ever survived when we have been cut down. They are all evil, everyone of those Walk-To's, and I, for one, think that we should come up with a way to end them all." Tall Tales shook with anger. "It is them or us."

"Yes, I agree. If there were no Walk-To's we would live much longer. They cut us down to build their lairs and then they cut us down to heat them in their lairs when it is cold. Then, once a cycle they cut us down for Christmas trees. Sometimes they even cut us down for no reason at all. You might think that it gives them some sort of twisted pleasure or a feeling of great power to strike us down the way they do., I hate them. I hate them all!" Predictor said, angrily.

"It is true. There used to be so many of us and now we are so few. If only there was something, anything, we could do to stop them. Why can't they just leave us alone? We do absolutely nothing to harm them or bother them in any way, yet they chastise us, carve on our trunks with those sharp things and they punish us as though we were their enemy." Old Log told them in a low voice.

"You are all just dreaming. There is no way to harm the Walk-To's. They are not like us. They can go places and do things that we cannot do. It is hopeless. For cycles and cycles all of us have wished that there was something we could do to stop them. And, it is not just our Thicket, but all the Thickets have been thinking about it. If we could only communicate with the Walk-To's and tell them of our plight maybe, just maybe, they would stop and realize what they are doing. We are living creatures, too. We have feelings. We have families. We have roots and they go deeper than any Walk-To's roots will ever hope to go," Many Branches told them, sadly.

"If we could communicate with them, do you really think that it would change anything? Think! All of you THINK! The Walk-To's are selfish and self-centered. Oh, sure, for a while they might stop tormenting us, but after the novelty wore off, they would continue like always. You are very naïve to think it could be any different," Tickler told them as he folded his branches in defiance.

"We came up with something to put that fire out, so maybe if we all think together and concentrate with all our knots on the Walk-To the next time he comes, maybe we can communicate with him," Fuzzy Moss offered.

"It is I who needs to come up with an idea," Weeper told them. "I know that I am but a day to day tree and my thinking processes are not on the same high level as the rest of you but, I need to try to be of some help. I feel rather useless at times," she whimpered.

"We must fight!" Rhymer surprised them all. "We must grab them and squeeze them until they end. I will trip them all when they come by me and then you can grab them and squeeze them with your mighty branches."

"All this talk is getting us nowhere. We must all put our knots together and come up with an idea to stop the Walk-To's. They are supposed to be very intelligent. We have existed much longer than they have. God created us first, and, therefore, we should be even more intelligent than they are. We must think.....think so that it really counts," Predictor instructed them.

"I tink I 'ave a way o' getting' rid o' dem!" Old Thunder Stick butted in on their conversation.

"Well, I'll be! Why aren't you asleep like the rest of the forest?" Old Moss asked his old buddy of many cycles.

"I might be askin' ya da same quesssssstionn. Ya do no' tink ya 'ave a corrnner on da marrrkit fer bein' awake, na do ya?" he asked, proudly.

"No, I guess we don't at that. Did you get hit by lightening or did we wake you up?" Old Moss asked him.

"No, I di' no' git 'it by lightnin' and, yah, ya di' wake me ooop, boot I forgivvvves ya. I di' no' like wha' I wuz drrrreamom' no how," he said as he cleared his throat. "Now, ta git back at wha' I wuz sayin", ya oout ta git um to cooom 'ere an' stand furrr ah whyle an' din mahbe sum of dem 'ill git 'it by lightnin' an we con git rid o' dem dat way," he said, hopefully as he stood proud and tall with his nose stuck up in the air.

"Oh, sure, that's a great idea. Only how are we supposed to get them to come up there? And, then, after we manage to get them up there, how are we supposed to keep them there until the day we have some lightening? Go back to sleep, Old Thunder Stick. You are not thinking at all," Tickler admonished him.

"I think it is time you all came to your senses" Many Branches told them. "Stop dreaming of things that can never be. It will only cause us more heartache in the end. If anything, we should pray to The Great God of All Things and ask Him to help us."

"Why are all of you talking about ending the Walk-To's? This is not at all why Old Moss woke you. Twiggy has ended! Doesn't anyone at all care that we have lost her? She will never return! We will never see her in this life again!" Little Bark finally lost his temper.

"Yes, Little Bark, you are correct in your thinking and we all feel as you do. We all feel very lost in our trunks and want our revenge for Twiggy's ending. That is why we have been talking as we have. Do not think for a minute that you are the only one who will miss her. We will all miss her very much. It is because of her ending that we were discussing how to rid ourselves of the evil Walk-To's," Many Branches told her son.

"What is to become of all of us, Old Moss?" Fuzzy Moss asked. "We are so few and the Walk-To's do not seem to notice. Soon there will not be a single tree left standing. Then what will they do without us?"

"I do not know. It is only for the Great God of All Things to know. He is all-wise and He sees our plight. He will reward us and punish our enemies someday. But, now we must clear our knots of all thoughts of revenge and we must have a Raften for Little Twig," Old Moss said, sorrowfully.

It was many hours after the Raften for Twiggy that Little Bark finally broke the silence.

"Why must we just stand here while the Walk-Io's get to move about whenever and wherever they please?"

"The Walk-To's are soft and do not live very long. They need shelter or they will end. They are very weak and do not have strong, long roots as we do. They have spindly little things they call toes. They aren't long enough to even hardly touch the ground, let alone root themselves in it. Besides that, they never get very tall and always only have two branches so they have to move around to keep from withering away and ending. They must go to the water and drink from a hole in their trunk. Their roots are too short to drink from the ground as we do. It is a wonder that they survive at all," Old Log told him as he looked down at his roots that were bulging from the ground in some places.

There was nothing in this that Little Bark found helpful.

"Someday, before I end I will see the Walk-To's punished for what they did to Twiggy and for all the wrongs they have done to us all," he told his Father.

"We have all said this at one time or another, my son, but few of us who have said it are alive today and the Walk-To's go unpunished. We all feel anger toward them, but there is nothing that any of us can do. We need a miracle. Ours is a life of patience and enduring. The Great God of All Things has promised someday to lift us up to Him and punish our enemies. We must wait and be patient. It will be done someday, for He has said it, therefore we must believe it.'

There was a long silence, a long, cold silence. One where thoughts were like ice cycles melting in the sun to become muddy and unclear.

At long last, Tall Tales broke the silence gently as he began his story. "There is said to be an old tree named Watcher somewhere. I don't remember where for sure, but I have heard through whispers of those far away that he was alive and considered very old when the Great God of All Things messenger came to this great land many, many cycles ago. It is said that this messenger from God talked of The Land of Sweet Waters And Cool Breezes and that we would all be lifted up and taken away to that land. And, those who remain behind here on earth would be our enemies and very evil. He said that He would punish them as He once punished us long ago."

"What were we punished for?" Little Bark asked him.

"Long ago we used to walk the land like the Walk-To's do now, but The Great God of All Things became very angry with us because the Great Oak trees did not like the Great Red Woods and the Great Red Woods did not like the Tall Firs and none of us liked any other trees but our own kind. We were prejudiced against one another because of a slight difference in our color or our bark or our leaves. We warred against one another like the Walk-To's are doing now. So, the Great God of All Things became very angry at our third world war and He said; 'Enough! You are constantly in battle and always you war among yourselves. No more! Your punishment is that each of you will be firmly planted where you now stand and you will no longer roam the hills and valleys and mountains. It is done!' And, from that day on, we no longer walked the earth. We learned to get along with one another no matter the color or shape of our leaves or needles," Tall Tales finished with a smile.

"Is this just one of your stories, Tall Tales?" Little Bark challenged.

"No, that one is true," Old Moss reassured him.

"No one liked anyone as around the world they scooted,

Now because of anger and war, we are all well rooted," Rhymer stated, bitterly.

Night came and laid its cold, icy hands on all the trees. Most of the Thicket had returned to their slumber and few were left awake. But, those few were being pulled into slumber like quick sand pulls whatever happens to be unlucky enough to fall into it. One by one they were all conquered except for Little Bark who clung desperately to consciousness and reality

All was quiet, like the inside of a tomb deep in the cold, dark ground. The wind blew the limbs of the trees and they made hideous shadows dance all around him.

As Little Bark listened, really listened, he thought he could hear the mournful howls of lonesome trees of by-gone days. Trees that seemed to be reaching out from their graves to grasp their icy cold limbs upon his heart to warn him of some untold danger, "What do they want?" he wondered as a dark shadow fell upon him as though he were the only tree left standing in the thicket and a huge giant had sought him out to devour him in his mighty jaws.

Suddenly he felt very small as though he were being squeezed from one world into another. It was an unwholesome, cruel world, a world of ill tidings and perils which were only felt, not seen.

To the left were many jagged mountains. Mountains the like of which he had never seen before, or had he? Something about this whole thing was very familiar. Had he been here before?

The mountains were purple and green and blue, striped here and there with white. In the middle was a giant cave with a subdued light shining out of its mouth. There was a vast deep chasm surrounding it with boiling red liquid rock to stay anyone from venturing too close.

To the right there was a great light buried behind some hills, unlike the sun as we know it today, and great shadows crept down the sides of the mountain. A cold and clammy mist clung to everything in its wake.

Directly in the middle was a cave-hole, a giant cylindrical mouth with stairs going almost straight down but with the slightest slant. Here and there it mildly turned to left and right with an empty room every now and then. Until, at last, it came to a halt at a huge doorway with great pillars to hold it up. Beyond the door was a great hall with many trees sitting around huge tables made of white marble.

The trees were feasting from great pots of stew and flat round cakes of bread. Each had a huge cask from which they drank an ill- smelling ale. All about them were Walk-To's doing this and that. Not Walk-To's as they are known today, but puny, skinny things with short arms and legs and long, long toes and fingers like the trees.

Some of the Walk-to's were combing the needles of the trees, others were washing their roots and still others were waiting on them, bringing them more stew and cakes and ale.

The trees were talking to one another in loud boisterous tones that almost always denotes drunken merriment. At their sides hung swords and great battle axes and knives, the tools of war.

Little Bark noticed that all the trees were of the same kind.

Then, suddenly, there was silence, a deafening silence, the kind that pierces your ears and makes them ring. The kind of silence that makes you wonder if you truly have lost your hearing.

"Ah, they have seen me," he thought to himself as icy fingers of fear tickled his trunk.

A tall, strong, bearded tree got up and came toward him. Little Bark's first reaction was to run, but, alas, he was still well rooted.

Little Bark stood his ground as the old bearded tree reached out to him and stared him eye to eye. Kind eyes, he noticed with wonder, and, were those tears?

"Tell them…. Tell them not to do it. Tell them it will only lead to pain and misery and heartbreak. Tell them that we….."

"Ahhhhhhh Chooooooooo! Ahhhhhhh Chooooooooo!"

"What? What is going on?" Little Bark said as he looked around. "I don't believe it" he said, angrily.

"Well, the least you could do is bless me," Tickler told him.

"Don't you realize what you've done?"

"What have I done? I just sneezed, that's all!"

"You woke me in the middle of an important dream. A prediction. How am I ever to find out what he wants to tell me? I am constantly being interrupted!"

"Who wants to tell you something?" Tickler quizzed him.

"Never mind. Just go back to sleep."

"That might help you, but I feel rather rested. Look! The Big Slumber is about over!"

"Oh, pooh! There is still snow on the ground. Go to sleep," Little Bark told him as he closed his eyes to return to the land of the walking trees.

Little Bark slept, as did Tickler, but he did not dream his dream again.

Jim had visited Wendy every morning and every evening with the same result. She had not responded to him. She didn't even seem to know him. It was as though she was in a trance, her own little world, where no one could penetrate.

"May I take her home now?" Jim asked the doctor as he looked down at Wendy lying in the hospital bed. She looked so thin and frail. She had lost a lot of weight and would not eat.

"Yes," he said, rubbing his chin with his fingers, "Maybe that will be best for her. But, you realize, of course, that she cannot talk and that she may never talk again?" Dr. Stewart warned him.

Jim sighed. "Yes, I do, but, maybe if I take her home and she is around familiar surroundings, she will come out of it and become the joyful, caring young girl that she once was."

"It is possible. We still do not know what caused this trauma for Wendy. It had to be something that she just could not deal with in the real world so she withdrew inside herself to her own private little world where unhappy things are not allowed to exist. She actually believes right now that nothing can harm her in her little world. Can you understand, Jim?"

"Yes, I think I can," he told the doctor as he helped dress Wendy to take her home.

"She may not ever be able to communicate, not even in writing," Dr. Stewart whispered in his ear as he put his hand on Jim's shoulder.

"I understand."

As they were driving home, Wendy watched out the window at all the houses and big beautiful buildings that seemed to fly by her as though they had wings.

Outside the city she saw beautiful meadows packed with the snow of a cold winter. Farther down the country road she saw houses and farms where chimneys were billowing with smoke from the warm fires within.

Then, she saw the trees and she began to cry. Not a loud cry, but a mournful cry as though someone dear to her had just died.

"What is it, Wendy?" Jim asked his daughter. "Can't you tell me what is wrong?"

There was no answer. She just continued to look at the trees as if to say, 'I am so sorry, so very sorry' with her eyes.

"What is wrong with the trees, Wendy?" he asked her. "Can't you tell me what it is that is bothering you? I love you so much and I want so much for us to be a family again. I've missed hearing your voice and see you run and play."

There was no response. It was as though she hadn't even heard what he had said. She just looked out the window at the trees with tears streaming down her face.

"Well, no matter, we will be home soon and everything will be okay again as soon as you are around familiar surroundings. Mandy is there, she is there waiting for you. She has missed you so much. She came to see you in the hospital too, but she said you didn't even look at her."

Jim looked over at Wendy. 'She has lost so much weight', he thought to himself. "Maybe we can put some weight back on you with some good home cooking. You loved Mandy's cooking, didn't you? I sure hope you get your appetite back because I can't eat it all, you'll have to help!" he said as he reached over and tweaked her nose between his two fingers.

There was still no response. It was as though there was no life left in her.

"I'll bet you are anxious to see your new bicycle! You haven't even had a chance to ride it, have you? Well, the snow is melting pretty fast and soon you will be able to ride all over the place," he said as he looked over at her. "It's okay, Pumpkin, everything will be just fine when I get you home," he reassured her, but he could not hide the doubt he felt in his heart.

At last Jim could see his farmhouse and a sharp twinge of excitement and hope suddenly shot through his whole body. Hope that Wendy would respond and hope that everything would be returned to normal.

As he drove up the driveway to the house, he could see Mandy standing there waving like a proud and happy flag.

"Look, Wendy! It's Mandy!" Jim tried to get her attention. There was still no response. "Honey, won't you please look at Mandy and wave to her? You can hate me if you want for cutting down your tree instead of digging it up, but Mandy had nothing to do with it," he said as tears poured down his face.

Wendy looked at her Father with tears in her eyes. She could not understand why she had lost her ability to talk, but she had. It was as though her mind wasn't connected to her mouth and voice anymore. She had blamed her Father at first, but, now she knew how much he meant to her. She loved him dearly. No one could ever take his place, especially not a tree. 'Oh, Daddy, I love you so much. I wish you could hear me. I wish you could understand me. I want to talk to you so much,' she thought at him as hard as she could as she reached out and hugged him.

"Oh, Wendy, if only you could talk to me," Jim said as he felt a spark of hope. "This is the first sign that you could ever understand me. Oh, Thank You, God! Thank You so very much."

Wendy climbed out of the car and ran to Mandy and gave her a big hug. Mandy began to cry. "How's my little angel? Are you feeling better now?" Mandy asked, as she looked first at Wendy and then at Jim.

"She still cannot talk, but she is showing improvement. She gave me a big hug in the car. I think she has forgiven me, but she still can't talk for some reason. We've got to give her time, I guess and lots of love and lots of prayers. She will be okay; I just know it deep down inside my heart."

CHAPTER FOURTEEN

Weeks passed since Twiggy's Raften. The snow was just about all melted with but a few spots here and there, desperately trying to cling to winter, but soon spring would win the battle as she did every year.

The Crocuses were pushing their way up out of the ground with their pretty blooms spreading open wide to greet the sun.

All the fruit trees began to bloom in their magnificent colors of pink and white. It seemed as though all life was renewing itself as if the old no longer existed.

All the trees in Old Moss' Thicket began to wake, one be one, from the Big Slumber.

"I feel as though I have had no sleep at all. Look at me....I'm just as thin and bedraggled as ever. You might think that some day I would wake up from the Big Slumber and be full of branches and at least thirty lippits tall!" Thin-As-Grass had awakened her usual complaining self. "Oh, dear, just look at me!"

"I try not to," Tickler teased.

"My! How you and Fuzzy Moss have grown!" Many Branches told her son, ignoring Tickler's remark. "Look at our Son, Old Log; he will soon catch up to us!"

"Not for many cycles yet, Many Branches. He has grown though, much more than I had anticipated." Old Log said, admiring his big, strong son.

"Yes, I have grown in many more ways than just height. I feel very old and burdened with many heavy loads," he said in a sad voice.

"I, too, am burdened," Tall Tales said in a tired voice, "I have too much feathers from the Angels Wings on my limbs. I cannot move! My limbs feel so heavy!"

"That is not the feathers from the Angels Wings, Tall Tales; it is old age setting in! You are just stiff like the pond from the long slumber. Move your branches all about and you will soon feel better," Old Moss told him as he, also stretched and groaned in stiffness.

"Look!" Weeper shouted, "See? Over there where Twiggy once stood? We have a new seedling poking its head above the ground!"

"Yes! Yes! I see it!" Fuzzy Moss shouted with joy. "Is it Twiggy? Has she come back to us, Tall Tales?"

"No, Twiggy is gone forever, I think. No, this is a new one, probably a Will-of-the-Wind like you were," Tall Tales told him. "We will know in a couple of weeks when it has learned to talk and I can tell it my famous stories!"

"That's all I need!" Predictor told him. "Why can't the Big Slumber last longer? That way we would not have to listen to all this so much."

"That is quite enough. We have just wakened and already you two are arguing. Can't you two get along? What is the new seedling going to think of us? I think it will be nice to have some fresh sap among us. You are both acting like seedlings," Old Log scolded.

"Yes, of course, you are right as always. We like to let each other know we are awake," Tickler apologized.

"Then, please find some other way to do it! We do not need the tension. It is spring! Enjoy it! How about a good welcome from all of us to our new member?" Many Branches suggested.

"Why? Just so that it can be cut down with an ax for a Christmas tree or maybe it will only be burnt down from a Walk-To's little stick-of-smoke. Or, better yet, maybe one of them will come along and cut it down for no reason at all," Little Bark said, bitterly.

"Not all Walk-To's are that way, Little Bark. I have heard in whispers from far away that there is a special place, a very special place, where trees like us are protected by the Walk-To's. The Walk-To's call it a National Forest and no Walk-To's are allowed to cut the trees down and they are not allowed to use their little sticks-of-smoke either. There the water is sweet and not sour smelling like the gud from the Walk-To's stinky-gos. Even the animals are protected and the Walk-To's are not allowed the hunt them down and end their lives. Wouldn't it be wonderful if they would make us a National Forest?" Tall Tales asked

Little Bark as he imagined how wonderful it would be, like the Land of Sweet Waters and Cool Breezes.

"Is this just another one of your famous tall tales or is it just something that you dreamed about during the Big Slumber?" he asked.

"No, this story is supposed to be true. But, sometimes I even doubt it. There just doesn't seem to be any reason to believe it, especially after what happened to Twiggy. The Walk-To's are mean and cruel and selfish. I just have a very hard time imagining them doing anything so noble," Tall Tales said with remorse.

"We have only seen the bad side of them. There must be some good in them, don't you think? A tree can be bad and a tree can be good. It must be so with the Walk-To's. We just haven't met any good Walk-To's yet," Rhymer said.

"Why, Rhymer! I do believe that is the longest thing that you have ever said without rhyming!" Many Branches congratulated him.

Rhymer blushed.

"Shhhhh! Something is coming, I can hear it!" Fuzzy Moss told them.

"I hope it is not a Walk-To. Walk-To's only mean trouble, and we have had enough of that lately." Little Bark told him.

"It is! I can see it! It is the same one that picked Twiggy out for its Christmas tree!" Many Branches said in a very worried voice.

All were staring down the path as Wendy came into view.

"Go away!" Little Bark shouted.

"No, I won't! I cannot. Not until I have told you all that I am so sorry, so very sorry about your friend, Twiggy," Wendy told them.

"What? What is this? The Walk-To is talking to us! And, she can understand what we are saying! I must be dreaming! Someone hurry and wake me up!" Old Moss shouted in disbelief.

"Hmmmmmm! Then, Old Friend, we all must be sharing the same dream because I, also, can hear it," Predictor said in disbelief.

"You are not asleep, and I can hear you and I can talk to you. It is because of Twiggy that I can talk to you. I heard her scream when my Father put her on the pile of leaves and he poured gasoline all over her and then lit her on fire with a match and she began to burn.........
Oh...........God.....how she burned! I'm so sorry...I couldn't do anything to stop him! I was too late! She just kept screaming.....and.....

screaming! I could not believe my ears!" she screamed as she threw herself to the ground and sobbed as though her heart was going to burst.

"Calm yourself, Little Roots. It is not your fault," Old Moss told her. "We all make mistakes. Yours was that you cut Twiggy down instead of digging her up as other Walk-To's do. She would have lived if you had dug her up and brought her back when you were done with her. But, now, we will miss her very much. What is done is done. Nothing can change the past. But, we can change what happens in the future."

"My Father was supposed to dig her up, but he couldn't. The ground was too frozen and he could not budge it with the shovel and he knew how much I loved Twiggy and wanted her for my Christmas tree. So, he went back home and got his ax and chopped her down.....If only I had been with him. I wasn't with him, you know. I was sick. If I had been with him, I would never have let him cut her down," she said as she hung her head in sorrow. "I am so very sorry. I know that just saying I'm sorry won't bring Twiggy back, but, I had to tell you. I wish I could make everything well again."

"I see now that it is not your fault," Little Bark told her as he searched his knots and his trunk in forgiveness. "Do not feel so lost in your trunk. Twiggy is in the Land of Sweet Waters and Cool Breezes with other loved ones that have ended. She is much better off there than here. All is well, again. We did hate you for what you did, but, now we can see that you are as upset as we all are. Therefore, you must care very much."

"I do care. I really do. I love trees so much," she said with a sparkle in her eyes. Then she frowned. "What is the Land of Sweet Waters and Cool Breezes?" she asked Little Bark.

"It is where we go when we end," he told her.

"Oh, I see. We call it Heaven. Do you believe in God as we do?" she asked.

"Yes, we believe in the One God of All Things. He created everything, you know. He even created you and me."

"How did you learn of Him?"

"Through whispers and from our parents or Thicket Councilors. We are taught these things when we are very small Seedlings." He told her proudly. "How did you learn of Him?"

"I go to church and our preacher tells us all about Him. My Mother taught me, too, but she is gone now. She is in Heaven. Daddy teaches me now," she said sadly. "What are whispers?"

"Well......they are what other trees tell us from far away."

"Oh, you must mean stories or news or maybe rumors. I see."

"What is a church?" Little Bark asked her.

"It is a place where we go to praise and worship God. We sing and pray and listen to our Preacher tell us of all the wonderful things God and His Son have done and are going to do," she said. "What does lost in my trunk mean?"

It is an empty feeling that you feel way down deep inside your trunk when you lose someone that you love," he explained to her. "Do you understand?"

"Yes, I feel that way right here," she said as she pointed to her chest. "I felt that way when my Mother died, too." She said, sadly.

"It will pass with time," Old Moss told her. "When did your Mother end?"

"It hasn't been too long ago. I think it was in the late spring or early summer many months ago. Why do you ask?"

"Because that was the same time that Predictor and I and others felt lost in our trunks and we couldn't think of any reason to feel that way. We were all happy and in good health. You have a special aura about you," Old Moss told her.

"Thank you, I guess." She told him wondering what an aura was.

"How come you are able to hear and understand us?" Old Moss asked her.

"I don't really know. I have always loved trees and many times I have wished that I were one of you, standing tall and sturdy, watching all the years go by, seeing all the many wonderful things that you must have seen," she said as she swayed back and forth in wonderment. "I think when Twiggy screamed and I heard her, it was because God wanted me to hear her. But, what I can't understand is why I cannot talk to people like my Father or Mandy any more. It doesn't make any sense. I don't even know how I am talking to you. My mouth is not moving. I do not exactly hear my voice. It is as though you can understand my thoughts. That's it, I think."

"Was Twiggy beautiful?" Many Branches asked her.

"Oh, yes! She was the most beautiful Christmas tree any of us had ever seen! People that we knew came from miles around just to see her!"

"Is it true that you put lights like fire dancing on her limbs?"

"Yes! Oh yes! And pretty colored balls and long silver ice cycles and strings of different colored popcorn all around her! Yes, she was so beautiful! We took a picture of her and I will try to bring it with me the next time that I come to see you," she told her. "I could not speak to her at that time, but she stood so proud and so tall as though she was proud to be a Christmas tree," she said, sadly.

"She was proud to be a Christmas tree," Old Moss told her.

"Even though she knew that she was going to die?" Wendy asked him with a quivering voice.

"Yes, if by dying you mean ending. Yes, she was still proud to be a Christmas tree. We think it is a very great honor, a very honorable thing, to be chosen by one of you for a Christmas tree," he told her.

"I guess it would be if people didn't chop you down. It is better if we get a shovel and dig you up so that we can re-plant you after Christmas," she told them sorrowfully. "How do you feel toward me now? Do you all hate me?"

"No, Little Roots, we don't hate you. I, for one, like you very much," Little Bark told her. He didn't really think that he would ever say such a thing to a Walk-To, especially this one, the one that had taken his beloved Twiggy away from him.

"We all like her, I think," Old Moss said as he looked around at all the others.

"Yes," Old Log said, firmly.

"We sure do!" Predictor told her.

"Me, too!" Rhymer said in a squeaky voice.

"How can I hear you change your voices? What makes me hear each voice in my mind differently?" Wendy asked them.

"This we cannot tell you. We do not know this ourselves, but, we can hear laughter, sorrow, crying, excitement, anger, whispers, and loud talk. It just comes to us the way the one who is talking means for us to hear it. Do you understand, Little Roots?'

"No, but there are many things that I do not understand. I have tried talking to my Father, but, nothing comes out of my mouth anymore, no noise, nothing. I think at him, but, he doesn't hear me like you do. It is very frustrating," she said as she frowned. "Why do you call me Little Roots?" she asked Old Moss.

"Ahhhh, Little Roots, do not be offended, but you have such tiny, skinny roots. They are barely visible, they are so small. I think you call them toes."

"Oh! Ha! Ha! Ha! Ho! Haw! Ha! That is very funny! Ha! Ha! Ha! Ho! Ha! No.......Ha! Ha! ...... I am not offended! Ha! Ha! I have never heard toes called roots before!" she laughed.

"Shhhhh! something is coming," Many Branches warned them.

"I hope it is not my Father. I have run away from home. I cannot talk to him anymore. I cannot talk to anyone anymore. I can only talk to you. My Father doesn't understand me any more." Wendy cried.

"Wendy? Wendy? Are you hiding? Oh, there you are! Thank God you are alright!" he sighed as he put his arms around her and gave her a big hug. "Are you okay?"

Wendy nodded her head.

"Can you understand what I am saying?" Jim asked her in surprise.

Wendy nodded her head again.

"Oh, Wendy! Why didn't you tell me that you could understand me?"

Wendy just stood there, helpless. She tried to answer him, but she could not.

"What's the matter, can't you talk?"

Wendy shook her head.

"It's okay, Sweetheart, it's okay. Everything is going to alright again, just as I had hoped and prayed for. You will talk again. Right now I am just so happy and thankful that you can hear me and understand me. I will only ask you questions that you can answer with a yes or a no, okay?"

Wendy nodded and reached up and put her arms around his neck and gave him a big bear hug like she used to do before Twiggy had died.

"Come, let's go home now. Mandy will be so happy to hear the good news. Don't you think she will be happy, Pumpkin?" he asked her.

Wendy nodded her head and smiled.

"I love you," he told her.

Wendy pointed to herself and then to her Father.

"You love me, too."

Wendy nodded and grasped his hand in hers as he led her down the path toward home.

"I'll be back!" she called back to them.

"Be careful, Little Roots. We don't want to lose you now," Little Bark called back to her. 'That's strange,' Little Bark thought to himself, 'A few minutes ago, I was ready to put an end to her and now I think I am actually going to miss her'.

CHAPTER FIFTEEN

"Well, what did you think of our new friend, Predictor?" Old Moss asked his good friend of many years.

"She was quite likeable, I think. She seemed pretty intelligent for a small Walk-To. She is very young, though. I think I like her very much. How about you? What did you think of her?" Predictor asked him.

"I liked her very much. She has a very tender heart and she also loves us very much. That is very evident. But, I wonder......why is it that The Great God of All Things has allowed us to be able to talk to her?"

"This I cannot even guess. Never before have I ever heard of such a thing. Oh, yes..... maybe in stories, but I never believed them, not for an instant. And, believe me; no one will ever believe us either. They will all think that we are crazy and that we grow too close to the loco weed."

"Nonsense! They will believe us! They will have to believe us!"

"No they won't! Would you believe them if they told you what happened here today?" Predictor asked him with raised eyebrows.

"Well, that's different. I don't trust anyone outside our Thicket."

"Yes, and they don't trust us either."

"But, she will be coming back and then we can prove it to them."

"What if her Father won't let her come back? What then?"

"I think that you are underestimating our new little friend. She will be back.......mark my words! She will be back!" Old Moss said, proudly.

"Old Moss, it is I, Little Bark, and I must speak to you of a matter of great importance."

"What is it?" Old Moss asked in a very important voice.

"I have thought on this thing that I am about to tell you for many long days. It has required much thought and now, alas, I can come up with no answer what-so-ever," Little Bark said as he cleared his throat. "During the Big Slumber, I had a dream and many months ago I had a vision or a dream and they were the same. In my dreams there were mountains, strange mountains, with a cave. And, in the cave there was a strange subdued light. I could not see into that cave, but there was another cave. It was in the ground in the middle of a field between the two mountain ranges. There were no trees on the mountains or anywhere else except down in that cave in the field. And, they were all sitting around a huge table and they were eating stew from great huge iron pots. And cakes......little round, flat cakes..... And they drank foul smelling ale. There were many Walk-To's in my dream.... but.... they were different than they are now and the Walk-To's were the trees slaves. The trees were not rooted like we are now, they could walk. And, in my dream, one of the trees with a great long beard came over to me and he said 'Tell them... warn them all before it is too late.... Tell them they must not..... tell them not to do it, tell them that it will only lead to pain and misery and heartbreak.....tell them that we...' and then I was rudely awakened by Tickler when he sneezed. The trees had swords draped at their sides and great battle axes and knives, all the tools of war. What could my dream possibly mean?" Little Bark asked.

"This will require much thought," Old Moss said as he frowned at Little Bark. "Were you awakened both times that you had this dream?"

"Yes......let's see..... The first time my Mother woke me because I was trembling. And, the second time I was awakened by sneezes from Tickler." Little Bark told him again.

"Ha! Ha! Ha! Ho! Ha!" Old Moss laughed.

This was the first time that Little Bark could ever remember Old Moss laughing.

"I really fail to see the humor," Tickler told Old Moss, indignantly. "As I recall, that young up start, Little Bark was very rude to me!"

"I apologize. Just don't sneeze when I am sleeping!" Little Bark told him.

"Stop….both of you! Isn't it enough that you argue with Tall Tales? You do not have to argue with everyone in the Thicket, you know." Old Moss told Tickler in a low warning voice.

"What about my dream?" Little Bark asked Old Moss once again.

"It is hard to say. I think there is supposed to be a warning of some kind in it, but, it is still very vague. If it means what I think it means, someone is in real big trouble."

"What do you think it means?" Little Bark asked.

"I don't care to say right now. I would rather be sure about it first."

"Can't you even give me a clue?"

"The only thing that I will tell you is that I think it has something to do with the Walk-To's"

"What could it possibly have to do with them?"

"Think, Young One, think. I have told you all that I am going to tell you for now. You must wait until you finish your dream some time."

"But, what if I don't ever finish it?"

"You have erred seriously in your thinking, Little Bark. Do you think the Great God of All Things has shown you this dream only to give you a fraction of it?"

"No….No, it would do no one any good just knowing what we know now."

"That is much clearer thinking," Old Moss complimented him.

"I do not think I am capable of clear thinking. I am afraid that my mind is not yet competent enough, for although I have had many facts shown to me in my dreams, instead of just one single one on which to think, I still have not come to any specific conclusions as you seem to have done."

"You are chastising yourself unnecessarily, Little Bark. I have more knowledge upon which to base my conclusions. You are young. Much time has been consumed in acquiring my knowledge."

"I think that the hardest thing that I have had to deal with so far is my youth!" Little Bark told him in an exasperated tone.

"Do you know what?" Tall Tales asked them both.

Neither of them answered. They just looked at him, waiting for him to begin his story.

"That Walk-To.....Little Roots, I think you called her, reminded me of a story I once heard about a tree named Communicator. This tree could talk to all the animals and one day a Bushy Tail came along, very excited, he was, and he was out of breath from running. He kept stopping and looking over his shoulder and screeching very excitedly, "It is coming! It is coming!" he said as he scurried by and disappeared into the bushes. Then, a few minutes later, a Stinker came loping up to him screaming, "It's coming! It's coming!" and before Communicator could ask him what was coming, he, too, disappeared into the bushes. Later, a Nibbler hopped and pranced up to him, "It is coming! It is coming!"....."What is coming?" Communicator asked him before he had a chance to scamper away. "A twister! A twister is coming!"... And he, too, disappeared into the bushes.

So the twister came as it crushed and slithered and churned its way, blackening the skies. Bounding through cities as it tossed and turned, ripping away at buildings and pulling up huge boulders. It threw Stinky-go's around like they were leaves in a breeze. It ripped away at bushes and drank up the streams as closer and closer it came. Communicator didn't know what to do. In its path it left nothing but debris and waste.

Finally, it reached out and grabbed Communicator and ripped him up out of the ground, roots and all. Two days later, it finally subsided and dropped him in a very strange country. All about him there was nothing but waste land. There was nothing except for an occasional tree here and there. There were bushes, lots of bushes and some Pocket Hoppers. The Pocket Hoppers spoke in a strange language that Communicator had a hard time understanding. The language was English, but, they had a strong accent. "It's coming! It's coming!" said one of the Fuzzy Pockets, and then it climbed up into his branches. And, another twister came along and grabbed him up and took Communicator back home again. The Fuzzy Pocket and Communicator became very good friends and the Fuzzy Pocket lived in his branches for the rest of his life."

"That has to be the longest story that I have ever heard you tell!" Old Moss exclaimed pompously.

"I agree, but I liked it. One thing, though what is a Pocket Hopper and a Fuzzy Pocket?" Little Bark asked.

"A Pocket Hopper is a giant Long-eared Fuzzy Hopper and it carries it's young around in a pocket in its stomach. A Fuzzy Pocket is a tiny Back Scratcher that also carries its young around in a pocket in its stomach. They come from a place called Australia, so I've heard."

"And, how do you know all of this?" Old Moss asked as he brushed some moss from his upper trunk where it began to tickle his nose.

"I've heard it from the whispers of many trees," he told him, secretively.

"Tap! Tap! Tap"

"What is that?" Fuzzy Moss asked.

"Tap! Tap! Tap! Tap!"

"Ouch! Stop that! That hurts!" Tickler shouted. "Go away!"

"Tap! Tap! Tap!"

"Shoooooo! Go away!" Tickler said as he brushed the Stiff Beak off of his trunk and it flew over to Tall Tales.

"Tap! Tap! Tap!"

"Oh….no you don't! Shoooooo! Go away!" He warned. "Thanks a bunch! Why did you have to Shoooooo him over here to me?" Tall Tales asked him.

"Tap! Tap! Tap!"

"Ouch! Those pesky little varmints!" Predictor shouted as he swatted at the stiff beak. "Everyone start waving your branches and maybe he will to away."

So they all waved their branches furiously, and the stiff beak finally flew away."

"What was that noise?" Weeper asked in a soft apologetic voice. "I am sorry if I interrupted anyone, but, I think this might be important."

"What noise?" Old Moss asked her.

"That humming, whirring sound! Can anyone hear it? Maybe it is just my ears that are ringing. Please forgive me for interrupting," Weeper apologized again.

"No….No… I think I can hear it, too!" Many Branches told her as she strained to hear.

"Ahhhhhhh! Yes! I can hear it now! It sounds like a flying Stinky-go. We should be able to see it soon," Predictor told them.

"It is flying very low, don't you think?" Old Log said. "They usually fly a lot higher than that."

"Yes, it sounds as though it is sick or something. Listen to it cough and sputter," Many Branches told them with a very concerned look upon her face.

"Something is wrong with it," Old Moss said. "There it is! It is coming almost directly at me! Look! Can you see it?"

"Yes! Yes! Something is terribly wrong with it! Look at the smoke puffing out of it!" Tall Tales said.

The plane flew very close to the top of Old Moss, barely missing his top branches as it crashed in the field next to him. If Old Moss had not ducked way down like he did, the plane would have hit him.

"Oh! Wow!" Fuzzy Moss said with eyes as big as the full moon. "That was some crash!"

"Wow, is not quite the word I had in mind but, it will do for now," Many Branches said. "I wonder if there are any Walk-To's in it."

"There should be. I don't think it can fly without a Walk-To in it," Old Log told her as he strained to see.

"I don't know. I don't see anything moving over there," Old Moss told them. "It would be terrible, would it not, to fall from way up high in the air like that?"

"Extremely hazardous to your health, I would imagine," Tickler joked.

"That, my dear Tickler is an understatement," Predictor told him.

"Help...Somebody help us!"

"Well, I guess that answers our question of whether there are any Walk-To's in it. At least one of them is still alive. What can we do to help it?" Many Branches asked.

"I have an idea," Little Bark said, excitedly. "We can send a message to Little Roots through the trees for help," he suggested as he looked around for some sort of approval.

"It sounds good to me," Old Moss said. "Tall Tales, you start the message. Give it to the next Thicket....Old Stiff Branches Thicket.... and tell them to tell the next and so on and so on."

"Okay, but they aren't going to believe me when I tell them who the message is for!" Tall Tales said as he turned and told the trees of the next Thicket.

"What? Have you all gone mad? Did you really think we would fall for such nonsense as this? Harrunph!"

"But, it is true! Just do it or be expelled and excommunicated from the Council of Trees!" he demanded.

"Oh, alright," and they in turn told others on down the line until soon the message reached all the way to the creek where the forest ended abruptly.

"Now what shall I do?" A tree named Twisted Trunk said.

"I will carry your message through the bushes!" said a little bush whose name was Sticky Bush.

"Would you? That would be so nice and friendly of you. Thank you. Way over there," he said as he pointed back into the forest, "there is a Walk-To that needs help right away. And, there is supposed to be a Walk To at that farm house, over there that can communicate with us. Ask her for help," he told him with a little hint of doubt in his voice.

"Okay, if you say so!" And, Sticky Bush sent the message through many of his friends and finally it reached a huge apple tree in Wendy's yard.

"Madam Apple Tree, could you, please, give a message to the little Walk-To who lives in the house for me?" Yellow Leaf asked her with utmost respect.

"How dare you address me? I am an apple tree, you know! I should not even be conversing with you! All of the other fruit trees would simply end if they knew of this! And, what was that you said? Did you say that you had a message for the Little Walk-To? Ho! Ho! Ha! Ha! You must be kidding! What are you, anyway, a tumble weed? And, maybe you have bumped your leaves one too many times! No one can talk to a Walk-To!"

"Oh yeah?" Think again!" Wendy said as she leaned out her upstairs bedroom window.

"My stars!.....It.....can....hear us!" Madam Apple Tree said as she nearly fell over in shock.

"Wow!" Yellow Leaf said as he looked at Wendy in surprise.

"What is the message?" Wendy asked.

"There has been an accident. A flying Stinky-go has crashed in the field in Old Moss' Thicket. There is a Walk-To in it. It is still alive, but we don't know for how long," Yellow Leaf told her still unable to believe that this was really happening.

"Send back a message that I will bring help as soon as I can," Wendy said as she shut her window and ran down the stairs.

Wendy walked over to her Father and took his hand in hers and tried to pull him up out of his chair.

"What is it? What's the matter?' Jim asked his daughter as he got up and began to follow her. "Where are we going?"

All Wendy could do was pull him out the door to the yard. There she pointed toward the forest.

"Is something wrong?" Jim asked.

Wendy nodded her head vigorously as she tugged at his hand once again.

"It's okay, I will follow you. You just lead the way, Sweet Pea, and I will follow you.....Okay?"

Wendy nodded her head as she began to run ahead of her Father.

"Wait! Wait for me!" he said as he ran after her with Ralph barking at his heels.

They ran through the field and climbed through the fence and over the little bridge.

"What is wrong in the forest?" Jim asked her, puzzled. "I smell smoke!" he said as he quickened his pace.

Wendy motioned for him to follow as she disappeared up the path into the trees.

"Someone is coming!" Many Branches cautioned everyone.

"It is more than likely Little Roots!" Little Bark said, excited that his message might have gotten through to her.

"Hello, everyone!" Wendy said as she ran up the path. "I got your message! What is this about a flying.......Oh! My!" she said in astonishment as she saw the plane that had crashed.

"Stay here Wendy. I don't think I want you to go over there. We don't need you going into shock again," her Father told her as he ran to the plane.

"Hello? Is anyone in there?" he called as he approached the plane.

"Oh, Thank God! Yes! Oh, yes! Please help us. My husband and our son are badly hurt. I'm okay, I think. I'm just pinned in here and I can't move." A woman told him.

"Don't try to move," Jim cautioned her as he looked at her husband and her boy. "They are both still alive. You are all very fortunate," he told her as he looked the plane over good. "No one seems to be in any immediate danger. I will go call for a doctor and an ambulance. Don't worry, I will be back soon."

Jim walked back to where Wendy was standing. "Stay here, Wendy, and don't go near the plane unless it is absolutely necessary. And, by that I mean, unless the woman calls out to you, okay?"

Wendy nodded her head as Jim ran back down the path toward home.

"Are all the Walk-To's still alive, Little Roots? I heard your Father say that there was more than one." Little Bark asked.

"Yes, I think so. I know one of them is, anyway," she told him.

"It is good to see you again, Little Roots, I did not think that it would be this soon, though," Old Moss told her affectionately.

"My Father is becoming used to me, now. We can communicate but he must ask me a yes or no question. Soon I think he will relax and I will be able to come here as often as I like. Did you see the plane when it crashed?" Wendy asked Old Moss.

"Yes, if that is what you call a flying Stinky-go, it made a very loud noise but, it did not burn like the other plane did that crashed a long time ago. We thought the one that crashed a long time ago might start a fire and burn us all down, but, the Walk-To's saw the smoke from it and came in a great hurry and put it out. This plane smoked a little but, not much," Old Moss told her.

"That is really something the way you got the message to me. I almost never got it, though, you know." Wendy told him with a worried look.

"Why? What happened?" Little bark butted in. After all, it was his idea to send the message in the first place.

"That old bag of a fruit tree that is outside my bedroom window did not believe the little bush when he told her to please give the message to me. Not only that...but, she was pompous, rude and stuck up! I didn't like her attitude at all! Who do they think they are anyway, some one special or something?" Wendy asked in a disgusted voice.

"They think that because they have fruit and we don't, that we are lower classed than them. They are nothing but a bunch of stuck up snobs pretending to be high class. They are funny that way, but, we just ignore them," Old Log told her.

"Oh! It is so good to see all of you again!" Wendy said as she slowly turned around and greeted everyone. "Oh, dear me! Look! You have a new member in your Thicket!" Wendy said as she pointed to the little seedling that had poked its way up out of the ground where Twiggy once stood. "Oh! And look! There is one coming up right beside it, not even an inch away!"

"There is? Where?" Many Branches asked as she leaned way over as far as she could without falling over and uprooting herself.

"Right there!" Wendy said as she walked over and touched it.

"Oh! Yes! Now I can see it!" she said excitedly. "Old Log, look! We have another Seedling coming up! Isn't it wonderful?"

"No, it is not so good, Many Branches. When two Seedlings grow in the same spot like that they both usually end," Old Log warned her. "Besides, no one will ever be able to take the place of our Little Twiggy," he said, sadly. Then he looked at Wendy. The expression on her face was no longer a happy one. Sorrow was written there now. "Do not feel so lost in you trunk, Little Roots, remember, we have all decided that it was not your fault. And, we must not ever forget Twiggy. We must be able to talk about her without feeling any anger at all. We will always feel lost in our trunks. Only time will heal that. Now, cheer up and smile. Today is a beautiful day," Old Log told her kindly. He had tremendous compassion for the Little Walk-To.

"Yes, it is a beautiful day, Old Log, but, I must make everything right between all of you and my Father. My Father is a good man, a very special person. He is kind and gentle. He does not know that the trees have families and friends. He doesn't know that you have feelings like we do. I really didn't even know for sure until Twiggy screamed that awful night, but, some how I suspected it. I had a feeling deep down inside of me that you trees were more than just wood and branches and leaves. And, my Father only cut Twiggy down because he loves me so much and he knew that I wanted her with all my heart for our Christmas tree. You must forgive him. He doesn't even know that he did anything wrong. He will never do it again, I promise. And, after all, he is the one that put the Forest fire out, you know?"

"He was?" Fuzzy Moss asked in surprise.

"Yes, he was. He had help, of course, but, he was their leader. He told them all what to do and he helped them do it," she said as she looked over to Little Bark. "Twiggy and you were very close, weren't you?" She asked him, her finger between her teeth.

"Yes, we were. I loved her very much. We were betreethed." he said, sadly, closing his eyes to keep the tears from flowing.

"Does betreethed mean that you were engaged to be married?"

"I guess that is what it means. It means that the two of us would love no others for the rest of our lives."

"Then it is you that I must convince to forgive my Father. I have a feeling deep down in my chest, right here," she said pointing to where her heart is, "That until you forgive him, Twiggy will never really be at rest in the Land of Sweet Waters and Cool Breezes. She would not want you to feel anger and hate toward him the way you do now. Twiggy wasn't like that, I don't think."

There was a long silence as each member of the Thicket searched their knots and their trunks. It was a pleasant quiet, though, as the Song-With-Wings sang and the Bushy Tails chirped and scolded as they ran up and down the trees limbs.

Old Moss frowned in thought as he looked at the Little Walk-To. Then his face cleared into a broad grin. "You know, Little Roots, that you are a very persuasive little thing. If I am not careful, you just might take my place as Thicket Councilor!" he said with a chuckle. "This, that you have asked us will require much thought and much discussion. We will let you know the next time you visit us. But, right now I think I can hear your Father returning. I hear only his footsteps though. I thought that he went to get help?"

Oh, I'm sure he got help. They just haven't gotten here yet," she reassured them as she ran up to her Father.

"Help is coming. They are flying a doctor and some paramedics in by helicopter. They should be here very soon. You stay here, I am going back over to the plane to see how they are," Jim hugged Wendy then ran over to the wrecked plane.

"Hello? Lady? Are you awake?" he called as he came around the front of the plane.

"Yes, yes, I'm still awake. My husband is waking up, too. He is in very much pain. I think his leg is broken. And, my son has a big gash on his head. It is not bleeding anymore, though; I put my bandana around it and tied it there real tight. But, I am still pinned in here under the dash. I can't move my legs........I can't feel my legs," she cried.

"The doctor is coming now, I can hear the helicopter. Be patient, we will have you out of there in no time at all." He tried to reassure her. But, the fact that she could not feel her legs was not good news as far as Jim was concerned. It was sounding more and more like her back or her neck might be broken.

The helicopter landed in the field right next to Old Moss. The doctor, two paramedics, two men and a nurse climbed out. The doctor and the nurse came running to the plane while the paramedics and the other two men unloaded a bunch of equipment. There were stretchers to carry the injured people on and tools to unpin the lady from the front of the plane. They brought fire extinguishers in case of fire and lots and lots of medical equipment, prepared for any kind of assistance that they might have to give. It all seemed very dramatic to Wendy, like she was sitting at home in her own living room, watching it all on television. It all seemed very unreal to her,

"The man and the boy are going to be just fine," the doctor told Jim when he pulled him aside out of hearing distance of the plane. "I am not so sure about the woman. I think her spine has been injured, but, I don't know for sure. I will have to wait for them to unpin her and then I can get her to the hospital to do some tests. Have you notified the FAA yet?"

"Not yet. I just called you and came back here immediately to be with them until you came in case they needed anything. I didn't know what I could do exactly, but if they needed me, I wanted to be here."

"I'm glad that you had the foresight not to move them, especially the woman. It could have been fatal," he patted Jim's back. "You had better notify them soon. There is nothing more to be done here for you, so you can go home if you want. The police are on their way to pick up any valuables and belongings they might have had on board. That way they won't get stolen by anyone or turn up missing. One of the men will stay here until they come," the doctor told him as he wiped his face with his handkerchief and started walking back to the plane.

"Yes, I had better get my daughter back home away from all this. It is not good for a child her age and in her condition to see this sort of thing. Besides, it is getting dark and a little too chilly. She didn't bring a coat and neither did I," Jim said as he looked over at Wendy.

"Well, thank you again for all you help," the doctor called back over his shoulder.

Jim walked over to Wendy who was standing at the edge of the field next to Old Moss.

"Shall we go home? I think the excitement is over for now," he told her, putting his arm around her to keep her warm.

"Is everyone alive?" she wanted to ask him, but couldn't.

"Boy! Those people are sure lucky to be alive!" Jim told her as though he had heard her question.

"Goodbye everyone! I will be back to see all of you very soon!" Wendy called to them as she and her Father walked down the path toward home.

"Goodbye! We will always be here!" Tickler chuckled."

"Now just what kind of remark was that?" Little Bark asked.

"A truthful one, I hope," he replied in earnest.

CHAPTER SIXTEEN

The sun was shining and pouring splashes of warmth on everyone in the Thicket. It was the beginning of a new day, perhaps something to look forward to. Hopefully no danger lurked nearby to unfold itself to make the day less perfect.

The snow was gone now and it left a soft, fresh ground where grass and flowers were poking their heads up with new sprouts here and there. The stream was swollen and overflowing its banks from the melting mountain snow, water rushing by with the eagerness and ferocity of spring.

"Little Bark, you grow taller with each passing day. My but you will soon be taller than me if you keep this up. You must have many knots by now," Old Moss told him in a proud voice.

"I have thirty-one, Old Teacher," he replied half-mindedly.

"THIRTY-ONE! That is almost as many as I have now and it has taken me many, many cycles to obtain them! You are a very special tree, Little Bark. The Great God of All Things must have a great purpose in mind for you," Old Moss told him as he brushed his trunk with one of his branches to rid himself of a pesky ant that had crawled up his trunk.

"Do you really think so? I don't think that I am so special. I'm just another tree standing in a Thicket enjoying the company and companionship of my family and friends," he said, quietly.

"You are, though, Little Bark. Can't you see that you have a great destiny and, the Great God of All Things must be in a hurry to have given you so many knots and so much knowledge, especially in such a short time? You and Fuzzy Moss will both be able to take the test soon. It will be a close one, mark, my words," he said as he brushed another ant from his trunk. Old Moss looked at Little Bark closely. "What is the matter, Little Bark? Your knots seem to be preoccupied today. What are you thinking about?"

"I had another dream last night," Little Bark told him, sadly.

"Was it the one about the bearded tree that spoke to you down in the big room in the cave?" Old Moss asked with anticipation.

"No, this one was different. Much different. I had it several times, over and over again. It seems as though I would just get done dreaming it and then, it would start all over again. It just kept coming back and coming back," he told his teacher with a sigh.

"What was this dream about that you had over and over again?" Old Moss asked, frowning in thought.

"I don't know exactly what it was. It was very hard to understand," he said looking very thoughtful for a moment before continuing. "It was horrible, and, well, all the trees…everywhere…as far as the eye could see…all of them became ill or something. And the Walk-To's tried to save us, but it was of no use. And, in the end something happened……I cannot quite picture it……it was too hazy…but, something happened, something that I think is probably very important. What does it mean, Old Moss?" he asked as he glanced uneasily at his Old Teacher.

"I don't really know, Little Bark," he said, trying to cover up the concern that was very evident on his face. "I'm sure that if it is a prediction, we will hear of it again. Put it out of your mind for now and enjoy the new season," he told him as he searched his knots for an answer to Little Bark's dream.

Dreams were not always as they seemed. Sometimes they had a hidden meaning and weren't at all what they had appeared to be in the beginning. Little Bark's dream could mean almost anything.

But, Old Moss was getting old, very old, and he should have paid more attention to Little Bark's dream.

"Something comes!" Many Branches warned them all.

"What is it?" Fuzzy Moss asked. Lately, every time someone or something came down the path, it meant trouble.

"I don't know yet. It has not come around the corner into my view," she told him, squinting and straining her eyes to see who or what it was.

"Is it Little Roots?" Little Bark asked in anticipation.

"No…… I don't think so. There, now I can see! Oh, My! It is two Walk-to's! I have never seen either of them before. Look! They are holding each others branches like we do, Old Log!' she told him with surprise.

"Oh, yes, I can see them, too!" Little Bark told her.

"I wonder what they want." Predictor asked in a skeptical tone, a worried look in his eyes.

"Just because a Walk-To comes down our path, doesn't mean that it is going to be something to worry about. They have been known to just walk on by, down the path without bothering us at all, you know," Old Moss said, thoughtfully.

"Okay then, why that skeptical tone in your voice?" Predictor asked.

"Well, there is one thing that I do know," Tickler speculated apprehensively, "and that is the fact that it won't be good, whatever it is that they want. And, another thing that I am sure about is that they will let us all know very soon."

"Look! They have stopped there by you, Tall Tales!" Old Log said, watching them uneasily.

"What is that sharp thing that the Walk-To has, Old Log?" Little Bark asked, thinking of the last time that a Walk-To had visited them with a sharp tool. The other Walk-To's tool was much larger, though.

"It is called a pocket knife. See how he unfolded it?" he asked, carefully watching the strange Walk-To with unblinking eyes.

"Does he think he is going to chop Tall Tales down with that puny little thing? It will take him days!" Little Bark said with a hint of sarcasm in his voice.

"Ouch! Stop that that hurts! You scrawny, dumb walking weed! Why on earth is he carving away at my trunk like that?" Tall Tales cringed, his breath short as he fought to control his temper. "Someday, someway, I will get my revenge on all these dumb, idiotic, stupid, brainless, unfeeling, walking weeds! How would they feel if I got myself one of those pocket knife things and carved on their bark? Don't they realize that it hurts?" he said, wincing with pain.

"Will he be alright, Old Moss?" little Bark asked, worried, looking over to his Old Teacher with tears in his eyes.

"Oh, yes," he said, a bit too cheerfully. "It happens all the time. Every now and then a Walk-To will come along and he will walk up to one of us and he will start to carve away at the bark on our trunks for no evident reason at all. The Walk-To's are bad that way. Maybe when Little Roots comes back, we can tell her how much this sort of thing hurts us and then she can tell all the other Walk-To's. And maybe…..just maybe, they will think before they do such foolish things," Old Moss said, hopefully. "Sometimes, but not very often, it can cause diseases to form in our bark."

"Do you really think that it would do any good to tell Little Roots? Do you actually think that anyone will listen to her?" Tickler asked.

"Perhaps I am dreaming, but we must always have hope. Without hope there is only desperation," he said, philosophically.

Soon, the Walk-To's disappeared back down the path from whence they came.

"I will be sore for days!" Tall Tales told them, looking around for sympathy.

"In more ways than one, no doubt," Old Moss chuckled.

"I wish that there was something that I could do to ease your pain," Weeper cried. "But, alas, my abilities are indeed small and I haven't the knowledge required to heal you. Wouldn't it be wonderful if we had a gold leaf from the tree named Healer in your story, Tall Tales?" she asked, absentmindedly.

Tall Tales gave her a weird look. "Maybe I will become like Old Tattoo who lives in a far away land across the big water. I have heard through whispers that he has been carved on for hundreds of years and that his carvings begin at his roots and they go all the way up his trunk to the very tip-top. I guess Walk-To's come from many, many searches (a search being approximately one mile) around the world just to look at him. But, they can't carve on him anymore because there is no more room on his trunk," he said, his thoughts wandering, wondering how that tree had suffered so much and still lived.

"You had better hope, Tall Tales that you do not become like him or else you would be constantly sore!" Tickler said with a chuckle.

"You would like that, wouldn't you?" Tall Tales felt his sarcasm and he responded in a cool, chilly voice. "It would complete your day to see me in constant pain, now wouldn't it?"

"Hey! There is no reason for you to be so nasty to me! I didn't carve on you, the Walk-To did!"

"Old Moss?" Little Bark interrupted them both as he called to his teacher.

"Yes, what is it, Little Bark?" Old Moss asked, paying only half attention to Little Bark. After all it was a beautiful day, a day that was meant for relaxing and enjoying the warmth of the sun, not concentrating on Thicket matters. Now was a good time to nap or at least do some heavy day dreaming?

"I have been thinking about the little Walk-To that we call Little Roots. You know the one that can speak to us and hear us?"

"Oh, for gnarled limbs sake, of course I know!" Old Moss said, indignantly. "What is the matter with you? Do you think that my sap doesn't run all the way to my knots anymore?"

'Ah–hah! That got his attention!' Little Bark mused, very proud of himself.

'What is the matter with Little Bark anyway? Does he think that I am getting so old that I can not remember from one minute to another?' Old Moss thought as he looked Little Bark up and down carefully. "Ah, but you are a sly one, Little Bark! You did that to get my full attention, did you not?" he asked in a sly voice.

"You are indeed a hard one to fool, wise, old, elusive teacher of many things," he complimented Old Moss.

"Why do you ask about Little Roots?" Old Moss gazed at him in wonder of what his answer would be. It was like a game of chess between the two of them sometimes, one trying to out-move the other.

"My day is now complete, Old One, for you have answered my question with a question again," he said with a sigh.

"Sorry," Old moss told him as he shrugged his branches.

"Apology greatfully accepted," Little Bark told him as he bowed.

"It was nothing. Please continue," Old Moss said, stuffily, his nose stuck up in the air like an aristocrat. "Why is it that Little Roots can talk to us and understand us?" he asked, curiously.

"It is hard to say why, although, many, many cycles ago, just after the Great Planting, there was an old tree prophet named Forsee's It. I think he is a distant relative of Predictor's, I don't really know. So don't quote me on that. Maybe I will ask him someday," he told him as his mind wandered. "Anyway, this old tree prophet, Forsee's It, foretold of a day in the last days of the trees when a Walk-To would be able to communicate with the trees. It is said that that Walk-To would try to get much accomplished in our last days to help the Walk-To's understand the many cruelties that they have made us all endure for cycles and cycles. And, maybe, our Little Roots is the one. I don't know. No other Walk-To has ever been known to communicate with us."

"Then you think, Old Moss, that there is little time left until we are all lifted up to the Land of Sweet Waters and Cool Breezes?" Little Bark sounded worried.

"Time is something that is measured differently by all things. The pretty Flying Flower measures time by mere seconds because its life is so short. And, we measure out time in cycles, many cycles, because most of us live for a very, very long time. It is hard to hold time in your limbs and say 'at this time or at that time'. Time eludes us all. Yet time is precious to all things. It can be your friend or your enemy, depending on what is happening at that moment. The time of The Great Lifting may be many, many cycles away or it may happen in the next few seconds. If The Great God of All Things had wanted us to know the exact time, he would have told us."

"Then, you do not think that Little Roots is the one that Forsee's It spoke of?" Little bark asked.

"Now, Now! You put words in my mouth that I did not say! That is not what I said at all, is it? I did not actually say one way or another! But, yes, I do think that she is the one. Many, many things indicate that she is. The main thing is that we used to number the earth like the stars number the skies, and now even the Walk-To's seem to out number us. We are very fast becoming extinct. Soon we will all vanish from the face of the earth without a seed left to carry on. It is sad in some ways to think about it, but, happy in other ways," Old Moss said in a far away voice.

"But, how can one small Walk-To help us? She does not even seem to be able to take care of herself, let alone the entire world!" Little Bark said, bitterly.

"You forget so quickly, Young One. Did not the Little Walk-To help us already with the flying Stinky-go?" he reminded him gently.

"Yes, but, that was different," Little Bark said, shyly.

"Why was it different?"

"Because it was to help other Walk-to's. It did not help us in any way."

"This is true, but, she still came to us when we needed her and she will again, too."

Little Bark was beside himself. Here he was, trying to gain as many knots and as much knowledge as he could so that someday he could be the next Thicket Councilor, and now he learns that there will be no trees for him to council!

Old Moss looked at Little Bark with compassion as though he knew what he was thinking. "One small Walk-To can grow into one very big, strong Walk-To, Little Bark. They do not remain small and puny all their lives. Of course, they don't get as big and strong as we do, either. But, I think that someday she will help us. It has been foretold, hasn't it? And, no other Walk-To has ever or will ever communicate with us. So it is only natural that she be the one."

"But, maybe her Father will not let her come back here," he said, challenging Old Moss again.

"Oh, I think you are underestimating the little Walk-To. She has much bravery in her trunk. She will find a way!" he promised."

"You like her, don't you, Old Moss?"

"Yes, I really do. I miss her, too. She is very special, just like Twiggy said a long time ago."

"Yes, Twiggy did say that, didn't she?" he said as his thoughts wandered. "Old Moss, help me if you will. My thoughts on this are all jumbled up. Maybe there was a great purpose for Twiggy's ending. Maybe she had to end so that Little Roots could hear her screaming. Didn't she say that she could not hear us or understand us until Twiggy screamed? And, didn't she also say that she can no longer communicate with other Walk-To's? How can she possibly help us if she cannot talk to other Walk-To's?"

"Only the Great God of All Things knows how Little Roots will help us, Little Bark. And, as for Twiggy, yes, I think her ending was but a beginning for all of us, though I think it will be a sad one," he said as he stretched his old limbs. "I am getting very old, too old, I'm afraid. My trunk is becoming weak and it no longer wants to hold up my branches. Such is the way of things," he said as he relaxed and slept in the warmth of the gentle spring sunlight.

"But, I have more questions, Old Moss!" he demanded.

"Not now. Later. I must sleep now."

Little Bark looked over to his Father. "Teachers, especially Old Moss, can be so frustrating at times. He is enough to shake my leaves to the ground!"

"HA! Ha! Ho! Haw!" Old Log laughed at Little Bark.

"How am I supposed to increase my knowledge if I cannot ask questions?" Little Bark asked in a frustrated voice.

"You will never learn anything at all, Little Bark, unless you first learn HOW to think. You cannot ask all your questions at once, because it would give you too much to contemplate. You must now think about and analyze what Old Moss has just told you. Then you can ask more questions. But, first you must THINK!"

What should he think about? The little Walk-To? The big Walk-to? Twiggy? Time? The Great Lifting? Maybe he would just sleep for a while along with Old Moss.

"I have had a dream, Old Friend," Predictor called to Old Moss in a quiet voice, just loud enough for him to hear. What he was about to say was not meant for everyone's ears.

"What was your dream about, Good Friend?" he asked, hesitantly, he had a feeling that Predictor's dream would be much the same as Little Bark's had been.

"This may sound a bit funny, but, I'm not quite sure what it was all about, some of it was very hazy, very hazy, indeed. It was a bad dream, a nightmare, if you will. It was very hard to understand. But I shall try to sort it all out into something we may be able to decipher and comprehend. You see all of us, all the trees in the whole world became very ill, very, very ill, and we began to end, one after the other and sometimes whole clusters at one time, as it were. The Walk-To's did everything in their power to save us, but, alas, it was too late. After the sickness had touched every tree, there were but two left alive in the whole world," he said, sadly.

"Do you know who the two were that were left, Good Friend?"

"No, to be sure, no, I do not. The image was too hazy and fuzzy like it had a strange mist hovering over it, but not on it. I could not see at all clearly."

"What happened to the two trees that were left standing? Did they end?"

"Again, Old Friend, I felt a need to rub my eyes as though a film had clouded over them, keeping me from seeing my dream at all clearly. All I could see, as it were, is what I have already revealed to you, nothing more."

Old Moss drew in a deep breath as though it were his last. "It is happening all over again, isn't it? We are doomed to end soon. I can feel it. It is like a great dark shadow has enveloped us or, perhaps a tunnel....a long, dark tunnel with a light way at the other end. And, no matter how hard we try to reach it, it remains just out of our reach."

"It seems so, yes, indeed. Hard times are upon us and maybe our very ending. I dare say, I wish I knew just how much time was to be allowed us...a sorry business, this....this short journey we call life. It seems as though there are to be no more good times allowed us. These, indeed, must be the last days that have been foretold."

"Yes, my fear finds identity with yours, I am afraid. We are always in constant danger, danger from fire, disease, the great winds, flooding and Twisters. But, most of all, the Walk-To's. We have little hope of surviving such odds as those. We have stood this ground for many cycles. It is time for a change," Old Moss said, wearily.

Predictor looked at Old Moss. Never had he seen his Old Friend so drawn out and weary. He realized that he must have felt helpless and inadequate. If he could bare his Old Friend's burden, he would gladly take it from him. But, as it were, only Old Moss could carry that load. "Old Friend, do you remember the time, long ago, when I was upset and I knew not what to do? Do you remember what you told me? You said that I must remain strong in my faith and keep up my hope. For, if we lose hope, then we are only left with desperation. The Great God of All Things has a purpose for everything that He does. I think the time of the Great Lifting is almost upon us," Predictor speculated as he stared at the little particles of dirt that were floating in the air in the stream of bright sun light in front of him.

"Again, Good Friend, you have snatched the thought right out of my knots. We are beginning to think alike. It is probably due to the years of constant association, don't you think?"

"That could be, yes, and in all probability it is. I wonder," Predictor frowned in thought, "what the next life will be like? Will we know one another?"

"Hmmmmmm......I have thought much on this matter and could probably think as long as three more lifetimes and not come up with an answer. We shall all know when that day comes, though."

Hours passed by as the two old friends spoke of old times and what may lie ahead in the near future, but, soon they both tired and slipped slowly into the land of dreams. A land where reality wasn't allowed, which was just as well for both of them.

"Old Log?" Many Branches called to her husband as she gently tapped on his trunk with her branch. "Do you hear something coming down our path?"

Old Log perked his ears up toward the curve in the path and listened for a moment. "Do you know, Many Branches, this path has become well worn with the many visits of the Walk-To's. It is almost as bad as the long gray road that they drive their Stinky-go's on. I suppose that some day I will get used to it, though at this time, I doubt it very much."

"Maybe we could get some stinkers to chase them all away. Wouldn't that be a funny sight to see them running in every direction?" Many Branches said as she laughed.

"Yes, it would be funny, but not for Little Roots. Everyone else is okay, but, not Little Roots."

"Everyone except our Little Roots," Many Branches agreed.

"Ahhhh! It is our special Walk-To! See? It's her, it's Little Roots! She has come back!" Old Log said, eagerly.

"Is it?" cried Little Bark in excitement.

"Hello, everyone!" 'Wendy told them all, cheerfully. "I'm back! See, I told you that I would be back, and I am!"

"See," Old Moss bragged to Predictor. "I told you she would be back to see us, remember?"

"Yes, I remember," Predictor smiled at his old friend.

"Old Mandy tries to keep me all locked up inside the house, but, sometimes I can out smart her," she said proudly as she sat next to Little Bark. "She thinks I am napping upstairs in my room. But, I'm not as you can see. I had an errand to run for myself. Here," she said as she dug around in her pocket for a moment and withdrew a piece of yellow paper, "This is for you, a present, just for you. I wrote it the other night when my Father took me back home. It's a poem. Would you like me to read it to you?"

"What kind of poem?" Little Bark asked, curiously.

"It's just a regular poem, I guess. It is from my heart to you. I wrote it because I feel so bad about Twiggy," she said, sorrowfully.

"Please read it to me then, I love Rhymer's poems."

"Okay" she said happily,

"Once there was this little tree,
Just about as perfect as it could be.
Once there was a man and his family
Who saw the perfect little tree.
So he took an axe and began to chop.
As the little tree shook from bottom to top.
'Ouch! Oh my goodness,' said the tree
'Why are you doing this to me?'
Twiggy was crying, her tears had begun,
Because as he chopped, her sap did run.
He chopped her down with axe to scar,
As she waved back to friends afar.
The man put Twiggy in a stand,
Decorated her and she looked so grand!
Twiggy stood there so proud and pretty
With all her balls and lights to see!
"I'm much prettier than any other tree!
If only my friends could see me!"
Christmas had soon come and gone,
And the man laid Twiggy out on his lawn.
"Now what has happened, they don't want me?"
Cried the perfect little Christmas tree.
"I'm not so grand anymore, not at all,
I could have lived so sturdy and tall

But, alas, it is over, all I can do is die

And the little tree began to cry."

"That was very beautiful, Little Roots. I have not heard so nice a poem in all my cycles. You must have loved Twiggy very much," Old Moss told her, compassionately.

"Yes, I did. I loved her so very much. She was so pretty and proud. Of course, I never did have a chance to talk to her, but, I always thought she was something special....very special, like a friend or something," she thought to herself for a moment. "I really can't quite put my finger on it. To me she was just very special. I could feel it in my....my.... Hmmmmmm.....I could just feel it, that's all. I guess it is just one of those things that can't be explained, only felt......here," she said as she pointed to the middle of her chest. "Deep down inside," she tried to explain.

"Ahhhh! She also said that very same thing about you, Little Roots. She could not quite come up with a reason, either, but, she said that there was something very unusual about you," Old Moss nodded as though to affirm his own convictions.

"She did? Hmmmmmm...Old Moss? That is your name isn't it?" she asked him.

"Yes, that is what I am called,' he told her proudly.

"Well...Old Moss....." she said as though she were testing his name on her tongue. "Why is it that you don't call me by my real name? My real name is Wendy, you know," she informed him.

"Yes, I have often wondered why your Father would call you such and inappropriate name. There is nothing about you that even suggests that you have anything to do with the wind," Old Moss stated matter-of-factly. "We name each other for the things that remind us of that one certain tree. Now, for example, Many Branches was named because she has an unusual amount of branches and Weeper because she cries a lot of the time. Thin-As-Grass is called Thin-As-Grass because she is so puny and sickly. Do you understand, Little Roots?"

"Yes, I think so....yes, I do understand. You called me Little Roots because of my toes, am I right?" Wendy asked him with raised eyebrows and a sparkle in her eyes.

"Yes, you are correct. Your toes.....funny little things..... Anyway, your toes are very tiny compared to our great roots," he told her, proudly. "I do not see how you can stand up even in a gentle breeze with such spindly little things. They don't look like they are much good for anything. Pardon me....Please don't take offense at what I have just said. I do not mean to make fun of them," he said, apologizing to her.

"Oh, don't worry about it at all; I take no offense at the truth. But, it's easy," she laughed. "We have what we call balance. We learn this when we are but little babies. It is our balance that holds us up, not our roots or toes, whichever you want to call them. Our toes help us a little, of course."

"If I may beg your pardon, and ask but one small question without being a bother and without being in the way, after all, I am but a day-to-day tree with very little knowledge and no sense at all. I would, please, beg your pardon, but, how do you keep your bark so clean, Little Roots?" Weeper asked in her apologetic voice. "You need not tell me if I have offended you in any way or if you deem my question not worthy of an answer, and in that case I beg your pardon once again and will be silent from now on."

"What?" Wendy asked, somewhat puzzled. "What do you mean?"

"I have offended you. I am so sorry. Please forgive me. Like I have stated previously, I am but a day-to-day tree and I am not at all well versed in my manners and I often hurt those I do not want to hurt. Forgive me, please," she cried.

"Oh, no, you have not offended me, I just don't know exactly what you mean," Wendy said, kindly.

"Your bark, how do you keep it so smooth and clean?"

"Oh! You mean my skin! Oh, I just take a bath!"

"What is a bath," Thin-As-Grass asked her.

"Hmmmmmm....." she thought as she held her chin in her hand and looked up at the sky as though her answer would come from the clouds. "Well....I have a big tub.....and I pour lots and lots of warm water in it....then I take all my clothes off and I get in it and I wash myself," she said, trying to explain as best she could.

"You mean swim, don't you?" Tall Tales asked her in a correcting tone.

"Oh, no...... the tub is not big enough for me to swim in. No, I just wash my skin off with a wash rag and soap and then I rinse the soap off and then I get back out of the tub and I dry myself off. Then, I put on some fresh, clean clothes. It makes me feel very good all over."

"There is a story, you know, of a tree named swimmer. He got his name from his Thicket because he loved to swim. And, one day, he left the Thicket and he went to the big water and he swam thousands of miles across to the other side to the East. And, there on the shore stood a huge tree with long, low limbs and in her branches there lived many colorful Songs-With-Wings. And…"

"Excuse me but, what is a Song-With-Wings?" Wendy interrupted him."

"It is one of those, up there," he told her as he pointed to a bird sitting on one of Old Log's limbs.

"Oh, we call those birds."

"Yes….well, anyway….where was I…Oh, yes…And higher up in the middle of her trunk, far out on her limbs were hundreds of Do-As-I-Do's scurrying around from limb to limb, chattering and swinging happily to and fro. Swim…."

"Excuse me, but, what is a do-as-I-do?" Wendy interrupted him again as Tickler burst out laughing.

"It is a strange animal that looks a lot like you, only it has hair all over its body and it has a very long tail with which it hangs in the trees upside down," he explained to her as he gave Tickler a dirty look.

"Oh, you mean a monkey!" she said, happily.

"Yes, if you say so…. Anyway, as I was saying, Swimmer liked the Do-As-I-Do's so much, that he decided to go ashore and stay and make his home there. So, he dug his roots down very deep into the sandy shore and then he waited for some of the Do-As-I-Do's to come over to him and play in his branches among his leaves. But, alas, a few hours later, a Cruel Ripper, the only one that Swimmer had ever seen in his life, came along…"

"Excuse me, please. What is a cruel ripper?" Wendy interrupted him, again as Tickler laughed so hard that he nearly toppled over to the ground holding his trunk as though he was in a great deal of pain.

"Tickler, you had better shut up or I will have Little Roots put lumps all over your trunk!" he said, menacingly.

"What is a cruel ripper?" she asked him again, impatiently, ignoring their arguing.

"It is a long and very large cat that roars. It doesn't meow. It has very long fangs, cruel eyes, long sharp claws and it has hair all over its body. Now…may I get on with the telling of my story?"

"Of course," she whispered in a sad, apologetic voice. Tears welled up in her eyes. She did not want to anger her new friends. "I'm sorry, but, how am I to know what your story is about if I do not know who and what the things are that you are talking about?"

"Well, it is okay," he reassured her as he saw how upset she had become. "Anyway, it came along and saw Swimmer standing there, tall, strong and proud. It looked him up and down all over. Then, it began to claw and scratch at his bark to sharpen its nails and to mark its territory. So, Swimmer uprooted himself and swam back to plant his roots in his own thicket, never to swim again. He still has no bark on one side of his trunk. So, now, they call him No Bark. So, you see, Little Roots, while the grass might seem to be greener somewhere else, it isn't always the actual case. It seems greener everywhere else when in all actuality it is better where you are right now. We all seek happiness and we think that by running away to another place, we will find it. Sometimes, very rarely though, we can find it elsewhere, but it is better to remain where you are and let happiness find you."

"What do you mean?" Wendy asked as her eyes narrowed in thought.

"I think what he is trying to say is that you should be satisfied with what The Great God of All Things has chosen for you in life and not long for something else," Old Moss explained, carefully.

"Oh," she said thoughtfully. "Kind of like me wanting to be a tree all my life and now I am very close to being one, but I had to give up something very dear to me to have my wish," she said, thinking about not being able to talk to her Father ever again.

"Yes, that's it, I think," Old Moss agreed.

"I don't mean to change the subject but, I have a very important question to ask all of you," she said as she glanced around uneasily from one to another. "I want to know if you have decided to forgive my Father."

"We have talked much upon this subject in your absence, Little Roots. We have all decided unanimously to do as you have asked. We forgive him. You were right when you said that Twiggy would have wanted it that way. Now, maybe, she will rest in peace," Old Moss told her absentmindedly.

"We have something to ask you, also, Little Roots," Old Log told her. "Go over to where Tall Tales is standing and look at his trunk."

Wendy did as she was told. "Oh, My! Who did this to you? Who would do such a terrible thing?" she asked him anxiously as she gently touched the spot where the Walk-To's had carved their initials.

"Two Walk-To's came here the other day and they stopped and carved on my bark. It happens to trees all the time, but it is the first time it has ever happened to me," he said, a bit snidely, looking at his bark where they had carved it away.

"They also take hard spikes and nails and they hammer them into our trunks as though we are bad and they are punishing us for it."

"Something must be done about this! It cannot continue!" Wendy protested, unable to hold back the anger and disgust she felt toward her fellow man.

"This is what we had hoped," Predictor volunteered. "We had all hoped that maybe you could tell all the walk-To's how much it hurts us when they carve on us like that. Tall Tales is still sore from it and he will be for a long time."

"But, how can I tell them? I cannot talk to them anymore," she told them as she threw her hands up in the air in frustration.

There was a long pause as everyone thought about the new obstacle they must somehow overcome.

"Might I offer a suggestion?" Little Bark volunteered as he looked around at everyone. "Did you not say, Little Roots that you wrote that poem that you gave to me today?" he asked as he rubbed his trunk in thought.

"Yes, I wrote it, all by myself, too! There might be a few misspelled words in it but I can read it very clearly. I am at the top of my class in spelling." She said proudly as she stuck her nose up in the air.

"Well, then, can you write notes to other Walk-To's? Can you give them messages the way you gave me the poem?" Little Bark speculated a bit apprehensively. He was afraid that maybe there were very few Walk-To's that could read and write.

"Oh, yes! Why didn't I ever think of that?" she frowned in thought. "And, I wonder why my Father never thought of it, either?"

she asked in a puzzled voice as though she was just speaking to herself. "Hmmmmmm.... I must ask him in a note when I return home. Maybe he is just like me and he just never thought about it," she concluded with a sigh.

"Will you tell the Walk-To's not to carve or hammer on us? Will you tell them how much it hurts us?" Tickler asked her wondering if she would do this for them.

"Sure! You bet I will! You know, don't you, that my Father is a Forest Ranger and he can get a lot done for you. He knows a lot of important peo.........Walk-To's," she said proudly. "Maybe he can get this whole Forest declared a National Forest! Do you know what a National Forest is?" she asked as she looked around at each of them.

"We have heard through whispers that it is a place where the trees and all the animals are protected," Old Moss said, not too confident that what he had heard was true.

"Yes, that is true! Wouldn't it be wonderful? Then no one could carve on you, or hammer nails in your trunks, or cut you down, or burn you or anything." she said as she twirled around in excitement.

"It has been but a dream that we have all shared but never expected to realize," Old Moss told her in an old, tired voice. "I hope I will live long enough to see it happen."

Well, I guess I had better go back home before they miss me and come looking for me. I will try, tonight when my Father comes home from work, to write him a note," She promised them all. "Well, goodbye everyone! I will be back!" she said as she started down the path. And then she suddenly turned around and came running back to Little Bark. I almost forgot about this" she said as she took something else out of her other pocket. She handed it to Little Bark.

"What is this...Oh, My God, it is Twiggy and she is all dressed up in lights and balls and everything you said that you had dressed her in, but, I don't understand? Where is she? How come I can see her on this piece of paper?"

"It is a photograph of her. I took it at Christmas time."

"My Twiggy, my little Twiggy. May I have this to keep for all time?" he asked her as he held the picture close to his trunk.

"Yes, you can, but I think the others might want to see it, too.

So Little Bark passed the picture of Twiggy around to everyone.

"Thank you for this image of Twiggy, I will always keep it close to my trunk just like I will your poems."

"Good Bye everyone. I am on my way home now." Wendy told them once again.

"Goodbye for now Little Roots, and thank you for the beautiful poem and the wonderful image of Twiggy," Little Bark called to her.

"I will bring you another poem when I return next time." She called over her shoulder as she disappeared around the corner.

And, when she had completely disappeared around the corner and out of sight, Tickler burst out once again in uncontrollable laughter.

"You had better be very careful who and what you laugh at, Tickler," Many Branches warned him. "Tall Tales has made himself a very valuable friend today."

"Ha! Ha! Ho! Ha! I…..cannot…quit……laughing!

"I hope some buzzers nest in your branches! Then you will not be able to get any sleep ever!" Tall Tales snickered, menacingly.

"You would like that wouldn't you? Your day would be complete, wouldn't it?" he asked glaring at Tall Tales in anger.

"Oh there is going to be a terrible argument. I just know there is and it is probably all my fault. I am the one that began asking questions, so it must be my fault. Forgive me please, for I am but a day to day tree, not knowing how to think clearly before speaking," Weeper cried in a worried voice.

"I think they are done arguing," Old Log said firmly as he stared them both down with cold steely eyes.

CHAPTER SEVENTEEN

It was late afternoon as the Songs-With-Wings were singing and fluttering, hopping from branch to branch as thy busied themselves with he yearly task of building their nests in the branches of the trees in Old Moss' Thicket. The Bushy Tails were scurrying here and there scolding anything and everything that happened to catch their mischievous eyes.

Life was still renewing itself as all the trees continued to burst with brand new fresh green leaves. And, even Rhymer looked perkier this spring.

Look! The Lady Bugs are out!" Rhymer said excitedly as he watched a little Lady Bug crawl on one of his leaves. "She reminds me of a poem I once thought up in my knots a long time ago. Would you care to hear it?" he asked apprehensively as he glanced around at everyone.

"I think that I would like to hear it," Tickler told him as he looked Tall Tales boldly in the eyes in defiance.

"Yes, I think I would like to hear it, also," Tall Tales said, undaunted by Tickler's steely gaze.

There was a long silence as everyone looked at Tall Tales in awe and wonder.

"What did you say?" Rhymer asked as he looked at him in surprise. "You actually want to hear one of my rhymes?" he asked as though in shock.

"Yes, yes, I do," Tall Tales said a bit too dramatically as he looked at Tickler.

"I don't know if I want to tell it now. You took all the fun out of it. After all, I only think them up to irritate you," he said, sadly.

"Please tell us your rhyme," Many Branches coaxed him.

"Well, okay," and he began his poem;
"Oh! Lady Bug! Oh! Lady Bug!
With spots along your wings
With little legs like little pegs
Clinging to countless things!
You walk along with wings like crowns
Among flowers with their rainbow gowns.
You waddle here, you waddle there,
And you are welcomed most anywhere.
Oh! Lady Bug! Oh! Lady Bug!
With feet so tiny and small,
With button nose and curled up toes
You climb a tree so tall!
You look like your neighbor,
The spotted frog
Who lives next door
To the dotted dog!
Oh! Lady Bug! Oh Lady Bug!
How carelessly you flutter by
To visit with the queen
Madam Spotted Butterfly.
Your freckled friends
Are up at dawn
The spotted leopard
The freckled fawn.
Your next of kin your freckled friend,
A polk-a-dotted pony.
A giant staff is a freckled Giraffe,
With neck that looks so phony.
Oh! Lady Bug! Oh! Lady Bug!
Freckled things are such silly things!
Go east! Go west! Go way up high!
Away you fly up in the sky!
Away, way far away!
Return to me another day!"

"That was very beautiful, Rhymer. Did you think that up all by yourself?" Manny Branches asked him.

"Yes, I did, and thank you, I'm glad you enjoyed it," Rhymer told her politely.

"We all enjoyed it," Tall Tales said as he glared at Tickler.

"Yes, we did, didn't we?" he retorted snidely.

"You two stop this instant!" Old Log ordered them in a cool chilly voice. "Tall Tales, you know you would feel very lost in your trunk if anything ever happened to Tickler. And, Tickler, you know you would feel the same way about Tall Tales if anything should ever happen to him. Why can't you two try to get along?" Old Log asked in a friendlier manner.

Tickler and Tall Tales just stood there looking at one another in shame like two small Seedlings who have just been reprimanded.

"I have another rhyme if you all would like to hear it?" Rhymer asked, hesitantly, afraid that someone would reproach him.

"We are all listening, Little Friend," Old Log said kindly as he looked sternly at both Tickler and Tall Tales.

And, Rhymer began, again.......

"A sprinkle of pink on a Cherry tree
And flowers blooming as far as the eye can see,
It must be Spring.
A nice cool breeze on a hot, dry day
And all the children outside to play.
It must be Summer.
There is a dash of green and a splash of gold
A few dots of red as the wind blows cold,
It must be Autumn.
A sprinkle of rain as the cold wind blows,
The fresh, fluffy flakes of the white fleecy snows,
It must be Winter.
The four seasons come and go,
From budding Spring to Winter's snow.
It must be the miraculous work of God."

"That, also, was very beautiful, Rhymer. You are very talented for such a short bush," Many Branches told him fondly with a smile on her face.

"Thank you....I try very hard," he told her, proudly.

Wendy ran home as fast as her legs would carry her after she had talked to the trees. It wasn't very late in the evening when her Father arrived home from work.

"Hi! Pumpkin!" he said as he pinched her nose, "How was your day? Was it good?"

"IT WAS GREAT!" Wendy wrote on a piece of paper and handed it to him.

"Wh….What's this? I didn't dare to hope that you could still write!"

Wendy smiled at him. She could see by the expression on his face that he loved her very much even after all the trouble she had been to him these past months.

"Oh, Wendy! I love you so much! And, now I can talk to you again," he told her as he hugged her, tears running down his face. Happy tears. "I didn't think you were able to write to me. Dr. Stewart said that you would probably never be able to communicate in any way at all as long as you were autistic."

"I CANNOT TALK YET BUT I CAN WRITE EVERYTHING. AND FATHER, GUESS WHAT? I CAN TALK TO THE TREES! I REALLY CAN!" she wrote on the paper and then she handed it to her Father.

"What do you mean, you can talk to the trees?" he asked, puzzled.

"I CAN TALK TO THE TREES! AND THEY CAN TALK BACK TO ME!"

"Maybe I should take you back in to see the doctor," he told her as he felt her head for any sign of a fever.

"I'M NOT SICK. REALLY I'M NOT. PLEASE FATHER…. PLEASE BELIEVE ME! I CAN PROVE IT TO YOU."

"How can you prove it to me?" he asked, worried that she was suffering from a mental breakdown.

"COME WITH ME TO THE FOREST AND I WILL ASK THEM TO DO SOMETHING SO THAT YOU CAN SEE. THEY WANT TO KNOW IF YOU WILL MAKE THEM A NATIONAL FOREST SO THAT NO ONE CAN CARVE ON THEM OR HAMMER NAILS INTO THEIR TRUNKS OR CUT THEM DOWN."

"Just making them a National Forest does not guarantee that no one will do these things, you know. People are not good in that way. Just because we post signs and warn people, doesn't mean that they aren't going to do it. There are people who don't care about such laws and regulations," he warned her.

"YES, I SUPPOSE SO. BUT IT CAN HELP, CAN'T IT?"

"Yes, it can help," he said thinking about how he was going to handle this manifestation she was having about being able to talk to the trees. It was a very delicate and difficult situation that he was in. What could he do? 'I guess I will just have to follow her out to the trees and then when they don't reply with anything, she will see that it was all a silly dream that she was having and then maybe she will be herself again,' he thought to himself.

"WELL CAN WE GO TALK TO THEM?"

"Tomorrow," he told her. "Okay?"

Wendy nodded her head sadly. She wanted to go then…right then, but, she was happy that her Father had even agreed to the next day.

That evening, Jim made many phone calls and wrote many letters. He didn't quite believe that Wendy could talk to the trees, but, he had decided that if it was important enough to her to make believe that she could, then he had decided it was worth his time and effort to petition the government.

Hours passed as the trees talked and joked among themselves of old times and what was ahead of them in the future.

"Pardon my intrusion into your thoughts, Old Moss, as I have a question of great importance, if only to myself. After all, I am but a day-to-day tree and my questions are frivolous and probably unworthy of your most slight attention. If it would be better to ask at another time, I beg your pardon, but, if this is an opportune time, I beg your indulgence, please," Weeper said, apologetically.

"What may I help you with?" Old Moss asked her gently. He loved Weeper very much. She was unlike any of the other members of the Thicket and he enjoyed talking to her. He really couldn't understand why she always belittled herself the way she did. He thought Weeper was really quite intelligent.

"Can you tell me, please, what is God's purpose in having us communicate with Little Roots?"

"This I cannot say for sure. I have thought of little else since she first spoke with us," he told her with a heavy sigh. "I do think, though, that the time is coming for the Great Lifting. Very soon, very soon, indeed."

"Yes, this is what I have concluded, also. Was it not said, long ago, that we would be able to communicate with a Walk-To just before the Great Lifting?"

"Yes, this is true, but, who is to say what a short time is to the Great God of All Things? It might mean a season or a cycle or a thousand cycles. What would time mean to the Great God of All Things? He is not governed by such things as time, He has all of eternity," Old Moss explained.

"Eternity is very hard for me to imagine. Something never ending is perhaps beyond comprehension for all of us."

"Yes, perhaps it is," he said, trying to imagine time never ending. His face saddened.

"I have upset you with my dumb questions. For this, I am very sorry. I should have thought of all the information that I had before I came to my conclusions. You are so right, so right indeed. It was never how long a short time is. Again, I have worried unnecessarily. But, I am but a day-to-day tree of no importance, what-so-ever," "So, please, forgive my intrusion."

"You did not intrude, Weeper. And, your questions have never been stupid. You belittle yourself unnecessarily."

"I do not mean to complain or belittle myself, but I do know my limitations. And, I do not like to intrude when there is a possibility that that tree might not want to be bothered at that particular moment. It is much easier to ask later at a more opportune time. If I have offended you by seeming to belittle myself, again, I apologize. My greatest aim in life is to please my fellow trees whenever I am able to," and, with that last thought, she cut her line of communication to Old Moss as neatly and as surely as a brand new razor cuts a strand of hair.

'She's a funny one,' Old Moss thought to himself, 'so different from everyone else in the Thicket.'

The sun was about an hour and a half from crawling behind the hills to slumber for the night. It left ever changing shadows from the trees and bushes as it slowly crept across the sky. It was fun for the trees to imagine what the shadows resembled.

"Shhhhh!" Old log warned everyone, suddenly. "I hear footsteps. And, there is more than one Walk-To, I think. It is not our Little Roots, either. The footsteps are too heavy for one so small."

All were looking down the path when two strange Walk-to's slowly approached them. They stopped at every tree along the way and looked them over very carefully, inspecting them up and down. One of them had a very strange, round, funny looking thing is its limb.

"I don't see any here, do you?" one Walk-To said to the other.

"No, I don't think so," he said as he looked around. "Ahhhh! Yes, I do. There is one over there," he said as he pointed to Old Moss.

"Better mark it, then, but make sure. We don't want to mark any more trees than is absolutely necessary."

"Okay," he agreed as he walked over to where Old Moss was standing and shook the round cylinder and sprayed yellow paint on Old Moss' trunk.

"What was that all about?" Old Log asked curiously as the Walk-To's continued checking all the trees as they continued down the path away from their Thicket.

"I don't know," Tall Tales said in a worried voice.

"I have heard….something…..cycles ago, about this, but, I cannot remember what it was. I think it was bad. It has to be bad…..Walk-to's don't mark trees because they like them, I'm sure. If a Walk-To does something like this," he said looking at the yellow mark, "I guarantee it is not good, no good at all. There is very little that the Walk-To's do that is good," Predictor warned them.

"Perhaps we should pick another Thicket Councilor soon," Old Moss said sadly.

"Do not talk that way. I, for one, am tired of hearing about ending. I have nightmares about it all the time," Weeper told him as she looked around at all of them. "Excuse me, please, my outburst is quite unpardonable, I'm sure. Pay no attention to me; my nightmares are of no importance. I was merely expressing my inner feelings. I think we should think about living for a change."

"I, too, am tired of hearing about sad things. First it was Old Sap and then it was Twiggy. Next I think that I shall wither and end from no sun and no water. Why, my roots are even brittle!" Thin-As-Grass complained.

"You do look unusually thin and scrawny," Tickler teased her.

"Now, don't be telling her that, Tickler. You will make her worry unnecessarily,' Many Branches told him.

"I, for one, will ask Little Roots when she comes back if she knows what it means," Little Bark stated matter-of-factly.

"I don't think that she will ever be coming back," Tall Tales told him, flustered at the thought of her interrupting him again.

"Oh, come now, I think you are wrong. I think she will be back," Little Bark stated, firmly, but good naturedly.

"You think that you are so clever, don't you, the way you cuddle up to her and hog her all to yourself!" Tall Tales told him, jealously.

"What do you mean? The last time she was here, you did all the talking!" Little Bark informed him, none too gently.

"Oh, no I didn't!" he retorted, testily.

"Oh, yes you did," Old Moss said as he broke his trend of thought.

"I did?" Tall Tales said as though he had been stuck by a pin in his trunk.

"Yes, you did. Don't you remember, she kept asking you questions and interrupting you all the time?" Old Moss asked him as he tried to refresh Tall Tales memory.

"Yes.....now that you mention it, I do, but, she was very interested in my story. That is the only reason she asked so many questions," he said, proudly.

"No, it wasn't," Little Bark told him, firmly. "She just didn't know what we call some things so she had to ask questions. The Walk-To's call the Song-With-Wings....birds, and the Do-As-I-Do's......monkeys and the......"

"Yes, yes, I know all that!" Tall Tales said rudely as he interrupted Little Bark in mid sentence. "But, if she wasn't interested in my story, she would not have listened and, therefore, she would not have asked so many questions!" he stated, folding his branches in front of him in triumph.

"Not so fast, Tall Tales, maybe she was just being polite," he suggested.

"Have you ever known a Walk-To to be polite?"

"No, but, there has never, ever been a Walk-To like our Little Roots, either. She is special and should, therefore, be thought of as special. And, I still say that she was just being polite," Little Bark snapped.

"Enough! Both of you! My nerves are wearing thin, almost as thin as Thin-As-Grass!" Tickler teased.

"Oh, please! Let's not start picking on poor Thin-As-Grass," Many Branches warned them.

"What started all this anyway?" Fuzzy Moss asked in a puzzled voice.

"The Walk-To started it, I believe, when he marked my trunk with that smelly yellow stuff," Old Moss said, sadly.

They all looked at one another, not daring to speak. That is....except for Old Moss.

"I really think that soon we should pick a new councilor for the Thicket. I feel a definite urgency about it, as though something dreadful were going to happen to me," Old Moss told them, sadly.

"There is still much time, Old Friend," Predictor consoled his friend of many cycles and many hardships.

"Are you sure, Good Friend?" Old Moss asked him in a very tired voice.

They all slept a bit fitfully as they dreamt about the Walk-To with the Yellow smelly stuff.

The next day was a slow day with everyone thinking about Little Roots and the fact that through her things might change for the better in their Thicket.

"It would be so wonderful if we could be made a National Forest," Thin-As-Grass said, smiling happily.

"Quiet! Everyone be quiet! Someone is coming up the path again," Many Branches said as she strained to see who it was. "It is our Little Roots, I think and she is coming very fast. Something must be wrong."

"Hello! Hello everyone!" she called as she came running up to them, out of breath.

"Hello, Little Roots, it is good to see you again," Old Moss told her kindly.

"Oh, I have such good news for all of you!" Wendy said, excitedly as she gave each one of them including Rhymer a big hug as though they were family that she hadn't seen in a long time. "I don't know quite where to begin!"

"Then it is always best to begin at the beginning," Predictor told her.

"Let her begin where ever she wants to," Old Log told him.

"Yes, by all means.......begin wherever you wish," he corrected.

"Wait! Wait for my Father! He will be here very soon. He wants to talk to you through me," she said, proudly.

"He does? What for?" Little Bark asked her, curiously.

"He has some very good news for you.....for all of you! I can't wait until he gets here, but I think it would be better if he was here when I tell you."

"Here he comes now!" Old Log told her.

"Wendy! You ran so fast! I couldn't catch up with you! Here," he said as he handed her some paper and a pencil, "you will need these to write with. You forgot, didn't you?" he asked as he held her chin in his hand and looked deeply into her big blue eyes.

"YES, I FORGOT," she wrote on a piece of paper. "MAY I TELL THEM NOW?"

"Yes, you may tell them now," he told her with a hint of doubt in his mind. It was very hard for him to believe that the trees could actually think and talk.

"Listen! All of you! I have such wonderful news! My Father petitioned the government of the state and you are all going to be a National Forest!" she said with great enthusiasm.

"Oh, Little Roots, that is such wonderful news!" Old Moss and Predictor said at the same time, laughing.

"Yes, it...is....good...news," Weeper cried.

"I di' no tink I vood everrrr see da day dat dis vood 'appin!" Old Thunder Stick sobbed.

"What are they all saying? Did you tell them yet?" Jim asked his daughter.

"YES I TOLD THEM. THEY ARE ALL CRYING, FATHER. THEY ARE SO HAPPY," Wendy wrote.

"I cannot hear them," Jim told her, doubtfully.

"THEY CAN HEAR YOU," she wrote again.

"Listen all of you, if you can hear me," Jim said doubtfully as he glanced around at all the trees. 'I've got to be losing my mind standing here talking to trees!' Jim thought to himself. "There will be many people like me that will come and inspect you. They will take samples of the earth around you. They will inspect the bushes and the animals.... things like that. Pay no attention to them; they are only doing as they have been told to do." Jim said as he looked back at Wendy. "Did they hear me?"

"YES, THEY HEARD YOU. THEY WANT TO KNOW WHY THEY ARE GOING TO BE INSPECTED."

"It is nothing at all to worry about," Jim said as he looked around at each of them. Jim was standing where he could not see the yellow paint on Old Moss so he didn't think he needed to mention anything about what it meant. "I feel stupid; you know that, don't you? I feel like I am talking to a wall. I'm just glad that none of the other guys can see me! They would have me hauled away to the funny farm!"

"Can't you give him a sign that you can hear and understand him?" Wendy pleaded.

"Tell him that we will all bow at once to him," Little Bark said. "I will count to three and we will all bow. Tell him this."

"THE TREES SAY THAT THEY WILL ALL BOW AT ONCE! WATCH THEM!" she wrote as she looked at him with eyes as bug as saucers.

"Okay, ready now," Little Bark said, "One......two....three!" and they all bowed for him. Rhymer shook his leaves.

"My stars! I didn't even know that a tree could bow without breaking! You really can hear and understand me! And, you really can communicate with my daughter! Well, I never! No one will ever believe me if I tell them!" he said in amazement. "This is very strange, very strange indeed," he said, shaking his head in disbelief.

"Ask him if this means that the Walk-To's cannot carve on our trunks with their pocket knives," Fuzzy Moss told her.

"Okay," Wendy told him as she wrote on her paper, "THEY WANT TO KNOW IF THIS MEANS THAT THE PEOPLE CANNOT CARVE ON THEM ANY MORE. IT HURTS THEM."

"Well, I cannot guarantee it, but, they will be fined if they do," he told them.

"What does 'fined' mean?" Fuzzy Moss asked, curiously.

"It means that the Walk-To's will be punished," Wendy told him eagerly.

"But, how will they be punished? Will someone carve on their bark to show them how much it hurts? I don't think that is a very good idea. I do not think that the bark of a Walk-To can withstand such abuse. You are quite puny, you know." Fuzzy Moss meant it as a statement of fact, not as an insult.

"No, they won't carve on them. They will find another way to punish them," she said as she decided not to try to explain what a fine was and then have to explain what money was. "Anyway, see, I told you that things would get better for you!"

"Yes, Little Roots, it is as you said. We are all so happy and so very proud if you," Many Branches complimented her fondly as a mother would compliment a child. "We have a lot to be thankful for today," she cried as she leaned on Old Log for comfort.

"Do the trees have names?" Jim asked her, not knowing that she was still conversing with the trees.

"OH, YES INDEED THEY DO!" she wrote as she introduced him to each of them including Rhymer.

"I guess we should be going home now, but we will be back soon," Jim told Wendy and the trees.

When they were out of sight, Old Moss turned and looked at Predictor. "It is as has been predicted, is it not, Good Friend?" he asked with raised brows.

"It would seem to be that way, wouldn't it?" Predictor speculated to his Old Friend.

None of them had remembered to ask the Walk-To's about the yellow paint.

CHAPTER EIGHTEEN

Old Moss woke early, for this was to be a very special day indeed. Only Tall Tales and Old Moss knew how very special it was to be. No one else in the Thicket had been told that today a new Thicket Councilor would be chosen to take Old Moss' place when someday he would retire.

One by one they all began to wake to a beautiful sun filled day. The Song-With-Wings were singing in the trees as the sun gently caressed their leaves and danced away to light upon the grass below.

All were stretching and touching as they greeted each other for a new day. There was the usual chatter among family and friends about the dreams of the night and what those dreams might have been trying to foretell, if anything.

All were busy doing one thing and another when Tall Tales called to Fuzzy Moss in a low voice, "Little One, there is a story of long ago that I wish to tell you," he began, as he whispered only to Fuzzy Moss. "Many cycles ago when there was less noise in the world and more greenery and when the trees were more numerous and taller and fuller than any building ever built by a Walk-To, there was a gigantic tree, very remarkable indeed. It was said to have had branches that reached out and scratched the shores of the Big Water in the east and the Big Water in the West. It also stretched from the Big Lakes of the North to the dry, hot, sandy desert in the south and he shaded all the country in between. He wasn't very tall for his width, but he could stretch his huge branches farther than the eye could see. And, now, Fuzzy Moss, you realize that we are all named because of some difference in our personality, the way we look, or the way we talk. So, now, Little One, tell me if you can what this tree's name was?" Tall Tales asked him with raised eyebrows. He hoped that Fuzzy Moss would think before he spoke. Neither Fuzzy Moss nor Little Bark was warned that this was THE TEST. The reason being, that a Thicket Councilor must always be alert to everything around him.

"This is it, isn't it? This is the test that I have been hearing about for so long, isn't it?" Fuzzy Moss asked as he began to tremble from top to bottom.

"Just answer my question," he ordered. "You know, you get more like old Moss with every passing day. He always answers everyone's questions with a question. I hardly ever get any answers to my questions from anyone around here! And, let me tell you something….if I were able to walk like the Walk-To's, I would leave this Thicket and go where I would be better appreciated. But, enough of this," he declared. "What is your answer? I will give you only three guesses, so guess wisely, Little One," he said as he took a deep breath and peered down at Fuzzy Moss as though to stare into the very soul of his knots.

Fuzzy Moss thought, thought as he had never thought before in his life. Everything depended on his answer. His whole future was at stake. What would he do if he didn't guess correctly? He would be no one; he would have the respect of no one in the Thicket. He would still be thought of as an outsider, a Will-of-the-Wind Seedling that no one cared about. No one even knew where he came from or who his parents were. 'Did anyone ever care about him?' he wondered.

"Is it Shadow Maker?" he asked in a voice that quivered with uneasiness.

"No, it is not Shadow Maker. You have but two more guesses. Guess wisely," he warned, "And, remember the story!" Tall Tales told him with much emphasis.

"You must give me time to think," he told Tall Tales. "This is very important to me. It is everything! It is my whole future!" he said as he continued to think. "My second guess is Shore to Shore."

"No, Shore to Shore is not correct, either. Listen to me, Little One, you have but one guess left. Remember, no one except Old Moss and Pitchy Bark have ever guessed correctly. If you guess correctly now, you will be the only one, other that them, that has ever guessed correctly in three guesses. So take your time…….and THINK……before you answer.

'Think? What does he think I have been doing all this time? My knots ache from thinking so hard! Think stupid! Think about the story,' he told himself over and over again like an echo in a canyon. 'What was it that he said? Oh, yes, the big tree shaded the countryside. That must be it, then!'

"My third guess, Oh Teller of Many Tales, is Shader. Am I not correct?" he asked with confidence.

"Yes! Yes! By all my Sap and all my knots, Yes! You are correct, Fuzzy Moss!" It was no secret that Fuzzy Moss was Tall Tales favorite. Tall Tales had always wanted Fuzzy Moss to be the next Thicket Councilor.

"Now you must remain quiet while I test Little Bark," he cautioned him.

He need not have warned Fuzzy Moss, because Fuzzy Moss knew that to give anything away now would mean to lose all chance of ever being Thicket Councilor.

"Little Bark," Tall Tales called to him in a cheerful voice. "I have a tale of wonder to tell you so be attentive."

And, so Little Bark turned from his Mother and paid attention to Tall Tales. That is, he paid a little attention with only half of his knots as he watched the Bushy Tail run from a noise and hide in a near by bush. It was hard for Little Bark to pay attention to Tall Tales stories; after all, he had heard them all at least once.

"Many cycles ago, when there was less noise in the world and more greenery and when the trees were more numerous and taller and fuller than any building ever built by a Walk-To, there was a gigantic tree, very remarkable indeed. It was said to have had branches that reached out and scratched the shores of the Big Water in the East and the Big Water in the West. It also stretched from the Big Lakes of the North to the dry, hot, sandy desert in the South. And, he shaded all the country in between. He wasn't very tall for his width, but, he could stretch his huge branches farther than the eye could see. And, now, Little Bark, you realize that we are all named because of some difference in our personality, the way we look, or the way we talk. So, now Little One, tell me if you can, what this tree's name was?" Tall Tales asked as he stuck one limb beside his face as though he were in deep thought.

"Scratcher would be my guess," he said, all too quickly and at the same moment he wondered why he had said anything at all? Tall Tales would surely tell him in time without any guessing on his part. Tall Tales was just that way, he could not keep back any secrets of any kind of any story he had ever told. But, this was a special question. About a special story with a special secret!

"Ahhhhhhh! But, that was an excellent guess, Little Bark. I am amazed! I would not have guessed so fitting a name as you have just ventured. Unfortunately, it is the wrong one!" he mused as he stiffened with pride at besting the young Prodigy of the Thicket.

"But, then, do I get another guess or am I limited to only one? Little Bark asked as he stalled for time to think. 'This must be the Test! It has to be!' he thought as he tensed up with worry and anticipation. He knew that he must think and think hard for he had already blown away one chance at guessing by not thinking before he spoke. Now was his chance to prove himself to be the wisest and most promising Mere Twig ever to be taught the duties of Thicket Councilor. He wanted with all his heart to be Thicket Councilor some day when Old Moss retired to sleep and sway gently in the cool breezes until his ending came in the far future.

'Reaches?' he thought to himself. 'Reaches could be the answer, but, what if it wasn't?' He knew by the way that Tall Tales was acting that Fuzzy Moss must have already answered the question correctly. 'Oh, I wish I had more time to think about it,' he thought as the excitement and wonder overcame him.

"My mind is not yet competent, I am afraid, for had I thought of all the facts, instead of just one, I would not have erred so grievously. However, now that I perceive all the facts and material you have given me, I shall build my conclusion and my next answer will be a worthy one," he concluded, stalling for more time to think.

"You have three guesses, Little Bark, only three and, remember, no one in the long history of Old Moss' Thicket, except Old Moss and his predecessor, Pitchy Bark, have ever guessed correctly," 'Within three guesses until now!' he thought to himself.

By this time, Old Log, Many Branches, Tickler, Predictor and all the others were listening intently to what was being said. All had waited for this day with the hope that Little Bark would be the one to best Tall Tales and his famous question.

"Well? What is your second guess, Little Bark? Or do you need more time to think?" Tall Tales asked with narrowed, glaring eyes with lips curled up in a slightly sardonic smile.

"Hey! There will be none of that!" Old Moss said, as he saw what Tall Tales was trying to do. "That isn't fair and you know it! Leave him alone and let him think!"

Little Bark stood perfectly still and as tall as he could so no one could see or feel him tremble inside with worry and anticipation. 'It could be Stretcher, too,' he thought as he scratched his young bark. 'Reacher? Stretcher? Strong Limbs? Shadow? Which one? It could be any of these or it could be something entirely different. Trees usually took on a name that either fit the way they looked or something special about their personality. What was it that he had said about that tree, anyway? Oh, yes, he said it was short for its width. Could it be Shorty?' Oh, he wished that he had listened more intently to the story. He had thought that it was just another one of Tall Tales dumb stories that he always told the Seedlings and Mere Twigs. So, he had not paid full attention to what he had said. And, he realized now that that was probably what Tall Tales had counted on all the time

'I must quiet my heart and think, really think, because my whole future, my whole life depends on my answer,' he told himself as he slowly relaxed and regained his confidence. He could hear Old Moss months ago telling him to keep his knots straight and not make any rash or hasty decisions. There was Old Moss now, over there, intently watching, hoping that Little Bark would best Fuzzy Moss and become the next Thicket Councilor.

Over on his left he could see his Mother and Father, Many Branches and Old Log, as they stood proud, but anxious while looking at each other with hope. At the same time, desperation was clouding their hearts with turmoil. They wanted desperately for Little Bark to succeed and answer the question correctly.

At last, Little Bark could stall no longer. He had to answer quickly or he would have been told he was like an old Walk-To that could not make any decisions.

"It is time," Old Moss told Little Bark in a low but gentle voice.

"For my second guess," he offered slowly, but with all the confidence of youth, "You said that he reached out and touched the Big Waters on both sides of the land. You also said that he was short and spread his branches from the Big Lakes in the North to the hot, dry, sandy desert in the South and that he shaded all the country in between," he paused and looked around him as he gathered his strength. "My second guess is Shader," he said, holding his breath as he waited to see if he was correct or not.

Tall Tales gasped as though stunned by a mighty blow from an axe to his trunk. He just stood there gazing at Little Bark in disbelief.

All of Little Bark's family a friends began to applaud and tremble with excitement. Little Bark had proven himself to be the best candidate for the position of Thicket Councilor. Even Fuzzy Moss was in awe of Little Bark's answer because he was sure by the way Little Bark was remembering the story that he would guess Spreader or Reacher or something! Anything but Shader! But, now, it was all over. 'Little Bark will be the next Thicket Councilor and what about me? What will become of me? I have no purpose now,' Fuzzy Moss thought to himself, sadly.

"Do not be so lost in your trunk, Fuzzy Moss, you did very well. You guessed the answer within three guesses, which is quite an accomplishment in itself. If anything should ever happen to Little Bark, then you would automatically take his place as Thicket Councilor. Do not feel as though you have failed. We all love you very much and we respect you for the intelligent tree that you are. Why, you even have more knots than I do and it has taken me cycles and cycles to obtain them while you have obtained yours in just seven seasons," Old Moss told him proudly as he tried to cheer him up and let him know that he still had a purpose to his life.

"I will need much counseling from you, Fuzzy Moss, about matters concerning the Thicket. When Predictor retires, you will take his place in the main council for decision making," Little Bark told him.

"Yes, there does seem to be a purpose for me after all," Fuzzy Moss said, happily.

This was a day that would be long remembered and lovingly told for many cycles to come. Not just in their Thicket but, in all the Thickets of the Forest. It was a day that Little Bark would remember for the rest of his life.

"We are so very proud of you, Son," Old Log told Little Bark with much emotion evident in his voice.

"Yes, you did very well. I am so very proud and happy!" Many Branches told her son with tears in her eyes.

"Aye, et iz a goot ting dat 'as 'appened ere tooo daaay! Aye wuz so verrrrrry eksited dat aye nearrrly forrrgot me sellllf un fellll oooovver!" Old Thunder Stick told them, cheerfully. "Et izn't everrry day dat ya gets ta vitness da big test bein' givvven, ya nu."

"You are quite right, you Old Rascal! Not much escapes your ears, does it?" Old Moss chuckled with a giant grin on his face.

"Ahhhhhhh, neow, and vould ya be accusin' me o' eavvvesdrrropin?" Old Thunder Stick asked with a twinkle in his eye.

"Yes, I would, you old burl! And, no I wouldn't!" Old Moss said.

"Vell, neow, which iz et ta be, ya auld poop! Ya soooounds liked ya can't make ooop yer miend!" Old Thunder Stick retorted.

"You know as well as I do that we have always considered you to be one of us. We have never even considered that you weren't. But, you knew that already, didn't you? You just wanted to hear me say it, you old Burl!" Old Moss teased him.

"Vell, I gooot me vish didn't aye?" Old Thunder Stick chided him in a friendly manner. "Say, aye 'ave a qvestion ta ask yas aboot. Da ooooother day, a Valk-Tuu came and sprrrayed me vit sume yella, stinky smelly stuff. Now, wha' vould he be vantin' ta doooo dat forrrr?" Old Thunder Stick asked as he frowned in thought.

Old Moss and Predictor just looked at one another.

"We have been wondering the same thing. The other day a Walk-To sprayed me with yella.......pardon me I mean yellow, stinky, smelly stuff, also." Old Moss told him, deep in thought.

"Vell, I'eel be darn! Ya dooooon't say? Did et sprrrray anyoooone else in da' Thicket?" Old Thunder Stick asked, curiously.

"No, just you and me, apparently," Old Moss said, absentmindedly.

"He wuz prrrobly jus' pinkin' oooooot da most onnnnry trrrees he coood find!" Old Thunder Stick said as he laughed so loud that it echoed through the hills.

"What was that?" Wendy thought as she opened her bedroom window. And, as she did, she heard her friends in the Forest laughing.

'I wish I could be there with you always,' she thought as she looked longingly at the trees of the Forest.

Wendy closed the window, and returned to her bed for a nap.

'I think that maybe God should have made me a tree, and then I would not miss my Mother so much,' she thought as memories of her Mother slowly put her to sleep.

CHAPTER NINETEEN

Weeks passed by as the warmth of spring turned to the devastating heat of summer with only a cool breeze every now and then to soothe the trees.

"Old Moss?" Little Bark gently called to his Old Teacher and Master.

"Go away! I'm sleeping! A little sleep is a great cure for ageing and I will take all the cure I can get!" and with that, Old Moss went hastily back to sleep.

Weariness had overcome Old Moss these past few months. He was ill and he worried constantly about the yellow paint that the Walk-To had sprayed on his trunk and the trunk of Old Thunder Stick. What could it possibly mean? He didn't know and he could only guess that it was probably something bad. He had forgotten to ask Little Roots when she had last visited many weeks ago.

"Oh, well, it is of little importance, Old One," Little Bark said as he, also, decided to nap.

The mountains and caves of his previous dreams came back to haunt him as he slept. And, the Great Bearded Tree came up to him again and looked him straight in the eyes as tears were pouring down his ancient face.

"Why are you crying Ancient One?"

"My heart aches for all of you, all the trees of the world. You must tell them....tell them that soon it will be too late...."

"Too late for what, Ancient One?" Little Bark asked, hoping that someone would not wake him again before his dream was finished. But, this time, Little Bark was not afraid of the ancient tree.

"The Walk-To's will destroy you all.... It will happen very soon. You must try to warn them. Though I fear it is already too late. Tell them to stop building weapons of war and convince them that peace is the only way the earth can survive." The Ancient Bearded tree told him, sadly.

"How will they destroy us?" Little Bark asked/

"Who knows? They are very clever, you know, just as we once thought we were......" he said, his voice trailing off as though his thoughts were far away. "A very long time ago we waged war against one another constantly like the Walk-To's do now. We were always fighting and warring against each other. At our third world war, The Great God of All Things told us in a huge, profound voice, 'I have seen enough of war, prejudice and hate. There will be no more! You have not proven yourselves worthy to walk the Earth. From now on you shall be firmly planted where you now stand and the Walk-To's shall have dominion over all the Earth. So I have said, so it is done!' and, from that very moment we were all planted. Our roots were set deep in the ground and we were never able to walk again. We have endured much hardship because of it. Many of us were separated from our loved ones forever."

"What shall I do, Ancient One?" Little Bark said, confusion clouding his thinking.

"I know not, Young One. Do as your heart tells you to do." And, with that the dream ended abruptly and Little Bark woke to a frantic call from Tickler.

"Hey. Little Bark! Wake up! You are too noisy!" Tickler called in anger.

"What is it?" Old Moss asked, excitedly.

"What's the matter?" Little Bark asked in annoyance at being rudely awakened from his sleep.

"You are both snoring loud enough to wake up the stones!" Tickler rebuked them harshly.

"How dare you wake us up from a sound sleep? I have half a mind to come over there and beat you from top to bottom with one of your own branches!" Little Bark scolded him, his temper aroused to the fullest.

"Well, at least you are partially correct. You do only have half a mind!" Tickler teased with a big grin on his face.

"Enough! Both of you! It is too hot for such seedling-like behavior and I for one will not put up with any of it today! Silence!" Old Log ordered them sternly.

"Little Bark?" Old Moss called to his student.

"Yes, how may I be of assistance to you, Great Teacher?"

"Look over there where Twiggy once stood," he told him.

"Yes, what about it?" he asked as a stabbing pain went through his trunk.

"Do you not see the Song-With-Wings? I think it is the same one that carried Twiggy's letters to Sticky Bark," he said as he watched the pigeon.

"It has a leaf in its beak!" Little Bark said, excited to see the Song-With-Wings.

"It is probably a letter to Twiggy from Sticky Bark. Can you reach it?" Old Moss asked him.

"Yes....Yes....I....think I can....Yes! I can!" he said as he took the letter out of the little Song-With-Wings beak. Little Bark held the leaf in his limbs afraid to read it. Afraid of the flood of emotions that would be reopened. He closed his eyes and took a big, long, deep breath. As he opened his eyes once again, he began to read the letter to himself. "To all the wonderful friends and family of Twiggy, I send my most sincere and heartfelt condolences. I have just learned of the great tragedy that took our beautiful Twiggy from us. I will miss her very much. We spoke of love many times, but we knew that it would always be a love that we would share through letters only. She wrote in her letters of another love, a very special love, shared by herself and a tree named Little Bark. You are very blessed indeed to have known such an angelic love. I pray that someday we might meet and talk of our beloved Twiggy. Until then, I will always remain your friend, Sticky Bark." Little Bark stood still, very still as tears poured from his eyes.

"I will not ask you to read the letter, Little Bark, it is written on your face already," Old Moss said in a sad voice, eyes cast down to the ground where Twiggy once stood.

Nothing was as it used to be when Little Bark was a Seedling. Things were happier then. There wasn't so much sorrow and today the sorrow hung over the Thicket like a great, huge, dark cloud.

Little Bark closed his eyes as more tears squeezed their way free and traveled down his trunk. "I must write and tell Sticky Bark that I received his message," he told Old Moss as he wrote his letter and gave it to the Song-With-Wings that was patiently waiting to return to Sticky Bark with a reply as it had done so many times for Twiggy.

Then, Little Bark closed his eyes tightly as though he could make the pain disappear. But, reality was always with him. He relaxed a little and let the exhaustion of pent up emotions pull him into the land of sleep and make-believe.

It was a beautiful day with a cool breeze to gently caress their leaves. The sun had hidden itself, momentarily behind a white cloud as Little Bark heard the footsteps of many Walk-To's. He strained his roots as he leaned over very far to see who it was. And through the haze, he saw three Walk-To's approaching....and...two of the Walk-To's were carrying axes! And the other had something smelly and ugly. "It is an old tree," one of the Walk-To's said as Little Bark shook with fear.

Many Branches hesitated before she called to her son. She did not want her son to be angry with her for waking him up while he was dreaming but, he was trembling so badly that she just had to take that chance. "Wake up, Little Bark," she called to him with no response. "Little Bark, wake up!" She called to him again. "You weren't dreaming again, were you?" she asked as he slowly awakened.

"Yes, and it was not a dream, it was an awful nightmare," Little Bark told her sadly as he looked around him to make sure it was only a dream and not reality.

"Can you tell me about it?" Many Branches asked curiously. She had learned that there were some dreams that you could talk about and others that you couldn't.

"No Mother, I cannot," he said as he looked at his Old Teacher with pity and sorrow. 'And, this is one dream I will not tell you either, Old Teacher,' Little Bark thought to himself as the tears returned to his eyes.

"Oh, yes it is really true!" Wendy had wanted to say but she couldn't speak.

"I did! I really did! I actually talked to the trees through Wendy!" Jim told Mandy.

"Are you sure you didn't dream all this one night while you were sleeping?" Mandy asked him, doubtfully.

"No, it actually happened! If I hadn't seen those trees bow.... I would not have believed it myself. But, I did! I did see them! Wendy can talk with them! They are very intelligent, as intelligent as you and I and Wendy!" Jim said, trying desperately to convince Mandy.

"Okay, if you said it happened, it happened, and I believe you. But, why did it happen? What is the purpose behind all of this?" Mandy asked as she looked to where Wendy was sitting. Wendy was writing something on a piece of paper.

"PLEASE BELIEVE HIM, MANDY. IT IS TRUE. I CAN TALK TO THE TREES AND THEY CAN TALK TO ME! I BELIEVE THAT GOD PLANNED IT THAT WAY."

"This may be true, child, but God never does anything without a reason or a purpose in mind," she warned her.

"Well, maybe there is some great purpose He has in mind for her," Jim said absentmindedly, his thoughts a million miles away. "We must try to do more for the trees. They are so sturdy and strong and beautiful. When I was a child and I thought about growing up and being strong, I always thought of the trees. They just always somehow seemed to have so much strength when I looked at them."

"You sound so very mysterious!" Mandy teased him.

Wendy got up out of her chair and walked over to the window where she gazed out at the sunshine and Ralph as he barked at the mail man. Her mind was only half comprehending as she just stood there and stared.

Suddenly her day dream was broken by a wave of the mail man's hand as she waved back in surprise. Then she slowly turned from the window and walked to the living room where she promptly turned on the television and plopped herself down on the floor in front of it as though she was completely bored with the whole world.

Wendy had not been able to attend school since she had become autistic and this made her even more moody than usual.

"Stay tuned to this channel for further details after this message from your local sponsors," a strange voice said, urgently.

Wendy wondered what all the excitement was about. She stared at the commercial wishing that they would hurry up so that her curiosity could be satisfied. 'Those stupid commercials!' Wendy thought to herself. 'I wonder if anyone actually watches them?' she mused.

"And, now to recap our story….. As we have already said previously, the Russians have had, and I quote, 'A TERRIBLE ACCIDENT' as they have described it. In an attempt to be the leaders in germ warfare, they have developed a serum that was said to kill only people, but, we have learned from our overseas correspondent that a plane carrying two scientists and the deadly serum has crashed in the Soviet Union killing both scientists. The metal box with the deadly serum contained in it burst open on impact. It is not, however, killing people. Let me repeat that…It is not killing people. It is in no way dangerous to the human population… But, as reports have it, the trees…all the trees are dying by the thousands. None have been spared so far in the area. Reports also have it that the serum seems to be absolutely harmless to bushes and other plant life. Wherever the wind blows, in whatever direction, it carries death to any tree that happens to be in its way. Scientists from all over the world are converging in the Soviet Union to find an answer or a cure to this deadly serum. It is said that had the two scientists, who developed the deadly serum, 06TY3, lived they would have been able to stop the spread of the deadly disease, but, as it is, all record of the serum and its formula burned in the terrible flames of the plane crash. This is Clint Weston, your local news caster signing off until further details are made available."

"Oh, please God, No! Not the trees! Anything but the trees! Anything! But not my family of trees. Oh, God, please don't let it harm my trees' Wendy prayed with all her heart and soul. 'I have never wanted something so much in all my life.'

Wendy got up off the floor and ran to her Fathers side. Jim noticed the tears on Wendy's cheeks.

"What's the matter, Pumpkin? Did you watch a sad movie on television?" he asked as he hugged her and wiped her tears away with his napkin. "It's okay, it was just a movie, only pretend," he told her lovingly.

'Could it just be pretend? Could it just have been part of a movie that she had seen…"No! This wasn't pretend!" she wanted to scream as she grabbed her paper and pencil and began to write.

"OH, FATHER YOU MUST COME AND LISTEN TO THE TELEVISION! THE TREES ARE ALL DYING BECAUSE OF A PLANE CRASH AND A DEADLY SERUM THAT THE RUSSIANS HAVE LET LOOSE!"

"Where did you hear this?" Jim asked her with a frown on his face.

Wendy tugged at his hand as she started toward the living room. Jim followed her and so did Mandy.

The reporter was back on the screen repeating everything that he had said previously as Jim watched and listened in astonishment.

"WHAT CAN WE DO?" Wendy asked him in another note.

"There is nothing that we can do. We can only watch, wait and listen to the news. I don't mean to dash any of your hopes, Wendy, but this is a very serious matter. I do not think that there is anything anyone can do, unless they come up with a counter-serum in a big hurry," he warned her.

"WE MUST TELL ALL THE TREES RIGHT AWAY!" Wendy wrote again.

"That is something that I will have to think about, Sweetheart. Give me a few minutes, okay?" he asked her as he stood up and looked at her tearful eyes.

Wendy nodded her head in response and then just stood there hanging her head.

An hour passed as Jim stood gazing out the window in deep thought. 'Why are people so destructive? Why do they create only to destroy?' Jim thought in anger. 'And, why is it that Wendy can all of a sudden talk to the trees? Was she to be the special messenger? Was she supposed to talk to the trees and tell them of this bad news? Was this the purpose for her losing her ability to communicate with people? And, if so, what is the reason. There was surely nothing that one small child could do?'

Wendy walked over and touched his hand with a questioning look on her face.

"Yes, get your sweater, Wendy, and we will go and tell the trees. I hope it is the right thing to do," he said, doubtfully. "It may be cool by the time we return, so be sure to bring your sweater."

Wendy ran and put her shoes on and grabbed her sweater as they both walked out the door. Wendy came to a sudden stop at the gate and ran back into the house to get her pen and paper.

"It's a good thing that you remembered it this time, because that is the farthest thing from my mind right now. I would have had to walk all the way back to get them," Jim told her.

"Dear me, I can't believe it! Someone is coming up the path again!" Many Branches warned her husband. "I wonder what it is that has made our Thicket so popular. The stream of Walk-To's lately doesn't seem to stop."

"Yes, I agree with you. It does seem that we are being bothered more frequently than a couple of cycles ago. But, I guess that it is just the sign of the times. We will probably be seeing more than fewer of them now that we are able to communicate with them. Well, at least we can communicate with one of them and she can tell the others. So I guess that it is the same as being able to communicate with all of them," Old Log said as though he was talking to himself, trying to clarify something in his mind.

"Little Bark! Old Moss! Predictor! Wendy called as she came running up the path with her Father close behind at her heels.

"What is the matter, Little Roots?" Old Moss asked. "Please calm yourself. Nothing can be so bad that you are that upset. You are trembling from top to roots!"

"Oh, Old Moss, I have such terrible news for all of you," she cried, tears pouring down her face. "Now that I am here, I don't know whether I want to tell you or not. I guess it won't make any difference if I do or I don't."

"It cannot be all that terrible. You are just high strung and nervous. Rest a moment and calm down and then when you think it is okay to go on, then you can tell us all about it," he told her, reassuringly.

"Oh dear, I am so afraid to tell you. I think I am more afraid to tell you than I was when I first heard the news. I don't want to spoil what little happiness that you have by bringing you bad news. I should have thought about it more before I so rashly made my decision to come here," she said, wishing that she had never come to tell them. But, it was too late now. Except maybe, if she could think up something to tell them besides the truth. No she couldn't do that, it wouldn't be right.

"Come, you are calmer now, Little Roots. You must tell us sometime," Predictor told her in an encouraging voice.

"I am so very sorry…..I have such tragic news," she began to cry again.

"What is it, Little Roots? You can tell me, I am your friend. We are all your friends. Nothing that you can say could ever change that now." Little Bark said as he tried to ease her misgivings.

"Oh, Little Bark, it's just awful! And there is nothing that anyone can do about it, nothing at all."

"Is it that we are not going to become a National Forest? Is that the news that you have for us?" Weeper asked, in a quiet, gentle voice.

"I only wish that that was all it was," she said as she looked down to the ground.

"That's okay, now, I want you to take a big deep breath and relax," he paused as she took a deep breath. "Now, tell us of this great tragedy that has you so upset," Little Bark told her patiently.

"It's the Russians and our country and a few others, I don't know….. But, they have developed a secret serum that was meant to kill people, only now, it is killing all the trees……nothing else….just the trees. And, it is spreading faster and faster, as fast as the wind can carry it. Oh, Little Bark, people are so stupid! Why can't they just let everyone and everything live in peace and leave us all alone?" she began to cry again.

"Where did you hear of this, Little Roots?" Old Moss asked her.

"On our television, the news man told us on the news," she said, rubbing her eyes with the palm of her hand.

"What is a television?" he asked her, curiously.

"Oh, I'm sorry….well….it's a….well…..a television is a….oh, boy! How can I explain what a television is to you?" she thought as she paced back and forth.

"What are the trees saying, Wendy? Have you told them yet?" Jim asked as he glanced around him.

Wendy nodded to him. "THEY WANT TO KNOW WHAT A TELEVISION IS," she wrote to him on her tablet.

"Oh, dear, I don't know how to explain that one to someone who has no idea of what one is!" Jim said, thoughtfully. "It is a big box with a picture in it," Jim tried to explain.

"Hmmmmmm. Does he mean like the picture that you gave Little Bark of Twiggy?" Old Moss asked.

"Yes, but a little different. A picture is absolutely still, it doesn't move. In the case of the television, it moves. So that won't help you at all," she said, thinking.

"Yes, I believe I understand a little. The picture of Twiggy is not moving, but the one on the television does move. I think I understand, vaguely anyway. Did the man on the television show pictures of the sick trees?" Old Moss asked her, not really wanting to know the answer.

"No, they didn't show anything. They just told about the tests that both our country and the Russians have been doing in germ warfare and....."

"What is germ warfare?" Little Bark asked her in mid sentence.

"Oh, well, it's where....... Well.....both the United States and Russia are enemies. And, the scientists of both of these countries try to develop new and better ways of killing each other with germs. They don't want to use bombs any more because the bombs that they have now would destroy all the life, every kind of life there is on the whole planet," she explained as best she could.

"I see," Little Bark said as though he thought that all Walk-To's had lost their knots.

"Anyway, as you were saying," Old Moss coaxed her to continue.

"Yes, anyway.... Where was I? Oh, yes, there was a terrible plane crash in Russia and the two scientists and the deadly serum were on board. And, when it crashed, it killed the scientists and the vial burst open that contained the deadly serum. Even the formula for the serum was burnt up so that they can't find out what was in it," she said, sadly. "And now because the Russians and the United States have hated each other so much, all the trees, thousands and thousands of them are dying."

"How far away is this.....this Russia?" Predictor asked her.

"It is thousands of miles away, at least I think it is," she said doubtfully.

"Well, then, maybe the wind will never reach us here. Maybe the serum will all be gone," he speculated.

"It is as has been foretold in Little Bark's and Predictor's dreams. How soon will it reach us?" Old Moss asked as he sighed. A heavy burden had been put on him and he did not know the answer this time.

"Not for quite some time yet, I don't think. Maybe you are right. Maybe it will all be gone by the time it reaches here. Wouldn't that be wonderful?" she asked.

"Yes, indeed it would, Little Roots. But, we must prepare for the worst. It is our way of doing things. Thank you so much for coming and telling us. It took a great deal of courage. We shall always be in your debt," Old Moss said in a tired voice.

"No, you are wrong there, I can never make up for what happened to Twiggy, never," she said, sadly.

"That is done. Forgotten. It is time for you to forget and forgive yourself. The healing will not begin until you forgive yourself."

"I don't think I will ever be able to do that, Old Moss," she said, seriously.

"Maybe, in time you will. You and your Father should be returning home now. It is getting dark and we would not want anything to happen to you," Old Moss told her as he looked up to the sky where the sun was trying to hide behind the hills. "But, please, come again, Little Roots, with more news of this tragedy for us."

"I will. Goodbye. I love you all so much. I would give anything for this not to have happened. And, I would give anything to be able to undo what has been done. But, I guess that that is in God's Hands now," she told them as she looked up to her father's face.

"I HAVE TOLD THEM EVERYTHING. THEY ARE VERY SAD, BUT, THEY DON'T BLAME US. THEY LOVE US. AND, THEY WANT US TO GO HOME BEFORE IT GETS TOO DARK. THEY ALSO WANT US TO RETURN WHEN WE HAVE MORE NEWS TO TELL THEM," she wrote to him on her little tablet.

"Goodbye, we will be back soon, as soon as we hear anything else," Jim said as he tugged on Wendy's hand and they began to walk down the path.

"He is a good Walk-To, is he not?" Tall Tales asked Old Moss.

"Yes, he is. We shall call him Strong Trunk because of his love for his daughter," Old Moss said, fondly.

There was a long silence as everyone looked first at one another and then at the ground. It was an eerie silence like the silence of an empty tomb, cold and clammy with the thoughts of the future. Was there to be any future?

"This is it, isn't it?" Thin-As-Grass whined as she broke the long silence like a giant hammer hitting a giant bell. "We are all doomed! There is no hope for us! We are all going to end!"

"Perhaps," Old Moss told her, "perhaps."

Old Moss had forgotten to ask about the yellow paint, again.

CHAPTER TWENTY

Wendy and Jim hurried home. The breeze had picked up quite a bit and there was a drop in the temperature which was unusual for this time of year. Wendy was shivering from the cold even though she had her sweater on.

"I'll build a fire in the wood stove and then I will make us some hot chocolate and some popcorn. How does that sound?" Jim asked her as he opened the front door and they both entered.

Wendy nodded her head in approval and walked over to the sofa to sit down. She was very tired both physically and mentally from this day that she had just gone through. Her heart was aching for her family of trees. She could only hope that they would be spared and that the serum would not reach them. But, then, again, maybe the scientists would find a cure in time for all the trees. 'Oh, I hope so,' she thought to herself.

"Here is your hot chocolate, little one," Jim said as he handed her a mug of hot chocolate with marshmallows in it, "just the way you like it. And, the popcorn has lots of butter on it, too."

He was trying to lift her spirits and cheer her up.

She smiled at him, thanking him with her eyes.

"Hey, what is this?" he asked when he saw a note laying next to the telephone.

Jim put his hot chocolate down on the table and picked up the note. It was from Mandy." Dear Jim, Sorry I had to leave before you returned, but my husband said that if I didn't do some grocery shopping soon, he was going to have to eat out at a restaurant! The real reason for this note is to tell you that the Sheriff called to tell you that the woman in the plane crash was going to be just fine. There was no injury to her spine after all! Isn't that wonderful news? See you both tomorrow! Love Mandy."

"Wendy, you will be happy to know that the woman in the plane crash is going to be just fine. Isn't that wonderful news?"

Wendy nodded her head and smiled. She leaned her head on her Father's shoulder and soon fell asleep. It was good news this time.

It was a cold morning, unusual for August. The night had been unusually cold, too. The clouds were gathering and thickening like huge fluffy marshmallows. The sky grew dark and gloomy.

It was still very early in the morning. The low fog was still clinging to the trees and bushes like a thick, gooey slime making giant shadows like huge birds flying overhead.

As the fog faded, the leaves of the trees and bushes were rustling gently in the breeze. No one had awakened yet as tiny drops of rain tickled and danced on their leaves and branches. A new day to clean the old one away.

"I dare say! What is this?" Thin-As-Grass said when she awakened with a start. "Quite refreshing, don't you think?" she said, gaily as Weeper woke and stretched to the new day.

"The rain, yes, the clouds, no. I do not like the clouds. They are so gloomy. They hide the sun during the day and sometimes they even hide the moon in its nightly journey. They creep and sneak across the sky in horrible shapes like the fists of a giant Walk-To. I am sorry if I have made you unhappy with my answer, but, I love the sun and the moon. Clouds make things seem dreary and unhappy. If I have offended you in any way, I am sorry. I am but a day to day tree and I often speak without thinking." Weeper apologized as she stood shaking in the chilly dawn, drops of rain slowly losing their grip on her leaves and branches as they fell to the ground below.

"Well, at least we are still alive. It is a wonder that the germs did not creep up on us in the middle of the night to slay us all. I fear we have only been granted a small reprieve. I do not think that we will be spared. These germs hold time in their limbs. They will strike when we are not thinking about them and then they will pounce on us," Tickler warned as he shook from head to roots to rid himself of some of the rain that had gathered in puddles on his leaves and branches.

"It is indeed unfortunate that our enemy, the germs, cannot be seen. We cannot fight something that we cannot see. If we could see them, we could take turns watching for them as the others sleep. That way we could be warned ahead of time. But, as it is, they are like the see-throughs. We cannot see them but, they can see us. They make no sound like the grass," Predictor said in a low voice as though he might wake the dreadful, creeping death.

The wind began to blow steadily, whipping and beating unmercifully against their limbs and branches. The ground was drenched as it eagerly soaked up every drop in grateful swallows. The clouds were advancing as though to smother and strangle any sunlight that was bold enough to try to peek through.

"Yes, we are all still alive," cried Rhymer

"I do not know about that!" Old Moss said as he creaked and groaned when stretching to rid himself of the kinks and lumps of the nights sleep." Sometimes I feel as though my roots are half in and half out of the Land Of Sweet Water and Cool Breezes. Part of me does not want to wake up in the morning any more. Part of me says 'Yes, let's get up!' and the other says, 'No go away!'. It is a constant battle every morning. Soon I think I shall fall asleep and never wake up again."

"Ahhhhhhh! Yer Jus' feelin' yur age! Why jes' luk at ya! Ya's luk azzz tho ya 'ave seen bet-er daze, me friend!" Old Thunder Stick teased him.

"Well, you aren't exactly in your prime either, you know!" Old Moss chuckled. He loved his friend of many, many cycles. Those were the days of happiness when trees were tall and majestic and unafraid of waking to a new morning. But, now, it was unknown to any tree whether they would wake at all. Times were dreary and sad, indeed.

"I'm ah bi' youngerrr than ye be, ya old poop!" Thunder Stick bellowed with joyful laughter.

"Not much younger!" Old Moss said while scratching his chin.

"Well, Old Moss, I wonder how far the disease has spread today?" Little Bark asked him as he shooed a bee away.

"I don't know, but, I am sure that Little Roots will keep us informed," Old Moss said in a tired voice. "I have a feeling of foreboding deep in my trunk today, an urgency that just will not be quelled. And, after much thought I have decided to retire from my office of Thicket Councilor.

From now on, Little Bark, your name shall be changed to Strong Bark as is fitting of your character. You have proven yourself worthy of the office of Thicket Councilor, over and over again. I now give up this position to you. I can carry the burdens of the Thicket no longer. My branches are weak and my bark is all falling off. I am old....older than old, I am ancient. I must put my memories to work for me now instead of the future. Old Sap was right, the world is changing and Old Sap and I cannot change with it....we are too old and set in our ways. That is why he didn't live through the Great Fire. You are wise, Strong Bark, wise enough to take on the duties and responsibilities I have so patiently taught you. You are strong and there is nothing that you can't do if you set your knots to it. I leave you with this thought, time is your enemy but it can also be your friend."

"I do not feel any wiser, Old Teacher. I feel confused and burdened. I feel as though life is going by while I am looking through a haze unable to reach the other side to grab some of it for myself," Strong Bark told him, sadly.

"Unfortunately, we all feel that way at times. But, nevertheless, we continue," he told him patiently. "This is supposed to be a time of great joy and celebration for you, Strong Bark."

"I know, but what is there to celebrate? Soon we will all end and I will have no one to council. I have worked so hard for what? Nothing! It will all end soon," Strong Bark said, discouraged at the thought of Old Moss retiring so soon.

"AHHHHHH! But there is a chance that we might survive. Did you ever think of that?" he asked him as he relaxed his branches and fell immediately to sleep, a restful sleep without the problems of the Thicket to hinder him. No more worries.

Strong Bark's mind was full of doubt. Doubt that he was ready, doubt that he was strong enough, doubt that he was smart enough. He was confused and he even doubted that he was thinking clearly at this moment. "Think of something else," he told himself as he realized that his thoughts were going no where but in circles.

The wind had stopped its fierceful pounding and was reduced to a mere breeze as it gently blew the clouds away over the mountains and let the sun peek out with its gentle caress of warmth. It looked like it might be a good day after all, a relaxing day. One of those lazy days that makes you sleepy and comfortable.

Tall Tales watched as a bushy tail ran into a nearby bush and a nibbler ran out the other side. "Did you see that, Old Log?" he asked him in surprise. "I wonder if that was Changer."

"Who is Changer?" Old Log asked as he opened his eyes to peep at Tall Tales, but only half open. He didn't want to let go of his half grasp on his dream. He was between two worlds, so to speak, wedged between reality and a world of dreams where all things were possible. And, if he were allowed a choice, he would rather be in a world of dreams, because dreams didn't hurt you the way things did in the real world.

"Changer was a small tree, not very old and not very handsome, but he was special. No other tree was ever like him. One day when he was but a seedling, a huge shiny golden Song-With-Wings perched herself in Changers branches and Changer was very afraid because he had never ever seen a Song-With-Wings like that before. She was beautiful. "You are very unhappy so I have come to grant you one desire and one desire only. What shall it be?" the golden Song-With-Wings asked him. "I wish to be anything I want to be," he told her. "So be it," she said. And, from that day on Changer could change his shape and become anything he wanted to be. He could be a Walk-To or any of the animals of the forest as long as he came back to his roots by the morning sun. Sometimes he was a huge black back scratcher or a small bushy tail. Once when he was a bushy tail, a big Song-With-Wings swooped down and grabbed him and started to fly away with him. So he turned himself into a huge cruel ripper and the Song-With-Wings dropped him from way up in the air. So, he turned himself into a bee and flew to the ground. And, then, one time, he changed himself into a huge, giant Walk-To and it was said, that he stood on the top of the tallest mountain of world and touched the moon as it scurried across the sky. But, he was too late getting back to his roots and so he remained a Walk-To for the rest of his life," Tall Tales told him. "I think the Walk-To's called him Paul Onion or something like that."

"Changer was a small tree, nothing like you and me.
One day when the sun was bright not dim
A beautiful Song-With-Wings perched on his limb.
'Unhappy you are so I have come from afar.

I have come through rain and I've come through fire
To grant you one and only one desire.'
'I wish to be anything I want to be!'
'So be it my funny little tree.'
A Back Scratcher, a Bushy Tail
Or a Song-With-Wings to sail,
A giant Walk-To he became
And that is what he shall remain
Because to his roots he did not go
Before the sun began to show," Rhymer smiled and looked up at
Tall Tales.

"That was quite good, Little Bush. I dare say that I like telling my
stories so that I can see what rhymes you can make of them. I wish I
had been more thoughtful before. They are rather good you know," Tall
Tales told him kindly.

Rhymer just looked at Tall Tales in astonishment.

"That was a good story," Old Log said with a smile on his face. "I
sometimes wish stories like that were true. It would give us something
to look forward to," he sighed.

"Old Friend?" Predictor called to Old Moss. "Old Friend, it is I,
Predictor. It is time to wake."

"Can't you let me sleep a while longer, Good Friend? I am very tired
and my limbs are very weak today," Old Moss called back to him.

Predictor's sap was running thin as he thought of the sad tidings he
must tell his old and very dear friend. "I am troubled deep in my trunk,
Old Friend. Dark times are upon us again. There is no other way to tell
you this except to do it and get it over with. It hurts….. I wish I were
a million lippets away from here and things were all okay again, but
that is not to be. They are coming today, Old Friend, from far away to
cut you down and end your life. They will say you are old and have a
rotten heart," Predictor said in a sad trembling voice as he lowered his
eyes in helplessness.

"What is there to do about it, Good Friend?" Old Moss asked
without wavering.

"There is nothing that anyone can do, Old Friend. I should have
known what was going to happen when that Walk-To marked your

trunk with that yellow stuff the other day. He has marked you to end, Old Friend, and I feel so helpless, so dreadfully helpless. If I could take the yellow stuff from your trunk and put it on mine, I would be ever so happy to do so and go in your place, but there is no way. There is nothing that I can do for you."

"Predictor!" Fuzzy Moss cried, "You might just have given us the answer!" he said, excitedly. "Rub your bark off, Old Moss, rub hard. Scratch it off if you have to. If there is no yellow stuff, they won't cut you down!"

Old Moss began to rub and scratch as hard as he could. The yellow stuff was becoming dimmer but it wasn't gone yet.

"There is also something else that we can do!" Strong Bark said, excitedly. "We can send a message to Little Roots and her Father, Strong Heart. Maybe they can stop the Walk-To's! I don't really understand why they want to cut you down anyway, we are all going to end if they don't find a counter serum for us," he said as he told Tall Tales to start sending the message. "I hope the message gets to her in time."

"Have a stout heart, Good Friend. What will be, will be. Nothing can change that now," Old Moss said as he made up his mind to the inevitable.

Predictor looked back to his Old Friend, "Do not feel bad or too lost in your trunk, Old Friend, for soon I shall join you in the Land of Sweet Water and cool breezes. I have known for quite some time now."

"What do you mean, Good Friend? The Walk-To's did not mark your trunk with the yellow stuff for your ending?" cried Old Moss. Old Moss was more upset about Predictor's ending than he was about his own.

"No....but, when they come to cut you down, they will see me and they will say that I am too tall and too skinny and brittle and they will say that they are afraid that I may fall on one of you during a strong wind and harm you. So they plan to end me very soon, also."

"But......you are still strong and well rooted, Good Friend," Old Moss told him in disbelief. "Why would they want to cut any of us down? I don't understand. Aren't we all going to end soon anyway? Must they hurry our ending? Are they that anxious to see us go?"

"I do not know, Old Friend. Maybe the wind will not blow this way and many trees will be saved." Predictor shook his trunk. "It does seem that they want to be rid of us though. The world will be a terrible place without us, I am sure," he told him as he sighed. "In a way I envy you, Old Friend."

"Why would you envy me? Am I not going to end? Didn't you say this but a little time ago? Do my ears deceive me?"

"No...I am afraid that your ending is coming very soon. I envy you because you are old and have seen many; many more cycles go by than I. So, you will end more quickly than I. I am yet considered young as trees go and it will take days for me to end as it must have taken our Little Twiggy," Predictor thought, sadly.

"Maybe the Great God of All Things will be merciful and grant you a swift and painless ending."

"There is no glory in ending unless you end for a friend. I would gladly take your place, Old Friend, but, alas, we shall both meet each other once again in The Land of Sweet Waters and Cool Breezes, I feel that it will be very soon."

"What is it?" Wendy asked as she leaned out her bedroom window to talk to Madam Apple Tree.

"The message simply stated for you to come to the Thicket of trees that you have been visiting quite regularly. They said that it is urgent and that they needed you immediately. That is all." And Madam Apple Tree cut the line of communication. She did not like the idea of talking to a Walk-To at all.

Wendy grabbed her sweater off the foot of her bed and ran down the steps and out the front door without even a word to Mandy. "I must get there, I must."

"Someone comes!" Predictor declared as he heard footsteps coming down the well worn path.

All of them watched anxiously hoping that it might be Little Roots and her Father, Strong Heart. But, they were disappointed as three strange Walk-To's came walking around the corner and up the path toward Old Moss. Little Roots or Strong Heart were not with them.

"It is an old tree," the tall Walk-To said to the fat one.

"Yes, it has been standing here since I can remember. It was here when I used to come to the forest as a young boy," the fat Walk-To replied, sadly.

"It is sad that we must cut down such an old friend, especially with what is going on over in Russia. You'd think that they would postpone cutting down any of the trees until that mess is over and done with. But, I guess orders are orders," the short Walk-To told them both.

"Yeh, orders…..sometimes I would like to disregard their orders, especially right now. I feel like something is dreadfully wrong about this whole business with Russia. I feel a foreboding like something terrible is going to happen," the tall Walk-To said wearily.

"Hurry, Little Roots!" Strong Bark called as he stared hopefully down the path.

"Hey, you guys, look at this!" the tall Walk-To said as he pointed to where Old Moss had tried to rub and scratch the yellow paint off. "Someone tried to take the paint off! I wonder who it could have been."

"I don't know, but I think that we have wasted enough time already," the fat Walk-To said as he began to chop away at Old Moss' hard, old trunk.

"Old Moss! What is happening?" Old Log called to his old friend. "What are they doing?"

"Oh, God, please hurry Little Roots," Old Moss said, his eyes closed tightly so that he didn't have to watch what they were doing to him.

"Please do something someone!" Many Branches cried in desperation.

"There is nothing that anyone can do now, it is already too late. You must all….. be strong now…and you…Strong Bark…..you must…be strong….for… all of them…..Tell everyone……..not to….feel so lost…… in their trunks…..I go…..to a better…..place…..with no…worry…. and……..no…sorrow….I shall…miss you all…….very much…..The Walk-To's…..are taking my……life away……I can…feel it…..running out……of me!….I loved…each one….of you….very, very……much…. Do not…..ever forget me……I am…..getting weaker….now….It is…… time…….for………..me………………..to………………… go…………….remember…………….me……….please?..I love………….you………all…………..so………………….much," he

275

said as he breathed his last breath of life and slowly fell to the ground as though he were but laying down to sleep for a while.

Everyone just stood there in shock, not knowing what to do, not knowing what to say.

Strong Bark just knew that he was going to break in two it hurt so badly. Why had he trusted the Walk-To's? He had been foolish to think that there were any good Walk-To's in this world. "Now I know the meaning of lost. It seems that it was only yesterday that I was asking Grandpa what it meant to be lost. Well, now I know three fold. First there was Grandpa. Then our beloved Little Twiggy and now, my dearest friend, Old Moss," he said, choking back tears, tears that he could not shed because he was now the Thicket Councilor whether he wanted to be or not. He had to be strong for his family and friends that were counting on him for support.

"Goodbye, Old Moss, I'll be seein' ya shortly," Old Thunder Stick called as his heart broke in two. "I wish that they 'ad took me first. Then I would no 'ave 'ad to watch dem."

"Well, there is one good thing to come out of all this, it will make good fire wood for someone. Look," the fat Walk-To said as he pointed to Old Moss' trunk, "it was going to die anyway, Look how rotten it is inside. That poor old tree has seen better days. We probably put it out of its misery."

"He was not rotten!" Strong Bark wanted to shout. "How dare they say such terrible things about such a strong, loving, courageous tree?" Strong Bark was angry, very angry.

The three Walk-To's turned and saw Predictor. "Ahhhh! Look at that tall tree over there; it looks very weak and brittle. I'll bet ya, if a good wind comes along, it just might fall over and harm one of the other trees or a person hiking this trail," the short Walk-To commented.

"Yeh, well maybe so, but we can't cut it down unless someone gives us permission. Besides, I feel bad enough about having had to cut down this one. I don't know why. It never bothered me before. It's probably because of all the trees that are dying over in Russia. Can you imagine a world without trees? I can't. It would be awful," the tall Walk-To answered as he picked up his axe and began to walk away, down a different path, up the hill to Old Thunder Stick.

"I do not think that I can bare the pain in my trunk," Predictor thought out loud. "I feel empty, almost afraid to feel anything. I will end soon, also, as I have predicted. My trunk is very heavy and I feel so lost. I feel as though I may split down the middle. I wish they had chopped me down, too, and got it over with so that I would be with my friend, Old Moss and I would not be here to mourn his ending," he said as he cried his first real tears.

Strong Bark looked over at Predictor with compassion. He knew that he might never live long enough to have such a wonderful friend like Old Moss was to Predictor, but he knew how it must feel. He had known Twiggy all his life, but that was just a very short time, indeed, just a moment in time compared to the length of time that they had known one another. "Old Moss asked us not to feel too lost in our trunks. We must try to obey his last wishes. It hurts so badly, though, that we all want to scream or yell at the top of our lungs about the injustices that the Walk-To's have so blatantly doled out to us. It is much easier to tell someone not to feel so lost in their trunks than it is to actually be the one left behind to mourn their ending. Will the sad times never end?"

"We must have a raften for him," Old Log told them sadly.

"I, too, am goin" now ta be vit Old Moss," Old Thunder Stick said as the Walk-To's came his way. "Do not forrrrrgetttttt me, too!" he cried.

"We won't, Thunder Stick. We promise that we won't. We will miss you so very much. We love you...." Many Branches called to him through her tears.

"This one should have been cut down ages ago. Look at it! It has only three limbs! It's been hit by lightening so many times, it's a wonder that there is any life left in the poor thing at all?" the tall Walk-To commented as he and the others began to chop away at Old Thunder Stick's trunk.

"I....love......you.... all......like...the......family......that I never.....had......remember.....me" he cried as he toppled over to the ground.

"Oh, God, I think I am going to end. I cannot take any more of this," Thin-As-Grass cried.

"I, too, feel as though I could end, here and now. I have not felt so completely lost like this in all my memory. I am but a weak minded tree, but I, also, feel the ache in my trunk. Maybe it is that I have been bad at some time or another and the Great God of All Things is punishing me," Weeper cried.

"No, Weeper, it is not because any of us have been bad. It is just one of those things that happens in life. We must muster up our courage to go on." Strong Bark counseled her.

"I don't think that I want to go on," Tickler told him, bluntly.

"We feel that way right now, but it, too, will pass," Strong Bark told him.

"I wonder what happened to Little Roots. I wonder if she ever got our message," Tall Tales asked with raised eyebrows.

And, as if she had heard them, she came running up the path and around the corner.

"What's the matter? I got your mess....! Oh, My God! What happened? Who did this?" Wendy cried as she threw herself on Old Moss' trunk and hugged him, sobbing her heart out. "Who did this?" she demanded as she clenched her tiny fists in anger.

"It was three Walk-To's. They came just a little time ago and cut Old Moss and Old Thunder Stick down. Our friends have ended; they are with us no longer. They are in The Land of Sweet Waters and Cool Breezes." Old Log said, sadly.

"It is all my fault! I should have run faster! I should have never left you alone until the men were done examining you! It is all my fault! I'm so sorry......so very, very sorry. I don't seem to be able to do anything for you. All I have done is harm you," she sobbed.

"Do not feel as though it was all your fault. There was probably nothing that you could have said or done that would have stopped them anyway. Besides, it was my fault for not sending you the message in time," Strong Bark told her sadly. He had vowed to himself that he would never talk to another Walk-To or look at one either, but, his Little Roots was so loving of all the trees, how could he blame her?

"I do not think that it is your fault, either. Who were they? Had you ever seen them before?" she cried as she continued to hug Old Moss' trunk. She squeezed him hard, hoping to squeeze some life back into him. She just laid there sobbing uncontrollably.

"Do not despair, Little Roots. He is better off where he is. He is in the Land of Sweet Waters and Cool Breezes now. He has no more troubles and no more sorrow. He is happy now. It's like I can see him if I close my eyes tight. He is with Twiggy and Old Thunder Stick and Grandpa. They are all smiling and very happy. I can see it no other way, so that must be the truth. They are all waiting on that sandy shore for the day when we will all go home to be with them," Strong Bark said, nostalgically.

"It is the story of my life," Wendy told them sadly. "Everyone that I love is taken away from me. It is as though it is bad luck for me to love anyone. Every time I think it is over, someone else dies," she cried.

"Calm yourself, Little Roots. This will do you no good. You are too upset, you must think of something else," Many Branches told her lovingly.

"I am thinking of something else and I wish that I did not have to tell you this, but I have more bad news for you," she told them as she got up off Old Moss and gave him a loving pat before turning around and looking at each and every one of them with sad eyes.

CHAPTER TWENTY ONE

"What bad news do you have to tell us?" Predictor asked her, wondering what could possibly be worse than what they had just been through.

"I'm so afraid," Many Branches told her husband as she nestled closer to him. "Our world is falling apart right before our very eyes."

Wendy looked around at each and every one of them once more. "The disease is still spreading. It will be here soon," Wendy told them in a far away voice." They have not, as yet, found a cure for it. And, I hate to dash your hopes, but, it doesn't look like they will find anything before…..before……before it gets here to you. Almost all the trees in the world are dying or dead from it. Wendy told them with much bitterness in her heart. "Are any of you sick yet?" she asked, worried that someone might say yes.

"No…….none of us is ill yet," Strong Bark told her. And, if we were, we would just have to be brave and accept it. What will be, will be. We cannot change anything. It is not in our power."

"It is too bad that I am not a wizard or a magic fairy. Then I could just wave my magic wand and all the bad would go away. As it is, the only thing that I can do is sit and wait. The disease is still as strong as the day that it happened. There was some hope that it would thin out and dissipate, but, it didn't happen. The scientists are baffled. They don't know what to do." Wendy began to cry once again, helplessness overwhelming her.

"Do not cry any more, Little Roots. We are all ready to meet The Great God of All Things. After all, isn't that why we are put on this earth, to purify ourselves so that we will be worthy of our place in the Land of Sweet Waters And Cool Breezes?" Old Log told her.

"Yes, I guess you are right. But, I won't know what to do without you. There will be no purpose for me. I will have no reason to live. I cannot even communicate with my own people. What good will I be to anyone?" she asked

"Your Father loves you very much, Little Roots. I can see it every time he looks at you. He is proud of you, very proud," Predictor told her.

"It is time. You must return home before you are missed. We must have a Raften for Old Moss and Old Thunder Stick," Strong Bark told her, lovingly.

"What is a Raften?" she asked, wiping the tears from her cheeks with the back of her hand.

"It is what you call a funeral, I think," Strong Bark replied.

"Oh, I see. And I'm just an old mean Walk-To and I have no feelings and I am not invited to stay," she said sorrowfully as she began to get up to leave.

"I'm sorry. Please stay, if you will. We would like to have you stay. I just didn't think that you would want to stay. It is a very sad time of remembering the ones that we have lost. Are you sure that you are up to it? You have been through so much today," he told her.

"I have not been through anything that you haven't been through. I will stay," she said as she dried her tears once more and walked over to where Old Moss lay.

After the Raften, Wendy said her good-byes and went back home to lie down and sleep for a while. She was exhausted, emotionally and physically exhausted.

"Do you know something?" Strong Bark broke the silence like the first song of a Song-With-Wings in spring. No one was startled, after all, what was left to be afraid of? "Little Roots is special, very special and I wish that I could do something special for her. She has become such a good friend, a treasure that I would not trade for anything in the world. I wish she were a tree," Strong Bark pondered. "If she were a tree she would be a lot like Twiggy, I think. They are both so much alike, perfect, fragile, considerate, loving, caring, thinking of everyone else before they think of themselves. Twiggy was so young and so is Little Roots."

"Yes, they are a lot alike," Old Log agreed. "I miss our Little Twig very much. Little Roots has filled the emptiness a little, but not totally. I still feel a void when I think of Little Twig."

"Things will never be the same as they once were, will they, Father?" Strong Bark asked, knowing the answer before he even asked the question. But, he had to hear it from someone else.

"No.….no.….I'm afraid not. I don't think they are meant to be the same, My Son. Change takes time and time means change. Things are always changing."

"I'm glad that the story about Old Time Ticker isn't true," Tall Tales said with a sigh.

"Who is Time Ticker?" Strong Bark asked.

"I never told you the story about Old Time Ticker?" he asked a bit sadly.

"No, I don't think so. I don't remember it anyway."

"Do you feel like listening to it now?"

"Yes, I think so. We need some cheering up," he told him.

"Okay," and he began his story. "Once, a long time ago, there was a large tree named Time Ticker. Time Ticker stood in front of a cave. It was a very special cave. He was the watcher of time and anyone who wanted to go back in time could go if they knew the secret word. Time Ticker was a shrewd old tree and he changed the secret word around every day. But, there were many trees who had guessed and there were many trees that were sorry that they had, because, for them, time stood still. Time was nothing but a constant circle. One tree went back in time one hundred cycles and when those one hundred cycles were over, he went back in time again, exactly one hundred cycles and it kept happening over and over again. Time, regardless of when it is, never changes; it always remains constant and the same. It is an elusive substance that dreams are made of. That trees wish was to go back in time exactly one hundred cycles and he got his wish, a wish that will never end because we already know that we can't change the future. So it is true of the past. Once done, it is done. We cannot change anything even if we relive it. That is why I am glad that we do not have Old Time Ticker here to tempt us to go back. We could not change anything that has happened. It would all happen just the same and I, personally, do not want to relive the last couple of cycles."

"It is something to think about, anyway," Strong Bark told him as his mind wandered. Maybe that tree didn't know how to change the things that had happened, but Strong Bark would like a chance to at least try.

Sun peeked through her bedroom window as Wendy woke to a brand new day. She laid there watching the little fuzzy things float around in the sunlight. "I wonder if we breathe all that stuff into our lungs?" she pondered as she threw her blankets off and put her feet on the nice warm floor. Her bedroom was right over the wood stove. The pipe went right through her room and through the ceiling and out the roof above.

Wendy dressed and ran down the stairway to find her Father already sitting at the breakfast table getting ready to eat his breakfast.

"Good morning, Sunshine!" he called to her as she came running to him with a big hug.

"GOOD MORNING, FATHER," she wrote on her tablet and smiled. "HI! MANDY!" she wrote again.

"Hi, Sweetie, did you sleep well?" Mandy asked her.

"NO, AS A MATTER OF FACT, I DIDN'T. I HAD A NIGHTMARE. IT WAS AWFUL. IT WAS ABOUT THE TREES AND FATHER AND A WHOLE BUNCH OF PEOPLE AND GOD AND HEAVEN AND JUST ALL SORTS OF THINGS. I CAN'T REMEMBER IT ALL, THOUGH. IT IS BLURRY. BUT, SOMETIMES, MOST OF THE TIME ANYWAY, MY MIND BLOCKS OUT BAD THINGS SO THAT I CAN'T REMEMBER THEM.

"Well, sometimes that is a good thing," Jim told her.

"Here's your breakfast, Wendy," Mandy told her as she put a plate of hotcakes and bacon in front of her. "Do you want milk or hot chocolate with your breakfast this morning?"

"I THINK I WANT BOTH," Wendy told her in a note.

"Okay, but, you will float out the door with that much to drink!" she teased her.

With breakfast done and out of the way, Wendy went to the living room and turned on the television. She didn't usually watch that much

TV but, now she watched it every chance she could get. She had to keep informed about the deadly serum and the trees that it was killing.

"FATHER, LOOK! THEY ARE SHOWING OUR HOUSE ON TELEVISION!" Wendy wrote and handed the piece of paper to her Father. Jim put his news paper down and watched the television with Wendy.

"AND, LOOK! THERE IS OUR FOREST! THOSE ARE MY TREES!"

"Turn up the television so that we can hear what they are saying," he told her.

"This is one of only three forests left in the whole world," the news reporter said as he flew over their house in a helicopter. "It was just recently made an National Forest through the efforts of Jim Wardly and his daughter, Wendy."

"WOW! DID YOU HEAR THAT, FATHER?" she wrote to him. "THEY SAID OUR NAMES RIGHT ON TELEBISION! ISN'T IT EXCITING?"

"Yes, it is exciting. I only wish it was under different circumstances," he told her as she sat down on his lap and continued to watch the television.

".........is spreading ever closer and closer. Nothing that the most brilliant scientists in the world have tried has stopped this creeping death. If you want to ever see a tree alive again, well, you had better all hurry. The disease is almost here; this is Jeff Laternly reporting for Channel 2 news."

"OH, FATHER! THEY ARE ALL GOING TO DIE, AREN'T THEY?" she wrote.

"Yes, I'm afraid they are, Pumpkin. But, don't feel sad, God always has a purpose for everything that He does," Jim said as he hugged her with tears in his eyes. "He will soon let us know what His Great Purpose is for taking the trees away from us. Although, I don't think I really want to know. I have a feeling of dread about all this. Now, you have to be strong for your tree friends if we go to them," he told her as he held her chin in his hand and looked into her eyes.

"I'LL TRY, FATHER."

It had been many days since the Raften had taken place for Old Moss and Old Thunder Stick. Strong Bark and the other trees continued to mourn their ending. There was nothing to look forward to anymore. They were even afraid to wake up in the morning and at night they were afraid to go to sleep, afraid that they would not wake up.

"I do not feel so good, Old Log. I feel weak and shaky as though I were very old all of a sudden," Many Branches told her husband in a weak voice.

"Yes, I too, am very weak. It could be from worry and sorrow and all the terrible things that we have been through lately, but, I don't think so. I think we have all been poisoned by the disease from the germ warfare. I think it has finally reached us," he told her sadly. "Our end is much sooner than I had anticipated."

"Someone comes, My Husband," she told him, quietly.

"Yes, I hear it also. But what does it matter any more? We are all going to end soon. Nothing else can harm us. Once you end, nothing can ever hurt you again."

"Yes, you are right, My Husband. We are lucky in a way, I suppose. Not everyone knows the hour of their ending."

"Little Bark! Tall Tales! All of you! Listen! I have sad news for all of you. Do you know that you are now the only Thicket left in all the Forest and in the whole wide world? You are the only ones left alive! There are no other trees!" she told them hurriedly, looking behind her, watching fearfully as though she were afraid of something.

"Why do you look behind you, Little Roots? Are you afraid of something? Is something trying to harm you?" Tall Tales asked her.

"No, but, many hundreds of Walk-To's are coming to see you! Thousands of them! They are here to make one last effort to save you. They only have one more thing to try. Are any of you sick yet?" she asked as she looked around at each of them.

"Yes, I think we all are except Fuzzy Moss and Strong Bark," Tickler told her in a weak voice.

"It is too late, then, for the rest of you. I am sorry, so very sorry for what the people of the world have done to all of you. We are all probably going to die also. We are about to have a war. It will be our third World War and it will happen very soon. If we do, there will be nothing left, nothing at all, just hot, barren land. The Russians are blaming us and we are blaming the Russians for destroying all of you. Our allies say go to war. It is such a mess," she sighed. "If there are to be no trees, then I, too, want to die," she said, sadly. "I can't imagine a world without trees."

"You must not think that way, Little Roots. We love you, too, and we want you to live," Tickler told her. "Our ending has been foretold for hundreds of cycles. We just never thought that it would come so swiftly. It has taken mere days to reduce our numbers to just a limb full. We did not end a few at a time, but, all at once."

"Well. I don't care. I still don't want to live without you," she said angrily as she turned to Strong Bark. "When did you change your name to Strong Bark?" Wendy asked him in a less angry voice.

"It was changed when I became the new Thicket Councilor," he said, sadly with just a hint of a tear escaping his eyes.

"Strong Bark is a perfect name for your personality," she told him. "Yes, we are all to blame for all your sorrows that have come on you lately. I thought that making you National Forest would help you and make it so that you didn't suffer any longer. But, I have brought you nothing but sorrow and anguish. I do not understand why you don't hate me," Wendy said, puzzled.

"We do not hate you because you had nothing what-so-ever to do with any of our hardships, except, maybe, Twiggy. But, now that I can see everything quite clearly, I don't believe that that was your fault, either. I believe that she would have been sacrificed in some other way if she hadn't become your Christmas tree. God wanted you to be able to talk to us and that is the way that He chose. Twiggy was so very proud to be your Christmas tree. If she had it to do over again, and knew that she was to end no matter what, she would still have chosen to be your Christmas tree," Strong Bark explained to her.

"I thank you for such kind words, but, I still feel responsible for most of it. I wanted to do so much for you. I wanted my Father to help make it a law that trees were not to be cut down for Christmas. Only dug up and replanted back where they got them. I wanted all of you protected from people carving on you and cutting you down needlessly. I know that we use an awful lot of you to build our houses, but we could start using bricks for most of it. I wanted to do so much, but, now you are all dying and I can do nothing to help you," she cried.

"It is as has been foretold many ages ago, Little Roots. It was said, generations ago, that we would be able to talk to a Walk-To in the last days. It was said that the Walk-To would try to do all manner of things for us and you have tried. Why, just think about it, Little Roots, it did not take you very long at all to have us declared a National Forest. I think that took a lot of courage in itself. Do not be sad.......be proud of yourself!" Strong Bark told her.

"You make it sound like I did something great. I would have done something great if I could have only saved you from this deadly serum."

"Well, I guess no one can do that. So, we will just have to deal with it, the way we always deal with things that we cannot change. Accept it and stop worrying about it," Tickler said.

"I didn't mean to make you angry," Wendy pouted.

"You have not made me angry. I did not mean to sound that way, Little Roots," he told her, kindly.

"Oh, I almost forgot. I have another poem. It is for all of you this time," she told them as she took a piece of paper out of her pocket.

"Please........read......it.......to........us..............." Many Branches told her weakly.

"It is about all of the trees, everywhere," she told them as she began:

"Take a good look at me,
I'm probably the last one you'll ever see.
You were the ones that made me so lonely,
And, now I am the one and only.
Along time ago you could see thousands of me.
We were there as far as the eye could see.
We were so tall we touched the sky,
As we watched hundreds of years passing by.
We out numbered you at one time,
And, on our limbs you used to climb.
But, out of man's lust for power, his greed,
Left barren the earth without a seed.
Yes, it is your doing and not mine,
And, it's really only a matter of time,
Before I am only a picture to see

Because this old earth is just too lonely for me.

So, quickly now, come and see

A very, very lonely tree," she said as she folded the paper and tucked the poem in a little knot in Strong Bark's trunk. "It is to all of you from my heart," she said as tears welled up in her eyes and overflowed down her cheeks.

Strong Bark looked at her with sad, unseeing eyes. "Many Branches and Old Log have ended," Strong Bark said quietly as tears crept down his face to trickle to the ground at his roots.

"So have all the others, except Fuzzy Moss and me," Predictor told him, solemnly. "It is just my lot in life to survive so that the Walk-To's can come and cut me down. But, alas, I am ill and will not last much longer. So, in all actuality, I have beaten them to it. It gives me great satisfaction inside to know that I have cheated them of my ending." He trembled. "I go now. I will be waiting for you with all of them in the Land of Sweet Waters and Cool Breezes. Do not be lost in your trunks, for I predict that you will be with us very soon. Good Bye......Little Friends, I go......." He said as he relaxed his branches and passed from this life to the next.

"No, please, don't go...." Wendy cried. "Come back! Please come back.....I love you so much," she sobbed uncontrollably.

"He has gone, Little Roots. No one can bring him back," Strong Bark told her.

"FATHER, THEY ARE ALL DYING! THE ONLY ONES LEFT ARE STRONG BARK AND FUZZY MOSS," she wrote to him.

"I am so sorry, Wendy, so very sorry. There is nothing that anyone can do for them now. I am just sorry that you had to witness them dying. It must be hard on you and all the trees," he said, sadly, holding Wendy in his arms to comfort her.

And, as he held her, the sky darkened except for a beautiful stream of sunlight that glowed through a hole in the clouds onto Strong Bark, Fuzzy Moss, Rhymer, Wendy and her Father.

"I am The Great God of All Things. I have come for you, Strong Bark and Fuzzy Moss. Come, it is time for you to come home where I have prepared a special place for you in The Land of Sweet Waters and Cool Breezes. There, no one will ever bother you again. There you will have peace everlasting. I have forgiven all the trees of the world and they shall be with Me this day. Come home."

"But, what will happen to the world?" Strong Bark asked Him, reverently.

"The Walk-To's are about to start their third world war as the trees once did. Long ago when you hated one another as the Walk-To's hate each other now, I stopped your third world war. I have had enough. Therefore, they shall now all be firmly planted as you once were. They will never roam the land and make war again. So I have said, so it will be done."

"But, what will happen to Little Roots and her Father?" Fuzzy Moss asked. "They had nothing what-so-ever to do with the wars."

"And, me, too!" Rhymer pleaded.

"All of the good Walk-To's and all of you, including Rhymer, shall come to be with Me in The Land of Sweet Waters and Cool Breezes this very day. Come, it is time."

And, God raised all the good people and all the good trees as had been foretold many years before by the whispers of far away, very old tree. And, from that day on, all the people who were left on the earth were firmly planted where they had stood.........rooted forever.

And, there was a great reunion in The Land of Sweet Waters and Cool Breezes that day. Rainbows on top gorgeous rainbows shining bright overhead. And, all were happy, including Wendy and Jim as they ran to hug Wendy's Mother who stood waiting with open arms.

LaVergne, TN USA
12 January 2010
169703LV00003B/3/P